Prevailing Love

3-IN-1 COLLECTION

Sealed with a Kiss
The Wedding Wish
Montana Sky

Loree Lough

PREVAILING LOVE

A 3-IN-1 COLLECTION FEATURING:
Sealed with a Kiss (© 1999 by Loree Lough)
The Wedding Wish (© 1998 by Loree Lough)
Montana Sky (© 1996 by Loree Lough)

Loree Lough
www.loreelough.com

ISBN: 978-1-60374-166-8
Printed in the United States of America
© 2010 by Loree Lough

Whitaker House
1030 Hunt Valley Circle
New Kensington, PA 15068
www.whitakerhouse.com

Library of Congress Cataloging-in-Publication Data

Lough, Loree.
  Prevailing love / by Loree Lough.
    p. cm.
  Summary: "Christian and romantic themes predominate in this collection
of three contemporary, inspirational novellas—*Sealed with a Kiss, The
Wedding Wish,* and *Montana Sky*"—Provided by publisher.
  ISBN 978-1-60374-166-8 (trade pbk.)
  1. Christian fiction, American. 2. Love stories, American.   I. Title.
  PS3562.O8147P74 2010
  813'.54—dc22

                          2009035857

2 3 4 5 6 7 8 9 10 11 ⨀ 17 16 15 14 13 12 11

Dedication

First, to my faithful readers, whose support and faith keep me writing.

Second, to Larry, light of my life and stirrer of my soul, for whom I'm happy to obey 1 Corinthians 7:10: "Let not the wife depart from her husband."

Special mention to my wonderful editor, Courtney, and the ever-capable Lois.

Finally, to my once abused, now spoiled dog, who put aside his Frisbee addiction long enough for me to write these stories!

Sealed with a Kiss

Prologue

May 31, 2009
London, England

S am Sylvester was dying, and he knew it.

When he closed his eyes, he could picture the huge red truck careening around the corner on two wheels, its chrome bumper aiming straight for the convertible's windshield.

Right before the impact, he'd glanced at Shari. As usual when they were driving, she'd had her nose buried in the pages of a romance novel. "It helps keep my mind off all the dangerous drivers," she'd once said. *It doesn't get any more ironic than that*, Sam thought.

He wondered where Shari was now. He'd seen the paramedics load her, bloodied and unconscious, into one of the ambulances at the scene. Had the Lord, in His infinite mercy, decided to take her home then and there, to spare her any suffering?

It was a struggle just to open his eyes, but Sam forced himself. Nothing in the bustling emergency room could possibly be as horrible as the pictures in his mind.

"Look 'ere, doctor," came the mask-muffled Cockney accent of a nurse. "'e seems to be coming round."

The broad, beefy face of a doctor peered at Sam from behind a surgical mask. "You know where you are, sir?" he asked, bushy brows drawn together in a frown.

Under other circumstances, Sam might have chuckled, because the doctor's breath was causing the pleats of his white mask to puff in and out like the bellows of a tiny accordion. Instead, Sam tried to muster the strength to nod. Yes, he knew exactly where he was—on his way to heaven.

But you can't go, he told himself. *At least not yet.* There was so much to do, so much to say, so many questions to ask before—

"M-my wife...." The words scraped from his parched throat like sandpaper across roughened wood. "W-where's my wi—?"

"Down the hall," said the nurse, patting his hand.

"Is she...is she—?"

The expression on her face told him everything he needed to know. Shari had already joined their Maker in Paradise. But maybe, just maybe, he'd read the blue eyes above the mask wrong....

He ignored the pain—pain that seemed to have no particular source, throbbing in every joint and every muscle. He screwed up his courage. He had to know for sure before he let go of this earthly life.

"Did she make it?"

In the moment of hesitation and silence that followed his question, Sam felt his own lifeblood seeping slowly onto the gurney beneath him. The doctors and nurses surrounding him were all perspiring, so why, he wondered, did he feel so *cold*?

Drowsiness threatened to take him far, far from the ER, but he fought it. "Did she make it?" he repeated with force.

"No, Mr. Sylvester," said the whisper-soft voice of the nurse, "I'm afraid she didn't." Another gentle pat. "But I can promise y' this—she didn't suffer."

Sam closed his eyes as a curious mix of gratitude and regret propelled a slow, groaning breath past his lips. Gratitude that his precious wife wouldn't be "up there" alone for long. Regret because their sweet little girl would have to live the rest of her days without them.

At least Molly will have Ethan, thank God.

Ethan…every bit as alone in the world as Molly would soon be.

For the first time since he'd regained consciousness, Sam felt a profound fear pulse through him. *Ethan…. They need to contact him right now because Molly's going to need him!*

With a strength that belied his condition, he gripped the nurse's wrist. "What…what did they do with…where are my things?" he choked out.

"In a locker, just down the hall." She fished in the pocket of her surgical gown as the corners of her eyes crinkled with a sympathetic smile. "I 'aven't 'ad a chance yet to file it," she said, withdrawing a key.

The way it caught and reflected the light made it look like a silvery cross, if only for an instant. In that instant, Sam pictured Jesus welcoming Shari home. "In my wallet," he said, struggling for air now, "there's a business card, and—"

Her blonde brows knitted with concern. "Please calm yourself, Mr. Sylvester."

"Why?"

He watched as she blinked and tried to come up with a rational reason for him to calm down. His mind started to wander, and he recalled how he'd been a volunteer EMT in Maryland before moving to London. He'd witnessed enough accident scenes to know what impending death looked like. He knew that the remainder of his life could be numbered in minutes, and that he had just one reason to conserve his remaining strength: Molly.

He thought about the joy she'd brought into his life, into Shari's. From the moment they'd picked up their round-faced infant at that crowded Korean orphanage eleven years ago, she'd enchanted them with her dancing brown eyes and elfin smile. And the first thing every morning since, Sam and Shari had thanked the Almighty for blessing them with their beautiful, raven-haired angel.

Life from now on would be hard for her. Very hard, especially at first. But Molly knew the Lord, and He would help her through those first sorrow-filled days. And she'd have her uncle Ethan to look out for her.

Molly adored Ethan, and Ethan had always loved Molly as much as if she were his own. Sam and Shari had discussed it dozens of times. The way he looked at Molly, the tenderness in his voice when he spoke to her—*that* was the reason they'd decided to make him godfather *and* guardian to their only child.

This would be hard for Ethan, too, Sam knew. But he'd be a good father to Molly. Sam was as certain of that as he was of God's boundless love.

From out of nowhere, a line Sam had read somewhere reverberated in his head: *In knowledge, there is power.* Knowing Molly would be in good hands gave him enough physical power to persist with the nurse. "The card," he said again, "will you...get it...for me?"

The doctor nodded his approval, and the nurse left to collect Sam's belongings. He closed his eyes. *Father,* he prayed, *let me hold on a little longer, for Molly's sake....*

"Is this it?"

Squinting, Sam smiled crookedly at the card held between the nurse's thumb and forefinger. "After all that fuss," he croaked out, "I'm ashamed to admit I...to admit that...that I can't focus enough....to read it."

"It says 'Burke Enterprises,' and under that, 'Ethan Burke, President and CEO.'"

A relieved sigh rattled from his lungs. "Praise God," he whispered. "Praise Jesus!"

For a moment, an odd stillness settled over the cramped, brightly lit cubicle, despite the blips and hums of the equipment monitoring his heart rate and pulse, despite the nonstop efforts of the medical team to repair his broken, battered body.

"What's your name?" he asked the nurse.

She raised her eyebrows high on her forehead, her stethoscope bobbing, as she pointed to her chest.

"Yes, you."

"Tricia Turner."

Reaching for her hand, he said, "Will you call him for me, Tricia?" Sam squeezed her hand.

"I'll see it gets done, soon as—"

Another squeeze, tighter this time, interrupted her. "I'd like *you* to do it." Sam spoke slowly, knowing he had to conserve his waning strength until he could be sure Molly would be with Ethan as soon as was humanly possible. "You know as well as I that I'm not walking out of here, Tricia, so say you'll grant me this last wish."

She blinked once, twice, and then said, "I—I'll try."

"No," Sam all but barked. "Promise me, before I die. Because my wife and I chose Ethan, there," Sam said, nodding toward the card, "to be our daughter's guardian, should anything happen to us. She's only eleven, you see, and I—"

"I understand. And you have my word. I'll phone him for you."

"I have your word?"

She nodded just once, but it was enough. A feeling of great peace settled over Sam, and, smiling, he let go of her hand. "Thank you. And bless you, Tricia, for your kindness...for giving me peace."

When she began to fade from view, Sam thought, *Not a good sign. Not good at all.* Good thing he'd given Molly an extra-big hug and an especially big kiss that morning. *Good thing you told her how much you love her. And how you taught her to turn to God in times of trouble.* The girl would need it—soon.

Soon, soon, soon, he chanted in his mind as a drowsy, dizzy sensation wrapped around him. The pain was gone now, and he felt nothing but the feathery weight of the stick-on patches that held the heart monitor wires in place on his chest. Sam closed his eyes and listened to the high-pitched one-note whine of the monitor.

"Code blue!" someone hollered.

"Crash cart, stat!" yelled someone else.

Their shouts didn't startle him. Sam was beyond fear now. Somewhere in the deepest recesses of his conscious mind, he remembered his days as a paramedic, when he'd seen the flat line on the monitor signal the end of a life.

This is the last time you'll have that *memory...last memory you'll have, period!*

Did the saints in heaven remember their days on earth? And if they did, were they granted permission to visit their former world? Sam hoped so, because he wanted desperately to know that he could look in on Molly from time to time.

The lead surgeon on the team applied electric paddles to Sam's chest, then bellowed "Clear!" as Tricia prepared a syringe for one last-ditch effort to save him. But Sam knew it was pointless. Soon, they'd realize the futility of their efforts, and by the time the doctor called time of death, he'd be with his Father, and with Shari, in Paradise.

Sam said one last prayer:

Lord Jesus, be with Ethan now. Guide his steps and his words, for Molly's sake, as well as for his....

Chapter One

Same day, Potomac Hills, Maryland

There'd been a time when Ethan had enjoyed hosting parties—the bigger, the better—especially right here on his own riverfront estate. But his heart wasn't in this one. Hadn't been "in" much of anything lately.

Not so long ago, his parties had been described in the society pages as "colorful affairs." But there hadn't been much color in his life lately, either. Even the sun setting over the Potomac seemed drab and washed out.

Ethan stood on the pier, hands in his pockets, and looked back toward the great expanse of lawn, where no fewer than a hundred well-dressed guests meandered from tennis court to swimming pool to dual-level deck.

You've got it all, he thought, frowning. And from all outward appearances, he did have it all—a successful, self-made business; a big, beautiful house on three acres of prime Maryland real estate; seven automobiles—a sleek, high-priced sports car (for impressing the ladies), a classy, imported sedan (for impressing clients), and five roadsters of various vintages to impress himself... and neighbors who were rich and famous, to boot.

So why did he feel like something was missing? Something meaningful, something *vital*?

There were two bright spots in Ethan's life: Burke Enterprises and his Korean-born goddaughter, Molly. The mere thought of the pretty preteen raised his spirits a bit. In another couple of weeks, Molly and her parents would arrive for a long, leisurely vacation, and already, he was counting down the days until the family would leave London for their annual trek to Maryland.

A woman's shrill voice broke into his thoughts. "Pee-wee-than!" she hollered. "*There you are!*"

It was Kate, the six-foot, blonde marketing manager his vice president had appointed a couple months back. She waved a hand of red-taloned fingers above her head, and he sent a halfhearted salute in return, then faced the slow-surging river and ran both hands through his hair. He'd been neatly dodging her blatant flirtations all afternoon, pretending the ice bucket needed to be refilled or feigning a must-have conversation with someone across the way. But now he felt trapped, like a captive standing at the end of the gangplank on a buccaneer ship.

Her high-heeled sandals clickity-clacked as she pranced across the wide, weathered boards of the pier. "Ethan, what are you doing over here all by yourself? People are looking for you."

Of course they were. And why wouldn't they be? Somebody, somewhere, was always seeking him out for any one of a hundred reasons—a favor, a raise, a piece of advice, an introduction to another mover and shaker. With shoulders slumped, he shook his head. *Quit feeling sorry for yourself, pal*, he chided. As his mother would have pointed out, God had blessed him with a lot—materially and otherwise. *But He's taken away a lot, too....*

"Ethan?"

You've got two choices, m'friend, he told himself, grinning slightly as he looked at the water swirling darkly around the pilings. *Jump, or pretend you're pleased to see her.*

Turning, Ethan took a deep breath and fixed a practiced smile on his face. "Kate, darling," he said smoothly, taking the goblet of iced tea from her hand, "looks like you need a refill. Let me get—"

Laughing lightly, she patted her flat stomach. "Please," she gasped, "one more ounce of *anything* and I'll positively pop!"

There was an awkward pause, and Ethan knew she was waiting for him to fill the void with some form of flattery about her figure. Unable to think of a single truthful thing to say, he let the moment pass.

A quick glance at his Rolex told him it was nearly four in the afternoon. Another hour or so and the party would be over. The crowd had already thinned considerably; once the last of them had gone, he'd call Sam and Shari to see if they'd made their airline reservations yet. Last time they'd talked, he'd promised to have a car pick them up at Baltimore-Washington International Airport. They were the closest thing to a family he'd likely ever have, so nothing but the best for them!

Kate linked her arm through his and led him back toward the house. "It sure was nice of you to throw a Memorial Day barbecue for Burke employees and their families," she purred. "I want you to know...I'm *especially* happy to be here."

Yeah, I'll just bet you are, he thought.

His vice president, Pete Maxon, had told Ethan what he'd overheard Kate say two days prior: "If I play my cards right," she told the gaggle of gals gathered near the water cooler, "I'll be Mrs. Ethan Burke by this time next year!"

Mrs. Burke, my foot! "Couldn't very well invite everyone else and leave your name off the guest list, now, could I?" was his bland reply.

By the time Sam and Shari had made him guardian of their only daughter six years earlier, Ethan had pretty much accepted the idea that Molly was the closest he'd come to having a child. He would have loved kids—a house full of them—but a man needed a wife for that. And every female he'd met so far had been like Kate, keeping her tummy flat and her sights firmly fixed on his checkbook. Hardly mother material!

"You look very handsome today," she said, then threw back her head and laughed. "Which isn't to say you don't *always* look handsome. I just meant that in those jeans and that white shirt—"

A gale of robust laughter interrupted her. "Ethan, m'boy! *There* you are! Seems I've walked every inch of this plantation you call a home looking for you." The silver-haired gentleman fixed his gaze on Kate. "Well, now, no wonder I couldn't find him," he told her, wiggling his eyebrows. Leaning in close, he lowered his voice to add, "I'd make myself scarce, too, if my date was as lovely as you."

Ethan heard the phone ringing in the distance. Without knowing why, he tensed. Everyone who might have a reason to call him at home had been invited to the cookout. "Kate isn't my date, Dad," he said distractedly. "She's—"

"Dad?" Kate interrupted. "This attractive young fellow is your father?" She flung an arm over his shoulders. "Why, you don't look nearly old enough to have a son Ethan's age," she cooed.

The older man attempted a W. C. Fields imitation. "My dear, you're an outrageous flirt!"

Kate kept her eyes on Ethan's father. "Now I see where you get your good looks *and* your charm, Ethan."

She turned slightly, aiming a haughty expression at her boss. "We-e-e-ell?"

His stiff-backed stance and tight-lipped expression spoke volumes. At least they should have. Kate didn't seem to notice at all how much her presence irked him.

"Aren't you going to introduce us?"

Poor Kate, he thought. *She somehow got the idea that Dad has more money than Donald Trump.* Shoving both hands into his pockets, he stared at the close-cropped lawn in an attempt to hide his grin. *If this is going where I think it's going, you two deserve each other.* "Dad, this is Kate Winslow," came his bored monotone. "Kate, meet Sawyer Burke."

During the introductions, he noticed that the phone had stopped ringing, and he wondered if Maria had answered it or if the machine had taken the call. Wondered, too, why a sense of foreboding still churned in his gut.

"It's a pleasure to make your acquaintance, my dear," Sawyer said, bowing.

Her hands clasped beneath her chin, Kate giggled like a silly schoolgirl. "Oh, but the pleasure is all—"

"Meester Burke! Meester Burke!"

All heads turned toward the deck, where Ethan's housekeeper was leaning over the railing with a portable phone pressed to her aproned bosom. "Hurry," she yelled, waving him closer. "*Muy importante!*"

Maria had worked for Ethan for years. The only other time he'd heard her carry on that way had been last Christmas, when the warmth of the fire had brought hundreds of praying mantis nymphs to life in the branches of the twenty-foot Douglas fir that dominated the living room. His heart pounding with fear and dread, Ethan took the steps two at a time.

There were tears in the eyes of the plump, gray-haired woman when she said, "Oh, Meester Burke...poor leetle Molly...."

Not Molly, Lord, he prayed silently. *Please don't let anything have happened to my sweet Molly....*

With a trembling hand, he accepted the phone and slowly brought it to his ear. "Ethan Burke here...."

"Mr. Burke? Um, my name is, ah, Tricia Turner, and I'm a nurse at 'ampton 'ospital in London? I, uh, well...."

He had a yard full of guests, so why was the little Brit hemming and hawing? But the instant she finished her sentence, Ethan wished he'd never rushed her, even in his mind. Because not even her crisp Cockney accent made it easy to listen to the rapid-fire dispensation of information that followed. Sam and Shari had been killed in a car crash at Trafalgar Square, and their daughter was home alone with her nanny.

"She hasn't been told yet?"

The long pause made him wonder if they'd been disconnected. But then she said, "No. Before Mr. Sylvester passed on, he told us you're the child's guardian. He said you'd take care of everything, including breaking the news about her mum and dad." Another unbearable pause ensued before she added, "'e was one brave chap, that pal of yours, 'oldin' on till 'e knew 'is li'le one would be in good 'ands...."

Ethan slumped into the nearest deck chair, one hand in his hair, the other gripping the phone so tightly his fingers ached. The nurse's tone of voice rather than her words themselves told Ethan that Sam had suffered in the end. *But how like him to bite the bullet until all the loose ends were tied up.*

Suddenly, the full impact of the news hit him. Sam and Shari, *gone*? Ethan struggled to come to grips with the stunning reality—the finality—of it.

"Mr. Burke? Are y'there?"

The oh-so-British voice snapped him back to attention. "Yes. Yes, sorry."

"'ow long d'you suppose it'll take you to get 'ere? I don't mean to be crass, but there's the matter of...of...."

"Identifying the bodies?"

"Yes. Rules, y'know."

The bodies. The funeral arrangements. Ethan was at a loss for words.

"So you'll be 'ere soon, then...?"

Ethan hung his head, shading his eyes with his free hand. Sam and Shari had trusted him to do what needed to be done should anything like this ever happen. Of course, he hadn't expected there would ever be a need for him to follow through; they'd always been so full of vim and vigor, always so *alive*.

The word reverberated painfully in his brain. If he'd known, when he'd signed the documents making him executor of their estate, that the prospect of making those hard, under-pressure decisions would turn his blood to ice, he might have suggested they hire a lawyer instead. An outsider. Someone who didn't *love* them.

"How soon d'you think you can be 'ere, sir?"

A mental image of Molly, alone in the Sylvesters' London flat with some barely-out-of-her-teens nanny, flashed through his head. She needed him, and if he had to pull every favor owed him, if he had to charter a private jet, he'd get there by morning. "I'll be on the next London-bound plane leaving Baltimore," he said. And, thanking her, Ethan hung up.

Propping the phone on the arm of the deck chair, he stared out at the Potomac. It wouldn't be easy filling Sam's shoes. The guy had made fatherhood look as natural as breathing. No matter how tired or overworked he had been, Sam had always dug deep and found the energy to spend time with his little girl.

Molly had told Ethan no fewer than a dozen times that he was her favorite grown-up. It was one thing playing part-time uncle. Being a full-time dad was something else entirely.

For that precious child's sake, he hoped he was up to the task.

Three months later

Through the two-way mirror in the waiting room, Ethan watched the therapist working with Molly. Miss Majors had been recommended by Pastor Cummings. Ethan had prayed before making the decision, and he prayed now that it had been the right one.

He'd been at his wit's end wondering how to cope with Molly's sad, stoic silence. Then Maria had suggested he turn to his church for help. He might have thought of it himself, except that church hadn't exactly been at the center of his life for the past few years. If not for Molly's refusal to speak, he might not have started attending again. But he'd had no choice. Her condition was his fault—no ifs, ands, or buts.

His head in his hands, Ethan closed his eyes, unable to watch the child's sorrowful expression a moment longer. He loved her as if she were his own flesh and blood; loved her the way he'd loved his sister Bess, his mother....

Why did it seem that whomever he loved deeply suffered?

With his eyes still squinted shut, he couldn't see into the next room, but he could hear every word thanks to the speaker overhead. The pretty, young counselor was pulling out all the stops. She'd tried everything short of a song and dance act to this point, yet Molly hadn't uttered a syllable.

Ethan slouched on the sofa. He kept his eyes closed and let his mind wander back to that terrible morning in London when he'd broken the tragic news to Molly. Despite the speech he'd practiced over and over during the red-eye flight into Heathrow Airport, he'd messed up big time when the moment finally came.

When he'd arrived at Sam and Shari's, it had been easy to smile as Molly skipped around him in a slowly shrinking circle, clapping her hands and squealing with glee that her uncle Ethan had come to visit. They'd played this welcome game since she had been old enough to stand on her own, and he cherished every giggly moment.

That morning, she'd wrapped her arms around him, just as she'd done a hundred times before...and then stopped. "Mommy and Daddy haven't called...."

Worry and fear were etched on her little face, and even as Ethan had prayed for the right words to erase them, he'd known no such power would be granted him that day.

"They always call," she'd said, looking up into his face. "There must be something wrong...."

He'd perched on the edge of the sofa, invited her to sit down beside him, and then, with one arm resting on her slender shoulders, looked into those dark, trusting eyes...and lost it.

What kind of a man are you? Ethan had demanded of himself as tears coursed down his face. *You're blubbering like a baby.... It's your job to comfort Molly, not the other way around!* He'd never felt more like a heel than during those long, harrowing moments when she'd patted his shoulder, saying, "It'll be okay, Uncle Ethan. Don't cry. Won't you tell me why you're so sad?"

A minute or so later, after his carefully chosen words had been uttered, Ethan realized that in the space of a minute, maybe two, he'd completely destroyed her safe little world.

He hated the old adage that said, "Hindsight is always twenty-twenty." However, looking into her shocked, pained eyes made him understand the truth of it as never before. He'd prayed for a kinder, gentler way to break the news. So, why hadn't God delivered on His "ask, and ye shall receive" promise?

He should have been gentler. Should have eked out the information more slowly. Should have brought in a professional to help deliver the awful, life-changing news....

The ugly memory made him groan aloud and drive his fingers through his hair. The all-business attitude that had kept his nose to the grindstone while building Burke Enterprises had given him the drive and motivation to work until he thought he might drop, watch the market with a shrewd eye, and study his competitors even more closely. "Tell it like it is" had become watchwords—no exceptions. Straight talk had never let him down before, but it had backfired miserably that morning with Molly. He wondered what Miss Majors would say about his pathetic performance as a parent.

Well, at least he'd done *one* thing right—he hadn't gone into detail about the accident. He'd been to the morgue and seen his friends' battered, lifeless bodies. The poor kid sure didn't need the image of *that* in her head for a lifetime!

Ethan didn't think he'd ever forget the way her dark lashes had fluttered as her deep-brown eyes filled with tears. She'd begun to quake, as if each tremor was counting the beats of her breaking heart. "B-but...but they *promised*," she'd whimpered.

"Promised what, sweetheart?"

"That...that they'd never leave me. Th-that they'd be here for me, *forever*." She'd punched the sofa cushion. "They can't be dead. It isn't true! It isn't!"

Not knowing what to say, he'd simply held out his arms, his own eyes filling with tears again as he sent a silent message with one nod of his head: *Yes, it's true.*

For a moment, she'd simply sat, staring. Then she'd thrown herself into his arms, and they'd cried together.

Ethan had no idea how much time had passed—minutes? half an hour?—before her rib-racking sobs and shirt-soaking tears subsided. Then, Molly had sat back, dried her eyes with the hem of her plaid skirt, and sucked in a huge gulp of air. "It's my fault," she'd whispered, staring blankly ahead.

She hadn't said a word since.

And now, despite Miss Majors' valiant efforts, Molly sat stiff and straight in the bright-red armchair, ankles crossed and hands folded primly in her lap, staring at some indistinct spot on the floor.

It would feel good, actually, to confess his faults and frailties to this stranger; it would feel equally good when she gave him the tongue-lashing he deserved, not that taking his lumps would change anything.

The counselor stood up and walked over to the two-way mirror, flipped a switch on the wall, and tapped on the glass. Up to this point, Ethan had been able to see and hear everything that was going on in the exam room without being visible to its occupants. But now, Miss Majors and Molly could see and hear him, too. The counselor's beautiful green eyes zeroed in on his, and she smiled softly. "Mr. Burke, I realize Molly's session has ended, but I'm hoping you'll stay a few minutes to talk with me."

Ethan blinked, unnerved by her intense scrutiny. *Here it comes,* he thought, *the dressing-down of your life-time.* "I—uh, well, sure," he stammered, running a hand through his hair. He had the sudden feeling that this nervous habit betrayed a deep psychological disorder, and she must have read his mind, because Miss Majors tilted her head and raised an eyebrow.

She opened the door in the exam room that led to the waiting room, then walked past him purposefully to her office, tossing Molly's file on the blotter on her desk.

He followed and stood in the doorway. "She'll be fine in there," the counselor assured him. "As you can see, Molly is all wrapped up in a book she found on the shelf."

He glanced back into the exam room, where, sure enough, Molly was sitting in that same red chair with an open book in her lap. *How long was I lost in thought?* he wondered. "She hasn't been that interested in anything since I brought her home," he admitted, meeting the therapist's eyes. "How'd you get her to do that?"

"It's my job," she said in the same no-nonsense tone he remembered from the telephone conversations that had led up to this appointment. "Please, make yourself comfortable."

She gestured to an upholstered armchair facing her desk.

As comfortable as a body can get in a contraption like this, he thought, sliding onto its seat. Ethan immediately leaned forward, balanced elbows on knees, and said, "So, can you help her or not?"

Miss Majors was standing behind her chair, her pale pink-painted fingernails drumming on the wood-trimmed headrest. When she smiled, the room brightened. He was taken aback until he realized why her smile looked so different, so special. It wasn't a flirty grin intended to knock him for a loop or a seductive smirk meant to advertise her availability, which were the types he'd grown accustomed to receiving from women of all ages. Her smile was honest, unpretentious. She was offering herself, all right...but on a caring, professional level.

Ethan found his respect for her growing, and he'd opened his mouth to compliment her when she said, "Yes, we can help her. But it'll take time, perhaps a lot of it, to find out why she stopped talking."

Pausing, she plopped into her chair. "And it'll take a major time commitment from you, Mr. Burke."

Her voice was soothing, rhythmic, like the calming sound of the Potomac lapping at the piling that supported his pier. Ethan sat back and crossed his legs, resting an ankle on his knee. "I intend to cooperate in any way I can. Tell me what to do, and it's as good as done."

Miss Majors wrote something in Molly's file, then stood up and walked around to the front of her desk. Perching on one corner, she said, "I'm glad to hear that."

His mind began to wander as she matter-of-factly outlined a course of treatment. *She's not much bigger than most of her clients*, he mused. His gaze shifted from her big, green eyes to the mass of long, carrot-colored curls framing her face, making her look like a cross between Julia Roberts and Pippi Longstocking. And really, what kid wouldn't be attracted to a woman like that?

Earlier, as she'd walked ahead of him into her office, he'd felt like a cartoon character floating along on the delectable scent of flowers and sunshine. The aroma reminded him of the hedgerow behind his childhood home...lilacs? Honeysuckle?

Ethan shifted in his chair, suddenly angry with himself. What sort of person was he, anyway, having thoughts like that about the woman who would help his little Molly escape her self-imposed prison of silence?

"If you're agreeable, I'd like to hold all future sessions at your house," she was saying. "At least, until we make some headway."

It appeared she hadn't noticed how far his mind had wandered from Molly, and after a quick prayer of thanks, he nodded.

"I think she'll benefit from being in familiar surroundings."

"I agree."

Miss Majors lifted her chin a notch and tilted her head slightly as those bright eyes zeroed in on his face.

"I think it's important for you to be available for the first few sessions, if at all possible."

"Of course, it's possible," he blurted out. "Nothing is more important than Molly."

"Not even Burke Enterprises?"

He clenched his teeth. Hadn't he just said that Molly came first? What did she mean by that crack, anyway? "Not even Burke Enterprises," he affirmed.

She'd said it to put him to the test. He could see it in her eyes, in the way one eyebrow lifted at his response. He'd used the tactic himself plenty of times during hard business negotiations. And from the looks of her approving smile, he'd passed.

"Good," she said matter-of-factly. She returned to the other side of her desk, sat down, and opened her daily planner. "Three times a week, an hour at a time, for starters," she said, clicking a ballpoint pen into action. And without looking up, Miss Majors added, "Mornings are usually best for the kids."

Most of Ethan's business meetings were scheduled first thing in the morning. But he'd just underscored that nothing was more important than Molly, and he aimed to prove it. Reaching into his suit coat pocket, Ethan slid out his electronic calendar. "Nine o'clock?" he asked, hitting the On button.

The upward curve of her full, pink lips told Ethan she hadn't expected him to agree so quickly.

"I owe you an apology, Mr. Burke."

Confused, he blinked. "What? But...why?"

"For appearing inflexible." She shrugged. "I've been at this long enough to know that people rarely say what they mean. Especially people like you—with plenty of money—who can hire others to do what...."

It seemed to Ethan that she hadn't intended to be quite *that* open and honest. Maybe that would teach her

not to judge all her wealthy clients by the abysmal behavior of a few.

"Most parents say they want to help," she continued,
"and that they understand therapy will take time, and
patience, and cooperation. But what they really want
is...for me to perform a miracle. Like I'm equipped with a
magic wand that'll fix everything with one quick stroke."
She gave another shrug. "It's not an altogether fair tactic, but I'll do anything, say anything, go to any lengths,
to help my kids."

Her kids? Was that something all the self-professed
child experts said to worried parents? Half a dozen other
specialists had said the same thing...and had failed to
draw Molly out of her shell.

Still, there was something about Miss Majors that
made Ethan believe she could no more look him in the
eye and lie than leap from the roof of this three-story
building and fly to the parking lot! It made him want to
give her a shot, if for no other reason than that time was
running out. The longer Molly remained in her wordless
world, the harder it would be to coax her out of it.

"You're the expert," he conceded. "So even when it's
inconvenient, or difficult, I'll make whatever changes are
necessary to help Molly."

With pen poised above her book, she smiled. "Just
so we can get things started sooner rather than later,
what do you think of my coming to your house at seven
tomorrow evening? And when we wrap things up, we can
schedule dates and times that work for all of us."

"Sounds like a plan to me." Without knowing it, she'd
spared him having to cancel and reschedule tomorrow's
early-morning meetings. Ethan got to his feet and extended a hand. She stood up, too, and reached across
her desk to shake it. The power of her grip surprised
him, especially considering her slight frame. If her ideas

about helping Molly were as solid as her handshake, things would right themselves in no time.

Ethan pulled a business card out of his pocket and plucked a pencil from a mug on her desk overflowing with writing implements. "It's tough to find my driveway if you don't know what to look for," he said, sketching a small, crude map on the back of the card, "so this should make it a little easier. Just watch for a gray mailbox."

Accepting the map, she thanked him and, nodding, watched him as he left her office and entered the exam room. He felt her eyes on him as he took the girl by the hand and led her down the hall. If he hadn't glanced over his shoulder as he and Molly were waiting for the elevator, he'd never have seen her wiping tears from her gorgeous green eyes. The sight of it touched something in him, though he couldn't say *what*, couldn't understand *why*. Her reaction should have roused deep concern. After all, weren't therapists supposed to remain aloof and unemotional if they hoped to obtain successful results?

It wasn't like him to let go of a suspicion that quickly, that easily. He'd sealed many deals with nothing more than gut instinct to go on. So no one was more surprised than Ethan when he said a silent prayer asking God to help him figure out if he'd made the right choice for Molly—or if he simply wanted to *believe* he had—because something about the pretty counselor called to something desperately lonely deep within himself....

Chapter Two

The sun had begun to set, reminding Hope of a brassy coin sliding ever so slowly into a slot on the glowing horizon. She rolled down her car window and let the air riffle her curls. But neither she nor the wind could distract her mind from thoughts of Molly Sylvester.

Professional detachment, she'd learned, protected her from letting what she *felt* interfere with what she *knew* was best for her patients. And that mind-set had guided her well so far.

But things seemed different this time.

Very different.

In the four years since she'd become a Christian counselor, Hope had worked with hundreds of troubled children, some barely old enough to walk, others whose teenage years were all but behind them. Some had lost a mom or a dad, and, with prayer and plenty of tender loving care, she'd helped them come to terms with their grief. But Molly had lost both parents at the same time.

The night before, while poring over psychology books and case studies in search of answers to the long list of questions raised by Molly's refusal to speak, Hope couldn't help but wonder if that fact alone explained the close connection she felt to the sad-eyed child.

Lost in her thoughts, Hope missed the Route 270 exit. She'd barely gotten back on track when the map Ethan had drawn fluttered out the window. Now she'd have to pull over to call him and ask him to repeat the directions. Groaning inwardly, she wondered if he'd worry about having made a mistake by putting Molly in the hands of a woman who couldn't even hold on to the map that would help her begin the girl's therapy.

It shouldn't matter what he thought of her. Losing the directions that way—well, it could have happened to anyone. But for a reason she couldn't explain, it mattered. A lot. Hope shifted uncomfortably in the driver's seat, and just as she was about to steer toward the road's shoulder to call him, she spotted a large, round-topped, gray mailbox.

Hadn't Ethan said his mailbox was gray?

She slowed down, instantly noticing BURKE spelled out in bold, black letters. And beneath the name, 435 RIVER VIEW.

Hope pulled into the driveway and headed down the narrow ribbon of blacktop, thanking the Lord as she neared the house for sparing her from having to admit she'd lost the directions. The quickly waning light of day was further dimmed by the thin canopy of trees overhead. Hope's heart began beating in double time. She'd conducted therapy sessions in children's homes before, so she didn't understand why this particular one was making her so nervous.

But you do understand, she chided herself, remembering that after arriving home from work the night before, she'd typed Ethan Burke's name into an Internet search engine. In an eyeblink, a lengthy list had appeared on the screen, and, in no time, she'd found herself skimming photographs and articles of Ethan arm wrestling with Harrison Ford, Ethan posing with Maryland's governor, Ethan munching a hot dog from the bench inside the Orioles' dugout, Ethan at the Kidney Ball, Ethan at the American Heart Association Ball...a different glamorous woman clinging to his tuxedo-jacketed arm at each event.

Next, Hope had read the "Hometown Boy Does Good" story in the magazine section of the *Sunday Sun*. And the *Washington Post* piece that explained how he'd renovated the dilapidated historic manor house on his Potomac River property. She hadn't needed to print out any of the photos to get a clear picture of his lifestyle: Ethan Burke was a self-made millionaire, and, no doubt, a typical spoiled, self-centered bachelor.

A squirrel scampered in front of her car, and Hope braked hard to avoid hitting it. The critter froze when her tires squealed. "Didn't your mama teach you to look both ways before crossing the road?" she gently scolded the rodent as it darted into the thick underbrush alongside the driveway.

Much as she hated to admit it, the near miss had been more her fault than the squirrel's. Her attention had been diverted by imagining what Ethan's house would look like on the inside. She continued down the drive, expecting a stately two-story colonial. White, no doubt, with dozens of multipaned windows and black shutters. Would it feature a semicircular portico? Or huge marble pillars supporting a white-railed balcony? Surely, there'd be a guardhouse, with a red-jacketed servant who'd ask to see Hope's driver's license before allowing her access to Ethan Burke's haven....

Through the trees up ahead, two massive brick columns came into view, each holding up a black, wrought-iron gate. Instead of a sentry on duty, Hope found a stainless steel speaker attached to a black post. She pressed the button marked Talk and waited.

"Can I help you?"

Despite the sputtering and hissing sounds, she recognized the masculine voice in an instant. No wonder he'd so easily wooed the women in those pictures! "Hi, Mr. Burke...Hope Majors, here for my seven o'clock appointment with Molly...."

A second of silence ticked by before his voice cracked through the box again. "Hey there! Just sit tight while I open the gate...."

She gave a haughty little nod. "Why, yessir," she said to herself, doing her best to imitate a British accent. "Whatever you say, sir." In a matter of seconds, the heavy bulwark began creaking and squealing, as if protesting even this slow-motion activity. "Looks like you don't get much exercise," she told it as she drove through.

Around the next bend in the drive, Hope finally caught sight of the house. No stone lions stood guard on either side of the front door, but the house didn't need any to be impressive. With mouth agape and eyes wide, she stared through the windshield. The front face of the house—three stories tall and at least as wide—was more glass than weathered wood. Low, sculpted shrubs hugged the façade.

As soon as Hope stepped from her car, a tail-wagging black lab greeted her, zig-zagging along the red brick sidewalk ahead of her and stopping now and then to make sure Hope hadn't lost her way. The dog led her over a wooden bridge and through a Japanese garden, complete with bonsai, stone benches, colorful lanterns, and a gently bubbling fountain.

This is Ethan Burke's house? she marveled, touching a fingertip to a small, shiny leaf on the ball-shaped boxwood beside the front steps. Never in a million years would she have pictured him in a—

The door swung open so quickly that Hope lurched with surprise.

"Sorry," Ethan said, smiling sheepishly, "didn't mean to scare you."

She giggled nervously. "Don't mind me," she said, accepting his one-armed invitation into the mansion. "I've been the jumpy type my whole life. Why, my folks used to say—"

Hope bit her lower lip. *Why are you chattering like a magpie? You're here to help that sweet little girl, not to pay this ladies' man a social visit....*

"Your folks used to say what?" he asked, closing the door.

What he doesn't know can't hurt you, she said to herself. She shrugged. "That I was jumpy...."

Ethan chuckled and grinned, and it took her off guard. Another item to add to her quickly growing "Why Women Love Ethan" list. But really, smile or no smile, he looked even more handsome now than when he'd come to her office in a dark business suit. Its cut and color had made it impossible *not* to notice his barrel chest and his narrow waist and hips. And the starched white collar of his shirt had only served to make his slightly tanned face all the more obvious. There was no denying he was a handsome man. His suit, his stance, his *style* made him look smart and sexy and successful all at the same time. But now, in maroon leather loafers, softly faded khakis, and a cream-colored silk shirt, he looked relaxed, casual, down-to-earth.

"Never mix business with pleasure" had always been Hope's professional motto, and she'd never broken the self-imposed rule. Had never been tempted to. Until now.

It was more than the clothes and the smile. Hope had pegged Ethan as an English hunt-club type. A guy who liked big, clunky wood furnishings and dark plaid upholstery. *Wrong again!* she thought, scanning the enormous foyer.

Skylights lit the room, making the pendant lamps of chrome and opaque glass unnecessary, even at this hour. With the lamps lit, a warm, golden glow shimmered down like muted sunshine, illuminating the large faux leopard skin tacked to one wall. On another wall, black-and-white photos of animals in the wild captured her attention. "Those are beautiful," she ventured, openly admiring the pictures of zebras, lions, and giraffes. "Where did you buy them?"

"Didn't."

She glanced over her shoulder at him. "Didn't what?"

"Didn't buy them," he said matter-of-factly. "I took them myself."

Hope faced the photo wall again. "*You* took those?"

He shrugged, as if aiming a camera at exotic creatures was no big deal at all. "I thought a safari might cure what ailed me a couple of winters back."

She gave the rest of the space a quick once-over. "And what could possibly ail a man like you?"

His left eyebrow rose as if to say, "A man like me?" Instead, he said, "Boredom, emptiness, lack of purpose... you name it."

Boredom? Hope was incredulous.

He gave another shrug. "When you've done it all...."

She couldn't help but wonder if he'd managed to leave the negative feelings behind on the African veld, or if he still coped with nagging pessimism—even while living in the lap of luxury.

Her hands clasped behind her back, Hope pretended to study the large, full-color shot of a lion pride sprawled paws-over-whiskers beneath a gnarled acacia tree. "Our lives are what we make them, Mr. Burke," she said quietly. "I think maybe it's up to us to create our own sense of purpose." She paused, then added, "So did it?"

He cleared his throat. "Cure what ailed me, you mean?"

Hope nodded.

Slowly, Ethan shook his head. "Not really."

She contemplated his words, remembering that out front, she'd parked her sensible sedan beside a racy, low-slung red convertible that was tethered to a shiny trailer carrying an iridescent blue hang glider. He owned acres of riverfront property, lived in a literal mansion, had the financial wherewithal to travel to faraway lands...surely, he wasn't serious about being *bored*!

Hope wondered what made him think he could raise an emotionally distraught orphan with an attitude like that. But then, guilt began to tug at the corners of her mind. *Give him a break,* she told herself. *At least he's willing to try.* Which was more than she could say for some folks....

She smiled and faced him, preparing to ask where Molly was and when they might begin their session. If she'd known how it would affect her—seeing the way he looked against the backdrop of life-sized wooden giraffes, zebra paintings, and towering plants—Hope wouldn't have turned around. It seemed to her that Ethan Burke *belonged* in that setting with his rugged good looks and Jack Hanna getup.

She recalled bits and pieces of the information gleaned from her online research: he'd raced stock cars. Had flown twin-engine planes. Climbed mountains. Sailed the seven seas. Yet he'd come right out and admitted that his thrilling life hadn't thrilled *him*. Now her heart ached for little Molly, and she wondered how Ethan would feel about a child who, with her grief and misery, would tether him to one spot indefinitely. If everything he'd experienced in life had left him feeling empty, what did he have, really, to offer a needy little girl?

Would Molly be made to feel like a ball and chain, the way Hope had felt as a child? Or, worse, would she be just one more possession to show off at summer soirees before being trotted off to some fancy, faraway boarding school?

Well, Hope thought grimly, *at least she'd be at the best boarding school money could buy.*

Ethan chuckled softly. "You look as though you've just stepped into the Twilight Zone." He punctuated his observation by whistling a few notes from the show's theme song.

Hope didn't know what to say, so she let a quiet giggle suffice as a reply. Just then, Ethan's big black lab rescued her by trotting up and sitting at her feet, his chocolate-brown eyes pleading for attention. An animal lover for as long as she could remember, Hope got down on her knees and took the dog's face in her hands. "So, what's it like living at the zoo, big fella?"

A quiet, breathy bark was his answer.

As she got to her feet, she asked Ethan, "What's his name?"

"Dino."

She looked at the dog and gave his head an affectionate pat. "Funny, he doesn't look Italian."

Ethan laughed. "I didn't name him. The neighbors did."

In response to her inquiring expression, he added, "He's here often enough to be mine, though." Pocketing his hands, he said, "All the perks of a pet without the vet bills. But best of all, Molly loves him."

"I'm sure he's good for her. Especially now."

"Molly's quite a kid. But I imagine you already learned that."

At the mention of the child's name, the dog's ears perked up.

"She's in her room, fella," Ethan said, bending to scratch Dino's chin. "Go on, and tell her she has company; you'll save me a trip upstairs...."

Dino bounded up the curved wooden staircase and disappeared through a doorway at the top. "Hurry, boy!" Hope called after him, feigning alarm. "Timmy's trapped in the well, and we've gotta get help!" Giggling, she added, "If he actually brings her down here, I'll eat my hat."

"You're not wearing a hat."

She matched his smile, tooth for tooth. "Then I'll get one."

No sooner had she spoken than Dino appeared on the landing. He barked once, then sat on his haunches and looked over his shoulder, waiting for Molly to join him.

Ethan put his back to the staircase and whispered, "The only time there seems to be a spark of life in her eyes is when she's with that dog."

Hope couldn't help but notice the way Ethan's smile brightened at the sight of Molly. He took a step forward, gripped the railing, and looked up at her, as if giving in to some unconscious, magnetic pull. He loved her like his own daughter, and it was written all over his face.

A magical moment ticked by before Hope broke the silence. "Well, there she is, Mr. Burke. Good for what ails you."

When counselor and patient emerged from Ethan's teak-paneled den at the conclusion of the therapy session, Hope's senses were overwhelmed by the steamy scents reminiscent of a five-star Italian restaurant. "I don't know about you," she said, giving Molly's hand an affectionate squeeze, "but now I'm *glad* I said I'd stay for supper!"

Her first inclination had been to politely turn down the invitation. Ethan must have read the latent response in her expression, because he'd quickly added, "I'm sure it will be good for Molly...."

Now, Hope glanced at the girl, whose only response had been the quirk of one dark eyebrow. On the chance that the minuscule change in Molly's expression had meant that she *wanted* Hope to stay, she'd said yes.

But she'd expected boiled hot dogs and pork 'n beans. Or grilled cheese sandwiches and canned tomato soup. Pizza, even, or subs, delivered by a teenage boy in a baseball cap.

"I hope you like stuffed shells," Ethan said as they entered the kitchen.

"If they taste even half as good as they smell, I think I'll like them just fine!"

For a second, she would have sworn Molly had mirrored his smile. But the girl quickly averted her gaze and focused on the black-and-white tile floor beneath her pink-sneakered feet. She looked so small, so vulnerable, that Hope gave in to the sudden urge to hug her. Getting on her knees, she placed her hands on Molly's slender shoulders. "You've taste-tested your uncle Ethan's stuffed shells before, haven't you?"

The instant of eye contact was deep and intense, and Hope knew better than to waste the precious moment. "You should've warned me," she added with a grin and a wink, "and I wouldn't have eaten those cookies he brought in earlier." She punctuated the joke with a light kiss on the tip of Molly's nose, then stood and draped an arm around her...and it warmed her to the soles of her feet when the child didn't fight it.

Ethan plopped a hot baking dish onto a wicker trivet, then removed his thick oven mitts. "You don't mind eating in the kitchen, do you?"

"Actually, I prefer it," Hope admitted. "The kitchen is my favorite room in any house."

Smiling, he nodded. "Make yourself comfortable while I pour the iced tea."

"What can I do to help?"

"Not a thing," he said, watching as Molly slid onto the caned seat of a ladder-back chair. The way she sat—eyes downcast and hands primly folded on the tile-topped table—made Hope wonder if she might be praying. *But what are you praying for, little one? Your mommy and daddy to come back?*

Hope understood that desire only too well. If she had a dollar for every time she'd said that same prayer....

She took a deep breath and sat down across from Molly, reminding herself that if she hoped to keep her professional distance, she'd have to watch herself closely. This kid reminded her entirely too much of her own childhood.

A cursory assessment would suggest that the sweet-faced girl had nothing at all in common with Hope. For starters, Molly had gleaming black hair, while Hope's freckled face was framed by a wild mane of fiery curls. Molly saw the world through dark, almond-shaped eyes; Hope's were long-lashed and green.

There, the most salient differences ended.

Both were tiny and feminine, and they moved in fits and starts like small birds skittering among fallen leaves in search of nourishment, companionship, *family*.

Both had been traumatized by the loss of their parents early in life.

Both were alone in the world.

But that wasn't entirely true. Molly had Ethan....

"Shall we say grace?" he asked, taking his place at the head of the table.

Hope blinked in surprise, which inspired a quiet laugh from Ethan. "I haven't been a regular churchgoer," he stated, flapping a white linen napkin across his knees, "but that's going to change." He glanced at Molly, who sat silent and still, staring into her empty plate. "She needs the community and support of a parish family. Never more than now."

Nodding, Hope said, "I couldn't agree more."

"And when I have to be out of town on business, I know just the family that'll give it to her."

If he doled out much more warmth, Hope thought, she might roast from the inside out!

He folded his hands and shot her an amused grin. "Let me guess...you're wondering what a guy like me sounds like when he talks to God...."

She blushed slightly and stared down at her own plate. How did he know precisely what she was thinking?

Without further comment, he closed his eyes and bowed his head. "Father, we thank You for this food and for blessing us with good health and the protection of a safe home."

When he paused, Hope found herself criticizing his words, because how would a footloose and fancy-free guy like him know the difference between a good home and a lousy one?

"Thank You, too," Ethan continued, "for sending Miss Majors into our lives. Bless her with Your loving wisdom so she'll know how to help my sweet Molly find her voice again." He reached across the table and laid one hand atop the child's. "'Cause I sure do miss hearing her say how much she loves me...." His smooth, resonant voice cracked slightly, and he cleared his throat. "Amen" came on the heels of a gruff, growly breath.

"Amen," Hope echoed.

Ethan grabbed a long-handled spoon and scooped up two shells, depositing both on Molly's plate. "Extra sauce on top?" he asked. And without waiting for a reply, he traded spoon for ladle and poured thick, spicy sauce over her meat-and-spinach-filled pasta. "Of course you do," he said, grinning nervously. "You love Italian food smothered in sauce, don't you?"

"I'd like to meet the person who *doesn't* love it!" Hope said.

"My father, for starters...."

Hope helped herself to a dipper of extra sauce while Ethan sprinkled grated parmesan over Molly's meal, then his own. "Why?" she asked. "He doesn't like garlic? Oregano?"

"No...Dad's just...different."

Was it her imagination, or did Ethan seem to harbor some sort of grudge against his father? Hope didn't dwell on the question long, because soon, she'd have the answer to that question—and more. And by the time she got Molly talking again, she'd know more about Ethan than he could ever have dreamed possible.

But she hadn't been right about him in any respect so far. What made her think he'd willingly open up and share personal, private information about his most intimate relationships?

"How's your iced tea, kiddo...sweet enough?" he asked Molly.

But the girl barely acknowledged him, poking sullenly at her food with one tine of her fork. The only sound she'd made since sitting down was the squeal of chair legs as she'd scooted closer to the table. Hope had noticed how she'd winced at the noise, as if it had disrupted the balance in her quiet, solitary world. She made a mental note to use musical instruments, television shows, CDs—a variety of sounds—at their next session to determine which of them elicited the strongest—and most positive—response.

Like a nervous mother hen, Ethan hovered. Sprinkling a little more cheese atop her sauce, he said, "Remember that time I found you sitting by the fridge with a spoon in one hand and your cheeks stuffed like a chipmunk's with Romano?" Laughing, he watched for a reaction.

Hope's heart ached for him, because despite his female magnetism, which came without much effort, he seemed to be putting his "all" into interacting with this girl—but to no avail. Most people in his situation would try for a few weeks, at best, before throwing in the towel. To his credit, he'd stuck it out for months now, and Hope knew with certainty he'd stick it out for the duration. She gave him credit for that.

Hope glanced furtively at Ethan. Was he aware that when he looked at Molly, his love for her was as evident as the dab of tomato sauce on his chin? Yes, he was trying, all right. Smiling, Hope tacked a line onto the prayer he'd said at the start of the meal: *Lord, help me reach her...for Ethan's sake, as well as her own.*

Chapter Three

E than eased the covers under Molly's chin. "You comfy, sweetie? Got enough pillows? Is the blanket too heavy?"

He heaved a sad sigh. *Might as well be talking to myself.* But he shouldn't have been disappointed; she hadn't responded in any way since that awful moment in Sam and Shari's London flat when she'd finally accepted the fact that her mom and dad were gone for good.

That was three long months ago!

He'd dedicated himself these past weeks to her one-on-one care. Except for the three to four hours every day when he absolutely had to be at the office—when Maria watched over her—he'd spent every moment with this precious child. He'd obtained permission to keep her out of school, at least until there'd been some progress with the counseling.

On his knees now, Ethan sandwiched her hands between his own. "Lord Jesus," he prayed aloud, "send Your strongest, smartest angels to watch over my sweet Molly tonight. Bless her with beautiful dreams, and let the sunshine kiss her awake in the morning. And remind her how very much her uncle Ethan loves her. Amen."

He tried to remember if she'd been three or four when he'd made up that prayer just for her. She'd loved it and had memorized it almost from the very first recitation. During Ethan's visits to London and the Sylvesters' trips to his place, she'd always say it with him, her lilting soprano harmonizing with his deep baritone.

Ethan had repeated the prayer every night since Molly had come to live with him, but the words always sounded hollow and flat without the music of her voice. So was it habit that made him persist in praying it? Or was it pure stubbornness?

Stubbornness, he decided as he got to his feet, *because I intend to say it every night for the rest of her life!* Bending down low, he pressed a paternal kiss to her forehead. "G'night, Molly, m'love," he whispered, and when she closed her black-lashed eyes, he kissed her again and then waited...hoping....

Each time Ethan had stayed with Sam and Shari in London, Molly had insisted that her uncle Ethan tuck her in every night of his visit. The ritual had started when Molly was still in diapers: Shari would feign impatience as she instructed the child to go to bed; Molly, dressed in a ruffly nightgown, would dawdle until Ethan lumbered up the steps behind her, pretending that the last thing he wanted to do was tuck her into bed.

She'd known as well as her parents how much Ethan treasured their little game, and, as if to prove it, she'd wrap her arms around his neck and squeeze for all she was worth. "I *love* you, Uncle Ethan!" would echo from every wall of her pretty pink bedroom as she snuggled into her blankets, wiggling her eyebrows with a mischievous glint sparkling in her dark eyes. "Will you read me a story?" she'd ask, a fingertip between her lips.

He'd "reluctantly" agree...and read book after book until she fell asleep.

They'd played the game last Christmas. Could it really have been just nine months ago? She'd been so happy and well-adjusted, secure in the belief that Mom and Dad and Uncle Ethan would always be there for her.

Would she ever feel that safe, that sheltered, again?

Ethan's fists clenched at his sides. *Yes, she will, he vowed, even if I have to move heaven and earth to make it happen!*

She looked so sweet, so innocent, lying in the middle of the queen-sized bed. He wanted nothing more than to shield her from all pain. But he couldn't do that, especially since she refused to tell him what was wrong.

He settled for a hug. "Ahh, sweetie," he said, gathering her close, stroking her silken black hair, "I sure do miss you. Miss you *so much!*"

Her only response was a long, shuddering breath.

Gently, Ethan tucked the covers back around her and plumped her pillows. "Won't you tell me what's wrong, darlin'?"

Silence.

Sitting on the edge of her bed, he lifted her chin on a bent forefinger until their gazes locked. "I'd do anything, *anything* for you. You know that, don't you?"

He'd said it before, hundreds of times in the months since Sam and Shari's accident, yet Ethan hoped that tonight, maybe, she'd say, "Yes, I know...."

Molly stared deep into his eyes, and for the first time since he'd brought her into his home, Ethan believed she was really *seeing* him. There was a certain light, a new intensity in the dark, shining orbs that he hadn't seen since....

...Since before he'd told her Sam and Shari were dead.

"Whatever you want, honey, you name it and it's yours. I promise."

Her brows drew together, as if to say, "Promise? Ha!" But even that slight response heightened his hope. "I've never broken a promise to you, have I?"

The little furrow in her brow deepened. He read it as a no, taking heart in the belief that she at least trusted him. The fingers of his right hand formed the Boy Scout salute. "I give you my word, Molly. Tell me what you want, and I'll get it for you."

She lay quietly, alternately blinking and staring, for what seemed like an hour. He watched with rapt attention as her chin quivered and she inhaled a shallow breath.

Was she...was she going to *talk*?

Ethan held his own breath and sat perfectly still. He couldn't, *wouldn't* risk a sound or movement that might cause her to change her mind. *Please, God*, he prayed silently, *please....*

Her eyes widened, and her lower lip trembled.

Lord Almighty in heaven, please....

Surely God had it in mind to answer Ethan's heartfelt prayers. Eventually. *Right, Lord?*

Molly's lips formed a thin, taut line as tears welled up in her eyes. She sighed audibly, gave a brief shake of her head, and then turned away, as if to say, "Don't make promises you can't keep."

Because, of course, she wanted only one thing. She wanted her mom and dad back, and he couldn't make that wish come true no matter how many strings he pulled, no matter how many dollars he spent. He understood, suddenly, that his repeated promises to give her anything sounded like the shallow, superficial oath of a desperate man.

But I am desperate!

He couldn't afford to wallow in self-pity, however. Molly would remain at the center of his focus. He'd be there for her the way he hadn't been for his mother, for Bess. He hadn't been man enough to save *them*, but by all that was holy, he'd do everything in his power to save this kid—or die trying.

On his feet again, Ethan brushed back Molly's bangs, hoping she wouldn't notice his trembling fingers. "Silly of me to make promises I can't keep," he said. "I should've known you're way too smart to fall for a line like that."

He swallowed and said a quick, silent prayer that God would give him the strength and the inspiration to say something, anything, that would comfort her—right this minute—because she needed comfort *now*.

"I can promise you this," he said, his voice rasping on a pent-up sob, "I love you, Molly-girl. I've loved you from the moment I first set eyes on you, and I'll love you all the days of my life."

For the second time in as many minutes, she looked at him. *Really* looked at him. He'd told her before that he loved her, probably thousands of times over the years. And except for those months before she'd learned to talk, she'd always echoed the words. Would she say them now? Was it too much to hope?

Lord, he prayed again, *please....*

As suddenly as she'd let him into her solitary, silent little world, she squeezed her eyes shut, turned toward the wall, and shut him out again. If God planned to answer Ethan's prayer, it obviously wouldn't be tonight. *She's in Your hands now, Lord*, he thought, pulling her bedroom door closed behind him. And as he shuffled down the hall, he wondered how many times he'd say *that* before this was over.

The soles of his sneakers squeaked as he made his way down the polished hardwood steps and headed across the foyer. He stopped for a minute, hands in his pockets, and stood staring at the intricate pattern beneath his feet.

In keeping with the jungle theme in this room, he'd sent to Malaysia for the wood. And it had taken nearly six months to interview a dozen craftsmen in search of the one who could turn Ethan's rough sketches into reality. It had been well worth the wait, because the man he'd hired was a true artist. The honeyed teak was inlaid with a lion and a lamb, carved from mahogany, lying side by side beneath a small tree. The scene was amazingly lifelike, from the light reflected in the animals' gentle gazes to the veins in each leaf above them.

Evidence of Ethan's ability to "pull strings" and "make things happen" didn't end there. Most of the carpets had been imported from Persia; hammered brass urns from Morocco and hand-blown glass vases from Italy decorated tables he'd purchased in Brazil.

When he'd made it known that he had his eye on a writing table that had once belonged to a czar, everyone had said he'd never talk the Russian government into letting him buy it, but he did. And no one had believed he'd ever convince the family of a silent-film star to part with the one-of-a-kind four-poster bed in which Molly was now sleeping.

"Put enough digits ahead of the decimal," he'd assured the doubters, "and *nothing* is priceless."

He ran a hand over the smooth top of the writing table that now stood near his front door. Yes, he'd gotten pretty good at pulling strings to get what he wanted, but his formerly prized acquisitions gave him no comfort, brought him no pleasure. And this time, being "connected" wouldn't do him a whit of good. This time, money couldn't buy what he was lacking.

What did the well-traveled businessman who lived in a riverfront mansion, who owned a garage filled with antique roadsters and pricey sports cars, lack?

His best friends, Sam and Shari, for starters.

And the soul-satisfying sound of Molly's voice.

He caught a quick mental glimpse of her, looking for all the world like a fragile porcelain doll against the starched white sheets. Shaking his head, he again tried to figure out *why* Molly's silence made him feel completely helpless.

But he knew the answer. It was his fault she'd stopped talking. He'd blundered into her flat like a bull in a china shop and had blurted out the truth like a clumsy oaf, shocking her so badly that it was possible she would never recover.

The admission made his heart pound.

Ethan ran a hand through his hair and headed for the kitchen, his footsteps echoing in the big, bright room. The refrigerator motor hummed. Ice *kerchunked* into the plastic bin in the freezer. The dishwasher droned. Fluorescent overhead lights buzzed. The cabinet door squeaked when he opened it to get a glass, and the crescent-shaped ice cubes clinked and cracked as he filled it with gurgling water. The Westminster chimes of the carriage clock in the kitchen hutch announced it was 8:45.

He'd never been aware of all this *noise* before. Why was he noticing it now?

He knew the answer to that, too. Usually, the house was brimming with guests.

If he'd invited government officials, visiting foreign dignitaries, entertainers, and authors because he'd enjoyed their companionship, it would have been one thing. But the fact of the matter was, he usually kept the house bustling with activity because he couldn't stand the silence. He couldn't stand being alone.

And who could blame him? If any of those VIPs knew what sort of man he truly was, they wouldn't want to be alone with him, either.

He didn't like himself, and the reason was simple. As he saw it, he had a character flaw of immeasurable proportions; a deficiency, a defect that cut so deep, he couldn't even come up with a name for it. Whatever it was, well.... *Three strikes and you're out, Burke....*

For the second time that night, Ethan shook off a horrible memory. He was about to take a sip of water when it dawned on him. The cut-crystal goblet was part of a collection that had belonged to a Hawaiian king. It hadn't been easy finding the matching pitcher in a Civil War shop. If he sold either, he could easily pay cash for one of those subcompact cars the teenagers were driving these days.

He started chuckling. It was ridiculous, really—his sitting here in the lap of luxury. What was the point of having it all if "it all" was useless in helping the people he loved?

Soon, his rumbling laughter was echoing off every wall in the cavernous kitchen. Tears sprang to his eyes as he wheezed and chortled, one hand repeatedly slapping his thigh, the other clutching the footed drinking glass.

He didn't know when, exactly, his tears of mirth turned into tears of another kind. All Ethan knew was that he didn't *like* feeling helpless. Hadn't liked it when his father had deserted his mother years back; hadn't liked it when she'd grieved herself to death over it.

There was no noise. No conversation. No "good host" duties to help him escape his dark thoughts this time. He'd deliberately cleared the house of partygoers and long-term guests to ensure that Molly had a tranquil haven where she could adjust to her new life and accept that....

...That the guy who's in charge of her doesn't have a clue. About anything.

As usual, the helpless feelings reminded Ethan what an irresponsible lout he was.

Bess's accident had been his fault, after all. He'd believed it at fourteen, and he believed it now. If he'd gone to summer camp with her that year, as he'd done every year before, she'd never have fallen on the pier. He would have seen to it that she didn't go where she shouldn't.

But you didn't want her tagging along everywhere you went. You didn't want the guys razzing you about your four-foot-tall shadow.

It was his own immature selfishness that he blamed for the accident that had left his sister wheelchair-bound and nearly deaf. And his stubborn streak had been the reason for her death ten years later.

Emotionally spent, Ethan put the glass onto the table with a *thump*. He'd let an awful lot of people down....

That belief had fueled his main ambition in life: to make money—more than anyone could imagine possible—to pay for the harm he'd caused.

In the years since Bess's death, he'd been doggedly determined to see that her memory, at least, lived on. So, he'd donated money to dozens of charities, funded the additions of new wings to hospitals, paid to put the latest equipment into school computer labs and the great works of literature in their libraries...all in Bess's name.

But just as his money couldn't erase his guilt and shame, it also couldn't help Molly. He'd called in every favor. He'd spent hours on the Internet and even more hours on the phone searching for *the* top specialist, the great expert, the one miracle worker who could get his Molly talking again and put her back on the path of the living.

He slumped onto the seat of the very chair in which Miss Majors had sat earlier. Ironic that her name was Hope—because she was his last hope. The even greater irony was that if she could help Molly, it would cost him next to nothing!

The carriage clock he'd purchased at Asprey in London began counting out the nine o'clock hour, each hollow note reminding him how truly alone he was.

But wait.

He wasn't alone.

He had Molly!

And she has you.

Ethan rubbed his eyes and shook his head. *What a wicked joke life's played on the poor kid*, he thought, *making an orphan of her first as an infant and then again when Sam and Shari died, then sticking her with a guardian who is helpless and powerless to do anything for her that really matters.*

Something shiny winked up at him from the floor, and Ethan crouched down to pick it up. "Hmm," he said distractedly, inspecting it, "a butterfly earring...."

It belonged to Hope Majors. Had to. Because Molly didn't wear anything but ladybugs and daisies, and Maria's choice of earrings had always been gold hoops.

He dried his eyes on the cuff of his shirt and pictured Hope—wide, green eyes and curly, coppery hair. He didn't think he'd ever seen longer, thicker eyelashes or a sweeter, more sincere smile. Her voice was softly soothing, every word reminding him of wind chimes...and those tiny, silver bells his mom used to put on the Christmas tree. And despite the fact that she was barely bigger than a minute, Hope seemed to have more spunk and spark in her curvy little body than any woman he'd known.

If anyone can get through to Molly, she can, he thought, closing his fingers around the butterfly.

Then he opened his hand and put the earring in his other palm. Had her father given it to her? A brother? He didn't like the possibility that it might have been a gift from a boyfriend. Or, worse yet, a fiancé. *You only just met the woman, Burke, and she's Molly's counselor, for the love of Pete.*

But given a choice between the green-eyed monster and self-loathing, he'd take the beast any day.

A slow smile spread across his face as he took another sip of cool water. Nodding, Ethan dropped the earring into his shirt pocket. *First thing in the morning*, he thought, giving his pocket a pat, *I'll call her.* "Anything missing?" he'd ask. And she'd probably say, "Only one of my favorite earrings...." And that's when he'd invite her to lunch, a two-birds-with-one-stone meal, during which he could quiz her about Molly's progress and return her little silver butterfly.

The carriage clock ticked quietly now, counting off the seconds with mechanical precision. He knew that it had never been more than eight seconds slow. If it said 9:07, then it was seven minutes after nine, meaning he'd have to wait nearly twelve full hours to make a call to Hope's Rockville office.

He turned off the overhead lights and headed upstairs, thinking that maybe tonight he would read one of the books that had been cluttering his nightstand for months. Maria would sure be glad to have one less book to dust....

Or maybe he'd watch some television—if he could remember how to make the flat-screen TV appear from behind the wooden panels covering its wall mount.

Carrying his water goblet onto the balcony off of his room, Ethan sat in one of the showy deckchairs he'd ordered from that high-priced outfit in New York and watched the moonlight shimmering on the Potomac. He caught himself praying this feeling would never disappear.

He was a fool. He knew that better than anyone. But he couldn't put the pretty little therapist out of his mind. She'd been aptly named, he thought.

And then an idea formed in his head....

Maybe hope was the thing he'd been searching for, that elusive, missing puzzle piece that always made him feel incomplete.

And maybe Hope Majors would help him find it.

Chapter Four

"Miss Majors, please."

"This is Hope...."

It wasn't quite nine o'clock, but it didn't surprise Ethan that she was already in her office. Nor did it surprise him that she'd answered her phone on the first ring. Ethan smiled, for he'd recognized her voice instantly. For one thing, he'd never heard another like it. For another, he'd been hearing it all through the night in his dreams.

Her small counseling practice was affiliated with Rockville General Hospital, and she probably didn't earn enough to hire a receptionist. "The reason I'm calling," he began, clearing his throat, "is that I found a butterfly earring under the kitchen table after you left. And since Molly hasn't pierced her ears yet, and Maria hasn't developed a fondness for this particular species, I figured it must be yours."

He could almost see her grabbing one earlobe and then the other to see which one was missing.

"So *that's* where it is!"

"Maybe if you have time for lunch, I can return it. I have a few questions to ask you about Molly's treatment."

He heard the unmistakable sound of Velcro and presumed she'd opened her daily planner.

"I'm free after one," she said, "if that isn't too late for lunch."

A quick glance at his own calendar showed a one o'clock meeting to discuss the expansion of one of his smaller holdings, a printing firm in Baltimore's enter-prise zone. The senator was a busy woman, and it had taken two weeks of telephone tag to get this appoint-ment. If he canceled now, there was no telling when he'd get another chance to speak with her. So Ethan couldn't believe his own ears when he said, "One is fine."

"Where would you like me to meet you?"

Right here, right now, he wanted to blurt out. "Ever been to Saxon's?" he heard himself say.

"No...where's that?"

He swallowed a note of disappointment. When he'd acquired the eatery a couple of years back, he'd launched a major advertising campaign, complete with television and radio ads. Obviously, they hadn't reached *all* of his intended audience. "It's on Rockville Pike," he said, "right before you—"

"Oh, you mean that place with the gigantic sword and shield on the sign?"

Amazing, he thought, *that tens of thousands of dol-lars didn't accomplish what a five-hundred-dollar sign did.* "That's the place!"

"I've heard they have a real French chef...."

She'd heard right. Ethan had flown to Paris to taste-test Henri's culinary concoctions before offering him the job. "So I hear...."

"Kinda weird, don't you think...? A French chef in a German-sounding restaurant?"

"Never gave it a thought," he admitted, remembering that Saxon's had a decent following when he bought it.

"...never been inside," she was saying, "so I hope I'm dressed appropriately." On the heels of a girlish giggle, Hope added, "Wouldn't want to embarrass you or anything."

Embarrass me? He pictured the sensible suit she'd been wearing the first time they'd met, followed by the slacks and light sweater she'd had on last night. *You could wear holey sneakers, raggedy blue jeans, and a bulky sweatshirt and still outshine most of the women in the place!* "I'm sure whatever you're wearing will be just fine."

From out of the blue, she asked, "Who's staying with Molly while you're at the office?"

It didn't surprise him that she asked. What surprised him was that it had taken this long for her to ask. "She's with Maria, my housekeeper." He hesitated. "The woman loves Molly almost as much as her own kids, and Molly feels the same way about her."

Hope must have heard his secretary's *buzz*, because she said, "Well, my nine-fifteen is here. See you at one!"

But because he didn't want to hang up, Ethan scrambled for something to say. "Right. One. I'll get there a few minutes early, try to snag us a booth near the windows so we'll have a river view."

"A river view?"

She sounded distracted, and he would've sworn he heard the sounds of an eraser, drumming on her desktop. *She's Molly's therapist, and you're carrying on like you just scheduled a romantic lunch!* As the heat of a blush warmed his cheeks, he said, "Right. One. See you then." And finally hung up.

He checked his Rolex and frowned. Quarter after nine. It wasn't like he didn't have plenty to occupy him between now and one o'clock. There was the meeting with the senator to reschedule, for starters. And his accountant would arrive any minute. Then, there was the matter of going over the household books with Maria....

But something told him it would still be a long four hours....

Hope parked beside Ethan's racy sports car and took a deep breath as she checked her lipstick in the rearview mirror. Between appointments and all during the drive across town, she'd rehearsed what she intended to tell him as soon as their lunch was delivered.

First of all, she practiced in her head as she walked across the parking lot, *I'd like to suggest that you warm up the atmosphere of that house a bit, even if only in Molly's room.* That wasn't to say it wasn't an interesting place with all the eclectic collectibles scattered about. But the sleek angles of wood and glass, combined with the wild animal décor, made it feel more like a museum than a home. And maybe he could plan a shopping trip to buy girlie clothes, some stuffed animals, and feminine toys to help her adjust more quickly.

During the tour he'd given her of the mansion, those ideas had been on the tip of her tongue, and it had taken all her willpower *not* to recommend that he turn one of the guest rooms into a playroom. Though it had been nighttime when she'd seen the house, Hope could tell that during the day, sunshine would stream in through the tall arched windows. And with that view of the river....

She spotted Ethan the instant she stepped into the dining room. He'd chosen a table near the windows, just as he'd said he would. Backlit by the blue, cloud-dotted sky and wearing a brown pinstriped suit, he looked like a male cover model.

"May I help you, miss?" the maître d' asked, giving her a quick once-over.

"I'm here to meet that gentleman," she answered, pointing at Ethan.

The man tucked in his chin as if to say, "I'll take you over there, but if you ask me, you're way outta your league, missy." He shot her a stiff, well-practiced smile and said, "Of course, my dear." Tucking a gold-trimmed black leather menu under his tuxedoed arm, he added, "Follow me, please."

As they made their way across the plush carpet, Hope noted the deep-green custom drapery treatments topping every window, the rich upholstery on every mahogany chair, the brocade linens atop each table. Silver flatware clinked against china dinner plates as other patrons ate their meals, and the crystals of a dozen chandeliers rained rainbow light upon the goblets at each place setting.

"Miss Majors," Ethan said, standing up when she arrived at his table. "So good to see you again." He pulled out her chair and then returned to his own while the maître d' flapped a heavy linen napkin across her knees.

"Have you been waiting long?" she asked, taking the menu offered by the maître d'.

Ethan shook his head. "No, no; not long at all." He nodded at the man. "Jasper," he said, "bring the lady one of our special menus, will you please?"

The man took back her menu and bowed. "Yes, yes of course, Mr. Burke. Will there be anything else, sir?"

"That'll do for now," Ethan said, smiling.

Hope watched Jasper hurry away and whisper something to a tuxedoed fellow at the bar. The two chanced a peek toward Ethan's table, then disappeared around the corner. A second later, when a server in a starched black uniform poked her head out from behind the gilded partition, Hope met Ethan's gaze. "You must come here quite often."

He shrugged one shoulder. "Not really."

"But...everyone seems to know you."

Grinning, he gave a nonchalant wave of his hand. "Only 'cause I could have 'em fired."

Fired? That could mean only one of two things: either he knew the boss or he *was* the boss. Something told Hope it was the latter, and for a reason she couldn't explain, it made her nervous. She took a sip of ice water from the goblet and tried to think of a sensible response. When she'd read those articles about him on the Internet, she had joked to herself that he must have more money than Donald Trump. But from the looks of things, it hadn't been a joke, after all.

Jasper returned and handed Hope a menu bound in white leather.

"Thank you," she said.

"My great pleasure, miss," he replied, then disappeared.

While she pretended to peruse the restaurant's offerings, Ethan fumbled in his coat pocket and withdrew a white envelope.

"Hope—may I call you Hope?"

"I thought we got that settled last night: Hope and Ethan, for Molly's sake...."

"You're right, of course." He shrugged again. "Just want to make sure I'm not overstepping my bounds." Then, "Before I forget, I have something here for you."

He slid the envelope across the table, and when she reached for it, their fingers touched. The contact was quick, slight, and barely noticeable, but the effect was electric. A shiver ran down her neck, and she felt her face begin to redden. Fortunately, Ethan didn't seem to have noticed. "Ahh," she said, peeking inside the envelope, "the missing earring." Tucking it into her purse, she grinned. "These are number seventy-eight in my butterfly collection."

"Butterfly collection?"

She nodded. "Pressed wings, stained-glass orna-ments, tapestries—" Hope stopped abruptly when she noted how intently Ethan was looking at her. With a self-conscious toss of her head, she said, "You'll learn in time that it isn't wise to get me started talking about but-terflies, because I could go on and on for hours!" Then, sitting up straighter, she folded her hands on the table. "But you wanted to talk about Molly...?"

"That can wait until lunch arrives."

Unnerved by his scrutiny, she sought refuge behind her menu. "Since you seem so familiar with the place," Hope said, peeking over it, "maybe you could recommend something? Otherwise, I'll just ask for my old standby."

"Which would be...?"

"Cheeseburger and fries."

Ethan leaned back and, smiling, looked out at the river. "I usually order the filet mignon," he said, meet-ing her eyes again. "Henri hand-selects the cuts, and I promise, you've never had a more tender steak."

When the server came back, Ethan spoke up for her. "The lady will have the filet—how do you like yours, Hope? Rare? Medium?"

She'd never had filet mignon for lunch in her life, but rather than admit it, she said, "Medium rare will be just fine."

"I'll have the same," he said. "And tell Henri to do his usual magic." Turning to Hope, he asked, "Would you like a glass of wine?"

"No, thanks. Never touch the stuff." She hesitated. "But don't let that stop you from—"

"Two fluted glasses of tonic water over cracked ice," he instructed the server.

"With a twist?" she put in.

Without missing a beat, he wrinkled his nose. "Nah. Don't feel like dancing."

"Thank you, sir," said the server.

And when she was gone, Hope smiled. *For a man about town, he sure has a corny sense of humor.* Admittedly, though, she found everything about him charming.

"You want to hear a good one? I actually own a vineyard here in Maryland, though I don't drink at all."

"Never?"

He shook his head. "Guess it doesn't fit the stereotype of guys like me, does it? Single, moneybags, teetotaler...."

She couldn't help but laugh. "I'm beginning to see that very little about you fits the stereotype, Mr. Burke."

"Ethan," he corrected her. "I thought we got all that settled last night."

"Touché!"

Suddenly, his expression grew serious, and he rubbed his chin as though he had something important to say but didn't know where to begin. On the heels of a deep breath, he leaned closer. "Do you mind if I ask you a favor, Hope?"

The way he looked at her with those soulful brown eyes of his made it hard for her to concentrate. "Of course not."

"Well, I've been thinking...." He stroked the broad chin again. "That house of mine is awfully...." He shook his head. "Well, let's just say it isn't the most child-friendly place." Reaching across the table, he blanketed one of her hands with his. "Do you suppose you could help me make it...." Now he frowned as if searching for just the right words. "...help me make it warmer, more welcoming, for Molly?"

Hope blinked. So, now she could add "mind reader" to the quickly growing list of his finer qualities. "Sure I will," she said, deftly slipping her hand from beneath his.

"And while you're at it, could you help me fill that big closet in her room? I mean, I know what sort of games she likes, but clothes?" He shrugged helplessly. "I don't have a clue."

Suddenly, a faraway look dulled his bright eyes, and his smile dimmed slightly. "I'll give you my credit card. Money is no object. And, of course, I'll pay you for your time, so that—"

"Ethan," she interrupted him, "I'm more than happy to help in any way I can, free of charge. It'll be fun filling her closet with cute outfits. But...."

"But what?"

"But you're going shopping with us. You're her father now, and it's important that you become an active participant in the things that affect her."

He stared off into space. "Okay, I'll clear some time on my calendar...."

Here we go, Hope thought, smirking inwardly, *the laundry list of excuses why he can't—*

His eyes met hers. "Is tomorrow too soon to start?"

"Tomorrow?!" Hope laughed. Once again, she'd underestimated him. "Tomorrow is Friday. I think we can wait until the weekend."

"Well, you're the expert. Whatever you think is best."

The arrival of their food interrupted the conversation, but once the steaks had been served and their glasses had been refilled, Ethan pulled out an electronic organizer and typed in "Hope and Molly, shopping" on Saturday.

"What time's good for you?" he asked, his slender finger poised above the tiny keyboard.

"Nine?"

And as he added it to the gadget, she hoped this wasn't just one of those "cooperate for a little while" things parents too often did....

After lunch, Hope realized she would be late for her first afternoon appointment. Ethan remained seated at the table as she rushed off, using the excuse that he needed to check on a few things in the restaurant kitchen before heading back to the office. But the real reason he'd lagged behind was so that he could watch Hope without her *knowing* he was watching.

He could see the parking lot from his seat, and he observed her through the window as she crossed the lot in half the time it would have taken most women, her high-heeled shoes hitting the pavement with the surety and grace of a model on a runway. She had curves in places where other women didn't even *have* places, and he doubted a more animated face existed, even in cartoons.

She was vivacious and vital, more alive than anyone he'd ever known. From what he'd seen, Hope didn't do anything halfway. And if her reputation as a children's counselor wasn't proof enough of that, he had only to remember the way she'd oohed at the delicate texture of her steak and aahed at the creamy richness of the hot fudge sundae he'd insisted on ordering as dessert.

The tastefully elegant outfit Hope had worn told him she knew the difference between quality and quantity—and that she valued quality. It might be true that she didn't earn as much as many others in her profession, but it was clear that she knew how to spend her dollars wisely, as evidenced by the trim, tailored dress that accentuated her petite figure. But Ethan didn't know which he'd say he admired more—the way she wore her clothes or the fact that she knew how to shop for them.

He'd been so thrilled when she'd suggested that he join her and Molly on Saturday that he'd almost bellowed "All right!" in the middle of Saxon's elegant dining room. Instead, he'd nodded somberly and said, "Good, that sounds good."

He watched Hope climb into her car and check the mirrors before backing out of her parking space with the deftness of a professional truck driver. He had to reel himself in as she drove off; he'd been leaning into the window as if doing so might allow him to ride along with her, if only for a moment.

Once she was out of sight, he sat back and exhaled the breath he hadn't even realized he'd been holding. And then his trusty Rolex beeped 2:15.

A quick mental calculation told him it would be a day and a half—nearly forty-eight hours!—until he'd see her again. He sneered at the watch and muttered, "For six thousand bucks, you'd think you could make time go a little faster."

"Excuse me, Mr. Burke?"

The heat of embarrassment pulsed in Ethan's cheeks as he looked into the questioning face of his maître d'. "Nothing, Jasper," he said, standing up. As he headed for the exit, he grinned to himself and muttered, "...except I think maybe I'm losin' it!"

Chapter Five

A t Hope's suggestion, Ethan called the pastor's wife on Friday to inquire about the children's Sunday school program at church. It was important, she'd said, to keep Molly engaged in normal, everyday life. Exposure to other kids—their activities and bright voices—might inspire her to open up.

Ethan wasn't surprised when Mrs. Cummings began talking about Hope. The elderly woman's reputation as a matchmaker went way, way back, and it gave him the perfect excuse to find out more about the pretty counselor.

Hope was working closely with his beloved godchild, after all, so it made sense for him to want to know everything possible about her as a professional. But, sadly, Ethan hadn't managed to learn much of anything about her on a personal level.

Over their dinner of stuffed shells two nights prior, he'd asked her a few seemingly innocuous questions about herself, but she'd dodged them like a woman who'd rather walk a mile barefoot in the snow than divulge even the smallest tidbit about herself. "Where were you born?" and "Where does your family live?" were sidestepped as artfully as if he'd asked for her ATM PIN.

"Such a lovely girl," Mrs. Cummings was saying. "She deserves a lot of credit, turning out the way she did, considering...."

When the woman's voice trailed off, the hairs on the back of Ethan's neck bristled. "Considering what?"

The pastor's wife lowered her voice. "You were probably too young to remember, but the story was in all the papers the year Hope was born. It was quite the scandal!"

If that was true, he could look it up online later. But something told Ethan that Mrs. Cummings might just be able to add something that wouldn't have appeared in the newspaper articles. "A scandal?" he echoed.

"Oh, yes...it was terrible, I tell you. Simply terrible! When her father found out that her mother was with child, he ran off and left her."

Ethan blew a stream of air through his teeth, thinking it was downright sinful the way some husbands felt no responsibility toward their wives and children. The fact that desertion happened as often as it did sickened him. If *he'd* been blessed with a loving spouse and kids, there was no way he'd leave them!

"It really bothers me," he admitted, "when husbands don't honor their commitments."

Mrs. Cummings's sigh rattled in his ears. "Her father was never married to her mother, poor dear. In fact," she whispered, "he denied even the *possibility* that Abbie's baby might be his."

Abbie, he repeated mentally. Hope was a real person now, with an identity, as well as a life story. "Was she... was Abbie...promiscuous?"

"I should say not! She was young, and like most people her age, thought she knew everything. It was foolish, getting involved with that *Josephs* fellow."

Wincing, Ethan shook his head. "Fathers abandon young mothers on a daily basis. Why would a story like that be of any interest to the media?"

The pastor's wife gasped with exasperation. "Honestly! Sometimes I wonder why the good Lord made men so *dense!*" She paused and then lowered her voice again as she said, "Now, mind you, I'm telling you all of this only because Hope is working so closely with your little goddaughter." She hesitated before continuing, then said, "And it isn't as if I'm telling you anything you couldn't easily find out on your own...."

She was doing a lot of talking, he thought, but so far, the woman hadn't said much of anything. "You have my word," Ethan told her, "that anything you share with me is in the vault, and you're the only one with the combination."

"If you promise...," she said.

Just get on with it, please! he demanded silently.

And as if she'd read his thoughts, Mrs. Cummings cleared her throat. "Hope's mother had a twin named Alice. The poor girls lost their parents when they were barely seventeen. Alice, the quiet one, seemed to go into a shell after the accident, while Abbie seemed determined to see how far she could push the limits of ladylike decorum. She was eighteen when she met Taylor. That leather jacket and noisy motorcycle were almost as attractive as his big, green eyes and thick, coppery curls. And it didn't hurt, I suppose, that he was a TV star...."

Taylor Josephs. *Now* Ethan knew why the name sounded so familiar. Hope's father had been the host of a major network talk show based in Baltimore.

"Well, the dear girl came to us one Sunday morning after services, sobbing hysterically because she was in a family way. At first, she wouldn't reveal who the father was. But once the truth was out, and everybody in town knew the lowlife had denied being the baby's father, she spent the remainder of her pregnancy—nearly six months—alone in her room."

Mrs. Cummings continued with a catch in her voice. "She got a job as a bank teller, don't you know, and one Saturday after work, while Alice was working at the diner, Abbie put little Hope in her crib with her favorite teddy and a bottle of milk...."

The woman paused, and Ethan could hear her sniffling. He wondered what, exactly, Hope's mother had done. Run off like Taylor, maybe?

"She went into the bathroom and hanged herself," Mrs. Cummings finally managed. "She left a two-page suicide note explaining herself. Alice found it, and she showed it to Pastor Cummings after the funeral. When I read it, I bawled like a baby, I tell you!"

Sniffing, she continued. "About a year after Abbie's death, I suppose it was, Alice married John Majors, the bank vice president, and they raised little Hope as their own. By the time she was old enough for school, John had legally adopted her. They were good people, Alice and John, but I don't think either of them ever got over what happened to Abbie. And intentionally or not, they took their frustrations out on little Hope. Not that they were physically abusive or anything, but they were awfully strict. And cold. You'd never have guessed a child lived in that house. Not a toy in sight, not even a doll baby.

"They were devout people," she added in a raspy whisper, "but their faith was expressed in an angry, bitter, self-righteous way." A sigh, and then, "I never have been able to understand how anyone could know the Lord—truly know Him—and not feel...*happy!*" Another sigh. "They meant well, I suppose, but Hope didn't have much of a childhood, I'm afraid."

"Are they still alive?"

"No. Boating accident, about five years ago...."

Ethan sat in stunned silence, trying to sort out his thoughts. No wonder Hope had taken such an immediate interest in Molly!

And just when he thought Mrs. Cummings had finished her story, she said, "When Hope was about fifteen, she heard something in the attic and went up there to investigate. Found some evidence of mice...and a dusty old box tucked under the eaves. Inside was her mother's suicide note."

Ethan hung his head and said a quick, silent prayer for the girl she'd been, for the woman she'd become.

"And like her mother had all those years earlier, Hope shut herself in her room. Refused to come out for over a week. Now, mind you, she'd been a happy-go-lucky child, despite how stern Alice and John were. Always smiling. Always trying to brighten everyone else's mood."

Picturing Hope's bright face, Ethan had no trouble believing that at all.

"After she came out of her room, she was still pleasant enough, still smiled a lot...but the smile never quite made it to her eyes...."

Like Molly, Ethan thought.

"Then she went away to college. Best thing that could have happened, if you ask me, because when she came home after graduation, Hope seemed more like her old self."

Ethan heard the implication loud and clear. She may have been "more like her old self," but she still wasn't the happy kid she'd been before finding that box in the attic.

It all made sense now—the way she'd fidgeted when he'd showed her around his neat-as-a-pin house, how she'd gasped quietly when he'd taken her into Molly's stark, grown-up room, the way she'd lit up like a Christmas tree when he'd asked her to help him fix up the place for Molly....

Ethan got it now. He knew her special connection with his goddaughter existed because she saw a bit of herself in the little girl's eyes, heard an echo of her own past in the child's silence. No wonder she'd chosen counseling as her profession. *Christian* counseling, no less, specializing in children's needs. He believed she hoped to prove to troubled children that God loved them, gently and tenderly, even when their own parents seemed incapable of doing so.

Ethan felt a jumble of emotions for Hope at that moment—empathy, admiration, respect—but not pity. Her loveliness went far deeper than her big eyes, her shining hair, her delightful smile. She'd worked hard to make something beautiful and redemptive of her ugly and difficult past. And for that, he respected her with all he had, down to the very marrow of his bones.

Hearing her story in a ten-minute time frame all but wiped him out. If his calendar hadn't been packed with back-to-back meetings, he might just have left the office and headed home to take a nap.

No...sleep wasn't what he needed. What he needed was to be with her.

"If everything goes well," he said to Mrs. Cummings, "I'll bring Molly to Sunday school this week. But you'll understand if we can't make it, right?"

"Of course," she said. "*'For everything there is a season....'*"

"*'...and a time for every matter under heaven.'*"

He'd always been partial to those verses from Ecclesiastes. And as he hung up the phone, another verse popped into his head—Romans 15:13: *"May the God of hope fill you with all joy and peace in believing, so that by the power of the Holy Spirit you may abide in hope."*

Hope.

For the first time since he'd brought Molly home, he had a glimmer of hope that she would survive this terrible trauma.

Hope Majors was his newfound inspiration. After all she'd gone through as a kid, if she could blossom into the beautiful woman he'd had lunch with today...well, he could now hope for the same miracle for Molly!

A stab of guilt hit him in the pit of his stomach. He was falling for Hope, hard and fast. But now—now that he knew all she'd suffered and endured without complaint, now that he knew what she'd become, despite the odds—

Don't add to her problems, Burke. A guy like you, who's never around when he's needed...the last thing she needs is somebody else who might let her down. And the sad fact set in that he'd been running from commitment his entire adult life. What made him think he could stop running now?

Maybe enough time had passed. Maybe his life of solitude and loneliness had finally atoned for all the times he'd been absent when those who loved him needed him. Maybe the tide was turning. After all, Sam and Shari had known him for years. Had been privy to every ugly detail of his miserable past. And yet they'd entrusted him with Molly, the closest thing to both their hearts. Would they have done that if they hadn't believed he was fit for the job?

He shook his head.

They'd loved Molly more than life itself. Not in a million years would they have consciously handed her over to someone whom they feared wouldn't be there for her anytime, anyplace, any reason she needed him!

"For everything there is a season...."

Maybe the seasons are changing, Burke. Maybe God's purpose is for you to finally need and be needed, to trust and be trusted, to love and be loved....

He stood at his office window, hands clasped at the small of his back, staring past the sea of cars in the lot below. Hundreds of vehicles were parked down there, all owned by the men and women who'd come to depend on him to provide for them and their families with steady paychecks, health insurance, Christmas bonuses. He owed these people a lot—owed them everything, in fact.

And that's why Ethan hadn't missed a day of work, not one, in the eight years since he'd founded the corporation. Whether they'd hired on as employees at one of his hotels, at one of his restaurants, or at any one of the dozens of other companies that were part of Burke Enterprises, they were family. He *liked* taking care of them, providing for them....

It was time to extend that attitude to Molly. Ethan had a long way to go to become the father Sam had been, but he intended to try to fill his shoes.

He wanted to be worthy of Hope, too, because she deserved a warm, welcoming home of her own, filled with children who adored her and a husband who thought she'd single-handedly arranged every star in the sky.

Lord, if You've seen fit to bless me with a daughter like Molly and a woman like Hope, surely You'll bless me with what's lacking in my character...so I'll deserve them.

A light rapping at his door interrupted Ethan's musings. "Yes?"

Kate poked her head into his office. "The graphics guy is here to discuss how you want the corporate brochure laid out this year."

He clapped a hand to the back of his neck. "Okay. Put him in the conference room and get him some coffee, and tell him I'll be there in a minute."

"Headache?" she said as she came further into the room.

"Nah." He started making neat stacks of the paperwork on his desk.

Kate inclined her head and, frowning, grabbed the tablet from the top of one pile. "What's this?"

Ethan's ears got hot suddenly. With sweaty palms, he grabbed the tablet back from the tall, blonde marketing manager. During his conversation with Mrs. Cummings, he'd absentmindedly doodled "Hope" all over the page. The repetitive scrawl reminded him of the time in fourth grade when his teacher had made him write the word *definition* one hundred times to fuse the proper spelling into his brain.

He tossed the pad facedown on his desk, adjusted the knot of his tie, and jutted out his chin. It wasn't easy ignoring Kate's indignant expression, but he managed. "Does Pete know the graphics guy is here?" he asked her.

She pulled herself up to her full six-foot height. "He's already in the conference room," she said, more sharply than necessary.

His embarrassment was cooled by the dawning realization that Kate was angry. Very angry. *What's your problem?* he wanted to say. Instead, he fished around on the desktop for the marketing campaign folder.

"So, are you thinking about buying the Hope Diamond?"

He looked into her narrowed eyes and said, "Hope is the counselor who's working with Molly."

"Ah-ha. So it's true that she's holding sessions in your den...."

He didn't like the direction this was going. Didn't like it one bit. "Kate, I believe we have people waiting?"

Pursing her lips, she turned on her heel and strutted toward the door. "Yes, sir!" she snapped, turning around and saluting. "Whenever you're ready, sir!" And with that, she left the room, slamming the door behind her.

Oh, great, he said to himself, *like you don't already have enough problems*. Kate's behavior only served to accentuate how different Hope was from every other woman he knew. He considered reprimanding Kate's insubordination but thought better of it. He was at least 50 percent to blame for the fact that Kate thought something more existed between them than a business relationship;

while he'd never encouraged her behavior, he'd never *dis-couraged* it, either. He was just shallow enough to enjoy her jealousy a little.

The admission made him wonder if Hope would ever care enough about him to feel jealous of another woman, and the possibility that she wouldn't caused an ache in his heart that reverberated throughout his soul.

Frowning, Ethan gathered his marketing file and a blank notepad and stomped to the conference room, determined to shrug off his mounting feelings of self-pity. He'd never been afraid of taking chances before. Risked everything to turn Burke Enterprises into a Fortune 500 company.

His head and his heart went to war:

She might reject you, said his head.

Maybe, answered his heart.

It'll hurt like the dickens if she does....

No doubt about it.

Think you can survive that? his head taunted.

And his heart responded, *I doubt it.*

He gave a moment's thought to how life might be with a woman like Hope—a woman who'd love him for the man he'd become instead of for the properties he owned. A woman who'd love him and their children completely, no holds barred.

How can you be so sure that's the kind of woman she is? asked his head.

In all honesty, Ethan had no answer for that one. At least, none that made sense, especially considering the short time he'd known her. "She'll be good for Molly and me," he mumbled. "I just *know* it."

He stood outside the conference room door, picturing her warm smile and bright green eyes, which sparkled with a love for life.

Then take the risk, said his heart.

And even before Ethan had seated himself at the head of the long mahogany table, he knew without a doubt that he would.

Bright and early Saturday morning, Hope showed up at the appointed time, ready for a day of shopping. She'd worn her favorite sneakers, thick, white socks, slim jeans, and a pastel pink turtleneck sweater. Just in case the weather turned crisp, as it often did in September, she'd slipped into a navy blazer.

As she locked her car door, she had the sense that someone was watching her. Looking up, she saw Ethan on the other side of the parking lot, one hand in his pant pocket, one foot crossed over the other as he leaned against the driver-side door of his low-slung sports car. He threw a hand into the air, and though she couldn't see his eyes behind the mirrorlike lenses of his aviator sunglasses, she could only assume from the width of his smile that he was happy to see her.

How was it possible, Hope wondered, walking toward him, that every time she saw him, he looked more handsome than the time before? Today, he wore crisp jeans and new running shoes, and the red of his long-sleeved golf shirt peeked out from beneath a lightweight bomber jacket. At lunch a few days earlier, she'd noticed how his dark hair had curled over his collar. He'd gotten a haircut....

"Where's Molly?" she asked, walking up to him.

When he nodded toward the car, Hope bent at the waist to peer into the backseat, but the sun's reflection on the tinted glass kept her from seeing inside. Straightening, she frowned. "Did you tell her what we planned to do today?"

"Yeah, I explained," he said dully. "Guess she's not into spending money." Shooting Hope a crooked grin, he added, "She's gonna make some guy a great wife someday if she holds on to that attitude."

She returned his smile. "Funny. Very funny." Walking around to the passenger side of the convertible, she opened the door. "Hey, Molly-girl," she said, "what say you unbuckle that seat belt and come with us so that we can do our best to send your uncle Ethan to the poor house?"

The girl did as she was told, then stood silently beside the car, hands clasped at her waist. To that point, Hope had been feeling pretty chipper, like this little outing might actually be fun. Just two ordinary people taking a preteen girl out for a shopping spree. What could be more normal and natural? But one look at the girl's wooden movements and expressionless face served to remind her just how big a task she and Ethan faced.

Hope sighed and sent a quick prayer heavenward. *Lord, put the right words into my mouth today.* Then, resting a hand on Molly's shoulder, she said, "Did you bring a purse, sweetie?"

No response...unless she chose to count frowning at the pavement as a reaction.

Hope lowered herself to Molly's eye level so that their gazes met. "Well, then, we'll just have to make sure Uncle Ethan gets one for you today, won't we?"

Molly looked straight into Hope's eyes, blinking once or twice before attempting to turn way. But Hope moved her own head accordingly, forcing Molly to continue making eye contact. *Kiddo, you're doing a swell job of acting stubborn, but whether you know it or not, you've just met your match!*

Casting a furtive glance at Ethan, who was leaning against the car and watching them, she smiled. "I hope you ate a good breakfast, because we girls intend to walk your feet off!"

He slid his sunglasses up onto his head. "Two eggs over easy, Canadian bacon, and buttered toast. That'll hold me for a while." Winking, he added, "But keep in mind, I'm six-one—"

"Yeah," she countered, hands on her hips now, "so?"

"So, my legs are longer than yours and Molly's. I think it's you two who'll be hot-footin' it to keep up with me!"

Hope turned to Molly, fully prepared to say, "Did you get a load of that?" But she saw that the girl had indeed been paying close attention to the exchange...

...and was *smiling*!

In an instant, as if she realized a bit of joy had squeaked from her, Molly looked down at the toes of her shoes. Hope glanced up to see if Ethan had noticed the fleeting transformation, too. The look of disappointment on his face told her that he had. She pointed toward the mall entrance. "Inside, Daddy Longlegs," she said in the cheeriest voice she could muster, "'cause we're burnin' daylight!"

Laughing, Ethan joined her and Molly on their side of the car and, taking each of them by the hand, started walking toward the wide glass doors.

Hope's heart beat hard and her pulse pounded as she wondered if he was squeezing Molly's hand the way he was squeezing hers....

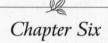

Chapter Six

W hew," Ethan breathed, flopping onto the family room sofa beside Hope. "I'm bushed! How do you do it, with legs as short as yours?"

Hope faced him. "The air is thinner up there where you are, smart guy, so naturally I have an edge." She toed off her shoes and propped both feet on the coffee table, then quickly lifted them. "Uh...it's okay to do that, right?"

His feet joined hers. "The thing is granite, darlin'," he said, chuckling. "It'd take more than those itty-bitty feet of yours to do it any harm."

Several moments of companionable silence passed before she sat up. "I have a confession to make."

"It isn't gonna make me blush, is it?"

"If it does," she said, laughing, "you're *wa-a-ay* too sensitive, Mr. Burke."

"Okay, but I have to warn you, I have no experience with absolution."

Grinning, she sighed. "Not that kind of confession, silly. I was just going to admit I've never actually snuggled into a leather sofa before. It's much more comfortable than I would have guessed."

Both his dark eyebrows rose on his forehead. "Why's that?"

"I guess I thought it would be cold. And that it'd make crackly noises. Like vinyl, y'know, and—"

His smile silenced her. "Okay, so I'm an unsophisticated twit," she said. "Sue me."

"From what I hear, you're plenty sophisticated."

Hope's heart began beating double-time as a flush crept into her cheeks. "What do you mean?"

"Just thinking of what Mrs. Cummings said when I called to enroll Molly in Sunday scho—"

"Mrs. Cummings!" she blurted out, leaping to her feet. "Why, if that old busybody actually knew half of what she professes to know, she'd put the TV news anchors to shame." She didn't want to be pacing, but it seemed she was powerless to make herself stop.

Soon, Ethan was on his feet, too. "Easy, girl," he said, placing his hands on her shoulders. "She thinks the world of you. Told me Molly couldn't be in better hands."

Now she felt like a goof for overreacting that way. "Oh," she said, biting her lower lip. "Sorry. That was a terrible thing to say about the woman. *Terrible!*"

He lifted her chin gently with his forefinger. "No need to apologize. I've known her for a while, too, y'know. And much as I hate to admit it, you're right. The poor old dear is a busybody."

Hope stared into his long-lashed dark eyes for a quiet, intense moment. There was no need to hide her past from him. She could see that in the understanding expression on his handsome face. Which told her he already knew everything. He *knew*, and now he felt sorry for her!

Hope wanted to turn and run. She thought about grabbing her blazer and purse and heading for the door, but the warm hands on her shoulders wouldn't allow it. The steady *ticktock, ticktock, ticktock* of the grandfather clock in the hall counted the seconds. With no warning whatever, Ethan pulled her close. She pressed her cheek to his shirt as the clock went *ticktock, ticktock, ticktock* some more. "She told you, didn't she?" Hope finally asked.

Ethan eased her gently to arm's length and nodded.

Hope's gaze slid toward the windows, then followed the gentle slope of the grassy hillside down to the ebbing river below. A blue heron sailed gracefully by, its wide wings outstretched to catch the crisp autumn wind as it searched for a suitable perch. She watched it disappear from view, wishing she could do the same. Oh, to have freedom like that, to sail off on an air current and leave behind whatever ails you.

Whatever ails you....

Hadn't she said something along those lines the first time she'd visited him here? *Ironic*, she thought, *that you were advising him about seeing the value in what was right under his nose, when it was you who didn't have a clue.*

"Hope?"

She sighed. "Mmm?"

"Does it bother you that I know?"

Maybe what he knows has nothing to do with your mother, or your father, or—

He ran the fingertips of his right hand through her hair as his left thumb drew lazy circles on her jaw. "What happened back then," he began, "had nothing to do with you."

Well, what else could the poor man say? In his shoes, she'd have said something similar.

In his shoes....

Ethan had just admitted that he knew about her miserable past. Maybe all his kindness and compassion were simply to soften the news that he'd found a more suitable counselor for his traumatized goddaughter.

Until today, Hope had thought she'd outgrown the humiliation of her past. But now, as she stood in the spotlight of his gaze, she knew she hadn't outgrown it. Probably never would outgrow it.

She hadn't admitted it to herself until now, but Ethan Burke had come to mean a great deal to her. Despite her "never mix business with pleasure" motto, she'd found herself hoping he saw something in her, so that when Molly's condition improved....

Well, fat chance of that happening now. Because now, all she had was his pity.

"You have to stop holding yourself accountable for—"

He stopped speaking so suddenly that Hope couldn't help but look up at him. She expected to find the sympathetic expression still darkening his eyes. But he'd clamped his teeth together so tightly that his jaw muscles were bulging. His generous mouth formed a thin, taut line, and his big dark eyes were mere slits. Didn't take a genius to figure out that he was angry. Very angry.

Was he mad that she hadn't told him more about her history? He probably would have liked to have found another counselor to work with Molly—one who hadn't been conceived in sin by a mother who consequently committed suicide. Did he think her past would somehow taint the innocent little girl?

"You deserved a lot better than that," he said sternly. "A whole lot better."

Surely, she was hearing things....

Gently, he pressed a palm to each of her cheeks, his fingertips combing the hair back from her face. "I don't make a habit of questioning the Almighty," he rasped, "but this is one instance when I can't help but wonder what inspired Him to give you *those* two for parents."

No question about it...she was hearing things....

"It wasn't *all* their fault," she said, quoting her mantra. "For years, I've believed there must have been something wrong with me, because why else would—?"

"I hope your use of the past tense means you don't still feel that way."

Her eyes met his, and she tried a half grin on for size. "I guess you'd have to say I'm a work in progress. My interest in psychology was rooted in questions about my past. When I went searching for reasons to explain why my parents hadn't loved me, hadn't wanted me, I discovered there were hundreds, even thousands, of kids who felt as I did."

Pastor Cummings, she told Ethan, had taught her many things in his infinite patience, but she held one lesson especially close: No matter what, *God* loved her. It was in His holy Word that Hope had found—for the first time in her life—true acceptance, unconditional love, mercy, understanding, and forgiveness.

"Forgiveness for *what*?" Ethan demanded. "You didn't *do* anything!" He let out a sigh of exasperation. "There's a little girl upstairs who's sleeping soundly on blue sheets with clouds on 'em because you somehow knew she wanted them. And that same little girl smiled today. *Smiled*, Hope. More than once. And you're the reason she did. In three long months, you're the first person who's managed to reach her, and that fact alone is enough to convince me that it'll be you who'll get her to open up all the way."

Ethan gave her another gentle shake and kissed the top of her head. "I've been thanking the good Lord for the past several days that you're here for Molly." He hesitated, then added, "And for me." He pulled her close to him again.

It was a lot to absorb in such a short while, but Hope had a feeling Ethan would give her the time and space she needed to get the job done. Standing in the protective circle of his arms with her ear pressed against his broad chest, she counted the beats of his heart.

And oh, what a big heart it was to have made room for a frightened little girl and a lonely young woman!

All the time they'd been standing this way, she hadn't even minded that his big shoe had been resting on the toe of her sneaker. Nor had she minded that when he'd kissed her head, her hair had somehow gotten tangled in the top button of his shirt.

"Ethan?"

"Hmm?"

"I think we have a problem."

"Nothing we can't solve with God's help."

His response sounded so sincere, so heartfelt, that Hope felt a little guilty about the giggles it inspired.

He tried to step back, no doubt to see what was so funny, and he froze when he realized what had happened. "Well," he said, mimicking Oliver Hardy, "isn't *this* a fine fix you've got us in?" Then, "Scissors are not an option. Anybody who goes near those gorgeous curls has to answer to me." And he punctuated the threat by pressing a kiss to her lips.

When they came up for air, she said, "Um, Ethan?"

This time, a note of suspicion echoed in his "Hmm?"

"We have another problem."

"I'm almost afraid to ask what—"

"You're...standing on my foot."

His attempt to glance down was halted by her hair, still firmly wound up in his button.

"Good gravy." And this time when he stepped back, he took her with him.

"Ouch!"

"Sorry...." With his hands on her shoulders, he looked deep into her eyes, then startled to chuckle deep and loud.

The sound was contagious, and soon the two of them were blotting tears of mirth from their eyes.

He couldn't very well discuss it in the doorway as he said good night to Hope. Not with Molly standing at the top of the steps, watching them—and giggling behind one hand. It had taken all the willpower Ethan could muster to keep from signaling Hope, but he didn't want to risk pushing Molly further from him by making too big a deal of her laughter.

After waving good-bye to Hope, he gave Molly a minute to scurry back to bed, then headed upstairs to peek in on his goddaughter. It was hard to believe that only this morning, the room had been somber and sedate. The bureau, rolltop desk, and four-poster bed still sat where he'd put them, and Hope had suggested leaving the deep-blue Persian rug on the floor and the wide-slatted blinds in the window. But the maroon valances and square-cut bed skirt were gone, along with the matching comforter.

Earlier, he'd wondered what Hope would do with the yards of gauzy creme-colored stuff she'd purchased at the fabric store, and now he knew. The filmy material hung in graceful billows from the headboard, and she'd flung it over the wooden curtain rods, too, giving the windows a soft, airy look that was feminine and classy...the perfect backdrop for the pale-blue quilt and ruffled pillow shams they'd picked up at the bed and bath shop.

The beady black eyes of two dozen stuffed animals stared at him from their new home on the cushioned window seat, and various board games, sketch pads, watercolor paint sets, and crayons decorated the low round table in the middle of the floor.

Huge silver-framed prints of ballerinas graced the walls. A tall lamp sculpted of white alabaster stood near the desk, and two shorter versions of it sat on the nightstands. A jewelry box adorned the bureau, its open glass lid exposing bangle bracelets, beaded necklaces, and faux gemstone rings. Inside the dresser were outfits Hope had chosen by watching Molly's reaction to every hanger she held up. And in the closet were a winter coat, knee-high boots, half a dozen dresses in assorted colors, and a tidy row of girlie shoes.

Ethan hadn't noticed any change in Molly's expression as the threesome had traipsed from one store to the next, dragging a dozen overflowing shopping bags. "That's because you were standing off to the side," Hope had said. "I had the better vantage point. Besides," she teased, "I'm closer to her size, so it's easier for me to gauge her reaction to things."

Now, he knelt down beside the girl's bed and took another look around the room. Part of Molly's childhood had been restored today, thanks to Hope. Tugging the covers up under her chin, he kissed her cheek. "G'night, sweet girl," he whispered, then tiptoed from the room. And in the doorway, he added, "I love you...."

He was halfway down the stairs when a small, soft voice stopped him dead in his tracks. "I love you, too, Uncle Ethan."

His heart pounding with hope and anticipation, Ethan needed almost no time to retrace his steps. But when he poked his head back into her room, the only thing he heard was Molly's steady, measured breaths, and he did his best to bite back bitter disappointment.

He stared at his Rolex. Nine twenty-three and fourteen seconds.

Ethan had already called Hope's number twice, though he conceded that it would make no sense for her to have made it home in such a short time. He decided to give her half an hour before trying again. Grabbing a glass of water, he headed for his study. The time was sure to pass quickly if he spent it with his Bible. Hopefully, the Lord would lead him to passages that talked about the word *hope*.

Sure enough, Ethan found verse after verse on the subject, though the first few were about hopelessness. Then he stumbled upon 2 Thessalonians 2:15–17: *"Hold to the traditions which you were taught by us, either by word of mouth or by letter. Now may our Lord Jesus Christ himself, and God our Father, who loved us and gave us eternal comfort and good hope through grace, comfort your hearts and establish them in every good work and word."* As he was about to jot down the Scripture reference for later memorization, the phone rang.

"Hi, there!" Hope said when he answered.

Man, but he loved the sound of her voice!

"I saw on my caller ID that you'd called a few times. Is everything all right?"

Everything is fine now.... "I was just wondering if you'd happened to notice Molly at the top of the stairs as you were leaving?"

"No...."

"I have no idea how long she'd been up there, but it was pretty obvious she'd been watching us."

He heard her quiet gasp.

"Saw her from the corner of my eye," he continued, "and she was grinning from ear to ear."

"Thanks to my hair getting snagged on your button, no doubt." And she punctuated the sentence with a merry giggle.

Ethan looked down at the few curly, coppery strands still clinging to his shirt and thought this one might never make it to the dry cleaner's....

"It's a good sign, Ethan, a very good sign. She made a lot of progress today. Before you know it, she won't need me at all!"

He'd never thought of it quite that way before, but, as usual, she'd hit the proverbial nail right on the head. When Molly was better and had resumed speech, the therapy sessions would end. Much as he wanted a happy, healthy godchild back—and he wanted that more than he could express—he didn't like the idea of less time with Hope. Didn't like it at all. "We'll still want to see a lot of you, though," he said. "I'm going to insist on it."

"Seems an unnecessary expense...."

"Holy cow, Hope. I never imagined you were so mercenary that you'd charge for friendship. Maybe I should bring you on board at Burke Enterprises. We can always use another hungry shark!"

She laughed along with him. "Say, does your company have a day-care program?"

"No," he admitted. "I'm ashamed to say I never even gave one a thought. Maybe when we get Molly squared away, you'll help me with that...?"

He heard her yawn. "I'd love to," she said around it.

"Well, I'd better let you go. You worked your pretty little fingers to the bone today. I'm sure you're exhausted."

"It was a hoot. I loved every minute."

"I still can't believe all you accomplished in just one day. You're a regular whirling dervish. A cyclone. A tornado. A—"

"You sure know how to turn a girl's head," she said, laughing. "Is that your gentlemanly way of telling me I'm just a lot of wind?"

"Is that what I did, Hope?" When she didn't respond, he added, "Did I turn your head?"

The ensuing silence was so long, so deafening, that he thought maybe they'd been disconnected. Or that she'd hung up.... Then, in a quiet, tentative voice, she said, "I don't know why you'd want to, but it's turned. Definitely."

Now he understood what the poets meant when they wrote about soaring hearts and singing souls. Ethan couldn't remember hearing better news.

"What about you?" she asked.

"What about me?"

"Is your head turned?"

"Like a hoot owl's! I'll have you know I've been walkin' into walls, thanks to you."

"I'm flattered," she said. Just then, he heard her doorbell ring in the background. "Now, who can that be at this hour?"

His free hand involuntarily formed a fist. "I'll hang on while you see who it is. And I'll call the cops if I hear anything that makes it seem somebody's up to no good."

"The deadbolt is in place, and I have a peephole. See you and Molly tomorrow!"

"Right." He didn't want to let her go. "Tomorrow."

This time when the bell sounded, it was clear the person on the other side of the door had grown impatient waiting for her to answer it. "I'd better go."

"Right. Sorry." He swallowed. "Hope?"

"Yes...?"

"Will you call me when the nutball who's trying to wear out your doorbell at midnight goes away...so I won't worry?"

Soft laughter filtered into his ear. "It's only nine thirty...."

"But you'll call?"

"If it isn't too late."

What did that mean? "Doesn't matter what time it is...."

"I really have to go, Ethan. See you tomorrow," she said, and hung up.

Ethan stared at the receiver until its buzzing sound prompted him to put it back into its cradle. He'd never been this way—possessive, protective, sentimental—with a woman before. Not with actresses or fashion models or corporate executives. So what was this crazy behavior all about?

"You're losin' your mind, Burke," he said, trudging toward the kitchen. Then, staring at the spot on the floor where he'd found her earring, he grinned. "Well, if you're gonna lose it, you might as well be with someone who can help you find it."

Chapter Seven

Hope immediately recognized the distinguished-looking gentleman at her door, because she'd seen his photograph on the mantle in Ethan's family room. But why would his father visit her unannounced at this hour? And how had he found her?

"Mr. Burke," she said, opening the door, "what can I do for you?"

"Please, please," he said, "call me Sawyer. Mr. Burke was my father's name!" He gave a hearty laugh and, despite the fact that she hadn't invited him to do so, stepped inside. "Nice place you've got here," he said, looking around the living room. "Lived here long?"

She closed the door and joined him near the coffee table. "Two years this Thanksgiving."

Ethan had apparently inherited his strikingly good looks from his mother's side of the family, because there was no physical resemblance between Sawyer Burke and his son.

The smile in the older man's eyes dimmed as he ran a hand through his silvery hair...the first similarity to Ethan that she'd seen. "I'll be blunt, Miss Majors," he said. "This isn't a social call."

Hope tucked the fingertips of both hands into the back pockets of her jeans, wondering why on earth he *was* here.

Lifting her chin a notch, she said, "I'm not surprised. You seem too much a gentleman to drop in so late, uninvited."

"Touché," he said. "Do you suppose I could bother you for a cup of tea while I tell you why I'm here?" He rubbed his hands together. "It's a mite brisk out there, and I'm afraid these old bones don't take to the cool weather like they used to."

Old? Other than the thick, snow-white hair, he could easily have passed for fifty. "Of course," she said. "The kitchen's right this way."

She was standing at the sink filling the teapot with water when he said, "You know, I had a feeling I was going to like you."

Hope shot a glance over her shoulder as he added, "And I was right."

What an odd thing to say, she thought, more curious than ever to learn what he could possibly want to talk about with her. She set the copper kettle on a front burner of the stove. "Please don't think me rude," she said, firing up the flame, "but it's getting late and—"

"I'll get right to the point, then," he said, taking a seat at the table. "I'm worried about Ethan. Very worried."

She dropped two tea bags into two red ceramic mugs, thinking that Ethan was the most in-charge-of-himself man she'd ever met. He was the last guy she'd think to arouse concern in his father. "What's the problem?"

"That child he's brought home with him is—"

"You mean Molly?"

"Yes. Of course. Forgive me. It's just that Molly is a reminder of some terrible times in my boy's past. With everything else that's on his shoulders these days, I just wonder if he can handle the extra pressure...and the memories."

She filled the mugs with steaming water and carried them to the table. "What memories?"

Sawyer frowned. "I'm afraid that in order to understand Ethan—and you'll need to do just that if the two
of you hope to help that little girl—I'm going to have to
tell you a few things about myself." He cleared his throat
and spooned some sugar into his cup. "Some rather...uh,
unsavory things, I'm afraid."

"I feel I should point out that I'm *Molly's* counselor,
not Ethan's." *Or yours*, she tacked on mentally.

"I'm well aware of that. He told me all about you
when I stopped by to see him yesterday." The man gave
a knowing little nod. "He depends on you far more than
you know."

"Because of the work I'm doing with Molly."

"There's that, of course, but what he feels for you
isn't entirely because of the child."

Hope didn't know how to respond to that, and so she
said nothing. But her mind whirled.... Ethan, who ran
a multimillion-dollar corporation, who employed thousands of employees, whose neighbors were rich and famous...*that* man depended on her?

"Since it's clear you're going to be a part of his life,"
his father continued, "there are a few things you should
know. To help you help him...and Molly."

"I don't know how big a part I'll play in *his* life," she
confessed, "once Molly is better."

"I know my son very well, Hope—though I'm sure
he'd tell you otherwise—and I can assure you that you've
become a very important part of his life." He chuckled,
reminding her again of his son. "Why, I wouldn't be the
least bit surprised, in a month or two, to hear that he's
popped the question."

Hope swallowed a gasp. She liked Ethan. Liked him
a lot. And if that kiss in his family room had been any
indicator, he liked her, too. But marriage? A nervous giggle popped from her mouth. "Really, Mr. Burke, I—"

"Sawyer, remember?" Another chuckle. "Or maybe you should practice calling me Dad."

She felt a blush creep into her cheeks. "Would you like me to warm up your tea?"

"Ah, a diplomat, I see," he said, winking. "In the line of work he's in, he needs a woman like you at his side."

It was ridiculous—no, ludicrous—to consider anything he was saying as logical! Still....

Sawyer cleared his throat. "Now then, I'll be as brief as possible...."

Too late for that, she thought.

He leaned forward, folded both hands on the table-top, and took a deep breath. "Did you know Ethan had a younger sister?"

She shook her head. "Had?"

Sawyer nodded. "She died when she was twenty and Ethan was twenty-four. Hard to believe," he said, his voice softening thoughtfully, "that it's been twelve years...."

Hope found herself leaning forward with curiosity. "How did it happen?"

From the look of desperation that shadowed his face, she knew nothing gentle had ended his daughter's life.

"Fire," he rasped.

"Oh, Mr. Burke, that's just awful. I'm so sorry!"

"Yes, awful. Especially considering Ethan blames himself for it."

"But—but why?"

He inhaled a deep, shaky breath, then slowly released it. "Bess was wheelchair-bound and mostly deaf when the, uh...when the fire happened." He shook his head. "And Ethan blames himself for *that*, too." His eyes met hers. "And I'm here to tell you that I'm the reason he blames himself for both.

"You see, by the time Ethan was fourteen, he'd grown pretty tired of having a ten-year-old shadow. His friends teased him because he couldn't go anywhere without Bess on his heels. The two of them had gone to summer camp together from the time Bess was four, and, naturally, Ethan couldn't have fun with his little sister hanging around all the time.

"So when he turned fourteen, he insisted he was too old for 'kid stuff' and refused to go to camp at all." Sawyer hung his head. "His mother and I saw no reason to make him go if he didn't want to, so that year, Bess went alone...."

The way his voice trailed off gave Hope a sinking feeling. She took a sip of tea and waited for him to continue.

"One rainy morning, she was running along the pier. She'd been told to stay inside, but Bess had a mind of her own. She tripped and fell into the pond." Wincing, Sawyer rubbed his face with both hands. "She hit her back on the edge of the decking, damaging her spinal cord. And she stayed underwater long enough to incur a three-quarter hearing loss."

He was frowning hard now and staring into his cup, as if he could see on the mirrorlike surface of the tea a rerun of that day. "When Bess regained consciousness in the hospital, she was paralyzed from the waist down."

Hope hung her head, feeling guilty for the judgmental thoughts she'd entertained about this man only moments ago. "I'm sorry, Sawyer."

He took a deep, shuddering breath. "Yes, well, such is life, right? But I'm afraid that isn't the worst of it." And, driving both hands through his hair, the man said, "In the hospital, I pinned Ethan against the wall. 'Are you satisfied?' I asked him. 'You couldn't be bothered to mind your little sister, and now look at her!'"

Hope's eyes widened as she wondered how he could have said such a thing.

"Believe me, I've asked myself ten thousand times how I could have said a horrible thing like that." A quiet moment passed before he added, "Then, from the moment we brought her home from the hospital, Ethan became *Bess's* shadow. He learned sign language and taught it to her. Taught her to read lips, too." He drained his cup and wrapped trembling hands around it. "And his mother and I, we let him. I spent less and less time at home. Got myself tangled up with a young woman whom I thought would help me forget all the miserable aspects of my life and—"

She saw the tears in his eyes and blanketed his hands with her own. "Sawyer, there's really no need to tell me all of this. I—"

"There's every need!" he all but hollered. "I have to make you understand, so you can help him. I owe him that much, at least!"

She sat back, stunned into silence by his outburst. Then, she said softly, "The Lord doesn't hold you responsible for what happened to Bess, and I'm sure Ethan doesn't, either."

Ethan's father harrumphed. "But that's just it, don't you see? He holds *himself* responsible, because when he was little more than a boy, I told him he *was* responsible."

Slipping his hands from beneath hers, he ran a fingertip around the rim of his cup. "Tragedy sometimes brings people together, makes them closer. Not my wife and me. I left Ethan's mother about a year after Bess came home from the hospital. Bought a little house on the river so I could be near the kids.... She died before the divorce was even final."

Hope wanted to ask how, to find out what had happened to Ethan's mother, but she held her silence.

"I insisted the doctors tell the kids she'd had a heart attack. Couldn't bear to heap the truth on them, after all they'd already suffered." He met her eyes. "Overdose," he said flatly. "Thankfully, I found the note before anyone else could...and burned it."

Hope had promised to call Ethan when her late-night visitor had left. But how could she do that now? What would she say? *"Your father was here, and oh, the stories he—"*

"So I sold the little house on the river and moved back in with the kids. And one night after they'd gone to bed, I went up to check on them and heard crying from Bess's room.

"It was Ethan—just sixteen at the time—on his knees beside her bed, praying with everything God gave him. She couldn't hear a word of it, of course, so I suppose he figured he was safe making his confession. And if I live to be a thousand," he said on a ragged note, "I'll never forget what that boy said...."

Sawyer closed his eyes and quoted his then teenage son: "'I'll take care of you, Bess,' he said. 'Always and forever, to make it up to you. I'll never leave you alone again. I promise.'"

No wonder Ethan had donated millions to children's charities. No wonder he'd built a burn unit at Bayview Medical Center and opened a long-term care facility for handicapped kids. Hope's heart ached for him—for the anguished boy he'd been, for the generous man he'd become.

It came to her in a flash. No *wonder* Molly's recovery was so important to him! Somehow, she believed, he'd found a way to blame himself for every tragedy in his life and had talked himself into believing Sam and Shari's accident had been his fault.

"He kept that promise," Sawyer went on. "Spent every spare moment right there beside her for years. Then, one day, while I was at work...."

Hope shuddered, remembering he'd said a fire had ended Bess's life.

"The neighbors told me they heard the kids arguing down by the pool. Bess wanted to go up to the house for a bowl of soup, and when Ethan wouldn't let her, she got furious and signed to say she wasn't a baby, and that he was making her miserable with his overprotectiveness. She told him if he loved her, he'd prove it by letting her do things for herself. So he did. And somehow, her clothes caught fire, and before he knew what was happening...."

He heaved a final coarse sigh and rubbed his eyes with his knuckles. "Well, there you have it, Hope. The whole sad and ugly Burke family saga." He forced a bitter laugh. "After hearing that, I don't know why you'd want any part of us—least of all me—but at least now you can make a decision based on facts. All of them."

She didn't know where he'd gotten the idea that marriage was a foregone conclusion for her and Ethan. Didn't understand why he felt that telling this tale would change her mind, one way or the other, even if a wedding was on the horizon. Not that it mattered. She'd already acknowledged that her feelings for Ethan had gone well beyond the bounds of "strictly professional."

So many things about Ethan made sense to her now—for starters, the way he pampered Molly and did things for her...from a distance. He was terrified that by getting too close, he might somehow put her in harm's way.

Ethan had accomplished so much in his life, and rather than hoard his millions, he willingly shared his wealth with those less fortunate. And now that she knew all he'd suffered and survived...well, Hope admired him all the more.

"Think you can handle him?" Sawyer asked.

She looked into his eyes and said, "I'm not sure, but I want to try."

Sawyer got to his feet and walked into the living room, and Hope stood up to see him out. At the front door, he pulled Hope into a fatherly embrace. "Thank You, God," he breathed into her ear, "thank You!" And, holding her at arm's length, he said, "I have a lot to make up for, and for *years* I've been praying He'd send someone to rescue Ethan from himself." He glanced up at the ceiling and chuckled. "Sure took You long enough!" When he looked at her again, he said, "So tell me, Hope, how does it feel to be the answer to a prayer?"

"Um, can I get back to you on that?"

"I wonder if your mother had any idea when she named you how well the name would fit."

She'd always just accepted that Hope was her name without wondering why or how it had been chosen. And now, she thought maybe she knew.

Chapter Eight

As Sawyer buttoned his jacket to go out, Hope's telephone rang. "Go ahead and get that," he said. "I can let myself out."

Maybe Ethan's dad *had* made a few mistakes—some terrible ones—but they were in the past. Clearly, he'd become a different man. A changed man. A *good* man whose concern for his son's happiness and well-being had driven him out into the night, alone, to confess his sins to a total stranger.

He pressed a quick, fatherly kiss to Hope's cheek as the phone rang again. "Seriously," he said, smiling, "answer it, will you, before the ringing drives me mad?" And with that, he was gone.

She'd barely uttered hello into the kitchen phone when Ethan said, "You *said* you'd call."

"I know, but...." How much should she tell him about her conversation with his dad? Should she tell him anything at all? "I–I...."

"Don't tell me your late-night guest is still there...."

"No—just left." The father-son relationship was already strained, and the last thing Hope wanted was to create more tension between them by telling him who her guest had been...and why he'd stopped by. At least, not before she had a chance to pray about it. "So, are you and Molly going to church tomorrow?"

"Yeah, of course," he said. "I talked with Mrs. Cummings about enrolling Molly in Sunday school, but I forgot to ask what time it starts."

"Nine, and so does the adult Bible study, followed by services at eleven. Think it'll be a help to Molly if I meet you two out front and walk her to the first class?"

"That'd be great." A pause, and then, "You locked up after your...uh, company left, right?"

She peeked around the kitchen door. "Not yet, but I'll get it when—"

"Do me a favor," he interrupted her, "and lock it now, will you? I'll hold on."

Oh, you will, will you? she thought, mildly annoyed by the way he seemed to think it was perfectly all right to order her around. But Hope put the phone down with a *clunk* and did as he had asked. "There," she said, picking it up again. "Done. Are you happy now?"

She didn't know what to make of the long silence that followed her question. Had he hung up?

"Very happy. In fact, I'm happier than I've been in a very long time."

Hope chewed her bottom lip. Could Sawyer have been right when he'd said Ethan had begun to care about her as more than Molly's therapist? Did his kiss signal a complete alteration in his intentions? Like it or not—and the professional side of her did not—Hope's heart fluttered in response to the possibility.

"Well, now that I know you're all safe and sound, I'll say good night."

"G'night."

"Sleep tight."

"Don't let the bedbugs bite." A yawn concluded her remark.

"Like Maria would allow a bug in this house!"

And the last thing she heard before the phone started buzzing was the music of his deep, delicious laughter.

Ethan wandered the quiet house for what seemed like an hour, hands in his pockets and head down. Where had this *jealousy* come from? He had no proof that her guest had been a man. But even if it had been, what right did he have to feel this way about it? Besides, if the guy meant anything to her, why had she invited *him* to church in the morning?

Logic raised its ugly head and told him she'd made the offer on Molly's behalf, not his, and his heart sank a little.

He turned on the TV and found and old black-and-white war movie. His hope was that the noise and action would distract him from thoughts of her. Despite the mayhem of cannon blasts and gunfire, he felt calm and serene, for her image floated in front of his face, and he saw instead the way she'd looked setting out napkins, cream and sugar, and teaspoons at his house the other night like a housewife on a 1950s television show.

Had she flitted round her kitchen setting out cookies, pouring tea, and making sure everything was just right for her recent guest, too?

Rubbing his eyes, he forced the question from his mind. Far better to think about the other night when she was bustling around *his* kitchen. "You cooked supper," she'd said, "so I'll clean up." When he'd failed at talking her out of it, Ethan had sat down again at the table, marveling that anyone could take such delight in mundane chores. It made him start to fantasize about life with a woman like that—a woman who took joy in doing little things for the people she cared about, who refused to do anything halfway, from arranging the placemats on the table to folding the dish towel after putting the last of the pots into the cupboard.

Not a woman like that, he thought now, *but that woman....*

He pictured the room she'd redecorated for Molly and thought of the little girl who, last time he checked, was sleeping contentedly on sheets of blue skies and clouds because of Hope's intervention. How much better would it be for Molly, when she fully recovered from the trauma of losing her parents, if someone like Hope was around, day in and day out, to see to her every need?

Molly had rarely met his eyes since arriving in the U.S., but as the counselor had been tucking the girl in, planting a kiss on her forehead, and wishing her sweet dreams, Molly had looked long and deep into Hope's.

His gaze slid around the family room to the spot where they'd been standing when he'd taken her in his arms and she'd melted against him. He'd taken a long look at the two of them, thanks to the reflection in the French doors to the patio. How good they'd looked together. How *right*. In the glass of the door, he had seen that she'd lifted her face to look at his, so he'd turned to meet her gorgeous green eyes...and had kissed her.

Just thinking about it took his breath away, and, shaking his head, Ethan chuckled to himself. Did she have any idea how captivating she was? Not likely. He might have kissed her a second time, and then a third, if he hadn't seen Molly hugging the newel post at the top of the stairs and grinning like a cat that had swallowed a canary.

One of the reasons he'd been able to turn a one-man, home-based company into a multimillion-dollar corporation was that he'd quickly learned to take the measure of the men he did business with. He had a feeling that if a man was lucky enough to work his way into that big heart of Hope's, he'd be there for life.

Better watch yourself, bud, he thought, *or you could drown in her—*

Drown.

He shuddered involuntarily at the word and prayed it would quickly flee from his mind.

In his bedroom, he kicked his sneakers to the back of his closet, draped his shirt over the arm of the big leather chair, and hung his jeans on the closet doorknob. The decorative pillows Maria arranged so artfully every morning thumped softly to the floor as he slid between clean, white sheets.

First, he praised God for allowing him to witness Molly's mischievous grin. Then, he thanked Him for a home that stood on a solid foundation and for the successful company that guaranteed he and his employees could keep their pantries stocked. *And if I dream tonight,* he added, *let me dream of Hope.*

Ethan dove into the lake headfirst and swam as fast as his legs would propel him. Bess was there, right there, just a few yards ahead. He could do this. He could get there, could pull her out of the pond and carry her to safety.

Her brown eyes were wide with fright as her long, dark hair snaked around her head like the fronds of their mother's Boston fern. Kicking frantically, she reached for him, and he could see her lips silently calling his name: "Eeeee-thannn...."

The dainty gold ring he'd given her for her birthday last year caught a beam of sunlight that pierced the depths. Almost there, he told himself, almost there.... Four kicks, then two more, and he'd be near enough to wrap his arms around her and then swim to the surface so she could fill her lungs with life-saving air.

He reached out, felt her fingers graze his, then watched helplessly as she drifted backward, floating farther, sinking deeper, out of his reach. And the harder he kicked, it seemed, the greater the distance grew between them. A terrified expression was on her face as iridescent bubbles escaped her mouth and rose to the surface, where Bess would be now if he'd been there to keep her from falling into the water in the first place.

He had to get to her, simply had to, because she'd always relied on him, always—

Ethan sat up with a start and sucked in a huge gulp of air. His heart pounding, he glanced around—at the bureau, the windows, the wall hanging that concealed his flat-screen TV, the clothes he'd worn today, scattered here and there.... As he consciously loosed his death grip on his pillow, he saw that he'd kicked the bedclothes into a tangle around his legs. He flopped back onto the pillows and willed himself to take slow, even breaths.

When he was fourteen and fifteen, that dream had tormented him nearly every night. It had come to the point that he would rather have done just about anything than fall asleep and risk a rerun. Before Bess's accident, he'd been a decent student. But afterward? All-nighters had helped him get onto the dean's list, marking period after marking period. And by the time he'd turned sixteen, Ethan had read nearly every book in his mother's extensive collection.

It had been many months since the last time he'd had the dream, because he'd learned that prayer kept the horrible images at bay. But tonight, when he'd asked the Lord to bless his night with dreams of Hope, he'd forgotten to ask Him to keep the nightmare away.

The dim, blue numerals of the clock on his bedside table said 2:43. He'd been down this road enough times to know that sleep would elude him until the alarm buzzed at 5:30, so he slapped the Off button and headed down to his study, stopping in the kitchen for a glass of water on the way.

Settling into his armchair, he allowed his Bible to fall open to a random page, and he read aloud the first verse his gaze settled upon: Mark 10:14. *"But when Jesus saw it he was indignant, and said to them, "Let the children come to me, do not hinder them; for to such belongs the kingdom of God.""*

Ethan could only shake his head in awe, for it had been Bess's favorite passage. He could almost see her sitting at the front of the church and signing it for the two other deaf children in the congregation. *"Truly, I say to you, whoever does not receive the kingdom of God like a child shall not enter it,"* he read on in verse 15.

Marking the page with his thumb, Ethan closed the Good Book as tears welled up in his eyes and sobs shook him.

For the nearly four months since her mother and father had died, Molly knew that her uncle Ethan had been trying.

Trying to make her feel welcome in his home.

Trying to help her come to grips with the horrible accident.

Trying himself to cope with the loss of his best friends, quickly, so he could devote himself to being the kind of parent he thought she deserved.

Trying to encourage her to tell him why she'd decided never, ever to talk again.

None of it had surprised her.

Molly didn't suppose that most girls her age knew much about things like honor and character, but she'd been hearing about her dad's best friend for as long as she could remember, and because words like *moral*, *ethical*, and *devoted* had been central to many discussions about her uncle Ethan, it seemed a good idea to look them up in the big *Webster's Dictionary* in the family room to find out what they meant.

Besides, if her daddy had thought Uncle Ethan was "good to the bone," as he'd so often said, then it must be true. And even if her dad hadn't thought the world of him, Molly still would have loved the gentle giant.

She remembered the time when she'd waited until the last minute to work on a science report. The result? A messy, inaccurate paper that earned her a low C. And when Uncle Ethan had seen it, he'd pulled her to him in a sideways hug and said, "Molly, m'girl, every time we do a thing, we leave our mark on it, so it's important to make sure that when folks see the mark *you've* left, they'll have no choice but to say, 'That Molly Sylvester, she always does her best!'"

If she hadn't loved him so, she probably would have shrugged it off. But she'd heard her dad say things like that—about Uncle Ethan—and she wanted nothing more than to hear him praise her that way, too.

Uncle Ethan had been doing his best ever since the double funeral for Molly's parents. And she knew that although he was the kind of man who seemed content to make rules, if someone didn't feel duty bound to follow them, he'd simply shrug and say, "Everybody has to live with the consequences of his choices." Molly understood only too well that this was the reason he hadn't been forceful or pushy about getting answers out of her.

He had a funny way of teaching lessons, and he wasn't anything like most other adults in that way. When he was visiting Molly and her parents at their flat in London, if her parents sent her to bed without dessert because she hadn't finished her chores, Uncle Ethan would always sneak cookies into her room when he came in to say good night. "Only *you* know if you've really earned them or not, and if you haven't, they won't taste good," he would say. It had taken just one bite of one cookie to discover just how right he'd been....

She knew full well that it was mostly her fault that he looked so sad standing beside her bed every night, saying the prayers solo that she used to say right along with him. If only she could tell him how much she loved him, how much she wanted to recite the words with him! Maybe then his dark eyes wouldn't fill with tears and....

Tonight, she remembered, right before he had tucked her in, Uncle Ethan had gone into her bathroom because she'd forgotten to turn out the light. "What's this?" he had asked, his deep voice echoing in the huge, tiled space.

If she'd known he'd go in there, Molly might have done a better job of hiding the figurine. She'd have buried it under a layer of tissues, or in some of the drawing paper Miss Majors had given her.

She thought Maria would be the only one who might ever find the shattered remnants of the adorable porcelain girl. And Maria, always smiling and happy, would naturally assume Molly had accidentally knocked the statue from its shelf....

"What happened?" Uncle Ethan had wanted to know, frowning as he stared down into the wastebasket. Then, he'd returned to her bedside and had gently taken her face in his hands, forcing her to look into his eyes. And she'd thought for sure he'd seen the truth written on her soul.

Oh, how she wished she could have thrown her arms around his neck and let him hug her, and oh, how she wanted to hug him right back! She'd wanted to tell him everything, wanted to answer all of his questions.

But she couldn't.

Because Molly believed she didn't deserve to talk—not ever again. And she didn't deserve nice things, either, like the beautiful Hummel figurines her parents had bought for her birthday every year. "You're such a big girl now," her mom had said, "and we know how well you take care of your things."

"That's right," her dad had agreed, "and that's why we're giving you an early start on the collection you've been wanting...."

But Molly believed she hadn't been a good girl. Hadn't been a nice girl, either. And she hadn't needed a better reason than that to smash the Hummel.

Uncle Ethan seemed so sad, so confused, looking at the splintered remains of the first figurine her parents had given her. "A little Hummel family," they'd said after she'd unwrapped it, "just like ours!"

She hated seeing him this way, but Molly couldn't tell him that it was *her* fault he'd lost his best friends, and she'd lost her mother and father....

Because she'd made a promise and intended to keep it.

Chapter Nine

"No way this was an accident," Ethan said. "If the Hummel had fallen, there might have been a few pieces of it in the trash can, but this...it's as if the thing was pulverized."

From the moment she picked up the phone, Hope could hear the distress and fear in Ethan's voice. It had always been part of her job description to treat family members as well as the children in her care, and so she assumed her "competent counselor" voice. "I'm sure there's another explanation," she said, "because Molly doesn't strike me as the type of child who'd deliberately destroy something so precious to her." But if she had, it meant Hope had a lot more work to do with the girl, she realized.

"If there's a reason, I'd sure like to hear it."

"We'll get to the bottom of it."

But he seemed not to have heard her. "It's as though she whacked it with a hammer or something."

"Hmm," she said, trying to raise his spirits, "the case of the pummeled Hummel...."

It took him a moment to react to her feeble attempt at humor. "Ha," he said. "A comedian counselor."

Did he think she was making light of the event? "I can hear that you're upset, Ethan, but I assure you, during our next session, I'll get to the bottom of it."

"Sorry. Guess I make too much out of anything that relates to Molly."

That wasn't the impression she wanted him to get, either! "You're doing a wonderful job with her. Your patience and dedication merit a parenting medal. Believe me, I've seen stress drive moms and dads to the point of going ballistic when things like this happen. Your tenacity astounds me."

"So," he said, "you're saying I'm a patient patient?"

She laughed a little. "I suppose one bad joke deserves another."

"I just wish the Hummel figurine was the first thing I've found...broken."

"What?" Her heartbeat accelerated. "What else have you found?

"Clothes torn, toys broken, stuffed animals destroyed...all things Sam and Shari gave her." He exhaled a long, shuddering sigh. "I don't get it, Hope. I just don't get it."

"How many times has this happened?"

"Over the past two or three weeks, I'd say eight, maybe ten times."

If only she'd thought to ask him earlier if anything of this nature had been going on between her visits with Molly. Her whole plan for therapy would have been different if she'd known—

"I should have told you earlier," he said, as if reading her thoughts. "At first, I chalked it up to ordinary wear and tear, since the things were all a few years old. But when she took to hiding the stuff...."

Hope listened as he described the way he'd found the dolphin Sam had carved for Molly from a piece of driftwood under the dock near the Potomac—minus its dorsal fin. And the sweater Shari had knitted for her, partially unraveled, in the kitchen trash. Sighing, she rested her forehead on a fist. This wasn't good. Not good at all. Picking up a pencil, she drummed her desk with its eraser. "Anything else you've neglected to tell me?"

Ethan cleared his throat. "I didn't neglect to tell you," he said, a defensive note raising his voice a notch. "The incidents were spaced apart at first, and seemed like... like innocent accidents."

Was he really so divided—running Burke Enterprises and monitoring Molly's daily activities—that he hadn't recognized the seriousness after the second episode? "Innocent accidents? An unraveled sweater and a broken carving, deliberately hidden? Come on, Ethan, get real!" She blew a stream of air through her lips. "Every time we've spoken, whether in person or by phone, what was the very first question I asked you?"

A second of silence ticked by before he droned, "If I've noticed anything out of the ordinary."

She sighed again. "And you honestly didn't see those acts of rage as peculiar—"

"Listen, missy," he interrupted, "there's no need to take that tone with me. *You're* the expert, for cryin' out loud. Why didn't you warn me what to look for? If I'd known she could start bustin' up the furniture, I might have seen it sooner."

"I told you at the start of my work with Molly that I'll do whatever it takes to help my kids. So if my tone upsets you, well, I'm sorry. But you hired me to help your godchild, not to baby *you*."

"Let's get one thing straight," he steamed. "Before my Molly became another one of your *cases*, I told you I'd do anything to help her, which is why I chose you instead of another of the hundreds of children's therapists in the area. Maybe...maybe I—"

Was he about to say maybe he'd made a mistake? That he was thinking of finding someone else? Someone older, or someone who'd racked up more cases during her years in the field? Being fired wouldn't bother Hope if she didn't know with absolute certainty how bad it would be for Molly, who'd finally started making progress and whose behavior proved she was, at last, beginning to trust Hope.

Hope had overstepped her bounds with Ethan just now because she'd overlooked an important detail in the case. He was right. She *should* have given him a list of things to be on the lookout for. She'd mentally accused him of being too distracted by business to notice the danger signs...but *she'd* allowed herself to become distracted—by her feelings for Ethan.

She couldn't afford to alienate him now. Molly's recuperation depended on consistency and steadfastness. "I owe you an apology," she began, "for not being more professional. What I said, the way I said it, was completely uncalled for, and I'm sorry. It won't happen again, I assure you."

"The only assurance I need from you is that you won't jump to conclusions in the future. I know what you're thinking—that I haven't spent enough time with her, that if I had, I might have realized the seriousness of—"

"No more blanket assumptions," she promised.

"The truth is, I don't *know* the difference between acceptable 'acting out' and dangerous behavior. Until Molly was foisted on me, my experience was limited to handing out presents at birthdays and Christmases. I wouldn't know a childhood disorder if it bit me on the nose."

It couldn't have been easy for a man like him—especially considering his background—to admit a thing like that. So why did her brain fixate on the word *foisted*?

As though he'd read her mind, Ethan blurted, "And, please, don't jump on your analysis bandwagon, judging every word that comes out of my mouth. I didn't mean that the way it sounded. I hope you know that."

But did she?

On the one hand, he'd overcome numerous obstacles to get to London immediately after the accident and had done everything humanly possible to make a good home for Molly. On the other hand, his whole life had been turned upside down. No more parties, no more black-tie balls, no more glamorous ladies on his arm at charity functions...because an emotionally distraught little girl had been *foisted* on him.

Ethan sighed heavily. "Listen, I have a meeting in five minutes. I know what that sounds like, believe me, but she's in good hands for the little while it'll take to get things taken care of." A pause, and then, "You're still coming over tonight for Molly's session, right?"

"Of course I am. What gave you the idea I wouldn't be?"

In place of an answer, he asked, "And you'll stay for supper, right?"

"Putting Molly at ease is of paramount importance. She's come to expect that, so it's not a good idea to deviate from—"

"See you at seven, then."

He didn't wait for a reply but simply hung up, leaving Hope to stare in dumbfounded silence at the buzzing receiver. *How have things gotten so out of control?* she wondered. They'd been getting along so well. She'd connected with him better than with any parent before him.

But then, she'd never been kissed by a patient's father before.

And she'd never kissed *back*.

She remembered how his big, strong arms had wrapped around her, and the way he'd looked into her eyes as no man before him had.

It had happened nearly four weeks ago, and Ethan hadn't made a single attempt to kiss her again. She took a deep breath, exhaled it slowly. Obviously, he'd realized the inappropriateness of their developing relationship even before she had, and he'd decided to call an immediate halt to it before it interfered with Molly's treatment.

Molly.

Right now, her feelings were all that mattered.

So Hope swallowed the ache in her throat and tidied the files on her desk. From here on out, she'd guard her reactions to Ethan. Not as much as a handshake would transpire between them. Yes, she'd do the right thing.

But that didn't mean her heart would be in it.

After an uncomfortably quiet supper, Hope led Molly into Ethan's office, where they had been conducting most of their sessions. Closing the door, she waited for Molly to sit down in the chair opposite hers, then she sat down and scooted forward until their knees practically touched. "Your uncle Ethan tells me he's been finding some strange things around the house."

The girl didn't normally make eye contact, but when Hope began listing the peculiar occurrences, she looked up.

"Who are you so angry with, Molly? Are you mad at your mom and dad for leaving you?"

She watched the child's dark eyebrows draw together in a serious frown and knew that if she didn't act fast—while she had Molly's attention—she might never get another chance like this. "Are you upset with them for dying, and forcing you to come here to live with your uncle Ethan? Is that why you're destroying every gift they ever gave you, one by one? Is that how you're punishing them for abandoning you?"

Molly blinked and clenched her teeth.

"I've also noticed you haven't been eating much lately. And your uncle Ethan and Maria have noticed it, too."

Now Molly frowned and crossed both arms over her chest.

Leaning forward, Hope rested her hands on Molly's knees. "You can behave like a stubborn mule if you want to, but it won't get you very far. And do you know why?"

She shook her head and stared at her hands, now fidgeting in her lap.

"Because I'm *way* more mule-headed than you are. Plus, I'm older. And I've had a lot more practice at being stubborn." She leaned down, forcing Molly to see her smile. "Just keep that in mind."

The girl's chin lifted a bit. "I can be more stubborn than you any day!"

That her first words were as a challenge was a good sign. *Let the games begin!* Hope thought. "I want you to know something, Molly Marie Sylvester...."

The pupils of Molly's eyes constricted to hear her full name, which told Hope that it had probably been a term of endearment used by one or both of her parents. Possibly Ethan, too. "I care a great deal about what happens to you, and I will stop at nothing to help you."

Now Molly's dark eyes clouded. Mistrust? Doubt?

"And your uncle Ethan loves you more than life itself. You know that's true. Your mom and dad trusted him to care for you because they believed he'd do everything in his power to do what's best for you. He's trying, Molly—trying so very hard. It's breaking his heart seeing you so miserable, not knowing how to comfort you...."

Molly blinked once, twice, then looked over at the window.

But Hope had meant what she'd said. She had no intention of giving up on this kid. Gently, she cupped Molly's chin in one palm until they sat eye to eye. "Tell me why you've been breaking things. Or why you haven't been eating. Or why you refuse to talk."

To this point, it had been Hope's job to establish trust, to get the girl accustomed to questions, even if none garnered an answer. Until now, she'd been busy building the bridge that would take her across the chasm Molly had constructed to separate her from human companionship and comfort, from reminders of her stable, loving past.

Well, the foundation had been laid, and now the time had come to complete construction on that bridge, word by word. "You're very angry with them, aren't you?"

Molly's eyes widened.

"You're *so* mad at your mom and dad, you're just speechless, aren't you!"

Molly shook her head as her eyes misted with tears.

"It's okay to be angry, sweetie. It's okay...and it's perfectly normal to be furious with them for putting themselves in danger that night."

Fat tears rolled down Molly's cheeks and plopped into her upturned palms.

"You believe if they had loved you more, they might have done something differently to prevent the accident. But they didn't, did they? And so you feel as though they let you down."

This time, when she shook her head, Molly's face was concealed by a veil of dark hair. She'd spoken only one line in all this time, but the words and the tears were proof Hope was getting through to her. Getting on her knees, Hope wrapped her arms around the child. "Oh, Molly, Molly, Molly," she chanted, struggling to stanch her own tears. "Don't punish yourself any more, sweetie. It wasn't your fault!"

Their gazes fused for several tense moments—Hope was intent on sending the message through her eyes that she would not give up, would *not* let up; Molly's eyes said the opposite. Her hands trembled. Her lips quivered. And with one heartrending cry, she wrapped her arms around Hope and began to sob.

"Oh, honey," Hope said, kissing her tear-dampened cheeks, "you're gonna be all right. Everything will be all right, I promise. We'll get to the bottom of this if it takes all night and—"

The door to Ethan's office banged open to reveal him standing there, fists clenched at his sides. "What's going on in here?"

Hope didn't need to turn and look at him to know how furious he was. What she didn't know was *why*.

He crossed the room in three long strides, wrenched Molly from Hope's arms, and wrapped her in a protective hug. "What's the meaning of this?" he demanded. "I hired you to help her, not hurt her!"

"Ethan," she began, surprised at the timidity in her voice, "you don't understand. Molly and I—"

"It's okay, sweet girl," he crooned, "it's all right. Uncle Ethan is here now...."

Despite his tender ministrations, Molly continued to cry...into Ethan's shoulder now.

Hope got to her feet and paced the plush Persian carpet in front of his desk. "Don't do this, Ethan," she said, stopping beside him. "If you usurp my authority this way, you'll—"

Holding Molly as if she were a toddler, he stared her down. "Usurp your authority? Let me remind you that you're in *my* house, Miss Majors, for one reason and one reason only: to help Molly." He hugged the girl tighter. "And from the looks of things, you're doing anything *but* that."

"Believe it or not, there was a purpose to my—"

"You're right. I don't believe it. I have no idea how the parents of your other patients behave at times like this, but I will not stand idly by while you torture *my* kid. She's been through enough. What she needs is—"

"What she needs," Hope said, slowly, deliberately, "is a guardian who will—"

"I'm not just her guardian!" he thundered. "Sam and Shari wanted me to be her father, and I want that, too!"

"Then act like one." She gave him a moment to react, then aimed a forefinger at him. "You need to leave Molly and me alone to continue our work. I know it isn't easy listening to her eternal silence, watching her cry, but…." She swallowed, praying that the Lord would help her find the right words—words that would console him while also comforting Molly. "You told me I was chosen from hundreds of therapists because of my success with kids like Molly."

He looked from her to Molly and back again.

"I know better than anyone that you want to do what's in her best interests. So trust me, Ethan." She laid a hand on his forearm and whispered, "Okay?"

She'd expected his angry expression to relax. Expected him to put Molly back in her chair. To stumble through a halfhearted apology and agree to leave her alone with the child to continue the session.

But none of that happened. In fact, she wouldn't have been at all surprised to hear him insist that she leave, right away, and never come back.

"I wish I could tell you this would all be over soon, Ethan; that it would be easy to reach a satisfying end. But I've been up-front with you so far, and I see no reason to be anything but honest with you now. I know what works. So you're just going to have to put some faith in—"

"Hold it right there," he barked. "Bullying my girl was never part of the plan. If I'd known browbeating and intimidation would be part of your therapy, I'd never have consented to—"

Hope gasped, cutting him off. "I know what it looked like, but you have to believe me, it—"

"Stop it!" Molly cried, clamping her hands over her ears and shaking her head. "Stop it right now!"

Ethan set her on her feet and got on one knee. Tears pooled in his eyes as he cradled her face with both hands. "Molly, darlin'!" he said, his voice gravelly with emotion, "you...you *talked*!" Pulling her close, he shut his eyes.

A moment later, he looked up at Hope. "She talked," he said, stunned. "Molly *talked*."

The argument, the accusations, the anger vanished as he and Hope both wrapped Molly in an embrace, their arms overlapping around her. Ethan linked his fingers with Hope's and gave a gentle squeeze. "Sorry," he managed to say around a sob. "I didn't know. I didn't realize...."

Hope was optimistic but guarded. She'd been down this road enough times to know that what had just happened was nothing to pin their hopes on. Molly's exclamation could have been a sign that she was close to recovery, but it just as easily could have been a fluke, a momentary flare-up, induced by the emotionally charged atmosphere in the room.

Although it went against everything she'd learned about psychological disorders and their treatments, about disappointments and expectations, she went ahead and hoped, anyway.

Chapter Ten

Hope had been letting him off the hook for far too long.

As she backed out of the parking space in front of her office building, she thought of the many occasions when Ethan had willingly participated in counseling sessions with Molly. Rearranging his overcrowded calendar had often required some fancy footwork, but he'd done it, quickly and without complaint. She drove toward his house, her mind abuzz with conflicting thoughts. He was a man to be reckoned with, to be sure. But did he really expect her to believe he was influential enough to put the governor on hold for Molly yet couldn't get out of an appointment in order to meet alone with Hope? *What's he afraid of?* she wondered.

Over the years, Hope had learned that a client's face—his facial expressions, his fleeting smiles or sneers—told nearly as much as the words he said. And if the stark look of dread on Ethan's face each time she suggested a one-on-one between them wasn't fear, she had no idea how to define it.

She recalled the article she'd read that claimed dentists are three times more likely than other professionals to commit suicide because they spend so much time looking into the eyes of fear. But frustration at not being able to help their patients surely put psychiatrists in a position of even greater likelihood of suicide. Hope shook her head. *I have three strikes against me without even trying,* she thought. Her mother had killed herself, she'd chosen psychiatry as a profession, and she spent her days drilling patients for information. *Thank God I have the Lord on my side!*

And she'd stay close to Him in the weeks to come....

She'd met Ethan in early fall, when the trees along the Baltimore Beltway were still green and full of leaves. Nearly two months had passed since then, and with each passing week, driving back and forth on I-695 between Rockville and Potomac, Hope had witnessed the subtle seasonal changes in nature. Now, the once-verdant trees glowed with blazing orange and burnt yellow.

But seasons past had taught her that the beauty of autumn is deceptive, for it is but a harbinger of winter's unwavering approach. In a little while, the limbs that now gleamed gold and scarlet would be stripped bare by blustery gusts, and, before long, the bright blue sky would dim to pale gray as the wind's frosty breath blew fall's cottony clouds to the far corners of the planet.

Ethan reminded her a bit of the wind—warm and soothing one day, cold and unnerving the next.

"We've been putting this off for days," she'd said on the phone that morning. "For Molly's sake, we need to talk today...alone."

And he hadn't minced words. "Then for Molly's sake, let's do it."

His emphasis on "for Molly's sake" showed how drastically their relationship had cooled since the argument. During their conversation, she had heard him popping the locks on his briefcase, rifling through its contents in search of his BlackBerry. "Tomorrow, six o'clock? Maria won't mind staying late just this once."

"She's a wonderful woman," Hope had said. "No need to put her to that trouble. I'll be there for my regular session with Molly at seven. Maybe we can talk after she's gone to bed instead."

"See you then," he'd said before hanging up.

Hope sighed heavily. "Help me, Lord. I'm at my wit's end. Please tell me what to do...for both of them."

As she neared the big house on the Potomac, her mind drifted to the articles she'd read about the self-made millionaire. One article in particular—"Nice Guys Finish First"—stuck out in her mind. "Like any other predator," Earl Shores had written, "Burke is cunning and stealthy, and patient enough to scope out the horizon in search of the young, the ailing, and the weak." Shores had filled an entire sidebar with the names of company presidents and corporations that had "fallen prey" to Ethan's incredible skills as a hunter. The facts, as presented by the reporter, made the headline all the more ironic, considering all that Ethan had done for his godchild.

Maybe when all this was over, once she'd put Molly on the path to healing and things were right between her and Ethan, Hope would take a much-needed vacation. She'd always loved the shore with its shell-strewn beaches and screeching seagulls. The quiet would be healing for *her* at this time of year, without scores of sunbathers hogging the beach and noisy children running around and splashing in the water. Long walks at the edge of the chilly surf soothed and calmed her as few things could...if she was careful not to wade out too far. She never had learned to swim.

She thought of Molly. Of Ethan. Of how very much she'd come to care for them both. And she prayed she wasn't in over her head.

❧

Maria had worked for Ethan for years and, even during her first week on the job, had never been the least bit shy about asking for—or telling him—what she needed. So the faint knock at the door of his study and the timid expression on her face when he told her to come in surprised him enough to say, "Maria, you—you look like you've seen a ghost!"

She looked furtively over one shoulder. "You have... you have company, Meester Burke." She pointed. "Downstairs, in the billiards room."

"Company?" The art deco grandfather clock behind her read 5:15. The only visitor he was expecting was Hope, but not until 7:00. Had she changed her mind about talking with him after her session with Molly? With more than a little impatience, he strode toward the door and caught a glimpse out the front window. "What are all those cars doing on the front lawn?" he asked Maria. "There must be thirty or forty—"

"Ethan!" said a sultry voice from behind him. "Happy birthday."

As he turned, Kate pressed a lingering kiss to the corner of his mouth.

"Kate," he said, placing his hands on her shoulders to keep her from getting any closer. "What are you doing here?" After the episode when Ethan had written Hope's name over and over on his notepad, Kate had turned up the heat in an even greater attempt to attract his attention. She'd stayed within the bounds of professional office propriety, yet she'd managed to let him know she had no intention of giving up without a fight.

She inclined her bleach-blonde head and smiled seductively. "Why, I've brought you a birthday present," she said breathily.

Ethan looked past her at Maria, who shrugged and held out both hands. "Don't look at me," she said. "I just work here."

Kate grabbed his arm and led him down the hall. "I'd blindfold you," she said, laughing as they reached the stairs, "but I've never been very good with knots. Besides, you could fall down—"

"Kate," he said, wriggling free of her grasp, "what's with all the cars out there?"

She kissed him again, this time on the lips. "It's a party, silly! You haven't done anything fun in months. What better excuse to kick up your heels than a birthday celebration?"

He took a deep breath, hoping it might help him summon the patience to keep from booting her out the front door. What made her think she could waltz into his home, uninvited, and behave like the lady of the manor?

It was clear he needed to stop focusing all his extra attention on Molly. And Hope. The distraction had allowed Kate to move in way too close. She was an excellent marketing manager, period. The time had come to make sure she understood they would never be more than employer and employee. "Kate," he growled, "you're overstepping your—"

"There he is!" someone shouted from downstairs. "Look, everybody, the birthday boy is here!"

Cheers bubbled up the steps as his employees gathered in the foyer. "C'mon down," someone said, and Kate added, "There's pâté and truffles and the most marvelous jellied mousse. All your favorites!" She leaned close to whisper into his ear, "And...some very special *presents*."

Frowning, he looked into her heavily made-up eyes. "Who told you it was my birthday?"

She'd always seemed so poised, so sure of herself, but under his scathing, demanding stare, Kate blinked and, for the first time since he'd met her, seemed uncertain what to do next.

She opted for humor. "I didn't realize your birthday was a corporate secret," she said, laughing. "Isn't this what you pay me for? To publicize you and Burke Enterprises?"

He hadn't noticed the TV cameras until that moment. Gritting his teeth, Ethan said, "Of all the...."

"Smile, Ethan," hollered a cameraman.

"We're live for the six o'clock news," said the reporter.

The media had never felt the need to stand on ceremony with him. He'd never been "Mr. Burke," because he'd encouraged the down-to-earth, friendly persona. Plastering a smile on his face, he slid an arm around Kate's shoulders. "Do you believe the gall of this woman, barging in here like she owns the place to throw me a birthday party?"

Amid the applause and laughter, Kate chose that moment to kiss his cheek.

"See if anyone needs a drink or some food," he said, stepping back. And to the reporter, he said, "I'll be down in just a second." He wiggled his eyebrows. "Few loose ends to tie up. Use the time to see what juicy gossip you can wrangle from my employees."

Maria was still standing behind him, looking confused and upset. "I did not know, Meester Burke. I open thee door, and Meese Kate, she shove right inside. I—"

"I know," he said, giving her shoulder a reassuring squeeze. "Bet now you wish you'd taken that class in night school...."

"Wheech class?"

"How to Avoid a Steamroller," he said, winking.

"They made a movie about theese one," she said. "I theenk it was called *Godzilla*."

Ethan laughed as the doorbell rang. "Tell whomever it is that we're at maximum capacity. I don't need the fire marshal breathing down my neck."

Kate opened the door as if on cue and ushered a caterer inside. Behind him was a group of black-suited young men and women carrying trays with white doilies into the kitchen.

"You theenk maybe Molly, she would like to join the party?"

He shrugged, wondering what Hope would recommend. "Don't suppose it could hurt any. If she wants to come down, it's fine with me," he said, heading back into his study. "I'll be only a few minutes," he added, closing the door.

With a glance at his Rolex, Ethan realized Hope would arrive in a little over an hour. And the party would be going full tilt by then. How would she feel about walking in on a birthday bash?

He got a picture of her face, wide-eyed with disbelief, and wondered how long it would take her to say, "We'll reschedule our session for a more convenient time...."

If she hadn't been there dozens of times, Hope might have thought she'd made a wrong turn somewhere. Why were a Channel Two van and a WQSR radio station car parked among dozens of others on his neatly mowed lawn?

The housekeeper threw open the door even before Hope could ring the bell. "Meese Majors," she said, hugging her. "I'm so glad you are here!" Looking toward the heavens, she raised her arms, then let them drop to her sides. "Meester Burke, he will need you. That *Kate* woman...ay-ay-ay-ay," she said, shaking her head.

Hope had never seen the spunky woman without a cheery smile on her broad face. "What's wrong, Maria?"

The unmistakable sounds of merriment filtered up from the lower level of the house. Voices engaged in laughter and conversation harmonized with the tinkling of ice cubes, the clang of flatware connecting with china, and the barely audible melody of music coming from the sound system. Maria closed the front door behind them. "You be careful of that one, Meese Majors," she whispered.

Hope swallowed a lump of nervousness without even knowing why she felt anxious. "Be careful? Why would I need to—?"

"That one, she eees trouble, I tell you." With one finger in the air, the woman said, "I am not at leeeberty to say more, but...please be careful, *si*?" With that, she disappeared into the kitchen.

Hope couldn't help but wonder why Ethan hadn't told her about the party. If he didn't want her here, surely he'd have come up with some excuse to postpone their session. She glanced toward the stairs, wondering where Molly was. Maybe—

"Well, well, well. What do we have here?" said a saucy female voice.

Hope turned as the woman thrust a limp, red-clawed hand in her direction. "How rude of me. I'm Kate, and I, um, *work* for Ethan...?"

Her emphasis on the word *work* hadn't been accidental, and Hope was left wondering why Ethan had never mentioned the woman.

"It's his birthday, you know," Kate continued.

"Oh. I—I didn't realize. I—we have.... I'm Hope Majors, Molly's counselor."

It made no sense to Hope why Kate's eyes narrowed at the mention of her name. Made no sense that her voice took on an icy edge when she said, "Ethan is terribly busy, I'm afraid, so perhaps you can come back some other time, when—"

"Of course," Hope said. "He must have forgotten about the party when he scheduled the appointment. Perhaps you'll be kind enough to let him know I was here?" But even as the words passed her lips, Hope knew Ethan would never hear from Kate that she'd stopped by. She headed for the stairs, intent on stopping in Molly's room. "I'll just get to work with Molly, and—"

Kate bit her lower lip, then said, "Oh, dear...he hasn't told you, then?"

Fear pounded in her heart. She had one foot on the first step, the other on the foyer floor, when she asked, "Told me what?"

The big blonde looked around as if checking for eavesdroppers. "I hate to be the one to break this to you," she said, "but I happen to know that Ethan has been interviewing other therapists."

How could Kate know such a thing unless Ethan had told her himself?

"Men!" Kate said, shaking her head. "They can be so self-centered. How rude of him not to call you. He could have saved you the trip over here." Stepping aside, she opened the front door. "When he gets to the office tomorrow, I'll be sure he calls you, first thing. He owes you a big apology!"

Hope remembered Maria's warning. "He doesn't owe me anything," she said, digging through her purse. "Least of all an apology!" Jangling her car keys, Hope smiled. "Nice meeting you," she said as Kate leaned on the doorjamb, one high-heeled foot crossed over the other.

When she was halfway to her car, Ethan's voice stopped her. "Hey, Hope! Where are you going?"

She turned, heartened by his warm, welcoming smile. But her feelings of elation died an immediate death when she noticed the unmistakable splotches of lipstick on his cheeks, on his lips...lipstick the same shade of red as Kate's....

Hope had admitted her feelings for Ethan to herself, but until that moment, she hadn't realized just how much she'd come to care for him. Seeing evidence that he and Kate had a relationship that was obviously more than professional—well, it made things painfully clear. That kiss? The warm hugs? She didn't understand what they'd meant, but she understood the possessive way Kate linked her arm through his.

Turning on her heel, Hope hurried to her car. She didn't bother to buckle her seatbelt or check her mirrors, and as she backed onto his circular driveway, she knew that it was by the grace of God she didn't collide with another car.

If she'd received Maria's message earlier, maybe she'd have been spared this humiliation.

Correction, she thought, fighting tears. *Heartache*.

Chapter Eleven

H ope!" Ethan hollered as she sped off. "Hope, wait up!"

He took a shortcut, high-jumping a boxwood hedge and zigzagging across the lawn in an attempt to cut her off farther down the drive. "Hope, for cryin' out loud, will you *wait*!" Whether she didn't hear him or was choosing to ignore him, Ethan didn't know. He understood only that she was bound and determined to get off his property as fast as possible.

Kate was waiting for him when he returned to the foyer. "What was that all about?" he demanded, slamming the door.

"I have no idea," she said, shrugging innocently. "I came up to check on the caterers and saw her at the bottom of the stairs. Guess she took it wrong when I said you and Molly were busy with the party and your guests."

Oh, she was good, real good. But Ethan was practiced at detecting guile, and he had dozens of corporate takeovers under his belt to prove it. Kate was attractive enough—if you liked girls big and blonde and pushy—and a year or so ago, he probably would have said she was just his type. But that was before he realized how much more he preferred a petite woman with freckles and green eyes, fiery red curls, and a smile that would melt the ice in his sarsaparilla.

He caught a glimpse of himself in the hall mirror behind Kate's head and saw the lipstick blotches around his mouth—Kate's not-so-subtle "brand." No doubt Hope had seem them, too. Had she run off like a scared rabbit because she'd been jealous?

The idea made him smile a bit.

But the moment didn't last long, because Kate reached out to tidy his collar with a haughty "I'm-too-sexy-for-my-party-dress" grin on her face.

Ethan didn't understand how Kate had known precisely when Hope would arrive, but he had no doubt that she'd timed the party to coincide with Molly's session. She'd never thrown a party for him before, so why now, after nearly five years' employment with him? It was a clever ruse, he decided, that allowed her to communicate her intentions. And, sadly, Hope had read the message loud and clear.

Kate's attitude might have made sense if he'd given her a sign that he was interested in her. How ever had she gotten the notion that they were more than employer and employee?

"What's going on inside that handsome head of yours?" Kate asked, sidling up to him.

He felt another caress coming his way and barred it with his forearm. "Trust me, Kate, you do not want me to answer that question."

"But of course I do, darling," she cooed, combing her long, painted fingernails through his hair. "You *know* I do!"

Despite his best efforts to prevent her, she managed to press herself against his side, so he put his hands on her shoulders and gave her a gentle shake. "That woman you just chased away?"

Kate read the wrong message from his hands-on approach and rested her hands on his shoulders. "Adorable little thing. Molly's counselor, right?"

"Adorable. Yes. Most adorable woman I've ever laid eyes on."

Her self-assured smirk faded.

"She's smart and talented, too, and sweet as cotton candy...."

Blinking, Kate took a small step back.

But Ethan was merely warming up. "With a smile brighter than the sun and eyes a man could get lost in, the voice of an angel, and—"

Giggling nervously, Kate licked her lips. "Ethan, *darling*, you'd better be careful, or people will get the idea you're—"

"That I'm in love with her?" One corner of his mouth lifted in a grin.

And Kate's blue eyes narrowed.

"I have to hand it to you, Kate."

She swallowed. "W-what?"

"Well, I knew pretty much from the get-go that I liked her, but until today, I never realized how *much*." He gave her a light kiss right in the middle of her forehead. "So thanks, kiddo, for helping me see what's been right under my nose all along."

"B-but Ethan," she stammered, "I thought, I—"

"I know," he said, turning her toward the door that led to the party downstairs, "you never expected that playing cupid would be part of your job description, did you?"

She stood alone on the landing, arms hanging limp at her sides.

"I believe in repaying deeds in kind," he said evenly, giving her a moment to mull over his meaning. "You'll find the best letter of recommendation you've ever read in your pay envelope next week and a big fat severance check, too."

Kate gasped as all ten fingers fluttered near her throat. "Recommendation? Severance? Ethan, surely you can't mean—"

He held up an index finger, commanding her silence. "I can, *darling*, and I do." Shrugging, he added, "It's one of the perks about bein' the boss." His stern expression was matched by the angry rasp of his voice. "I don't have to work with people I don't trust."

"But when you hired me, you said I was one of the best marketers in the business. It's what you said when you gave me my last raise, and—"

"Your work for Burke Enterprises has been impeccable," he said, cutting her off. "But you can't seem to grasp the boundaries of your job. Now, why not go downstairs, cut yourself a big piece of the birthday cake I probably paid too much for, and enjoy the party you threw to help me celebrate the fact I've finally come to my senses... about a lot of things."

As he turned to go downstairs, she said, "They're right about you. You *are* heartless!"

Ethan stopped dead in his tracks, made a slow pivot, and looked her right in the eyes. "The word is 'ruthless,' *darling*, and I earned it by knowing whom I can—and can't—trust."

Hope was going to wear a path in the carpet if she didn't stop pacing back and forth across her living room. *I behaved like a little ninny—a jealous little ninny!* was her mental self-castigation.

She had come so close to making a breakthrough with Molly, and now her unprofessionalism was threatening to blow everything up. It would be a miracle if Ethan allowed her to spend another moment with his girl!

What must he think of her, running off as though she had a pit bull on her heels? Hope got a quick mental picture of his face, spotted here and there with the imprints of Kate's kisses, and her stomach twisted into a knot.

Several times, she'd come close to admitting out loud that her feelings for him ran deep. But each time, she'd reined in her emotions. Excused them. Rationalized them. Pretended they were nothing more than the natural consequences of a schoolgirl crush...the direct result of too many years spent dreaming that someday, a white knight would carry her off to a rose-covered cottage.

She knew what she had to do.

But first, a little sustenance....

Hope fell to her knees right there in the middle of the living room, bowed her head, and folded her hands. With eyes closed, she prayed aloud. "Dear Lord, give me the courage to face my fears and own up to my mistakes. Open my heart and mind to accept Your wisdom and guidance, so I'll know what to say when I see...." Her heart pounded with dread at the mere thought of facing him. "...When I see him again."

The last thing she wanted to do was to get into her car, drive down that dark and deserted road to his riverfront home, and admit what a fool she'd been—and how horribly it would impact poor, innocent little Molly. But it was the right thing to do.

Hope had to convince Ethan to give her another chance, because she was close, so close, to reaching Molly. She'd give him much assurance to convince him to let her finish what she'd started.

"Almighty Father, bless me with the grace to do what's best for both of them, because I...."

Opening her eyes, she held her breath as the truth crashed around her like waves on the shore. "I love her," she whispered. "God help me, I love that little girl!"

She'd violated just about every rule of professional decorum ever written, but Hope knew she couldn't blame it all on her feelings for Molly. Admittedly, the child's history and her own were similar, but the real source of her departure from professional behavior was rooted in how she felt about Ethan.

Tears sprang to her eyes as she admitted, "Lord help me, I love him, too...." Then, on the heels of a shuddering sigh, Hope prayed, "Put my mind right, Lord. Help me focus on the important things in life, like obeying Your Word and helping *all* my patients find solace."

A sense of peace engulfed her, and she believed she would find the strength to do the right thing, for the right reasons. On her feet now, she crossed to the stereo and popped in a CD, letting the soothing, Spirit-filled music bring her an even greater calm. She decided to do something with her hair, repair the damage her tears had done to her makeup, and then change into something comfortable before heading back to Ethan's. It was a weeknight, after all, and the partygoers had to work the next morning. Surely, they would be gone by the time she got there.

The drive to the river seemed to take far less time than the usual twenty minutes, partly because she recited the Twenty-third Psalm the entire way.

It wouldn't be easy.

But she'd do it.

Maybe, by the time she arrived at his house, she would actually believe that.

Ethan knocked softly on Molly's door. "Hey, sweetie," he called, "mind if I come in?"

No response...par for the course. So, he turned the knob and slowly peeked into the room.

She wasn't at her desk or on the window seat, nor in the closet or the bathroom. Puzzled, he headed back down the hall to find Maria. The woman never missed a thing. Surely, she'd know where the girl had gone.

He found his housekeeper in the kitchen, loading the dishwasher. "You should have left hours ago," he admitted.

"And leave you weeth theese mess? Not me, Meester Burke," she said, laughing.

"I don't know what I ever did to deserve you. You're the best." Then, "You haven't seen Molly, have you?"

"Eeen her favorite place. Where else?"

Ethan grabbed his jacket from the wooden peg behind the door and headed outside. Pocketing his hands, he walked down the gentle slope of lawn toward the riverbank and soon heard the unmistakable *plink-plunk* of pebbles plopping into the murky water. Molly came into view, sitting on the pier with her bare toes dangling in the water.

"Kinda cold to be doin' that, don't you think?"

When she didn't answer, he hunkered down beside her. "So, what brought you out here in the dark, all by yourself?"

She shrugged.

If he'd asked her that before Sam and Shari died, she might have said, "I'm not alone. God is up there in the sky, with the stars and the moon; there are birds roosting in the trees...and there's you."

He made a move to sling an arm over her shoulders when he noticed the duffle bag stuffed to overflowing beside her. "Hey, what's this?"

Another shrug.

"Planning to run away from home, are you?"

Molly sighed.

Ethan pretended his heart wasn't aching with dread. If he hadn't come out here when he had, would she have gone? Ethan cleared his throat and put his fear into words. "How far do you think you could go...li'l gal who refuses to talk?"

Silence.

"Well, I hope you packed money. Plenty of it."

She nodded.

"Good, good, 'cause a girl needs money when she's on the run."

More silence.

"Might be kinda hard, though, going into a diner, trying to get a meal...."

She turned slightly.

"I mean, what're you planning to do, point at the menu to order?"

Molly blinked and tucked in one corner of her mouth.

"Ahh, I see," he said, nodding. "You hadn't thought it through that far, right?"

She shook her head.

"Then I wonder if you gave any thought to where you'd sleep. It's November. Gets pretty cold, 'specially at night, y'know...."

Her shoulders slumped.

"Hmm...hadn't thought of that, either, I take it...."

She shook her head again.

"Well, I know that a smart kid like you would have taken the time to think things through...if something hadn't distracted her. Was it that awful, noisy party?"

One shoulder rose in a half-shrug, and Ethan got to his feet. "Tell you what," he said. "Put your shoes on, and we'll head inside. Maria hasn't left yet, so maybe we can talk her into whipping us up a pot of her famous hot cocoa, and some of that amazing popcorn...."

When Molly looked up at him, the stars glinted in her dark eyes. He wanted to gather her close, hug her tight, and promise her the world would right itself soon. But like he'd said...she was a smart kid. No way she'd believe it, especially after all she'd been through lately.

Ethan settled for the feel of her warm little hand tucked into his big one. Side by side, they walked across the decking at the end of his yard. They'd just passed the gazebo when she blurted out, "My suitcase!"

A sob ached in his throat at the sound of her voice, hoarse and craggy from lack of use. But he bit his tongue and thanked God silently as she ran back to fetch the duffle. When she caught up to him again, he took it from her and dropped it on the lawn. "Remember how we used to sit in the gazebo for hours, just watching and listening for critters?"

Smiling, she nodded.

"What do you think...in the mood to do that now?"

Smiling wider, she nodded again.

He carried the bag inside as she settled on the bench facing the river, then came back out and sat down beside her, drawing her close in a sideways hug. Almost instantly, she rested her head on his shoulder.

"Last week," he whispered, "I saw a deer, right there in the woods." He pointed at the spot. "Big, burly buck with antlers as wide as this gazebo!"

"Hmpf," she said, grinning suspiciously. But he noticed that she'd immediately begun scanning the tree line for a glimpse of the big deer. "Uncle Ethan?"

It startled him more than he cared to admit, hearing her soft whisper so near to his ear. "What, sweetie?" he whispered back.

She pointed, and he followed her gaze to a spot beyond the brush where three does, their white tails flicking like warning flags, stood looking straight back at them. "How many?" he asked, hoping to coax more conversation from her.

"Just three...."

"Just three," he echoed, wishing Hope were there to share the joyous moment.

Chapter Twelve

F ollowing the directions Maria had given her, Hope headed down the path leading to the Potomac. She'd expected to hear Ethan's voice by the time her sneakers hit the weathered wood decking or to see Molly and Ethan, silhouetted by the moonlit sky. Had the housekeeper been mistaken? Maybe Molly hadn't headed for her favorite spot at her uncle Ethan's house after all....

Just then, his manly baritone floated toward her on the crisp November air. "I love you, sweet girl," she heard him say. She stopped walking, trying to pinpoint the direction from which his voice had come.

"You know that, don't you?"

The gazebo, she realized, but she saw no reason to move closer. Standing under the umbrella of the bare-branched willow was a bit like being in her own private auditorium.

"That bag you packed," he was saying, "is pretty heavy."

Hope read the silence to mean that Molly hadn't answered.

"Felt pretty good, didn't it," he continued, "when you got some help lugging it back up the walk?"

Hope took a step forward, which enabled her to see the shadowy figures of Ethan and Molly, huddled together in the darkness. When Molly nodded, Hope saw Ethan close his eyes and look up as if thanking God for the response, however silent.

"How much do you know about Miss Majors?" Ethan said next.

The blood froze in Hope's veins.

"Did you know she's an orphan, just like you?"

Molly turned on the bench to face him.

"She hasn't had a mom or a dad since she was a baby. Her aunt and uncle raised her." He kissed Molly's forehead. "Gotta admire somebody like that...."

Tears welled in Hope's eyes, and a sob ached in her throat. Had she misread the scene earlier between him and Kate?

"It's my fault," Molly said.

And Ethan asked, "What's your fault?"

"Mom and Dad...the...the accident...it was my fault."

Hope tensed, wondering what he'd say or do, wondering if she ought to join them.

"Why would you say such a thing?" Ethan asked.

"Because. It's true."

He gathered her closer and lifted her chin with his forefinger. "How 'bout explaining it to your poor old uncle Ethan...."

"I was at Sally's house that night. I was supposed to stay till morning." She sighed. "But Sally and me had a fight and I wanted to go home. So I called them, told them to come get me."

"Nothing wrong with that," Ethan interjected.

"But Mom said Dad had just got home, that he was extra tired. And I knew she never learned how to drive that new car, but I didn't care. I wanted to go home."

For a while, neither of them spoke. Hope was formu-
lating in her mind how she might handle the situation
in his shoes when he said, "Taking the blame for something like that? Well, that's a pretty heavy bag to carry
all by yourself."

Molly sniffed.

"Maybe you oughtta let me help you carry it."

Silence.

"...Like you let me help you carry your suitcase."

More silence.

"You packed that thing pretty full...."

The only sound was the water, gently slapping the
shore.

"It was nice, wasn't it, having help?"

"Yes...."

"So, what do you say, Molly-girl? Will you let me help
you with this one, too?"

The wind rustled through the underbrush. *It's what
angels' wings must sound like*, Hope thought, watching the answer to a prayer unfold before her eyes. As a
girl, the thought had calmed her when the night wind,
soughing past her windows, made her huddle under the
sheets, feeling alone and afraid. *The breath of God*, she'd
tell herself. And, in no time, her fears would evaporate.

The same serenity enveloped her now. "Be not afraid,"
Jesus had promised, "for I am with you."

Christ was with Ethan now, too, guiding his every
word.

"I aim to help you see it wasn't your fault. Okay?"

Suddenly, Hope felt every bit like the spy she was.
She had no right to be here, trespassing on this profound, private moment. Turning, she headed back to the
house, where she would hide out in the powder room
until her eyes were no longer puffy from crying tears of

relief and joy. Then, she'd do what she'd come here to do and apologize to Ethan.

It would be an uphill battle from here, this business of going on without him, alone.

No...not alone. She'd always have the Lord.

Ethan didn't need her. He'd never needed her. Hope knew that now, and the proof had been in his voice, in his words, in every action he'd taken moments ago...and since they'd met.

The inky sky overhead twinkled with the gleam of a million stars, and Hope looked up into the knowing eyes of God, whispering her request....

Ten years later,
in the home of Mr. and Mrs. Ethan Burke

"Molly, would you call your father for me, please?"

The young woman gave her mother a gently playful elbow to the ribs. "Sure, Mom. What would you like me to call him?"

Hope laughed. "Quit fooling around, silly girl. Supper's getting cold!"

Molly's smile was mirrored in her dark eyes. Giggling, she headed for the family room. "But I'm not even hungry yet! It's three hours earlier at Stanford, y'know."

"Well, you can at least sit at the table and visit with us, Miss I'm-Gonna-Be-a-Pediatrician." Hope gave her a sideways hug. It seemed the girl hadn't stopped talking—not even for a minute!—since that night in the gazebo when Ethan had promised to be there for her always, to help her carry her burdens.

Now, Ethan sidled up behind Hope and wrapped his arms around her in an affectionate hug. "Whatcha thinkin', pretty lady?"

She leaned against him. "Oh, just remembering by-gone days, that's all."

He turned her to face him. "You don't mean...?"

Blushing, she said, "What?"

"You've been in la-la land for days now. At first, I chalked it up to Molly coming home for the summer. But now I'm not so sure."

Her flush intensified. He'd always known her better than anyone, so it shouldn't have surprised her that he suspected something. She sighed. "I'd hoped to make the announcement over dessert."

He clamped a big hand on each of her shoulders. "Are you saying what I think you're saying?"

"This one's due on Valentine's Day."

Gathering her close, he chuckled into her ear. "Well now, how 'bout that?" He kissed her cheek. "Maybe we ought to name him Cupid."

Hope crinkled her nose.

"Okay, you're right." Stroking his jaw, he gave it a moment's thought. He pointed his forefinger in the air and said, "I've got it! Candy if it's a girl, Valentino for a boy!"

She wrapped her arms around him. "And what if it's twins again?"

"Hmm...you've got me there." After kissing the tip of her nose, he said, "You make me so happy. Repairing the relationship between my dad and me, convincing me that what happened to Bess and my mom wasn't my fault, getting Molly over her emotional hurdles...."

"These have been the best years of my life," Hope said.

"Mine, too." He paused, frowning slightly. "You're not sorry that you gave up counseling? Not even once in a while?"

"Are you kidding? It's all I do around here, breaking up squabbles between the twins! Seriously, look what you've done for *me*: giving me Sawyer as a substitute father and Maria as a dear friend, putting me in charge of day care at Burke Enterprises, and—"

"Well, just 'cause you're in charge of the program doesn't mean you have to fill every classroom single-handedly!"

"You had a little to do with that, need I remind you?"

He wiggled his eyebrows. "No, m'dear, you never need to remind me of anything so blessedly glorious."

She snuggled closer to him. "God has been very good to us, hasn't He?"

"Sure has." Chuckling, Ethan added, "We've been pretty good to Him, too."

Hope leaned back. "What?"

"Well, the church softball team was four players shy last season, and the Burke family filled every empty seat in the dugout."

Hope shook her head. "I'll make you a deal," she said, one palm pressed to each of his cheeks. "Stop saying sacrilegious things like that and I'll fix your favorite dessert—anytime you want it—for the rest of your life."

"Homemade apple pie, fresh from the oven, with a slab of cheddar cheese on top? For the rest of my *life*? Are you serious...?"

"Serious as a judge."

"Then you've got yourself a deal, baby."

She studied his face and, grinning, said, "Now, why don't I trust you?"

"Maybe because we need to seal this deal with a kiss."

"Oh, you!" she said, laughing. "I love you."

"I love you, too. And I like this system."

"What system?"

"The way we seal every deal with a kiss. Now, close your eyes and pucker up, lady, 'cause I'm about to plant one on ya!"

The Wedding Wish

Prologue

June 5, 2008
Ellicott City, Maryland

In his years as an oncologist, Ron Peterson had given patients bad news before, but it never got any easier than this.

Something told him it never would.

"Are you sure?" Leah asked, her voice a scratchy whisper.

He met her gaze...not an easy feat considering what he'd just told her. "You can go the holistic route, as we discussed a while back—"

"Been there, done that," she said flatly. Then, nodding, Leah took a deep, shuddering breath. For a moment, she sat still as a sculpture. "Well, then," she said, getting to her feet, "I guess I'd better be on my way." And more to herself than to the doctor, she added, "I have a lot to do."

Experience had taught him that words can be woefully inadequate at such times. And so, Ron laid a hand on her shoulder as that oh-so-familiar feeling of helplessness surged through him.

She sent him a weak half-smile, her blue eyes glistening with unshed tears as she gave his hand a comforting pat. "Aww, don't look so sad, Doc. It isn't your fault."

Then whose fault is it? he demanded silently. *Some-one needs to accept responsibility for ending a young mother's life!* With his jaw clenched in grim acceptance, he slid a business card from the brass holder on his desk and scribbled a number on the back. "If you need anything, anything at all," he said, handing her the card, "this is my private line."

She dropped it into her purse with barely a glance. "Thanks, Doc. You're a peach."

He had had a dozen or so patients who, like Leah, demanded straightforward answers to their questions. Ron admired them all, but none more than Leah. She'd put her life in God's hands—her words, not his—and no matter how negative the news or how painful the procedure, she wore that grin-and-bear-it demeanor like a protective cloak—not around herself, but rather around her little girl. Even now, she faced the ugliest of truths with dignity and grace. *Amazing grace*, he thought, because it *was* amazing that she insisted on the possibility of a miracle. "And you're a piece of work, Leah Jordan."

He walked her to the door. She had no parents, no siblings, no husband...just a two-year-old beauty named Fiona. "So how's that little angel of yours?"

A loving, maternal smile lit up her face. "I'm afraid she's entered the 'mixing stage'...."

A furrow of confusion lined his brow.

"At lunch today, she stirred ham and peas and mashed potatoes into her fruit punch...and ate it!"

Chuckling, Ron feigned an upset stomach. "And to think that just this morning, I was complaining about not having any kids." He shrugged and opened his office door. "Go figure."

"Yeah," she sighed, a wan and wistful smile tugging at the corners of her mouth. "Go figure."

He watched her walk down the hall toward the reception room, nod politely at the nurse, and wave good-bye to the receptionist. *You'd never know she just received a death sentence*, Ron thought. Her tenacity reminded him of his mother, whose courageous battle against breast cancer had been the reason he'd become an oncologist in the first place. At least he'd had eighteen wonderful years with her before she lost the war. Leah's daughter was only two....

"How do you prepare a toddler for the death of her only parent?"

His nurse looked up from her clipboard. "I'm sorry," she said distractedly, "did you say something, Doctor?"

Shaking his head, Ron frowned, realizing he'd unintentionally spoken the question aloud. Then, gesturing toward the examination rooms, he added, "How many more?"

"Three."

Heaving a sigh, he nodded. His eyes still on Leah Jordan's retreating form, he said, "Give me five minutes."

Closing his office door softly behind him, Ronald Peterson, medical doctor, slumped into his chair. And, his head in his hands, Ron Peterson, ordinary man, wept.

It was hard to believe a month had passed since the prognosis.

Just as Dr. Peterson had predicted, it was happening fast, very fast. Leah had, at best, a year; at worst....

She chose not to waste time thinking about that. She had no idea when the cancer would completely deplete her energy to the point where she could no longer care for Fiona, and she couldn't afford one moment of self-pity.

Far better to dwell on the many things she could be grateful for. Like the motorized wheelchair that helped conserve her waning strength, donated by fellow parishioners. Hot, nourishing meals, prepared every Sunday by the good ladies of the church. Biweekly housekeeping, provided by neighbors. Thanks to the mortgage insurance John had purchased before his death, the house was paid off, and Leah had more than enough in the bank to keep food in the pantry and oil in the furnace tank for years to come.

Trouble was, Leah didn't *have* "years to come."

She had a plan, though, and after countless hours in deep and heartfelt prayer, it had become clear that God agreed with it, too.

There wasn't a moment to waste. So, after rewriting her last will and testament, Leah began putting her plan into action.

In high school, Leah, Jade, and Riley had been known as the Three Musketeers. The caption beneath the yearbook photo of them standing arm in arm outside the cafeteria read, "Friends for Life!"

For Jade Nelson, Student Council President, and Riley Steele, star quarterback for the Eagles, the association had gone deeper than friendship....

But both had sworn Leah to secrecy independently, and, being the type who believed in keeping confidences, Leah had never let on that Jade loved Riley...or that Riley loved Jade. Ignoring her friendly advice to "fess up" to Jade about his feelings for her, Riley went off to veterinary college in Virginia, while Jade followed her hoped-to-be fiancé to California.

Their lives were busy and full, and both seemed happy...on the surface. But Leah knew better. They'd never stopped loving each other. She knew this because in every conversation with Jade, Riley's name came up...and vice versa. They were perfect for each other—always had been.

Leah had faced the truth about her future, and it was time for Jade and Riley to do the same.

Because Fiona needed them as much as they needed each other.

Chapter One

All during the long flight from California to Maryland, with plane changes in Chicago and Atlanta, Jade alternated between feeling overwhelming grief—how could she be losing Leah, her best friend for twenty years?—and rage—hadn't the poor woman suffered enough in her past?

Jade had never been one to question life's dizzying twists and turns. Simple acceptance, she'd learned, steadied things. But Leah was dying. Did the Lord really expect her to accept *that*?

She daubed a tissue to red-rimmed eyes and took a deep breath. *Get a grip, girl; you have to be strong for Leah.*

And for Fiona.

Fiona had been one of the main reasons she'd decided to move back to Baltimore. Why should Leah pay for full-time, live-in help while she was waiting for God to perform a miracle when her best friend had a nursing degree? Besides, things weren't working out as she'd planned in California, and it wasn't just because of Hank Berger, either.

Fiona....

She pulled out her wallet and looked at the photograph Leah had enclosed in her Christmas card. Chubby, stockinged legs poked out from under the ruffled hem of a red velvet dress that was mostly hidden by the huge stuffed bear Fiona was puckering up to kiss. She had her mother's honey-blonde hair, her father's aquamarine eyes, and "a smile so sweet it could rot your teeth!" as Leah was fond of saying.

Jade had been honored when Leah and John had asked her to be Fiona's godmother, and she took her duties seriously. At least once a month, she sent books, toys, and DVDs by way of "The Package Man," as Fiona referred to him. Every time she talked to Leah—and she could count on placing or receiving at least one long-distance call a week, in addition to the e-mails they regularly exchanged—Jade insisted on talking to her godchild. It amazed her how quickly Fiona had grown, from a quietly cooing infant to a nonstop chatterbox.

Much as Jade loved the little tyke, she knew that no one on earth loved Fiona more than Leah. When she'd called to ask for Jade's help, the last thing Leah had said was, "I'm really gonna miss that little monkey!"

"Can I get you anything, miss?"

Jade looked into the sympathetic eyes of the flight attendant. "No, thanks," she said, smiling as she blotted her eyes. "I'm fine."

The pretty young woman put an extra bag of pretzels on Jade's tray and gave her a compassionate smile. "Death in the family?"

Leah wasn't blood kin, but she'd been family since that dreadful day....

It had been one of those freaky in-the-wrong-place-at-the-wrong-time situations that had made Leah an orphan. She had been in Jade's family room, teasing Riley for losing at Monopoly—again—while her parents and younger brother were buying soft ice cream to celebrate a Little League victory. A gunman had barged into the

store, panicking the clerk and causing customers to top-
ple like dominoes as he fired round after round into them.
And Leah had lived with Jade and her family ever since.

The flight attendant took Jade's silence as a yes.
"Heading to or from the funeral?"

Funeral. The word sounded forlorn, final. That awful day could come in a month, six months, a year. Jade
had no choice but to hope and pray, right along with
Leah, that a divine phenomenon would take place. "Excuse me," she muttered around a sob, then got up and
hurried down the aisle.

"We'll be landing in just a few minutes," the attendant called after her.

In the safety and seclusion of the tiny restroom, Jade
pressed her forehead to the cool metal wall. *You'll be
landing soon,* she thought, *and Riley will be waiting at
the gate.*

Riley...big and burly, dark-haired and brown-
eyed....

"He's been here every day since I got the news," Leah
had told Jade on the phone, "running errands, cooking,
cleaning, taking Fiona out so I can rest...."

That was Riley, all right. Though she'd been back in
Baltimore dozens of times since moving to California,
Jade hadn't seen him since Leah and John's wedding five
years earlier. He had been dating a cover girl at the time—
no surprise to Jade, since every one of his dates had been
tall and voluptuous and gorgeous—more evidence for her
"Why I'm Not Beautiful Enough for Riley Steele" list. By
now, she'd pretty much resigned herself to the fact that
they'd always be friends and nothing more.

Now, though, even calling him a friend was a bit of a
stretch. Neither years nor miles had come between Jade
and Leah, so why had time and distance separated Jade
and Riley?

Had it separated them? Or had she only imagined the gap?

No. It was there, as broad and deep as the Grand Canyon. And Jade knew exactly when the crack had begun to widen into a chasm....

For years, she'd managed to hide her emotions behind jokes and grins and playful shoves. But on the night of their high school graduation, when excitement and pride and joy had propelled her into Riley's arms, she had kissed him. The gesture was supposed to say "Congratulations," nothing more. But she'd felt so good in his arms, so complete. When the kiss had ended, he'd gazed into her eyes, and in that unguarded tick in time, Riley must have recognized the look on her face for what it was: boundless love.

It must have terrified him, she'd figured, because he'd nearly taken a pratfall as he'd backed away from her. Two days later, Leah had told her he'd headed south to find a job and an apartment near the University of Virginia's School of Veterinary Medicine. Why hadn't he said good-bye? And why, whenever he'd visited his parents, had he made one excuse after another to avoid seeing Jade?

When Leah had called the week before to break the sad news, she'd said, "Riley will be so glad to see you!"

"Yeah, right," had been Jade's dry reply.

"No, really. He asks about you all the time."

"Uh-huh. Hoping I've finally married and settled down...outgrown that silly schoolgirl crush—"

"It wasn't a crush, and we both know it."

And there, in the jetliner's minuscule bathroom, Jade admitted it was true. Always had been, always would be....

A baritone voice interspersed with static interrupted her thoughts. "Ladies and gentleman, this is Captain

Tenet. We're making our approach to Baltimore's Thurgood Marshall International Airport, so if you'll all fasten your seat belts, we'll begin our descent...."

Her heart beating in double-time, Jade glanced at her watch. *Right on schedule, Captain*, she thought, swallowing the lump of fear that had formed in her throat.

Riley would be waiting at the gate, and she didn't know for the life of her what to say to him after all these years, after all this time.

Riley had been pacing back and forth in front of the window for nearly thirty minutes, hands in his pockets, and glancing at the monitor every minute or so. Flight 2254 from Chicago's O'Hare to BWI was right on time.

A quick check of his wristwatch told Riley he had ten to fifteen minutes before Jade deplaned. He'd called her from Leah's house—at Leah's insistence, now that he thought of it—to finalize the pickup arrangements. "I'm having most of my things shipped," Jade had told him, "so we won't have to stand around waiting at baggage claim."

She'd sounded every bit as sweet as he remembered. And, oh, he remembered!

His little black book was chock-full of names and phone numbers. He'd been engaged once and had come mighty close to marriage a second time. Some of the women he'd dated had been beautiful. There had been smart girls, successful ones; some who liked to cook for him, others who seemed to take pleasure in tidying his house.... But none had hair like spun gold or eyes the color of a summer sky. When *they* talked, he didn't think of angels; when *they* smiled, he didn't see rainbows. In short, they weren't Jade.

Folks were beginning to gather near the large window overlooking the runways. "It's here!" a little boy squealed. "Grandpa's plane is here!"

Riley watched the little family huddle near the glass, pointing and chattering excitedly as the jumbo jet wheeled up to the terminal. Either their enthusiasm was contagious or he was looking forward to seeing Jade even more than he'd allowed himself to admit.

Watch it, he warned himself, *or you could be in for one doozy of a roller-coaster ride.*

He reminded himself how, just before they'd graduated from high school, Hank Berger had announced that he'd been offered a job as a news anchor for a small TV station in Southern California. "And Jade says she'll come with me!" the big-shot college man had proclaimed. She'd dated Hank on and off over the years, but Riley hadn't paid the so-called relationship much mind. He saw Hank as a big-mouthed show-off...totally wrong for a girl like Jade. Riley had turned eighteen two days earlier, and he couldn't remember hurting like that before—not once in his life. Hank had gone on to explain how, since the best nursing school in the country was located near the studio, Jade's dad and his had put their heads—and their finances—together and bought a duplex for their kids to share. "She'll live in the left-hand unit, and I'll live in the right," Mr. TV Personality had crowed. "Brides stand on the left and grooms on the right at the altar, y'know...."

Jade had always been a happy, energetic girl, but that night, her blue eyes seemed to glow brighter, her smile to stretch wider. And when she threw her arms around Riley and kissed him....

Every time he'd kissed a date hello, good night, or good-*bye*, Riley had thought of that kiss. Her lips had been so soft, so warm and sweet and inviting, stirring something in him that he'd never experienced before...

...and hadn't felt since.

She'd gone off to California, just as Hank had said she would, returning for Thanksgiving and Christmas every year and for her parents' silver anniversary a few years back. She always made a point to call him when she was in town, and he always made a point of avoiding her. *Couldn't let her see that she'd broken my heart!*

The little boy interrupted Riley's thoughts, jumping up and down and clapping his hands. "Grandpa!" he hollered. And, turning to his parents, he pointed down the carpeted tube connecting the plane to the gate. "He's here! Grandpa's here!" The family surrounded the white-haired man, smothering him with hugs and kisses.

But Riley barely noticed. Leaning left and right, he searched for Jade.

And then he saw her.

She'd pulled her long, golden hair into a loose po-nytail that swayed pendulum-like as she moved toward him on tiny, white-sandaled feet. She was wearing a form-fitting jean skirt, a short-sleeved white shirt, a wide bangle bracelet, and dangly earrings.

Of course, dangly earrings, he thought, smiling at the fond memory. Silver with turquoise, brass, coral, feathers, or flowers had adorned her lobes for as long as he could remember.

He hadn't seen her since Leah and John's wedding five years ago. Hank had still been in the picture then, and the big oaf had hung on her like a permanent ap-pendage. What she saw in him, Riley didn't know. But he knew what Hank saw in her....

She'd walked into the room in her pale pink maid-of-honor gown and turned every head, her long hair woven in—what had she called it?—a French braid, smiling a smile that brightened the room like the photographer's giant telescoping lamp. He thought she was even prettier now, if that was possible.

Riley stepped aside. *The better to see you, my dear*, he mused, grinning.

Jade spotted him the moment he moved. He knew because her eyes and smile widened, and one tiny hand rose to send him a silent hello.

The next moment reminded him of that old margarine commercial with a guy and girl running toward each other in ultraslow motion across a blossom-studded field, arms outstretched. Except Jade wasn't running, and her arms weren't outstretched. *Well*, he thought, grinning at the irony, *at least there are flowers....*

Life in California had changed her in small, subtle ways. Though time had been very gentle with her—she didn't look twenty-five, let alone thirty—a wounded, lost-little-girl expression had replaced her look of carefree, innocent, little-girl naïveté.

"Hi," she said breathily.

"Hi, yourself."

She thanked him when he took her suitcase, then thanked him again when he handed her the flowers. "Riley, how sweet. You remembered."

"Remembered what?"

She fell into step beside him. "That daisies are my favorite flowers."

He remembered something else: at five feet two inches, she'd always had a hard time keeping up with his six-one stride. Riley slowed his pace. "They're really nothing but weeds, you know."

"I know. That's why I like them. They're pretty and delicate-looking, but tough and hardy, y'know?"

Yes, he knew. Because *she* was a lot like that.

"So, how was your flight?"

"A little turbulence over Atlanta, but—"

"Atlanta?"

She gave a little shrug. "Don't ask me how the airlines figure their routes. All I know is, we had a one-hour layover in Georgia before another change of planes in Chicago."

"Buy any peaches?"

Jade rolled her eyes. "Same old Riley, I see."

He feigned hurt and shock. "Old? Who you callin' old? I'm, what, six months older than you?"

Laughing, she shoved her face into the flowers. "Thanks, Riley," she said when she came up for air. "For these, and for picking me up, too."

"Hey. What are friends for?"

Lord, he thought, *why was that so hard to say?*

Because, came the answer, *you're crazy about her; always have been.* Riley exhaled. *If I have to settle for friendship....*

A blast of damp, hot air hit them the moment the sliding doors opened. "I'd almost forgotten how humid Baltimore can be in June," Jade said, wrinkling her nose. "In California—"

"I'm parked right on the other side of the road there," he interrupted. He didn't want to hear about California or anything that had to do with it. Hank Berger, in particular. Although he had to admit...he *did* wonder why she'd never married the big blowhard. Leah had been tight-mouthed about the breakup, saying only, "Things didn't work out, that's all."

Leah was like that, too. Telling her a secret was like dropping a penny down a well; chances for retrieval were slim to none. *I'm sure gonna miss her,* Riley thought.

"Speaking of Leah, do you suppose we could stop somewhere before we go to her house?"

Speaking of Leah? But they hadn't been speaking of Leah!

And then Riley recalled the way Jade had always been able to finish his sentences, and he hers. It had been one of the things that sometimes got them laughing so hard that it was all they could do to keep from drooling. Jade had explained it by saying their minds worked alike, and Riley had agreed. At least until Hank had dropped his California bombshell. He didn't think he'd *ever* figure out why Jade had followed Mr. Stuck on Himself to the West Coast. "Sure we can stop. They've remodeled the Double-T—"

Jade groaned. "Don't tell me they made it upscale!"

"No. Just a face-lift. It still looks like a vintage fifties diner." He pointed. "That's my car over there."

"The convertible?" Jade wiggled her eyebrows. "Ooh la la," she cooed, grinning. "How many poodles did you clip to afford *that*?"

Chuckling, he unlocked the trunk. "Oh, couple hundred, I guess." He stuffed her suitcase into the small space.

"Are you going to put the top down?"

He stared at his own reflection in her mirrored sunglasses. He could only assume by the upturned corners of her mouth that Jade would enjoy feeling the wind in her hair. He could name only one other female who liked riding with the top down...Fiona, his godchild. Jade's, too, although some sort of Hank-related emergency had kept Jade from being able to come home for the ceremony, and one of Leah's neighbors had filled in for her.

Thinking of the baby only made him think of Leah. There would be plenty of time for that...later. Riley unlocked the passenger door. "Don't get in yet," he instructed, "till I get the AC fired up."

"Air conditioner...fired up." Jade got into the car. "Real funny, Riley. Real funny."

"Hey. You know me," he said, sliding in behind the steering wheel. "I got a million of 'em. Ha-cha-cha-chaaaaaaaa."

"You aren't old enough to remember Jimmy Durante."

"Then how'd I just do an imitation of him?" He paused. "A *really good* imitation of him?" he challenged.

Jade peered at him over the wire rims of her sunglasses. "Reruns?"

This small talk was beginning to wear thin. Sooner or later, she was going to ask about Leah. Jade would be her round-the-clock caretaker, after all, starting tonight. And if Riley knew Jade, her head was swimming with questions. "Did they feed you on the plane?" he asked, hoping to put it off as long as possible.

Grinning, she nodded. "Yeah, but you know me... those little trays just stimulate my taste buds, make me hungry for a real meal."

Yes, he knew her, all right. She'd cost him the lion's share of his allowance more times than he cared to remember. Riley gave her a quick once-over. She probably didn't weigh a hundred pounds soaking wet. *How does she do it?* he wondered, remembering how she could eat a linebacker under the table.

They drove along in companionable silence until the polished stainless-steel exterior of the diner came into view. She made no comment about its newer, sleeker look; didn't remark about the big, blacktopped parking lot. "I wonder if they still serve breakfast all day long?"

"They do."

"Good, 'cause I'm in the mood for bacon and eggs. Hash browns. Rye toast. And tomato juice."

Riley held open the door, and as she walked inside, he said, "Mmm-hmm, 'Heart Attack on a Plate.'"

"No, that's fettuccine Alfredo."

Her soft, sweet voice had taken on a distinctive edge, and Riley had a feeling the small talk had just about ended. They followed the hostess to a booth in the back of the restaurant and ordered ice water and decaf coffee. The scent of the server's perfume was still in the air when Jade leaned forward on the Formica tabletop. There were tears in her eyes as she folded her hands as if in prayer.

"All right," she said, "give it to me straight. How long do you think Leah has?"

Riley blew a stream of air through his lips and shrugged. "I haven't talked to her doctor lately."

She narrowed her eyes and lifted one tawny eyebrow. "So, what does *Leah* say?"

He shrugged again. "You talked to her last night. What did she tell you?"

Jade rolled her eyes. "I've talked to her every night for a week, and I don't know a thing!" She began counting on her fingers: "She's holding her own. She's doing great...considering. She's lucky to have been given these last months to get everything in order." Running a hand through her ponytail, she sighed. "I put a call in to her doctor, but we've been playing phone tag all week."

"Leah thinks the world of him."

"Yeah, well, it remains to be seen if her loyalty is well placed."

It wasn't like her to be so cynical, and Riley said so.

"You'd be skeptical if you'd been doing what I've been doing for the past eight years."

He leaned on the table, too. "What have you been doing, Jade?"

"Watching people die, mostly."

She was angry, Riley noted, and didn't seem to be making any effort to hide it. Her eyes were flashing like blue diamonds, her full, pink lips thinned in exasperation.

"Most of the people I attend don't walk into the emergency room of their own accord—they're flown in by helicopter."

"You mean like shock trauma?"

Jade nodded. "I can't keep count of how many patients I've lost." Tears clung to her long, dark lashes. Her gaze fused to Riley's as she laid her hands atop his. "I don't want to lose Leah," she whispered haltingly.

Leaning forward as they were, Riley and Jade's faces were separated by mere inches. He wanted to wrap her in his arms, crush her to him, and offer all the consolation she needed. He wanted to kiss away her tears and promise that one day soon, everything would be the way it used to be between the three of them. But he couldn't, because Leah was dying. And because of that, nothing would ever be the same again.

Gently, he pressed a palm to each of her cheeks. "I don't want to lose her, either," he admitted, surprised at the sob-thickened huskiness of his own voice.

Jade closed her eyes, sending a silvery tear down one cheek. Riley caught it with the pad of his thumb and wiped it away. She rubbed her cheek against his hand, then turned slightly and kissed his wrist.

Oh, how he'd missed her, missed everything about her—from the heart that was bigger than her pretty head to the inner strength that had her trying, even now, to rough things out. She'd always been a scrappy little thing, and it was apparent to Riley that Jade was still a fighter.

She hasn't changed all that *much,* he assured himself.

When Jade sat back to look in her purse for a tissue, he felt the chill as surely as he'd felt it when they'd walked from the muggy July heat into the air-conditioned diner. He looked at his hands, empty now, save for a glimmer of dampness put there by her tears, and acknowledged silently that his heart had felt just as empty all these years without her.

Everything in him warned, *Back off, before you get kicked in the heart...again.*

"I'm sure gonna miss her," she said, sniffing and blotting her eyes with the tissue.

"Me, too."

She took a sip of her water. "How's Fiona doing? You think she knows?"

Riley shook his head. "Nah. She's too young to know more than her mommy rides around in a 'wee-cha'," he said, mimicking the child's baby talk.

The parody put a slight smile on Jade's face. "Wee-cha," she repeated, giggling softly. True to form, she shook off the cloak of sadness. "She really is a cute li'l monkey, isn't she?"

"Couldn't love her more if she were my own."

If they noticed the curious stares of nearby diners, neither Jade nor Riley commented on it. *This is our time*, seemed to be their message to the other Double-T patrons.

The server returned, and they placed their orders: Riley, a bowl of chili; Jade, a full country breakfast.

"How does she look?" Jade asked when the server was out of earshot.

Grinning, he held his hand parallel to the floor. "About two feet tall. Big, blue eyes. Rosy cheeks. And short, squatty legs that—"

"Not Fiona," she said, smiling, "*Leah.*"

At the mention of their friend's name again, their smiles evaporated and an awkward silence enveloped the table. He'd known exactly what Jade had meant. But he hadn't been ready to talk *death*. Not when he felt fully *alive* for the first time in years.

You self-centered jerk, he chided himself. *Leah is the only one who matters now. What she needs...that's the important—*

"I want you to promise me something, Riley."

How was it possible for her eyes to be bluer than he remembered? He waited for her to define the pledge.

"Promise you'll continue stopping by every day, and calling when you get a chance...."

"'Course I will." He tucked in one corner of his mouth, wondering why she'd even suggest such a thing.

"Not just for Leah," Jade said softly. "For me, too."

Now he was really confused.

"I've been right there, hundreds of times, when people died. Some wanted to be held, you know, like babies, when the end was near; others just asked me to hold their hands. I've watched the life light in their eyes fade away, heard them exhale their last breaths...."

Riley winced. "Gee. That's gotta be tough. *You've* gotta be tough, to do that...."

"Not really. They need to be with *someone* at the end...." Jade sandwiched his hand between her own. "But this is different."

"Different? How?"

"I've never lost anyone close to me before. I—" She bit her lower lip and looked across the room toward the window wall. "I don't know if I'm strong enough to handle this alone." Jade met his eyes again, tightening her grip on his hand. "I'm going to need you at the end of the day." Shrugging, she sent him a feeble smile. "In the middle of the day, sometimes, I imagine...."

"Then I'll be there. I promise."

She tilted her head and gave his hand one last squeeze before letting go. "I'm gonna hold you to that."

He was about to say, "No need for that" when the server arrived with their food. When she was gone, Jade leaned forward and whispered conspiratorially, "I was dying to ask you this at Leah and John's wedding...." She tugged gently at his beard. "What's *this* all about?"

"About an inch, I'd say, give or take a hair."

She laughed. Then, changing the words to the once-popular song, Jade sang, "How long has this been *growing* on?"

"Eight, ten years. Why?"

She tilted her head again. "I was just wondering...."

"Wondering what?"

"What you're hiding from."

"Hiding!" Riley laughed. "Just 'cause a guy grows a beard doesn't mean he's hiding from something."

"Or *someone*." She winked. "Leah tells me there's someone special in your life these days."

"Yeah. Right."

"No one?"

Was that *relief* flashing in her eyes? *Well, a guy can hope....* "No one." He grinned crookedly. "Unless you count...."

She stopped chewing, stopped dipping her toast in her egg—stopped breathing, it seemed. Riley's heart pounded at the possibility that there *was* hope for them. "...Unless you count Fiona," he finished.

His answer seemed to ease her concern, for she smiled around a mouthful of bacon. *Only time will tell*, he said to himself, *so take it easy...real easy.*

Chapter Two

Riley wheeled the convertible into Leah's driveway. "I have nothing but confidence in you." He stepped out of the car, walked around to Jade's side, and opened the door.

"Thanks," she said, patting his hand. "I'm lucky to have such a loyal friend."

Something flickered in his dark eyes. Was it relief that she'd finally accepted their relationship as platonic, or something else? Jade wasn't sure.

"You'll be fine. And I'll help."

As the jumbo jet had been rocketing toward Maryland, Jade had prayed that God would provide a miracle for Leah, give her a flight without turbulence, and dim her feelings for Riley. It remained to be seen whether the doctors would find a cure for Leah, and the plane had flown through a series of rough air currents. And if her thudding heart was any indicator, the Lord had decided not to douse the flame flickering in her heart for Riley... at least, not yet.

He winked and gave her bicep an affectionate tap. "I promised, remember?"

"I'm counting on it."

She stood beside him, hands resting on the door, and gazed at the gathering thunderclouds overhead. "Looks like we're in for a doozy of a storm."

Riley got back into the car. "Go on in without me," he instructed her. "You must be dying to see Leah."

Dying.

The word hung in the air like the rusting blade of an ancient guillotine. Their eyes met—hers misting, his glittering with self-reproach. Riley slapped his forehead with the heel of his hand. "Sorry," he groaned. "I've got to learn to be more careful about what comes out of my mouth."

She sent him a sad smile.

"I'll get your bag after I've put the top up."

Looking toward the front door, Jade hesitated, remembering what Riley had told her about Leah's appearance. Her once-beautiful, blonde hair was all but gone. Too weak to stand at the vanity to put in her contact lenses, she wore glasses instead. Her movements had always been so graceful, so feminine...difficult to accomplish from a motorized wheelchair....

She closed her eyes and bowed her head. *Lord,* she prayed, *give me the strength to be whatever Leah needs. Make me an instrument of Your—*

"Jade?"

"Hmm?" came her distracted reply.

"You're gonna be fine."

She lowered her head and met his gaze. "So, you said...."

"Did you ever see that old Humphrey Bogart movie?"

"Which one?"

"I don't remember the title, but it's the one where Lauren Bacall tries to teach Bogie how to ask for help."

Her brows drew together in confusion.

"'Just pucker up...and blow,'" he quoted Bacall.

Smiling, she closed the car door. "So, you're saying—"

"If you need me, just whistle."

She grabbed her purse from the passenger seat, then headed up the walk. When her finger was poised to ring the bell, his voice floated to her on the sticky breeze. "I'm almost finished here...." She turned in time to see him disappear beneath the convertible's canvas top.

Jade was still laughing under her breath when Leah opened the door. "What are you doing out there in this heat?" she scolded teasingly. "Get in here where it's cool and dry, and give me a hug!"

Bending at the waist, Jade wrapped her wheelchair-bound friend in a long, generous embrace. "Oh, Leah," she whispered, "it's *so good* to see you."

"All right, all right," she muttered into Jade's shoulder. "Turn me loose so I can have a look at you."

Jade stepped back to allow Leah to inspect her. Instead, Jade trained her nurse's eye on Leah....

She'd lost weight, thirty pounds or more—a huge amount for a woman who'd never weighed more than 125—and while Leah wasn't completely bald, her shiny, white scalp was visible through her thinning blonde strands. Once, Leah's cheeks had glowed naturally with good health; now, Jade could see, the blush had been powdered on.

But loving warmth still radiated from deep within Leah's soul, a fact that couldn't be hidden by the convex lenses of her tortoiseshell glasses or the lipstick that brightened her pale-lipped smile.

"Well," Leah said, grinning and spreading her arms wide, "what do you think? Should Miss Wheelchair America get ready to hand over her tiara, or what?"

"You're beautiful," Jade said truthfully, "and a sight for sore eyes, too."

"Why are your eyes sore? You've been lookin' at Riley for nearly four hours!"

"Four hours? It hasn't been—"

"It most certainly has. Your flight arrived right on time. Three o'clock sharp. I know," Leah said, wiggling her brows mischievously, "because I checked."

"You checked?" Jade pursed her lips. "Um, so where's Fiona?"

"Don't try to change the subject on me, young lady!" She crossed both arms over her bony chest and, tapping slippered toes on her wheelchair's footrest, added in her best maternal voice, "It's nearly eight thirty, half an hour past Fiona's bedtime. Now, then, where have—"

"Take it easy, *Mom*," Riley said, barging through the front door.

"Fiona's asleep...don't sla—"

The slamming door punctuated Leah's abbreviated warning.

"Sorry," he whispered, chin tucked into his collar.

"Well?" Leah asked.

He looked at Jade, who shrugged and made a face that said, "I don't know, either."

Riley looked back at Leah. "Well, what?"

"Where have you two been all this time? *That's* what!"

"Oh." He chuckled. "Jade wanted breakfast, so—"

"So you took her to the Double-T." She sighed. "There are plenty of restaurants that aren't as far away, you know."

He nodded, looking every bit the tardy teenager. "But Leah, Double-T is my favorite—"

"Oh, *this* is going to be an interesting assignment," Jade interrupted him, laughing. Propping one fist on her hip, she aimed a maternal digit of her own. "Well, let's get something straight right up front, girls and boys...."

Leah and Riley exchanged a puzzled glance, then focused their full attentions on Jade.

"This may be your house, Leah Jordan, but starting right now, *I'm* in charge around here." She zeroed in on Riley next. "Got it?"

"Got it," he and Leah chimed in unison.

She softened her tone. "It's for your own good, you know."

Leah rolled her eyes. "Oh, I get it. This is one of those This-hurts-you-more-than-it-does-me scoldings, eh?"

Jade laughed. "Something like that." She clapped her hands once. "Now then, first order of business.... Leah, when did you last have something to eat?"

Leah tapped a forefinger against her chin, squinting her eyes as she considered the question. Brightening, she pointed her finger in the air. "I had a chocolate bar at six...."

"And?" Jade coaxed.

"And what?"

"And soup? A sandwich? Some salad?"

Leah lifted her shoulders and grinned. "I can't hold down rich food like that."

Jade shook her head and raised a skeptical brow. "Mmm-hmm. But have you had *anything* nourishing today?"

"Fiona hand-fed me a fish stick at lunchtime," she said in a small, defensive voice.

Sighing, Jade grabbed the handles of the wheelchair and rolled Leah down the hall toward the kitchen. She parked her near the table, then began rummaging in the refrigerator, in the pantry, in the cupboards. Ten minutes later, a steaming bowl of canned soup, a ham and cheese sandwich, several oat bran pretzels, and a sliced apple sat on a platter between the spoon and paper napkin on Leah's placemat. "And you'll drink every drop of that milk, young lady," she said, setting a tumbler down at the two o'clock position above the plate.

"But Jade," Leah whimpered, "I'm not hungry."

"Eat a few bites, at least; you'll sleep better with food in your stomach."

Pouting, she took a tiny bite of the sandwich and popped an apple slice into her mouth. "Don't even like ham," she mumbled.

Jade gave her a sideways hug. "Then why did you buy it, sweetie?"

"Didn't," she muttered, grinning. "Church ladies brought it over."

"Which reminds me," Jade announced, "tomorrow, we're going shopping."

"For what?"

"Healthy, wholesome foods that *aren't* chocolate, for starters. And makeup, and a wig...."

"Makeup? Wig? It's nearly the Fourth of July, not Halloween."

Frowning, Jade shook a finger under her nose. "I know how important your appearance has always been, so we're going to make you feel as pretty as you are!"

Leah looked to Riley for support.

"Your bedside manner could use a little work, Jade," he said out of the corner of his mouth. And in response to her well-aimed stare, he held out hands in mock surrender. "Sorry, Leah, but Jade's in charge," he said in a singsongy voice.

Bit by bit, the food on Leah's plate disappeared as the trio chatted. But despite the makeup on her cheeks and lips, her face paled. And despite the food she'd consumed, her shoulders slumped with weariness.

Jade faked an exaggerated yawn.

Leah patted her hand. "Aw, are we keeping you awake?"

"Must be jet lag," she said, stretching.

"California is three hours *behind* us, Jade...." Then, grinning, Leah added, "You know, I'm a little bushed, myself. Think I'll go to my room and watch some TV," she said, winking at Riley, "so our sleepy pal here can get some much-needed shut-eye."

"Look at the pot calling the kettle black," he said.

Jade's brow furrowed with confusion.

"Your little patient there has been burning the midnight oil, night after night."

"Getting my affairs in order," Leah said in her own defense.

"Yeah, well, whatever. You haven't been getting much sleep these days...."

Jade stood up and started pushing the wheelchair toward Leah's bedroom. "Well, then. It's off to bed with you, Leah. But there's a catch."

"A catch?"

Don't go yet, Jade mouthed to Riley over Leah's head.

He nodded in agreement as Leah said, "A catch?"

"Riley is going to help me get you into bed, and then you're going straight to sleep. No TV for you tonight, young lady."

"Says who?"

"Says me." Jade leaned down to place a kiss on Leah's cheek. "That's who."

As if on cue, she yawned. "You gonna let her push me around this way, Riley?"

He grabbed the wheelchair's handles. "She's the boss," he repeated, rolling Leah down the hall.

"All right, but don't keep Jade up too late. She has jet lag, remember?"

Behind her, Jade's eyes widened and Riley's brows rose.

"I might be weak as a newborn kitten," Leah said, "but I'm really a *mother* cat, who has eyes in the back of her head and sees everything." She aimed a warning finger over her shoulder.

Riley gently lifted her from the chair as Jade pulled back the covers on her bed. Once Leah was in bed, he fluffed pillows, then Jade tucked the sheet under Leah's chin. Riley leaned down to kiss the tip of her nose. "Yeah, well, it's time to get some rest, *Mommy,* so close all four of your eyes and go to sleep."

Jade had ducked into the guest room to change into a T-shirt and sweatpants. "Think she's asleep yet?" she asked, padding barefoot into the kitchen.

He nodded. "I think she was sawing logs before we even turned out the light—" One look at Jade was enough to cut short his sentence. "Why the long face, kiddo?"

Jade wrung her hands. "Oh, Riley, she looks so weak and pale. I hope I can do what she needs me to do right now."

"You're doing plenty just by being here." He hesitated. "Leah told me you quit your job and sold your condo so you could be with her until...." Wincing, he gave a helpless shrug.

She sighed. "Don't feel bad. I can't say it, either." Then, almost as an afterthought, she added, "I'm not as noble as you think. Being here is sort of my grown-up way of running away from home."

"But...Baltimore *is* your home."

Jade merely nodded.

"I made us a pot of decaf," Riley said, changing the subject. "Everything we need is in the family room."

She hated seeing him like this, sad and powerless but trying his best to hide it. He stood a head taller than Jade and likely outweighed her by seventy pounds, and yet something about his demeanor brought out the mothering instinct in her. She wanted to comfort and reassure him, to make him smile again.

Humor had always worked when they were kids....

And so, crouching like a sprinter, she said, "I get dibs on the recliner!" and darted out of the kitchen.

The last time she'd visited Leah, the family room had been a warm, cozy place. The homey touches that were uniquely Leah—potted plants, a collection of ceramic vases, dozens of old books—had been moved aside to make room for the huge hospital bed. Jade stood at the foot of it, arms limp at her sides, and took it all in...the IV pole, the oxygen tank, the adjustable rolling dinner tray, the green plastic cup and straw, the stainless-steel bedpan.... Shaking her head, she pressed both palms to her temples and closed her eyes tight.

Riley turned Jade to face him, pried her hands from her head, and wrapped her in his arms. "I know, I know," he offered, stroking her back. "It's awful, isn't it? Almost like a hospital."

"The only thing missing," she muttered into his chest, "is the antiseptic smell."

"And that annoying squeak the nurses' shoes make on the linoleum."

"Yeah," she giggled, "and that *ding-ding* from the PA system."

"What about those nasal voices that *follow* the *dings*?" He pinched his nostrils shut. "Paging Dr. Kildare," he said in a mock falsetto, "Paging Dr. Kildare...."

"...Those ugly stripes they paint on the floors."

He chuckled softly. "And a monster of a TV hanging from the ceiling in every room."

A ragged sigh escaped Jade's lungs. "First thing tomorrow, I'm going to make this look like a real family room again."

Smiling, he held her at arm's length. "I thought you were going grocery shopping first thing?"

She bobbed her head from side to side and then rolled her eyes. "All right...second thing."

For a moment, Riley simply stood there, hands clamped around her waist, gaze locked on her face.

"Why are you looking at me like that?"

Blinking innocently, he grinned. "Like what?"

"Like I have spinach in my teeth or something."

"Because you have—"

Jade gasped, covering her mouth with both hands. "I wonder where Leah keeps the toothpicks," she said, trying to dislodge herself from his embrace.

But Riley refused to let go. "There isn't spinach on your teeth...."

She rested both hands on his chest and frowned. "But you said—"

Laying a fingertip over her lips, he continued, "As I was *about* to say, you have the most beautiful blue eyes...."

Involuntarily, her eyes widened.

And her heart hammered.

And her pulse pounded.

She'd had this dream dozens—no, hundreds—of times: standing in the comforting circle of Riley's arms while he said things like, "You have the most beautiful eyes...." Was she dreaming now?

Or had the dream come true?

"I'm glad you're back," Riley said.

"It's good to *be* back."

"Missed you, too."

He looked genuinely surprised after his admission, and Jade wondered why. "Leah needs you," he added.

Her smile faded. *That's what I was afraid you'd say,* she thought. And then, *How can I be thinking romantic thoughts when Leah is in such terrible shape?* Jade heaved another sigh. "She needs us both."

Riley nodded. "Yeah, but you can do things for her that I can't."

"Well, that's no surprise. I'm a nurse, after all, so—"

"I don't mean those things. I mean friend things." Scrubbing a palm over his bearded chin, he shrugged one big shoulder. "I'm pathetic at girl talk."

She brightened a bit. "What do you expect, with a voice like James Earl Jones?"

If he had heard her compliment, Riley was choosing to ignore it.

"And I hate sitting through all those chick flicks that Leah likes to watch...over and over and over...." With one forefinger, he drew a circle in the air.

Laughing softly, Jade reminded him that he was a master at Scrabble, which Leah loved to play, too. "And I can't rack up a hundred points for the life of me!" she added, smiling.

"Yeah, well, you more than make up for it in Monopoly. Remember how you used to beat the stuffing out of us?"

Jade nodded. "I still have the silly tycoon trophy you made me out of that old softball award of yours. I'm afraid I'd lose it if we played again, though, 'cause I haven't even *seen* a Monopoly board in years."

"But it was your favorite game...."

All this talk of fond memories was having a positive effect. Jade wanted—no, *needed*—those feelings now. Then, she looked at the stack of pillows at the head of the hospital bed, a stark-white reminder that Leah was dying. *Your needs aren't important*, she scolded herself. *Only Leah matters now.* Lifting one shoulder, she said, "Hank thought it was a waste of time."

"What was a waste of time?"

"Playing games."

Riley blew a stream of air through his lips. "Well, remember how Leah used to beg you to sing?"

She shifted her weight from one foot to the other and said nothing.

His brows dipped low in the center of his forehead. "Don't tell me he thought *that* was a waste of time, too...."

"He—"

Riley held up a hand to silence her. "But you have the voice of an angel...."

"Let's just say his taste in music and mine were—"

Riley gripped her shoulders and gave her a gentle shake. "What did you ever see in that pencil-necked geek, anyway?" he demanded.

She recognized that tight-lipped, narrow-eyed stare; it told her he was angry. She hadn't seen the look since Leah's wedding. That day, Jade had blamed it on Riley's date. She'd never liked clingy girls, and that one seemed glued to him. But why was he angry now? He'd always seemed so indifferent about the boys she dated. And on graduation night, when she'd told him Hank had asked her to come to California with him, Riley hadn't voiced a protest—much as she'd wanted him to. In fact, he'd been in such a hurry to catch up with Prom Queen Suzie Anderson, he hadn't said anything about the move at all!

"He isn't a pencil-necked geek," she said.

"I stand corrected." Riley's hard-eyed stare softened slightly as a silly smirk lifted one corner of his mouth. "Actually, his neck is more like one of those big, fat crayons of Fiona's...."

Jade tried unsuccessfully to bite back a giggle. "It isn't nice, you know, making fun of someone who isn't here to defend himself."

"And it isn't nice to ask the prettiest girl in school to follow you thousands of miles from home with a promise of marriage...and not deliver."

Shaking her head, Jade stared at the picture of Leah and John on the table beside the hospital bed and recalled her last conversation with Hank. He'd developed a loyal following during his WIME-TV years, and they'd convinced him to run for state senate. "What will people say?" he'd demanded when he'd seen her suitcase near the door.

"Leah needs me."

"*I* need you!"

And it was true, after all. Hank *did* need her—to organize parties to impress the bigwigs, to initiate rounds of applause when he gave speeches, to help him entertain corporate officials and political dignitaries....

Riley's voice came to her as if from the end of a long, hollow tube, interrupting her reverie. "So why didn't that lout marry you?"

Jade hadn't given the matter much thought until then. Her work and volunteer activities, along with taking care of Hank's business interests, had left very little time for pondering questions like that. But sometimes, in the quiet darkness before sleep overtook her, the truth seemed an easy thing to recognize. "Because he didn't love me, and he never would."

It surprised her, saying it out loud for the first time. But it didn't hurt. *Shouldn't it have hurt?* she wondered. *Especially considering how I dedicated myself to Hank's happiness for nearly a decade?*

"You left your family and your friends, started a whole new life for him. You don't seriously expect me to believe he never said—"

"Of course he *said* it." She met his eyes. "But people say things they don't mean all the time." His intense scrutiny was unnerving, and Jade looked away. "I'm tired, Riley," she said quietly. "I think—"

"*I* think," he cut in, "that Hank Berger is a stupid, idiotic fool."

She took a deep breath and let it out slowly.

Riley gathered her close again, kissing the top of her head, and added, "The biggest and stupidest idiotic fool on two feet."

Being a firstborn, she didn't have an older brother, but Jade believed she knew how having one might feel.

Riley was behaving as any protective big brother would under the circumstances. *"A friend loves at all times,"* she thought, silently reciting Proverbs 17:17.

Friend....

During the course of her flight home, she had worried that time and distance might have damaged their friendship. But the moment she'd stepped off the plane and spotted his warm, welcoming smile, Jade had known that her relationship with Riley had survived despite years of misunderstandings that had led to neglect. She sent a prayer of thanks heavenward, because in the months ahead, as they watched Leah slip further and further from them, they were going to need each other as never before.

"I'd better head out," Riley said. "I've got an early morning tomorrow."

Jade walked him to the door. The clouds they'd seen earlier had finally begun to make good on their threat, and the refreshing scent of damp earth swished in on a summer breeze. "You be careful, now," she warned him. "More accidents happen on newly wet roads than on icy and snowy ones."

His smile warmed her all over.

"Something to do with oils on the blacktop, I think," she added.

"I'll be careful," he assured her. "And you get some sleep. You have a pretty full day ahead of you tomorrow, too."

"Get a move on, Mr. Sandman...."

He chuckled. "I'll call you around lunchtime, see if you need anything...?"

Another nod.

"...I'll bring it by when I come over for supper."

He said it so matter-of-factly, as if he belonged here in this house, as if they were a family. The idea warmed Jade, and she smiled. "Okay."

He started for the car but stopped in the middle of the walkway and turned around. It was raining harder now, the sound of it hissing and sputtering around them like water on a hot griddle. "I'm really glad you're back," he said again.

Thunder rumbled overhead. "And I'm glad to be back. Now get going before you get soaked."

Riley snapped off a smart salute and jogged to his car. She watched as he slid in behind the wheel and fired up the engine, watched twin shafts of light perforate the darkness when he turned the headlights on....

...and continued staring after him until his taillights were nothing but tiny red dots in the darkness.

Fiona was on her hands and knees pushing a hand-carved wooden train around its oval track when the doorbell rang. "Now, who can that be?" Riley asked.

Fiona answered by giggling and beaning him with a stuffed bear.

Riley rolled onto his back, taking her with him. "Hey! You know what happens when you mess up my hair...." He quickly proceeded to blow air bubbles in the crook of her neck. The baby was still giggling when the bell chimed again.

Jade stood on tiptoe and peered through the peephole. A tall, good-looking blond man stood on the porch, a well-worn black doctor's bag in one hand, a battered brown briefcase in the other. She opened the door as far as the chain would allow.

"Hi," he said. "I'm Ron Peterson."

Jade unlatched the chain and swung the door open. "Of course. We've been expecting you. Won't you come in? Leah is napping," she said, glancing at her watch, "but I don't expect her to sleep much longer."

He set down his briefcase near the door and followed Jade into the family room as she said, "I'm—"

"Jade Nelson," he finished for her. "Leah told me all about you."

She cleared a spot for him on the loveseat. "You'll have to forgive the mess. I'm trying to make the place a little more homey for Leah, since she'll be spending so much time here until...."

Ron nodded as a look of silent understanding passed between them. "Never gets any easier...."

"No. I'm afraid not."

Riley was sitting cross-legged on the floor with Fiona in his lap. "So, how's it goin', Doc?"

"Not bad. Yourself?"

"Can't complain."

Jade hid a frown. They were being civil with each other, but it was obvious by their cool, detached facial expressions and stiff body postures that there was bad blood between them. "Can I interest anyone in a glass of iced tea?" she asked. "I made some fresh this morning."

"Tea?" Fiona repeated, bounding out of Riley's lap and toddling up to Jade. "Me, tea?"

Smiling, Jade scooped the child into her arms. "Sorry, sweet girl, the tea isn't decaffeinated. But I have something I think you'll like even better." She started for the kitchen, then stopped in the doorway connecting the rooms. "I know how you like yours, Riley...easy on the sugar, easy on the ice." Looking at Ron, she asked, "How do you like yours, Dr. Peterson?"

He put his medical bag on the arm of the loveseat and shrugged out of his suit coat. "Surprise me," he said, winking.

"I'll just give her a hand," she heard Riley tell Ron. "Will you be okay in here alone for a minute?"

"Why wouldn't I be? Isn't like this is my first visit...."

In the kitchen, Jade gave Riley a stern look. "What's with you two? You're acting like old rivals."

"That's 'cause we are. Sort of."

She passed Fiona to him and filled a sippy cup with fruit punch. "There y'go, sweet girl," she cooed, handing it to the baby. Then, as she dropped crescent-shaped ice cubes into three identical tumblers, she zeroed in on Riley. "How do you 'sort of' become rivals?"

Riley exhaled, and Fiona copied him. So he inhaled, and again, the baby mimicked the sound.

"You two sound like a couple of broken-down accordions," Jade teased. "But you haven't answered my question...."

Shrugging, Riley kissed Fiona's cheek. "I went out with his fiancée a couple of times."

Gasping, Jade opened her mouth in shock. "You... you did *what*?"

"Well," he said, wincing, "I didn't *know* she was his fiancée. She came into the clinic 'cause her poodle had mange, see...and, well, one thing led to another, and before I knew what was happening, I was accepting an invitation to have dinner at her apartment."

"She invited you to her place while she was engaged to Dr. Peterson?"

Riley nodded. "It gets worse." Looking left and right, he added, "We were right in the middle of a very sweet good-night kiss when the good doctor walked in."

Jade tamped down the jealousy coursing through her. "Wait—you mean to tell me he had a key to her place, and yet she invited you to—"

"Seems she'd been looking for a way to break it off with him for some time." He shrugged nonchalantly. "And Mr. Brilliant here was her ticket to freedom."

"How awful," Jade whispered, "for her to have used you like that." Then, in an even quieter voice, she asked, "How did he take it?"

"Let me put it this way: there's no love lost between Ron Peterson and me. Never was."

"You mean, you knew him before the—"

"Yup. We were on the basketball team together at the University of Virginia." Riley wiggled his eyebrows and, making a monster face, gave Fiona a noisy peck on the neck. She was giggling as he added, "Old Ronnie-boy wanted to be team captain."

Jade loaded the glasses of iced tea, a plate of cookies, and some paper napkins on a tray. "But you got the job."

He held out one palm. "I was a better player, and...."

"And what?"

"Well," he said, shrugging, "the guys liked me more. What can I say?"

She pursed her lips as she lifted the tray. "You can say, 'I'm the most humble man I know.'" Jade leaned closer. "'Course, it wouldn't be true...."

Riley rolled his eyes and gave Fiona another kiss.

"Here we go," Jade said in sing-song as she carried the tray into the family room. "Nothing like a nice tall glass of refreshing iced tea on a hot, humid July day, I always say."

"I never heard you say that," Riley said.

She saw the teasing glint in his eye and sent him a look that said, "Watch it!"

"Thanks," Ron said when Jade handed him his drink. He took a sip, then added, "You weren't kidding when you said you brewed this yourself, were you?"

She wrinkled her nose. "Never cared much for that powdered stuff. Besides, it really doesn't take longer to make it with tea bags."

"Now there's what I like," came Leah's voice from the hallway, "a rip-roaring, intellectually stimulating conversation!" She rolled into the room smiling. "Hi, Doc," she said. "Good of you to come all the way over here."

"My pleasure," he said, holding up his glass. "Care for some iced tea? Or should we get right down to business?"

Leah rolled her eyes and gave a sigh of resignation. "I'd just as soon get it over with, if it's all the same to you."

Standing up, he handed her his doctor's bag. "You hold on to that; I'll drive."

Ron steered Leah down the hall and into her bedroom, closing the door behind them. "What's this?" he asked, rattling the contents of a small brown bottle.

"You know very well what that is. It's the medicine you prescribed."

He popped the cap off and dumped the pills into an upturned palm. "But Leah," he said, meeting her eyes, "you've taken only two."

"I'm saving them. For emergencies." Grinning mischievously, she added, "You don't want me to get addicted, now, do you? What kind of life would that be?"

He inclined his head. "Leah...don't be flip. This is serious busi—"

"Aw, Doc, they make me all groggy and dopey."

He returned the pills to the vial and gave it another shake. "They're not doing you any good in here."

"And I'm not doing Fiona any good half asleep from pain medication."

"But...how do you stand it?"

She pointed to the corner of her room, where a small stereo sat on a wooden stand. "'How Great Thou Art,'" she said.

With furrowed brow, he admitted, "I don't get it."

"'The Old Rugged Cross,' 'In the Garden'....music," she explained. "It soothes me. My favorite song is 'Amazing Grace.'"

Smiling, he perched on the corner of her bed and took her hand in his. "I remember thinking once that *you* have an amazing amount of grace...and dignity."

"Oh, go on with you," she said, waving a hand. "I bet you say that to all your bald patients."

"Nope." He gave her hand a pat. "Only the brave, bald ones." Ron opened his bag and withdrew a stethoscope.

"So, what do you think of Jade?"

He hung the instrument around his neck. "She's gorgeous." Then, as if the answer embarrassed him, he cleared his throat and quickly added, "She seems very efficient. I'm sure she's an excellent nurse. We're going to have a little talk, she and I, when you and I are through here."

"About what?"

"You."

"What's to talk about?" Leah asked flatly. "I'm dying—unless God comes through with a major miracle pretty soon...."

Frowning, he listened to her heartbeat. "You sure don't believe in beating around the bush, do you?"

Leah shrugged. "Seems like an awful waste of time to me. Besides, it's unnecessarily hard on the shrubbery."

Ron shook his head as his long, thick fingers palpated her neck. "So, tell me...how long has Jade been a nurse?"

"Ten years, give or take."

He aimed the beam of his doctor's light into her right eye. "Does she have a boyfriend? Is she engaged?"

"What's with all these Jade questions? You sweet on her already?"

"Of course not!"

She watched his Adam's apple bob up and down as he swallowed.

"I'm only asking because I want to make sure she has the time to devote to you."

"I can assure you, she's totally dedicated to me, Dr. Peterson."

"Ron," he said, looking into her left eye. "You agreed to call me—"

"Ron. I know. Sorry." She gave the diaphragm of his stethoscope a light tap and set it to swinging like a pendulum. "Look, *Ron*—we both know all this examination stuff is a colossal waste of time, 'cause, hey, what are you lookin' for, anyway?"

"Irregular heartbeat, fluid in your lungs...."

"Ah," she said, nodding, "that dreaded pneumonia. I've read all about it. That's why I spend as much time as possible sitting up. Still," she said, riveting him with her gaze, "you don't need an excuse to come and see me." Wiggling her eyebrows, Leah smirked. "Go on. Admit it. It isn't Jade you're sweet on. You have a crush on skinny ol' bald me."

Ron chuckled. "I've said it before, I'll say it again: You're a piece of work, Leah Jordan."

"Yeah, yeah." Leah dismissed the compliment with a wave of her hand. "So, what do you think? Do I have a couple of months left in me, or what?"

He straightened, then busied himself with tucking his flashlight and stethoscope back into his bag. "I wish I knew. Could be six months, or two, or—"

She held up a hand to silence him. "I know—or I could go in my sleep tonight." She sighed heavily. "It's just that it's tough, you know? Most people have no clue when the end is going to come. Those of us who have a fairly good idea...well, we like to plan out what's left of our futures."

He knelt in front of her wheelchair and took her hands in his. "And what are you planning for your future, Leah?" he asked softly.

Leah glanced toward the closed bedroom door. "Not my future, Ron. Fiona's."

Chapter Three

I love what you've done in here," Leah said, stretching. "Sometimes, when I look around, I almost forget that I'm—"

Jade looked up from the book in her lap. "I thought you were sleeping."

"I was."

She laid the book on the end table and quickly went to her friend's side. "What's wrong? Are you in pain? Is that what woke you?"

"No. I'm having a pretty good day, actually." Leah leaned forward as Jade plumped her pillows and smoothed the sheet over her knees. "Where's Fiona? Napping?"

"She's with Riley."

Leah nodded. "Oh, yeah. It's Saturday...how could I forget their summer Saturdays? Taking walks in Centennial Park, playing on the swings at the tot lot, eating ice cream cones at Soft Stuff...."

Jade returned to her chair. "He's really good with her, isn't he?"

"The best." Leah sighed dreamily. "It's a shame he never married. He'd be a great dad. He told me once he'd like to have about a dozen kids."

Laughing, Jade said, "Maybe that's why he never married."

"What do you mean?"

"Well, that's nine years of pregnancy. Maybe he couldn't find a woman willing to *give* him twelve kids!"

She paused, leaned forward a bit, and added, "And while we're on the subject, why *doesn't* he have a wife? I mean, he's loving and thoughtful, handsome and successful, smart and—"

Leah pursed her lips. "Hmm...if I didn't know better, I'd think you were applying for the job."

"Ha! As if the Perpetual Bachelor is even looking...."

"I happen to know that he is."

"He told you that? Riley Steele said he's ready to settle down?"

"Actually, he said it years ago."

"Really." Jade did her best to appear only mildly interested and busied herself re-tidying the covers.

"Yup. Right after he enrolled in veterinary college."

"But that was...." Jade began counting on her fingers. "That was over eight years ago. What's he looking for? Mother Teresa, Ivana Trump, and Susie Homemaker all rolled into one?"

"Hmm...."

"Hmm *what*?"

"Nothing."

Jade crossed her arms over her chest and lifted her chin in stubborn defiance. "I'm not interested, if that's what you're thinking."

"Of course not."

But it was obvious by Leah's smug expression and teasing tone of voice that she believed exactly the opposite. "I'm serious!" Laughing, Jade slapped her knees and, smile frozen in place, added, "I mean, I want what's best for him, of course—he's a *friend*, after all! But I'm certainly not *interested* in him...not in a *romantic* way."

Nervous laughter punctuated her statement, because even as she told it, Jade asked God to forgive her lie.

"What was it Shakespeare wrote? 'Methinks this lady doth protest too much,' or something like that."

Jade opened her mouth to contradict her, but Leah held a finger in the air, commanding silence. "Shh, you'll just prove my point."

Leah was right, and Jade knew it. She did as she was told.

"You and I have talked at least twice a week since you moved to California, and every single time, Riley's name has come up at least once." Leah raised her right eyebrow. "How is it you're only now asking about his love life?"

Love life? Her heart pounded at the mere thought of it. She didn't want to know anything about his *love life*. Because, in all honesty, Jade hoped he didn't *have* a love life...unless she was a part of it....

"You're still crazy about him, aren't you?"

Again, the nagging guilt that had attacked her earlier from thoughts of a relationship with Riley came to mind. Much as she wanted it, it couldn't be. Maybe not ever, and certainly not now! *I'm not going to sit here and discuss such things*, Jade told Leah silently, *while you're lying there, helpless, and....* It was time to change the subject. Period. "How about a cup of tea? Or a nice glass of lemonade?"

Nodding, Leah smiled knowingly. "I was right—you *are* still in love with him!"

Jade hid behind one hand. "There's no talking sense to you today. Now, what'll it be?" she asked. "Hot tea or lemonade?"

"How about the truth for a change?"

With a gasp, Jade's mouth dropped open. "The truth... *for a change?* You've always said I'm one of the most honest people you know...that I use diplomacy and avoidance so I don't have to lie, even to spare people's feelings."

There was a moment of absolute silence before Leah asked, "What are you so afraid of, Jade?"

"Afraid? I don't know what you're talking about."

"Are you scared that if you tell him how you feel, he'll reject you?"

Yes, I've always been afraid of that, she thought, staring wide-eyed at her friend. "This is neither the time nor the place to be discussing such—"

"Did you ever consider that maybe he feels the same way?"

It was so preposterous, Jade could only laugh and roll her eyes. "Who? Riley? In love with *me*?" Another short burst of laughter, then, "I'd say you were high on painkillers...if you were *taking* painkillers...because that's just about the most ridiculous—"

"Look me in the eye and tell me you never gave it a thought."

Jade swallowed hard. She'd managed to avoid the truth with others, but never with Leah, who could be ruthless when on a quest for information. "As I said," Jade began, patting Leah's pillow, "this is neither the time nor—"

"It is *precisely* the time and place." Then, softening her tone a bit, Leah added, "Humor me, Jade. I've been a pretty good patient so far, haven't I?"

"You've been a very patient patient," she teased, smiling lovingly. And, looking into Leah's nearly lash-less blue eyes, Jade shook her head. *You never could refuse her anything*, she reminded herself. *What makes you think you could refuse her now?*

She took a deep breath and plunged in. "You know very well that I used to think about Riley and me not just as friends, but as...as...a couple. I thought about it all the time."

"Seems to me I recall a couple of prayers, too...."

Jade squared her shoulders. "True. But as you can see, they haven't been answered," she said without thinking. And upon hearing her blatant confession, Jade quickly added, "Besides, I was young and stupid then. Very young, and naïve, too."

"Oh, and you're *so* much older and wiser now...."

Jade tucked in one corner of her mouth and frowned. "You always did think you knew it all, didn't you?"

Shrugging, Leah said, "Hey, I believe in that old maxim...."

"Which is?"

"Tell it like it is."

Jade exhaled a sigh of frustration. "If I didn't know better, I'd say you were deliberately trying to make me mad." Grinning, she repeated, "And besides, it's 'as,' not 'like.'"

"Whatever," Leah laughed, waving the grammar lesson away. Yet there wasn't as much as the trace of a smile on her pallid face when she said, "I'm not trying to make you *mad*, Jade. I'm just trying to make you see what's right under your nose."

"What I see," Jade said, standing straighter, "is that Riley likes sultry, mysterious women. You know the type—tall and voluptuous, with big, brown eyes and long, black hair...." She spread her arms wide. "Look at me, Leah. I'm the complete opposite of that."

Leah regarded her with a careful eye and, nodding, said, "Can't see the forest for the trees, can you?"

Growling with frustration, Jade feigned a scowl and rolled her eyes, then laid a hand on Leah's forehead.

Leah giggled. "Stop that. What're you doing?"

"I thought maybe you'd spiked a fever. How else am I to explain why you're spouting platitudes like some delirious—"

"You're the one who's crazy," Leah interrupted her, grabbing Jade's wrist, "if you can't see how he feels about you." She paused, then continued, "I've seen the way he looks at you when he thinks no one is looking. He's feet-over-forehead in love with you, sweetie!"

Jade perched on the edge of the hospital bed and took Leah's hand in hers. Her heart pounding with joy at the mere possibility, Jade closed her eyes. *This is neither the time nor the place*, she reminded herself. *What kind of person discusses issues of her own romance with a dying woman?* She took another deep breath. *A selfish, self-centered....*

"Leah, you know that Riley has always treated me as though I were his silly little sister. He's protective and sweet, but he thinks of me as a friend—*just* a friend." She held a warning finger in the air. "That's the way it's always been, and I see no reason to believe he feels differently now."

"Maybe you need to look harder."

"What?"

"Maybe you don't see a reason to believe he feels differently because you're not looking hard enough." She squeezed Jade's hand. "*'O foolish men, and slow of heart to believe all that the prophets have spoken!'*"

Jade smiled to hear Luke 24:25 and looked up at the ceiling. *Lord,* she prayed silently, *help me put an end to this nonsense!* "Oh, and now she thinks she's a prophet, Lord," she said aloud, shaking her head. Grinning, Jade returned her attention to Leah. "I think I'll just fix you that tea now. A nice big mug of chamomile. Maybe it'll put you to sleep so I won't have to listen to any more of this nonsense!"

Laughing, Leah shook her head. "You can run," she called to Jade's retreating back, "but you can't hide."

"I can't hear you...," came Jade's voice from the kitchen.

Tapping a finger on her chin, Leah gave a self-satisfied nod. "Well, Lord," she muttered, "what do You think? Are things ticking along just fine, or what?"

Suddenly, she sucked a huge gulp of air between her teeth and grimaced. The pain always hit her this way, with no warning whatever. It was one of her only complaints, because if she had felt it coming, perhaps it could have been forestalled.

Trembling with agony, Leah leaned over and popped a CD into the stereo, then pressed Play. As the familiar notes of "Amazing Grace" floated around the room, she snuggled deeper into the pillows and focused on the words of the song, waiting for them to take effect.

Don't be angry, she told herself. *Be loving, like Jesus was at the end....* Smiling slightly, she remembered Jade's English lesson. As *Jesus was*, she mentally corrected herself.

"I once was lost," she sang along with the CD, "but now am found...."

Think about the plan instead of the pain....

That the Lord had blessed her plan was obvious. God had put the notion into her head, and Leah had never been more certain of anything in her life.

She took a deep, cleansing breath. "Thank You, Lord Jesus, for giving me the idea that has imparted to me such peace and contentment during this very trying time." And, grinning, she silently tacked on, *Who says you can lead a horse to water but you can't make him... and her...drink?*

Jade had left a message for Riley at the clinic, and when he returned her call at the start of his lunch break, the heaviness in her voice could have been weighed on a scale. "Just wanted to warn you," she said, "that Leah isn't doing very well today."

He'd made Jade promise to let him know whenever their buddy was having a bad day so that he could gird himself against letting Leah see his shock or sadness at first sight of her.

"I almost talked her into taking some morphine today," she added, "but Fiona woke up from her nap, and the minute Leah heard her voice...."

Her own voice was waning, and he could almost picture her standing in that stiff-backed way of hers, shaking her head in frustration.

"What can I bring you?" he asked.

Her answer echoed softly in his ear. "Just you." She cleared her throat, then asked, "What time can we expect you for supper?"

"Depends on what you're making."

"Spaghetti and meatballs, a giant Caesar salad, and cheesecake for dessert."

He knew she was teasing because of her lighthearted tone. Besides, these days, Leah couldn't hold down anything but bland foods—chicken, turkey, mashed potatoes—and Jade refused to cook anything spicy. "If Leah can't eat it," she said time and again, "*we're* not eating it. It just wouldn't be fair."

"Spaghetti and meatballs, eh? That's right...torture me with talk of what I *can't* have," he said, laughing. "Promise one of my favorite meals and fail to deliver. I have a good mind to do something just as mean...."

"Such as...?"

"Such as, I'll have spaghetti and meatballs for lunch, and give you a big fat kiss when I get there so you can smell it on my breath."

She giggled at that, a sound he'd come to treasure almost as much as the beautiful smile she always wore to greet him.

The rest of the day slogged by, and Riley couldn't wait to see her again. He'd seen almost as much of her lately as he had when they were kids, stopping by once, sometimes twice, a day since Ron had given Leah the final verdict.

The final verdict....

They'd gone round and round over that one, he and Ron, Riley demanding to know if the so-called medical professionals had truly exhausted every possible avenue of treatment, the doc insisting they were doing all that could be done.

It wasn't that Riley didn't believe Ron. The man had a tendency to hold a grudge, but he'd earned his stellar professional reputation. Still, Riley couldn't help but question the doctor's confidence in his diagnosis. Cancer went into spontaneous remission all the time. Why wasn't Ron looking into that to determine if something had been overlooked? Leah had no one else to look after her interests; if his persistence made Ron uncomfortable, so be it!

He'd made it his business to study the disease that was eating away at her, and he'd stood beside her every step of the way, which was exactly how he could be so certain that Ron *had* done all that was humanly possible.

That, and he'd been praying about it every chance he got since Leah had given him the awful news. Mostly, Riley prayed for a miracle. If the eyes of the blind could be opened, the ears of the deaf unstopped...if Christ could raise Lazarus from the dead and feed the multitudes from a few loaves and fishes, then there was hope for Leah.

Wasn't there?

Riley had long ago given up expecting an answer to why this had happened to his dear friend. *"Hear, O Lord, when I cry aloud, be gracious to me and answer me!"* he'd read in Psalm 27:7. All his life, he'd been an obedient follower who loved the Lord. Still, Riley thought he understood how Saul must have felt when he said to Samuel in 1 Samuel 28:15, *"God has turned away from me and answers me no more."*

He didn't know why cancer had invaded Leah's body.

And he didn't understand, or pretend to understand, why it couldn't be cured. But he knew this: Leah was in God's hands now. *"For thou, O Lord, art my hope, my trust, O Lord, from my youth."* Psalm 71:5 had become part of his daily prayers.

And he would continue to pray for Jade daily.

Because he still wanted her, now more than ever, and he believed it might well take a miracle to make *that* happen, too.

Riley winced inwardly as he parked his convertible in Leah's driveway. *What kind of cold-hearted lout thinks about his own love life when his best friend is dying?*

He let himself into the house quietly so as not to disturb Leah or Fiona, should they be napping. Jade was in the living room, lying in front of the fireplace beside Fiona, a tattered copy of *Green Eggs and Ham* open on the floor between them. Neither of them had heard him open the door, cross the foyer, or enter the living room.

Riley leaned a shoulder on the door frame and put his hands in his pockets, smiling and shaking his head, watching and listening....

"'...I do not like it, Sam I am; I do not like green eggs and ham,'" Jade read.

As she pronounced the words, her voice was every bit as animated as the rest of her. And he loved every minute part of her.

He'd never been the least bit envious of Fiona...till now. What he wouldn't give to have Jade snuggled up beside *him*, reading a story in that sweet, musical voice of hers!

Without looking up at him, Jade said to Fiona, "Tell Uncle Riley that staring isn't polite."

The little girl rolled over and, at the sight of him, scrambled to her feet and tottered over to where he was standing. With arms outstretched, she squealed gleefully, "Wye-lee!"

He gathered her up and chuckled as she rubbed a chubby hand over each of his bearded cheeks. "Wye-lee fuzzy," she said, giggling. Turning to Jade, she repeated, "Wye-lee fuzzy."

"Wye-lee hungwee," he said, and blew air bubbles on the baby's neck.

"You really shouldn't talk baby talk to her," Jade scolded him gently. "It's hard enough for a child to learn English, let alone a language she can't speak once she's out of diapers...."

He gave her a long, appraising stare, then nodded as a smile slowly tugged at the corners of his mouth. "You're gonna be a terrific mommy someday." Riley watched her blush and fidget.

"Well...well, thank you. That's quite a compliment, coming from you."

"Coming from me?" he asked, taking Fiona's finger out of his ear. "What's that mean?"

Jade shrugged. "You're a confirmed bachelor, and it's been my experience they're the hardest men to impress."

"I still don't get it," he mumbled past the tiny pink fingers wedged between his lips.

"You know what you want—and what you don't—and knowing makes you choosy."

Fiona pressed her lips to Riley's. "Wye-lee *kiss*," she babbled. "Wye-lee *kiss*."

He made a loud smacking sound against Fiona's chubby cheek. "How'd you know I had come in? I didn't make a sound."

Inclining her head, Jade wiggled her eyebrows. "You shouldn't ask a girl to reveal her secrets...."

"Secrets?"

"You know," she said matter-of-factly, "the wiles and ways of a woman...."

But he didn't know. In fact, Riley didn't have a clue.

It must have been written all over his face, because she smiled and said, "Oh, don't look so confused. From down there on the floor, I could see your reflection in that brass flowerpot on the hearth."

Chuckling, Riley shook his head. "You're a piece of work, Jade Nelson."

"Wok," Fiona repeated. "Wye-lee go wok?"

"No, sweetie," he said, grinning, "I'm off for the day. In fact," he added, digging in the outer pocket of his sports coat, "they can't even beep me."

"Beep, beep, beep," Fiona said, reaching for his cell phone.

Quickly, he shoved the gadget back in his pocket and gave Fiona to Jade. "More story?" he said, pointing at the book.

Reminded of what they'd been doing when he'd come in, Fiona bounced up and down in Jade's arms. "Book," she said. "Book!"

"Why the sudden handoff?" Jade asked, setting Fiona on the floor.

"Wipe that smirk off your face," Riley kidded as the child began flipping pages. "It's just that sometimes, like all females, she scares the daylights out of me."

"Scares you?" Jade laughed. "Dr. Dates-a-Lot, afraid of women?"

"Not *all* women. Just pushy, aggressive ones who poke fun at their friends...and poke their fingers in my ears."

"I didn't mean to poke fun at you."

She might have convinced him she was sincere... if she hadn't giggled and added, "But...you're scared of *Fiona*?"

He gave a shy nod. "No. Well, she can be real bull-headed when she sets her mind to something. And I happen to know she likes my cell phone. Took forever to re-download all my numbers last time she got ahold of it." Riley shrugged. "I didn't know how else to distract her."

Jade glanced at Fiona, who was contentedly leafing through the pages of the book. "Seems to me you know exactly how to distract her." Meeting his gaze, she smiled. "Leah's right...you *would* make a wonderful dad."

Riley felt the heat of a blush beneath his beard and rubbed a hand over his face. There was nothing he'd like more than to be the father of four, six, a dozen kids like Fiona...provided Jade would be their mother....

"So when's supper?"

"The table is all set, and everything is ready to go the minute Leah wakes up from her—"

"She's up," Leah interrupted her, rolling into the living room.

Riley took one look at and crossed both arms over his chest. "Did you just lie there reading, or did you sleep?"

"I slept, Mr. Clean," Leah insisted, "so wipe that scowl off your face and gimme a hug."

Immediately, his demeanor softened and he leaned down, letting her wrap him in a bony hug.

"What's cookin'?" she asked Jade over his shoulder.

When he straightened up, Jade said, "Turkey, mashed potatoes and gravy—"

"Ack. I'm not very hungry. Would you mind very much if I watched the TV news while you guys eat?"

It was the very reason Leah had put a hospital bed in the family room—so that she could feel like a part of the household and still rest properly. It didn't seem like such a bad idea to Riley, until he glanced at Jade....

Her stern expression and stiff posture made it patently clear: Leah had been skipping meals entirely too often to suit Jade. It could mean only one thing, and Riley didn't want to think about that.

"Oh, don't look so serious, you two," Leah scolded them in her typical, playful way. "I'm not dying...yet."

Gasping, Jade ran to her side and wrapped her in her arms. "Don't say things like that. Not even in jest!"

"Sweetie, you're a nurse. You know the signs even better than I do. Isn't it time you faced the facts?"

"I may be a nurse," Jade conceded, hugging her tighter, "but I'm a Christian, first and foremost." On her knees in front of Leah now, Jade grasped one of Leah's hands, reaching out to Riley with the other. "We're praying for a miracle," she said emphatically. Looking to Riley for support, she added in a softer voice, "Aren't we, Riley?"

He knelt down beside Jade and took Leah's free hand in his. "Jade's right," he agreed. "There's no reason to believe God won't come through for you."

There were tears in Jade's eyes when she said, "That's right! You can't give up, Leah. Fiona needs you, and...and so do we."

Leah sat back and gave Jade a long, appraising stare. "I know what you're trying to do, Jade, but I'd like you to stop it, okay?"

"What am I trying to do?"

"You think you're reviving my hope. Well, I have plenty of that." She shook her head. "I ask you, what's wrong with this picture?"

Riley could see that Leah's speech had cut Jade to the quick. She'd been working night and day, getting very little rest in the process. Surely, it was taking a toll on her.... He wanted to wrap her in his arms, as he'd done the night she'd come home, because she looked every bit as frightened as a small child who'd gotten separated from her mother in the supermarket.

"I see that I'm going to have to answer my own question," Leah said, wriggling her hands free of their grasps. "I used to be the weakling, the one who needed comfort and consolation."

"You were never a weakling," Jade insisted.

"You're sweet to say that," Leah said, "but we both know it isn't true. I moped around for months when I lost my family and whined every time my heart got broken by whichever boy I had a crush on at the time. I was impossible to live with when my SAT scores kept me out of Stanford, and when John died...."

Leah looked up at the ceiling, as if the description of that sad time in her life had been written up there in bold, black letters. "I don't know what I would have done without you two. Well, yes, I do," she added with a giggle. "I'd have fallen apart, that's what."

"Stop it, Leah," Jade scolded her. "You're wearing yourself out with all this talk about—"

"I won't stop it. I have to make you accept this." She held out her hands, indicating first the wheelchair, then her puny body. "*I've* accepted it."

Jade bit her lower lip. "But you can't just accept it. You have to fight this thing!"

"I *am* fighting it, sweetie." Her voice, soft as a whisper, caught on a pent-up sob. "Don't you think I'm praying for a last-minute reprieve from this death sentence? Don't you think I want to be here when Fiona loses her first tooth, when she goes off to school for the first time, when she dances at the prom, and gets married, and has babies?"

Angry now, she backed the wheelchair away from Riley and Jade. "I don't *want* to die, Jade...surely, you know that. But," she said, whirling the chair around to face them again, "if I have to...." She licked her lips. Swallowed. Bowed her head. Then, meeting their eyes again, she added, "If I have to die, I want to do it with as much dignity as this blasted disease will allow."

Shaking her head, she covered her face with both hands. "I'm sorry for losing my temper," she said into her palms. "It isn't your fault this is happening to me." When she came out of hiding a moment later, Leah was fully composed again. "Well, Jade, you never answered my question."

Jade's voice trembled when she asked, "What question?"

"What's wrong with this picture?"

"Oh. That." Jade blinked and sighed. "I don't know, Leah. What's wrong with it?"

It was the first time Riley had seen any evidence that the cancer—and the horrible effects it was having on Leah—was affecting Jade, too. She looked emotionally spent, standing there slump-shouldered, arms hanging limp at her sides as she tried her best to put on a happy face for her best friend. More than ever, Riley wanted to hold her, promise her that everything would be all right.

But he couldn't. Because if God didn't come through pretty soon with that miracle they'd all been praying for, Leah was going to die.

"Well," Leah said, grinning, "since you asked...." She folded her hands. "Feels odd, me giving comfort to you guys for a change."

The grin never quite made it to her eyes. Still, Riley noticed, the effort was there.

"Weird, huh?"

He shook his head. "I've told you dozens of times over the years that you have a convenient memory."

When she aimed those lashless blue eyes of hers at him, Riley thought he might just cry himself.

Leah propped her elbow on the arm of her wheelchair and rested her chin in her hand. "What does my pitiful memory have to do with anything?"

"I can't speak for Jade, of course," he began, sliding an apologetic gaze in her direction, "but as for me...."

He'd never taken much credit for the fact that he could bench-press double his weight; big bones and strong muscles were something he'd inherited from his father's side of the family. Since childhood, he'd hoped the solid, stable strength of his mother's people flowed in his veins. But he'd never really been tested...before now.

Lord God, he prayed, *show me what to do; tell me what to say to prove to Leah that I'm with her, all the way.*

It dawned on him that what she needed most right now was to feel stronger, despite the cancer—or maybe because of it—than himself or Jade. So, he put male pride aside and lay his head in her lap. And as she combed long, delicate fingers through his hair, Riley felt her relax, heard her take a deep, unwavering breath.

"I love you guys," she whispered.

"We love you, too," they said in unison.

Fiona toddled up and pushed Riley aside to climb onto Leah's lap. "Me wuv Mommy, too," she said, hugging her.

Connected by hearts and minds and clasped hands, the foursome formed a tight circle of love.

Chapter Four

S he let me give her something to help her sleep," Ron said when he joined Jade and Riley in the family room.

Jade was balancing on one end of the sofa, and the doctor sat down on the other. "Well, that's welcome news," she said. "How did you talk her into it?"

He gave a halfhearted shrug and stuffed his stethoscope into the black bag on the cushion between them. "She told me Fiona is going to a birthday party tomorrow...her first, as I understand it."

"That's right," Riley stated. "My brother's little boy is turning three. I'm picking her up at noon. We're going to spend the whole day together."

Ron buckled the satchel, all but ignoring Riley's comment. "I convinced her that a good night's sleep might just give her enough energy to snap a few pictures before Fiona leaves for the shindig."

Jade ran a hand through her hair. "Well, you deserve a medal. Riley and I can't even get her to take as much as an over-the-counter sleep aid. I honestly don't know how she's stood the pain all this time."

"A little stubbornness," Riley inserted, "and a whole lot of faith."

"Faith!" Ron's bitter laugh cracked the quiet. "Faith in what?"

Riley leaned back in the easy chair and held up his hands in mock self-defense. "No need to bite my head off, Doc. Some of us got it, some of us ain't. Looks like you're standing in the ain't line."

"And I'm standing there willingly," he blurted out, "because, in my opinion, faith is for fools."

"I always say that people in the sciences are hardest to persuade...of *anything*. You think because you can't measure Him in a test tube or read Him on an X-ray, God doesn't exist?"

"My attitude toward faith in God has nothing to do with medicine," Ron said curtly. "The way I feel is the result of years of hearing people pray for divine intervention—to ease their pain, to cure their illnesses, whatever—with absolutely no results. Faith is for fools, especially blind faith, and your attitude proves my point."

"You honestly expect me to believe you've never witnessed a miracle? Never had a patient who, for no apparent reason, got better?"

"Sure, I've had patients recuperate," he said. "But there are all kinds of rational explanations for it. And I resent that you're always questioning my professional opinion."

"I really don't give a hoot what you resent and what you don't. And in my opinion, your bedside manner could use a little work. Leah needs to know you believe she'll survive. *I* resent that your so-called professional opinions are proving just the opposite!"

"When I want your opinion, Steele, I'll ask for it... but don't hold your breath. As for my bedside manner, I reserve that for patients only. And while you're definitely trying *mine*, I—"

"Stop it!" Jade's hoarse whisper interrupted their argument. "Stop it, right now! What if Leah were to overhear the two of you, bickering like a couple of rowdy boys over the only swing in the schoolyard? It's important for her to stay calm. How's she supposed to do that if she hears you talking like this?"

Standing up, she glared openly at each in turn. "I know there's bad blood between you, but for the love of angels, can't you act like grown-ups for now and set it aside?"

Riley leaned forward, elbows propped on his knees, and hung his head. "Sorry," he said, clasping and unclasping his hands.

Ron huffed out a deep sigh and moved his doctor's bag forward an inch, then back again. "Yeah," he said nervously. "Me, too."

Jade massaged her temples. "And I didn't mean to come off sounding like a grumpy old crone, either."

"You didn't," Ron asserted. "We were behaving like a couple of spoiled, self-centered kids. We deserved a good scolding."

"Hey," Riley injected, grinning, "speak for yourself."

Jade watched as the men nodded courteously, thin-lipped smiles and smug-eyed stares declaring that, although it hadn't been announced formally, a temporary truce had been declared. She laughed softly, hiding her eyes behind one hand. "You two are priceless."

"Priceless?" Riley repeated.

Ron's confused stare echoed the question.

"You looked like a couple of wolves just now, teeth bared, squaring off to determine who's leader of the pack." She put Ron's bag on the floor at his feet and slid onto the center cushion. "C'mere," she said to Riley, patting the one she'd just vacated.

When he was seated, she grabbed his right hand, then Ron's. "Friends?" she asked, forcing them together.

"Friends," Riley said sullenly.

"Yeah," Ron echoed, "friends."

Begrudgingly, they shook on it.

"There, now," Jade said, smiling. "That wasn't so hard, was it?"

Too late, she discovered it was a question better left unasked, for the feral stares returned to their faces. *Well,* she told herself, *Rome wasn't built in a day, and neither are friendships.* For now, the focus should be on Leah....

"So tell me, Dr. Peterson—"

"Ron," he corrected her.

"Ron." She smiled. "How's Leah today? I hate having to ask you the same thing every single time you come by, but if she doesn't want me in her room when you examine her, what am I to do?" She lifted her shoulders in a dainty shrug. "I mean, I'm her friend, first and foremost, but I'm a nurse, too." She was rambling, and she knew it, but she seemed powerless to stop the flow of words once they'd started. "I'm *Leah's* nurse, for goodness' sake! How can I take proper care of her unless I know what's—"

"No need to explain your concern to me," Ron said, smiling gently. "I can see how much you care. As long as you don't ask me to violate doctor-patient confidentiality, I'll be happy to tell you anything you want to know."

"So cut to the chase, Doc," Riley butted in. "How's our girl doin'?"

Ron aimed a hard stare in Riley's direction but softened it a bit when he looked back at Jade. "Not well, I'm afraid."

Jade bit her lower lip. "It's close, then?"

A deep furrow formed on his brow. "Very close...."

"How much time does she have?" Riley wanted to know.

The doctor shook his head. "A month, maybe."

The three exhaled a collective sigh, ruminating over what seemed to be an irrevocable ruling regarding the person whom they all had in common—Riley and Jade had their friendship with Leah; Jade and Ron shared a medical concern for her; Ron and Riley shared utter sadness.

"Well," Ron said, shattering the moment of somber silence, "I'd best be on my way." He stood up and gathered his things. "I'll stop by again tomorrow at about this time," he added, heading for the front door, "if that's okay."

"Of course it's okay," Jade said, grasping his hand. "And if you don't mind an ultra-bland diet, since that's all Leah can eat these days, you're more than welcome to join us for supper."

His smile brightened at the invitation. "I might just do that." He gave her hand a little squeeze. "See you tomorrow, then."

She turned toward the family room and found Riley standing with his hands in his pockets, one foot crossed over the other, and a shoulder pressed against the door frame. She blamed his disapproving countenance on the supper invitation she'd extended to Ron Peterson. He didn't want to share a meal with the man, and the proof was written on his face, in his stance.

But Ron had seemed so lonely and lost, despite all his tough talk. She'd worked with doctors for more than a decade now, and while some allowed themselves to care beyond the bounds of pills and treatments, most held to the theory that arm's length emotional involvement was the most professional way to behave.

The sadness in Ron's eyes and voice told Jade that he considered Leah a friend. She believed he *wanted* to trust in faith, in the possibility of miracles. But he'd chosen oncology as his specialty, a discipline associated more often with death and dying than with life. With oncology patients, faith in miracles could sometimes seem hopelessly impossible....

As a nurse, Jade understood it only too well. She was about to explain it to Riley when he lifted one eyebrow and tucked in a corner of his mouth. "I'm gonna pour myself a glass of iced tea. Can I get you one?"

"Sure, thanks."

As he rattled around in the kitchen, Jade checked on Leah, who was sleeping peacefully in her bed. After the bickering fest between Ron and Riley, she needed a moment of quiet rest herself. She returned to the living room and settled into Leah's recliner, leaned back, and closed her eyes. She'd given a good deal of thought to what Ron's fiancée had done—used Riley to end their engagement—but something told Jade that the ex-fiancée fiasco was only a small part of the problem. *As long as their quarreling doesn't affect Leah, it doesn't matter how Ron and Riley feel about each other.*

If it had been that simple, why was she trying so hard to manufacture a friendship between the men?

Because, she admitted to herself, *helping build a relationship between them isn't sick and demented, like hoping that Riley will—*

She forced the thought from her mind and focused instead on the hard work it would be to bring them together. *But even if they never become friends, at least in the meantime you'll have something to distract you from your feelings toward Riley.*

Her eyes snapped opened, and she sat up straight.

How *did* she feel about him?

Her fingertips drumming on her knees, she counted his finer qualities. *He's gentle and kind, and thoughtful, too. And terrific with kids. And except for that run-in with Dr. Peterson, he's always been easy to get along with....*

Plus, Riley was completely devoted to his family, helping them in any way he could, every chance he got. He'd always had a way with animals, so it had come as no surprise when, in eighth grade, he'd announced that he wanted to be a veterinarian when he grew up.

Stubborn determination is what had given him the stick-to-itiveness required to turn his dream into reality.

And an old-fashioned attitude toward hard work and dedication had made his animal clinic one of Baltimore's most successful.

And then, there was his "way" with women....

Leah had often teased Riley by calling him a girl magnet, as much for his flirtatious charms as his dark good looks. And was it any wonder? It didn't matter one whit to Riley whether a female was five or ninety-five, overweight or not; he made every woman feel beautiful and intelligent, as if she were the center of the universe.

She sighed dreamily. *He makes me feel like that*, Jade admitted to herself. *Maybe you're just another one of his many admirers, basking in the warmth of his handsome gaze....*

There was no denying the attraction of his physical attributes. Why, Jade had never been overly fond of facial hair, but Riley looked so good in his neatly trimmed beard that she'd completely forgotten her preference for clean-shaven men!

And he was a terrific kisser, too. There had been only two kisses between them—the one after graduation and another he'd given her the night she'd come home to be with Leah. But Jade knew she needn't kiss a hundred men to be certain that *this* was the man she wanted to be with, morning and night, for the rest of her life.

The rest of your life....

Would she have had such a thought if she didn't love him?

The answer, quite simply, was no.

All right, so I admit it—I love Riley Steele! But she couldn't admit it aloud, especially not to Riley.

A creepy-crawly sensation shrouded Jade. It happened every time she had romantic thoughts about him. *You're a hideous, despicable human to be contemplating a future with Riley at a time like this!*

Prayer was the solution. The only solution. She would cleanse her mind and heart of Riley...by praying him away.

The idea made her grin a little, and a creative spin on a line from a *South Pacific* song jangled in her head: *Gonna pray that man right outta my hair....*

"Care to share the joke?" Riley asked, handing her an icy glass.

The smile and mood that had caused it disappeared. "Thanks for the tea," Jade said. And to herself, she added, *You're going to have to be more careful—a lot more careful—because he's always been able to read you like a—*

"I peeked in on Leah."

"Asleep?"

Riley nodded. "Yeah. I guess whatever Doc gave her finally kicked in."

"Good. She needs her rest."

"What she needs is a miracle."

The only sound in the room was the cracking of ice in their glasses. Riley broke the silence. "Will you pray with me, Jade?"

Her heart fluttered in response to the intimacy of his invitation. "Of course."

He sat down in the easy chair beside the recliner, and they bowed their heads and folded their hands. With eyes closed, Riley began, "Lord Jesus, we thank You for our blessings...good friends, satisfying careers, all our material needs met. But we have a need that has not been satisfied....

"You said that with faith the size of a mustard seed, we could move mountains. You can read our hearts, so You know the size of our belief. And You know how much we need Leah in our lives!

"We believe You have the power to heal her, if it's Your will. We ask it now, in Your most holy name. Amen."

"Amen," Jade echoed.

She'd never realized that Riley became a different person when he prayed. He did not attempt to impress or educate, as when speaking before colleagues; he wasn't trying to comfort or console, as he often had to do when talking to pet owners in his clinic; and he seemed to have no desire to dazzle and fascinate, as when wooing a lady. In prayer, he was more appealing than ever, because he was 100 percent the man God intended him to be.

Jade picked up her glass and clinked it against his. "To miracles," she said softly.

He nodded gravely. "To miracles."

Leah had heard the door open, and out of the corner of her eye, she'd seen Riley peek into her room. She hadn't dared stir for fear he'd take one look at her eyes and register the tormenting pain that was racking her body.

He'd tiptoed up to the bed, and she'd sensed him hovering over her. "Ah, Leah," she'd heard him sigh, "*why?*"

It had taken every ounce of self-control to remain silent and still, to keep up the pretense of sleep, because she'd wanted to grab him by the scruff of the neck and shout, "If only I knew!" She'd wanted to hold him close and comfort him, saying, "Don't be sad, Riley...."

The sound of his running shoes padding across the thick carpet had been the only indicator of his departure. Leah might not have opened her eyes at all if she hadn't needed to find a tissue to blot her tears.

She didn't want to die. At least, not at thirty. *How ironic*, she thought with a grin, *that the Flower Power generation said you couldn't trust anyone over thirty, and here I am, just reaching the age when I can't be trusted, and I'm dying!*

But in all seriousness, Leah knew that she would die—soon, if she was reading the signs correctly—despite the thousands of prayers she'd sent heavenward pleading for a cure.

She would hold fast to the possibility that she'd recover, right to the end. But never having been one to leave things to chance, she also believed in being prepared. It was what prompted her to carry with her everywhere a purse the size of a carry-on suitcase, filled with bandages and antibiotic ointment, baby aspirin and wet wipes, just in case Fiona needed something when they were away from home. The same attitude drove her to keep the pantry well stocked, the laundry washed and folded, and the house tidy at all times.

And the mind-set of preparedness was also responsible for her plan.

If she wanted things to turn out well for Fiona, Jade, and Riley, Leah knew she must act *now*.

She eased herself into her wheelchair and rolled quietly toward the sound of voices in the family room. Riley's prayer stopped her, though—a prayer that was both poignant and powerful as he asked God to perform a miracle.

She'd come out of her room, fighting the effects of the medication Ron had given her, to lay it all on the line—to ask Jade and Riley to help her put the finishing touches on that plan. But hearing his heartfelt appeal only served to underscore her own worries. Yes, she would continue hoping to win her battle against cancer, but still, the likelihood of victory was slim, at best.

Cancer was a woeful, wretched disease. "The Great Pretender" is what Leah called it, because, while it stimulated the camaraderie of friends and neighbors who gathered around to comfort and console, it left its victims to suffer in silent solitude the fears and doubts of a precarious, unpredictable future.

Leah could not face them this way—afraid, uncertain, and vacillating between the strength of her convictions and the weakness of her human spirit. In order for the plan to work, it had to be presented as the only viable alternative left to them; it had to be presented in a clear, convincing voice that established the very *rightness* of it.

She maneuvered the chair backwards down the hall, rolled up to the bed, and climbed back under the covers. *Help me hold on, Lord, until I've seen to Fiona's future.* When she could see for herself that things were firmly in place, Leah told herself, she could exchange alarm for assurance, cowardice for courage. *Then* she could face Jade and Riley, present her case....

With a trembling hand, Leah lifted the telephone from the nightstand, put it in her lap, and dialed the number she'd memorized on the day when Dr. Peterson had told her she might die.

"Jules?" she said when a man answered.

"The one and only...."

He was a kind man, an honest man, and when he'd promised to help her in any way he could, Leah had taken him at his word. "It's Leah Jordan. I'm sorry to call so late, but—"

"It's only eight thirty," he said, chuckling. "What can I do for you?"

"I...I need to talk with you. As soon as possible."

She read the lengthy pause to mean he was considering possible reasons for the urgency in her voice. But only one reason mattered....

"How about if I stop by day after tomorrow, around lunchtime, with the paperwork? All we need is your signature on a couple of documents, and everything's ready."

"Everything?"

"Well, there's one that isn't quite complete, but you can't sign that one."

"And I'm working on that."

"Any luck?"

Laughing softly, she whispered, "Well, there are a few signs and symptoms that it'll be a success. Now, if I can just keep it together a few more weeks...."

She heard a woman's quiet voice in the background asking, "Who is it, Jules?"

The lawyer must have put his hand over the mouthpiece, because his reply was muffled. "Leah Jordan," was his whispered reply.

"Oh, that poor young woman!" said his wife. "Tell her she's in our prayers...."

"Melissa sends her love and prayers," Jules told Leah.

"Thank her for me, won't you? I can use all the help I can get."

Death is a funny thing, Leah thought during the uncomfortable pause. *We all know we can't escape it, and yet it terrifies us...even when it's not our own death we're facing.* "Hang in there, Leah. We'll get you through this. I promise."

"See you soon, then," she said around the lump in her throat.

She put the phone back on the nightstand and collapsed into her pillows. Never before had Leah felt she could relate on a personal level with Christ's life. Even when He had walked the earth as a man, He'd been so pure, so perfect.

But one incident stood out in Leah's mind—when He'd seemed to behave more like a human than at any other time...at Gethsemane....

Afraid, sorrowful, and in anguish at the knowledge that He would be betrayed, Jesus left His disciples so that He could pray. Falling on His face, He called to the heavens, *"My Father, if it be possible, let this cup pass*

from me; nevertheless, not as I will, but as thou wilt"
(Matthew 26:39). He said it three times that night, alone
in the garden. And yet, though His plea was hopeful and
heartfelt, He was not spared.

He *could not* be spared, for He was the Savior! His
blood, shed at Calvary, had been a requirement to
cleanse the sins of all men, for all time. It had been the
supreme sacrifice, the most glorious of loves...dying so
that others might live. Humbled by such devotion, Leah
gave thanks to the Lord, as she did every morning and
every night.

But she was no one special. Her only accomplish-
ment in life had been Fiona. *What possible good can
come of my death?* she'd demanded time and again.

The thought had forced her to seek the Father's forgiveness time and again, too, for even asking the question. It wasn't for her to second-guess God's plan, after
all. Though, for the life of her, Leah didn't know how her
death was part of His plan....

She'd asked all the typical things: Why me? Why
now? She didn't know why cancer had invaded her body,
eating away at her like a ravenous beast. And it wasn't
likely she'd ever know any of those things. At least, not
while she walked the earth....

But Leah knew this: the Lord loved her, and if He
chose to take her home now, she would not fight it.

Oh, she'd continue asking the questions and crying
for answers, to be sure! And she'd keep right on praying
for a miracle. Mostly, though, she'd stick to the appeal
that brought her the most peace: "Father in heaven, give
me the strength to endure, uncomplainingly, whatever
awaits me...."

She turned out the light and rolled onto her side.
The pillowcase was damp with her tears, but Leah didn't

mind. She looked at it as proof she was still alive enough to shed them.

"I'm not afraid to die, Lord," she whispered, "but I am afraid to leave Fiona without loving parents." She paused, chewing her knuckle until the pain lessened enough to allow her to continue. "Thank You, Jesus, for helping me to come up with a way to protect her."

She closed her eyes and held her breath to forestall another wave of pain. "I'm tired, Lord. So tired of fighting, of pretending it isn't so bad. Bless me with strength and energy, at least until...."

The room was dark and quiet, except for the sound of her own ragged breathing. And yet, from deep in her memory, she heard the lovely notes of an old hymn. Leah sang the first line softly, then recited the second in her mind.

She was asleep before she could intone her favorite part, but its echo carried her toward peaceful slumber nonetheless: "I will cling to the old rugged cross, and exchange it some day for a crown."

"Riley will be a little late," Jade told the doctor as he stepped into the foyer. "He had an emergency at the clinic."

"Emergency?" He set his medical bag down near the door. "What kind of emergency?"

Jade ignored his tone of exaggerated concern. "Riley was getting ready to leave when he saw a little boy crossing the parking lot. He was carrying a small dog wrapped in a blanket. Seems the pup had been run over by a car. There isn't much hope, Riley says, but he had to try, for the boy's sake."

Ron tucked in one corner of his mouth. "Okay, so he has a heart, after all."

"You'd be surprised just how big it is," Jade said, leading him into the kitchen. She poured him a glass of iced tea.

He thanked her and sat down at the table. "So tell me, Jade, what are your plans for the Fourth of July?"

"I'm making turkey burgers and chicken hot dogs served with boiled potatoes. I figure if I decorate with red, white, and blue, no one will notice there's no cole-slaw or baked beans...."

"Planning to see the fireworks?"

She sat down across from him, a glass of tea in her hand. "Yes," she said, nodding excitedly. "The neighbors say you can see them from the backyard. I'm going to pad Leah's patio chaise lounge with blankets, and Ri-ley's going to carry her to—"

"Riley," Ron interrupted her, "our hero."

Jade raised one eyebrow. "Can I ask you a personal question?"

He shrugged, wrapping both hands around his tum-bler. "I guess...."

"Why don't you like him?"

Ron proceeded to tell her the story of how he'd walked in on his ex-fiancée lip-to-lip with Riley.

Jade waved it away. "That isn't why you dislike him."

It was Ron's turn to raise an eyebrow. "Oh, really?"

"You know as well as I do that Riley had no idea she was engaged." She hesitated, then added, "Don't you?"

"Yeah. I guess I do," was his response.

"Then what's the *real* reason you look as though you've just sniffed a rotten egg whenever he walks into a room?"

Chuckling, Ron shook his head. He stared into his glass and poked an ice cube with a beefy fingertip. "Sometimes, things don't have easy answers, Jade." Only then did he meet her gaze.

"Sometimes, the problems of two people don't amount to a hill of beans in this crazy world...."

"Huh?"

"*Casablanca*...?" She paused. "The point is, there are bigger problems than your hurt feelings."

He nodded.

"So...what are your plans for the Fourth, Doc?"

"I haven't any to speak of. I have an open invitation to several friends' cookouts...."

"Well, good for you! But don't you have any family in town?"

"No family, period."

"My folks used to live here in Ellicott City," Jade said, "but they moved to Colorado when my dad retired."

"Not Florida?"

"Nope. They went out West for their anniversary several years ago and fell in love with the place."

"So, being different runs in the family, eh?"

Jade's brows drew together in confusion. "Different?"

"You're hardly what I'd call typical. Not in any way, shape, or form."

"Is that so?"

"I'll say. Your approach to nursing would drive most docs nuts. You've questioned everything I've done...and some things I haven't," he said, counting on his fingers. "You refuse to accept the inevitability of Leah's future, and—"

"I don't refuse to accept it, Ron. But more than anything, Leah needs hope. And I can't give her that unless I have it myself."

"You mean, a miracle?"

"Why not?"

"Because there's no such thing, that's why not."

Jade shook her head. "If you really believe that, then I feel sorry for you."

"Sorry? For me?" He met her gaze. "*You're* not the one who's dying."

"We're all dying, Ron. If we're lucky, we'll be old and gray and go in our sleep. But some of us get cancer, some of us have heart attacks, some of us get hit by trucks." She paused, then gave the tabletop a light slap. "And some of us die long before our souls leave our bodies—of fear, and lack of faith."

"I have faith," Ron said. "Plenty of it."

"In science, yes. So you said."

"What's wrong with that? It's trustworthy. It's predictable. It's—"

"It's safe," she finished for him, "and doesn't require belief in the impossible."

He looked into her eyes for a long time before saying, "Maybe you've got a point."

"Maybe?" She grinned.

And so did he. "My grandfather on my mother's side was a born-and-bred Texas cowboy. He had a saying for folks like you."

"Folks like me?"

"People who dig at a thing till they unearth the answers they're looking for."

"Bullheaded?"

Ron chuckled. "He would have said you're like a puppy to the root."

"Hmm," she said. "It's sure a lot nicer than being called stubborn as a mule."

He took another swallow of tea.

"Why don't you join us tomorrow?" Jade asked.

"For turkey burgers and chicken dogs?"

"And vanilla pudding pie and fireworks."

He wiggled his eyebrows. "Maybe 'sparks' will fly—"

"Don't get your hopes up."

"Can't blame a guy for tryin'."

"Now then, why don't you tell me what you don't like about Riley?"

"I declare!"

"Puppy to the root?"

"Exactly."

"Want a refill on that tea?" she asked, standing up.

He shoved the glass nearer. "Sure."

"That's what I like," Jade said, winking, "a man of few words."

"Well, I'm not going to tell you what *I* like," Ron countered.

She dropped three fresh ice cubes in his glass. "Why not?"

"Wouldn't be professional. At least, not right now...."

Chapter Five

I tell you, Leah, he's in love with Jade!"

"Don't be silly, Riley. Ron is a—"

"Professional? I hope that isn't what you were going to say, 'cause doctors have been falling for nurses—and the other way around—for centuries. I don't know what it is...maybe all those starched white uniforms are a turn-on...."

Leah smiled weakly. "Well, even if you're right, and Ron *does* feel something for Jade, there's no reason to believe she feels the same way about him."

"You didn't see what I saw," he growled. His voice deepened—and so did his sarcasm. "They were sitting in the kitchen, talking and making googly-eyes at each other." He shook his head and threw both hands in the air. "She invited him to our July Fourth celebration, for the love of Pete!"

"Maybe Jade knows something we don't know."

"Like what?"

"That Ron is lonesome?"

"Don't make me laugh."

Leah smiled. "I don't think David Letterman could make you laugh right now," she said with a sigh, "because you're jealous."

"Jealous?" He scowled. "*Now* who's being silly?"

"Go ahead, admit it. You're in love with Jade, and the very idea of another man being interested in her is making you crazy."

In love with Jade.

He'd never put it quite that way before. And yet....

For as long as he could remember, Leah had been reciting clichés and platitudes. The more commonplace they were, the more she liked them. *In love with Jade, eh?* One of her favorite idioms fit this situation perfectly: *You've hit the old nail on the head this time, Leah.*

But admitting that he loved Jade only served to remind him that any thoughts of romance now were out of the question. "I just don't want him taking advantage of her. She's vulnerable right now, what with Hank breaking off the engagement and—"

"Whoa there, big fella," Leah interrupted him. "Where'd you get a nutty idea like that?"

"What? About the breakup, you mean?"

She nodded.

His brows drew together in a puzzled frown. "From Jade. Where else? She seems so sad and disappointed when she talks about leaving California. I just naturally figured it was because he'd ended the relationship."

"Hank would have been more than happy to keep Jade on a string forever," Leah said. "In my opinion, he wanted a mother more than he wanted a wife. If she told me once, she told me a hundred times how she saw to it that he ate well and exercised, got plenty of sleep, rested up after each long, hard day...."

Riley swallowed. "I didn't know they were, uh, living together."

"They weren't." She leaned forward in her wheelchair. "Oh, my goodness, you thought they *were*, didn't you?"

Clicking her tongue, Leah said, "Riley, I'm surprised at you. She was raised a good Christian girl. She would never—"

"I thought I knew her once, but she was living in LA, don't forget. And besides, we haven't exactly been close all these years. People change...."

Leah gave an exasperated sigh. "Don't I know it!" Frowning, she shook her head. "Wait. I retract that. Granted, you two haven't had much contact, but you have *too* been close." Leah pressed a palm to her chest. "You've kept her right here, and that's where she's kept you, too. People can't get much closer than that."

"You look tired, Leah. I'm so sorry."

"For what, sweetie?"

"For bothering you with my pathetic concerns." He stood up and leaned down to lift her from the chair, intent upon putting her back in bed. "Now, let's get you—"

"Stop it, Riley."

Her stern tone surprised him. "Stop what? You don't want to go to bed?"

"As a matter of fact, I do. But that isn't what I'm talking about."

Gently, he positioned her in the center of the mattress, then pulled the covers up over her knees. "You'll have to forgive me, Leah, but I'm just a thickheaded Irishman, and I don't have a clue what you're talking about."

"You're only half Irish, so drop the thickheaded routine. What I'm talking about...." She inhaled sharply, closed her eyes, and clamped her lips together.

Riley wrapped her in his arms. "What? Is the pain worse? Can I get you something? What can I do?"

"Ooo ann ett eem oh, orr arrtrrs," she mumbled into his shoulder.

He loosened his hold. "What's that?"

"You can let me go, for starters," she repeated, comprehensibly this time. Grinning mischievously, she added, "Wouldn't it be ironic if you smothered me before the cancer could kill me?"

Riley winced. "Leah, that's not funny."

"It left me breathless," she said, still grinning. "I'm fine," she assured him, patting his hand. "Really. But this is precisely what I'm talking about, actually. I know it's getting harder and harder to act as if I'm not sick, but you have to try. Pampering and protecting me won't help a bit. In fact, it'll hurt, because I need to feel like I'm still a whole human being who can conduct normal conversations with my friends, who's able to give advice, and—"

"And take it?"

She gazed deep into his eyes, so deep that Riley was tempted to squint, for it felt as though she were reading his soul.

"And take it," she conceded.

"All right, then," he said, dropping a kiss on her forehead, "here's some friendly advice: Get some sleep so you'll have enough energy to sit at the table with us for a change. Jade will have supper on in an hour or so."

She grinned crookedly. "Keep that up and I'm going to get the idea you guys miss havin' me around."

"We do." *We will*, he added silently to himself.

The next afternoon, Leah waited for Jules to close the door to her room before sliding the big envelope from her nightstand drawer. She'd barely finished signing on the dotted lines when they heard footsteps coming down the hall. "Put it in there," she whispered, pointing at the narrow drawer. "I don't want them to see this yet."

Jade had just returned from a quick trip to the grocery store, and she seemed surprised that Leah had a
male visitor when she entered the room. "I don't believe
we've been introduced," she said, extending her hand.

"Just call me Jules," he said. "I'm a friend of Leah's."

"How did you get in?"

"Leah told me the back door would be unlatched."

"But...I'm sure I locked it when I left...."

"And I *unlocked* it," Leah said. If her cross tone hurt
Jade's feelings, well, she felt bad about that, but what
choice did she have? Jade and Riley had to be kept in
the dark until everything was set to go, or nothing would
turn out as she wanted...as she *needed* it to. "Thanks,
Jules," she said, "for stopping by."

"Call me in a couple days," he said carefully, "and
I'll...uh, I'll come back. No need to walk me to the door,"
he told Jade. "I'll let myself out."

When he was gone, Leah said, "Would you mind very
much fixing me a cup of soup?"

"It's ninety-five degrees out there. Wouldn't you rather have something cold, like yogurt or applesauce?"

No, Leah thought, *because soup takes longer to prepare!* "Oh, it's nice and cool in here, thanks to the air
conditioning. No humidity, either. So...."

With hands up in surrender, Jade backed out of the
room. "Okay, all right. I'll be back in a flash."

Leah did her best not to let a sigh of relief escape
from her lungs. With any luck, she'd have a few minutes
of undisturbed privacy to go over the paperwork.

Rifling through the envelope, she scanned the deed
to her house. *Correction...the deed to Jade and Riley's
house*, she thought, grinning. The title to her car now
bore their names, as did her savings and checking
accounts at the bank. When her husband had died,
Leah had invested the insurance money, and her stock

portfolio was now registered to Riley and Jade. But the Certificate of Adoption, in her opinion, was the most important piece of paper in the file, for it would guarantee that her precious little girl had a chance at a stable, loving family, with parents who shared her last name.

Of course, none of it would be possible unless Jade and Riley signed the paper she was holding now....

Footsteps alerted her that Jade was on her way back. Leah would know the sound of that sure-footed, energetic walk anywhere. Hurriedly, she stuffed the documents back into the file and slid the file in the envelope. There wasn't time to put the folder back into the drawer, so she tucked it under the covers instead.

First, there came the familiar soft knock, followed by Jade's pretty face peeking between the door and the doorframe. "Your soup's warming up on the stove," she said. Then, entering the room, she probed, "Why do you look like the cat who swallowed the canary?"

"Because I just woke up from the nicest dream," Leah said. "I made a wish some time ago, and it's about to come true."

"A wish?" Jade came in and plumped the pillows, then sat down in the chair beside the bed. "What kind of wish?"

"A wedding wish."

Giggling, Jade rolled her eyes. "A wedding wish! Who's the lucky couple? Anyone I know?"

"My stomach has been growling for half an hour," Leah said, hoping to change the subject. "When will my soup be ready?"

Jade eyed her suspiciously. "In a few minutes, if you still think you're up to it."

"You know how I have good days and bad days?"

Jade nodded.

"Well, this is a pretty good day, all things considered."

"I'm glad." She gave Leah a sideways hug. "Want me to get Riley? Have him help you to the kitchen?"

"That'd be nice."

The minute Jade was out of sight, Leah stuck the file in the Jordan family Bible, which she buried under the stack of magazines in her nightstand drawer. She'd barely gotten the drawer shut when Riley strode into the room.

"Ready to eat?" he asked, rubbing his hands together.

"Ready."

He slid one arm under her knees, wrapped the other around her waist, and lifted her gently from the mattress. "You'll let me know if I hurt you...."

Leah nodded. But since *everything* hurt these days, she saw no point in singling out any particular activity. Especially one that brought her out to join the family again.

The pain was almost constant now, and to hide it from Jade, Riley, and especially Fiona, Leah had been spending more and more time in her room. Jade seemed to recognize the signs, but Leah had continued to deny any discomfort. Only Ron knew the truth, and he'd promised not to tell. She'd have to find a way to conceal it in the coming weeks, because the sands were quickly sifting to the bottom of her hourglass. As her grandma used to say, "You've gotta make hay while the sun shines."

She would tell them everything tomorrow, right after the fireworks.

Because something told her the sun wasn't going to be shining on her much longer....

Jade was proud of Riley and Ron, and as they stacked the paper plates and plastic cups and carried them inside after dinner, she told them so.

"Aw, shucks, Miz Nelson," Ron said, "you're gonna make me blush."

The comment prompted a laugh from Riley, and unless he'd been taking acting lessons lately, it seemed genuine.

"I hope she's strong enough to stay out there till dark," Jade said. "It seems she gets paler by the minute."

Riley closed the trash bag he'd filled and secured it with a twist tie. "Which is exactly why we have to let her stay out there. What do *you* say, Doc?"

"Much as I hate to agree with anything that comes outta your mouth," Ron said, forcing a grin, "I think you're right."

"Fiona is awfully cranky today. Do you think she knows?" Jade asked.

"Jade, honey," Riley said, kissing her cheek, "everybody is cranky in this humidity. I've done a lot of reading on the subject, and from everything I've seen, Fiona's too young to understand what's going on."

"He's right," Ron said. "I've seen this dozens of times. Kids under the age of three have no preconceived notions about life and death, so they accept things at face value."

"Well, Mama pin a rose on the experts." Jade put the last of the serving dishes and silverware in the dishwasher and turned it on. "While you two read up on what she's feeling, I think I'll ask her myself." She paused, then added, "For example, she knows that she loves her mother."

"What's goin' on in there?" came Leah's voice from the other side of the screen door.

Despite the hum of the refrigerator and the churn of the dishwasher, the room seemed suddenly cloaked in deafening silence.

"Where's Fiona?" Jade asked to change the subject.

"On the swing set with Riley's sister-in-law," Leah answered.

Ron pocketed both hands. "She's something with the little guys, isn't she? I told her she ought to have a whole passel of young'uns."

"The weatherman says we're in for a humdinger of a storm tonight." Riley ran both hands through his hair. "I hope it holds off till after the fireworks."

"For goodness' sake," Leah scolded them, "I wish the three of you would stop behaving like you're guilty of something. Remember what I told you, Riley...."

"Yeah."

"What?" Jade whispered. "What did she tell you?"

"That we have to treat her as if she's healthy as a horse. No pampering, no trying to protect her from the truth."

"That's right. Now, either get back out here," Leah instructed them, "or let me in. I miss you!"

It seemed to take an eternity for Riley and Jade to tuck Fiona in. Leah drummed her fingers impatiently on the mattress, stopping only to rearrange the file folder on her lap. They'd always paid her a brief visit after putting her little girl to bed, but Leah had never specifically invited it before. If she didn't know better, she'd say they somehow knew what she was plotting and were stalling deliberately.

You should have rehearsed it, she said to herself. *At the very least, you should have written down what you wanted to say....*

She took a deep breath and let it out slowly. The matter was entirely in God's hands, and the success or failure of her plan depended upon the words He would give her to speak.

Jade's familiar knock sounded on the door, startling Leah from her reverie. Suddenly, she found herself wishing they *had* been stalling...and that they'd done a better job of it. *Be with me, Jesus*, she prayed.

"So, what's up?" Riley asked, pulling a chair closer to the bed.

"The ceiling? The sky? The price of gasoline?" Leah joked.

"Very funny," Jade said, sitting cross-legged at the end of the bed. "You've been acting funny all day. Fess up, girl."

Riley stifled a yawn. "Yeah, quit stonewalling. It's late, and I need my beauty sleep."

Leah took another deep breath, then slid the folder from its envelope. "I have a few things here that I'd like you to look over."

"Legal documents?" Riley asked, nodding toward the stack.

"Legal documents," Leah echoed. "I've given the matter a lot of thought and prayer, and I've come to the conclusion that this will be the best for all four of us."

"All four of us?" Jade said.

"You, Riley, Fiona, and me." She handed Riley the deed, then gave Jade the Certificate of Adoption. "But for any of this to work, I need both your signatures on everything."

"Our signatures? On everything?"

Leah stuck a finger in her ear and wiggled it. "Is there an echo in the room, or have I lost my mind?"

"I'm sorry," Jade said. "It's just—"

"Surely, you didn't expect me to let Fiona end up in foster care. You had to know *one* of you would get custody...."

Jade and Riley continued to fidget with the papers.

"Really, now," Leah went on. "Whom did you think I'd leave her with? You two are my only family."

Riley flipped the first page of the deed. "Leah...."

"Yes, sweetie?"

"It says here you're leaving your house to us."

"That's right." She grinned. "I don't want my little girl living with homeless people."

"But," Riley put in, "I already have a house."

Leah lifted her chin and assumed a smug demeanor. "You can never be too thin or too rich," she said. "I read that in one of my gossip magazines. And," she added, her grin growing, "you can never have too many houses."

She took one look at their expressions and said, "Don't look so shell-shocked! What I'm suggesting isn't all that strange. There was a time when arranged marriages were as common as dirt. Back then, only the fella was given a dowry; in this case, you're both getting one! You can invest the money for your children's education."

Jade gasped involuntarily. "Our—our children?"

Riley showed her the first page of the deed. "She's serious," he said, pointing.

"Mr. and Mrs. Riley Steele," Jade read aloud. With eyes wide and mouth agape, she stared at Leah.

"No, it isn't a mistake. You read correctly." Leah gave an affirmative nod of her head. "I may be near the end of my life, but I want to be part of giving you two a new beginning. You'll get the house and everything in it... once you're man and wife."

Jade wanted to look at Riley to see if he was having as much trouble with this as she was. But she couldn't seem to tear her eyes away from the title line.

"There's an organization," Leah said, commanding their attention. "I don't remember the name of it, but I know it exists expressly to grant dying children one last wish."

Jade covered her eyes with one hand. "Good God," she muttered.

Riley merely shook his head.

"Oh, stop feeling sorry for yourselves," Leah scolded them. "I know this makes you uncomfortable, but it has to be done. We all know that." She smoothed the top sheet and lifted her chin. "Now, listen to me, kids. I'm no child, but I have a last wish."

Riley put the deed back on the bed and sandwiched Leah's hands between his own. "But I thought you said the organization was for—"

"*They're* not going to grant my last wish. *You* are."

"*We* are?" said Jade.

"How?" Riley asked.

Leah stared him straight in the eye, then zeroed in on Jade. "I want to schedule a wedding."

Jade swallowed. "For...for Riley and me, you mean?"

"Exactly." The corners of her mouth turned up in a trembling little smile. "I just so happen to have a calendar here...."

They watched her slide a pocket-sized date book from the folder before looking at each other. "But Leah," Jade said, "we're not—"

"Yes, you are," she said emphatically.

"You don't even know what I was going to say." She'd been about to say, "We're not in love," which was only half true, since Jade had admitted weeks ago how she felt about Riley.

"Whatever it was," Leah said with a wave of her hand, "I can explain it away."

She beckoned them closer, then held tight to their hands. "Look. You guys are all I've got. More important, you're all Fiona has. Or will have." Blinking away tears that had pooled in her eyes, she summoned a halfhearted grin. "Tell you what—don't give me an answer right now. Go out there, talk it over some. Pray about it." She winked. "See if you don't come to the same conclusions I did."

Leah gathered up her legal documents and shooed them away. "Now, scram. It's been a long day, and I need some shut-eye."

Riley and Jade stood up slowly, still stunned, and moved woodenly toward the door.

"Go on," Leah waved, "and don't come back till you can tell me you're getting married." She turned off the light and put her back to them. "Close the door, will ya, so I'm not tempted to eavesdrop."

Riley and Jade sat down across from each other at the kitchen table, shaking their heads and frowning in silence.

Finally, Jade spoke. "I kind of expected her to ask one of us to adopt Fiona," she began, "but I never dreamed she'd do anything like *this*."

"Me, neither." He got up and filled the teakettle with water. "I don't know why, but I'm in the mood for something hot."

Jade nodded. "Warm things are comforting at a time like this."

"I guess...."

"She's sure stirred up a tempest this time, hasn't she?"

He turned on the flame under the kettle. "You can say that again."

But aside from that, they didn't seem to know what more to say about Leah's shocking proposal.

"Here's a question for you." Riley looked left and right, then scooted his chair nearer to the table. With a lowered voice, he said, "Just between you and me, if she hadn't been cooking up this scheme all these weeks, which one of us do you suppose she'd have wanted to adopt Fiona?"

Jade sighed. "It was a toss-up, really. At times, I was positive she'd choose you because you're so playful, and Fiona simply adores you. Other times, I believed it'd be me, since I'm a nurse, and a woman, and—" She matched his grin, dimple for dimple. "Okay, out with it. Whom did you think she'd pick?"

He feigned a look of arrogant certainty. "Me, of course."

They shared a brief round of hearty laughter, which came to an abrupt end when the teakettle started to whistle.

Jade dropped tea bags and sugar cubes into two over-sized mugs. "Hmm," she said, pouring water into each.

"Hmm, what?"

"Never thought about it before, but we have a lot in common with these herbs."

Chuckling humorlessly, Riley nodded. "What, we suit each other to a...tea?"

"I was thinking more along the lines that we're in hot water right about now." Grinning, she set the mugs on the table. "What are we going to do, Riley?" she asked, grabbing his hands.

He brought hers to his lips and kissed her knuckles. "I don't see how we can refuse her, kiddo."

Jade felt her heart hammering, and her eyes widened. She'd dreamed of becoming his wife so many times, she'd lost count. But not this way.

Riley turned her loose, then wrapped his hands around his mug. "Well, we have a couple of things going for us, right from the start."

"Like what?"

"Well, we're best buds. We already know each other's quirks and faults, so—"

"Faults?" she asked, grinning. "Everyone knows I have no faults."

"Everyone but me...."

His hands, still warm from the hot mug, covered hers like a comforting blanket.

"I know that you're scared of thunderstorms," he began, "and that you're terrified of anything that stings. You hate lima beans, and after you sweep the floor, you always leave a pile of crumbs in the corner behind the broom."

She hid a blush behind one hand. "Only until I get around to finding the dustpan...."

"No need to defend yourself to me." He tightened his hold on her hand. "I'm not complaining. I love everything about you." He winked. "Even the way you insist that the toilet paper absolutely must roll *over* the top."

"Only because that's the right way to do it!"

"Unless you prefer it the other way...."

"Well," she countered, "what about the way you make a huge mess out of the Sunday paper and flip through the TV channels at breakneck speed? And the way you never push in your chair when you leave the table?"

"You've got me dead to rights, there," he admitted, "and you've just proven my point."

Jade wrinkled her nose. "I'm afraid I've forgotten the point."

"We won't annoy each other while we're getting used to all that stuff."

She rolled her eyes. "What an annoying thing to say!"

Again, they shared a moment of quiet laughter.

"Riley...?"

"Hmm?"

"Let's pray on it."

"Good idea." He took her hands as they bowed their heads and closed their eyes. Two, perhaps three, seconds passed before he said, "Amen."

"Amen?! You mean that's it? Riley, you barely spent a—"

"We were talking to God. How much time do you think He needs?"

After taking one look at her serious expression, he said, "All right. Let's try this again. Lord," he began, "give us a sign...if this *isn't* Your will."

Jade waited a moment, then opened one eye. "That's it?"

He shrugged his shoulders. "What more is there to say?"

Smiling, she shrugged, too. "You make a good point."

"I'd say God just answered our prayer."

"He did?"

Riley nodded. "I asked for a sign, didn't I?"

"Yeah, so?"

"So when I told you why I didn't say a long, drawn-out prayer, you agreed with my reason."

"Okay...."

"We're gonna get along great, Jade," he said, grinning, "as long as you continue being so agreeable."

Jade rolled her eyes. Outwardly, she went along with his little joke. But inside, where her heartbeat had doubled and her pulse was pounding, Jade acknowledged the comfortable compatibility that had always been part and parcel of their relationship.

"Seriously," Riley said, interrupting her thoughts, "it's sure gonna be nice, knowing you'll be with Fiona while I'm at the clinic."

"And that you'll be with her when I'm at the hospital."

He raised both eyebrows. "You're going to continue working after...."

"...After we're married?" she finished.

Riley nodded. "Yeah. After that."

"Would you mind?"

"No. Not if it's what you want to do. I'd never stand in the way of your happiness."

"Actually, if it's all the same to you, I'd *rather* stay home. For a while, at least. I think it'll take us all time to adjust...Fiona, especially. It's important to build a firm foundation for her, a stable routine." She shrugged. "Maybe in a year or so, I'll go back, but for now...."

Smiling, he gave her hand an affectionate squeeze. "I was hoping you'd say that."

"Really? Why?"

"Like I said...it's gonna be nice, knowing you'll be here, waiting for me...."

Waiting for him?

Jade read the warm light emanating from his dark eyes, the soft smile that turned up the corners of his mouth. If she didn't know better, she might have said they were signs that he loved her. But Riley hadn't said it. Hadn't as much as hinted at it. He was doing this for Leah, for Fiona—because he loved them both deeply. Always had.

He was right, after all; they had half the battle licked even before they exchanged vows. They'd gotten along well as kids, and they had been getting along well since her homecoming. That should be enough.

So why *wasn't* it?

Aw, who knows? Jade thought. *Maybe we'll be like one of those mail-order marriages that started out as a matter of convenience and blossomed over the years into a full-blown love affair!* She sighed wistfully. *A girl can dream....*

"When do you think we should do it?"

"Yesterday, if Leah has her way," Jade kidded.

"She's probably got a preacher and a church all lined up."

She bobbed her head back and forth, mimicking an empty-headed Californian surfer girl. "Do you suppose she sees me in a long, flowing gown? Or a simple two-piece suit?"

He looked completely serious when he said, "Oh, a gown, by all means." His expression turned sour when he added, "I wouldn't be the least bit surprised if she's already rented me a monkey suit." He groaned. "But I draw the line at a top hat and coattails. There's only so much a guy will do for a pal, y'know."

"Well, if you can put your foot down, so can I: I refuse to drag a fussy train behind me down the aisle."

A small grin slanted his mustache. "This is weird."

"All this wedding talk?"

"Yeah." He nodded. "Weird," he said again. "But you know something? I feel good about it, like it's the right thing to do. And I really think we can make a go of it."

Jade's heart did a little flip. He looked genuinely happy saying that. So happy that she couldn't help but wonder yet again if maybe he *could* fall in love with her... in time.

She'd be a good wife to him—as good a wife as she knew how to be. Which wouldn't be hard, because Riley had always been easy to please. "Three squares and clean sheets," he used to tease, "that's all I want outta life." Well, she'd give him that, and so much more. She'd see to it that his lab coats were always bright white. He hated floral-scented soaps, so she wouldn't buy them. Ruffles anywhere drove him to distraction, so they'd have none in their home.

Their home.

The picture made her breathe another wistful sigh.

Though male pride forbade him from admitting it, Jade had always known that he enjoyed flowers. "Stinky posies," he'd called them to hide his appreciation. But she remembered the way he'd always lingered in her mother's rose garden, and the way he would always drive a little more slowly up the streets in springtime when the cherry blossoms were in bloom. Jade intended to plant petunias and marigolds and zinnias...so many he'd go colorblind looking at the blooms!

His favorite meal was lasagna with garlic bread and Caesar salad, so she'd fix it every year on his birthday, along with his favorite dessert—fudge-frosted brownies. She'd be sure to keep plenty of milk on hand, because he drank a gallon a day, it seemed, and a steady supply of peanut butter, because....

"So, what do you say?" he asked, standing up. And, holding out his hand, Riley added, "Should we see if Leah is still awake?"

Nodding, Jade put her hand into his and hoped he wouldn't feel it trembling. "If this news doesn't give her a peaceful night's sleep, nothing will."

Chapter Six

J ust as they'd expected, Leah had, indeed, lined up a
preacher. But, much to their amazement, she'd arranged to hold the ceremony in the backyard rather
than a church.

"Look at you," Leah remarked when she rolled into
Jade's room. "You're gorgeous!"

Jade stood in front of the mirror, hands clasped under her chin. "You think so?" she asked, adjusting the
mesh veil that covered her face.

"Yup. I think so." She gave an approving nod. "Something told me you'd prefer a simple suit to a frilly dress.
I can see I was right."

Tugging at the hem of the fitted white jacket, Jade
grinned at her reflection. "It's beautiful. I don't know
how to thank you, Leah."

"Thank *me*?" Laughing, she shook her head. "*I*
should be thanking *you*—and Riley, too, of course—
for going through with this. You don't know how happy
you've made me."

Down on one knee, Jade wrapped her arms around
Leah's shoulders. "Hush. You'll wear yourself out, and
we have quite a day ahead of us, thanks to you."

"Boy. Don't I know it."

Standing up, Jade smoothed the slim skirt. "What I
want to know is, where did you find time to arrange all

this?" She pointed toward the window looking over the backyard, where giant bells of white paper and huge bows of white satin decorated the fence posts, gazebo, and deck rails. She'd had the grape arbor painted white, accenting the miniature red rose vine that clung to its slats. Three dozen white folding chairs stood in straight rows alongside the wide, white cloth path that split the yard in two, and white pillars flanked the arbor, the bright green fronds of a potted fern dangling down from each.

"It was taken care of even before you came home."

"But how did you know we'd agree to this?"

"Because I had God's assurance." Leah snickered behind a gloved hand.

"God's assurance?"

"You didn't think I did all this on a whim, did you?"

Jade took another look at the beautiful yard. "No, I suppose that would have been taking an awful chance."

"Riley's gonna flip when he sees you."

"I doubt that...."

"And wait till you see *him*. I'll tell you what...not every man looks good in a tux, but *that* guy...." Leah shook her head. "Mmm-mm-mm. He could make the cover of *GQ*, I tell you!"

Jade had seen him in a suit before and had thought he was quite striking. She could only imagine how much more handsome he'd be in a tuxedo.

"Stop worrying, sweetie."

She thought she'd been doing a good job of hiding her anxiety. "You know me too well," Jade said.

"Which is precisely why I know you'll be fine."

"I'll take good care of her, Leah. I promise."

"Fiona? Of course, you will! I'm talking about Riley. Things are going to be swell between you two. You'll see."

Jade only sighed.

"He loves you, you know."

A nervous giggle popped from her lips.

"He who laughs last," Leah quoted, shaking a finger of warning in the air. "Mark my words, before you know it, you're going to have to admit that I'm right!"

Another sigh.

"The flowers ought to be here by now. You want me to roll on into the kitchen and check on 'em?"

"No, there's plenty of time for that. Just sit here and talk with me for a minute." Jade sighed. "Next time we have a chat, I'll be a married woman!"

"The more things change," Leah said, "the more they stay the same."

"Have I told you how pretty you look today?"

"You think?" Leah struck a model's pose in her chair, tilting her head to emphasize the pink silk scarf she'd tied around her scalp. False eyelashes and drawn-on brows gave her back a semblance, at least, of her former natural beauty. "I'm going for the gaunt look."

Jade winced.

"Aw, sweetie, I'm sorry. My sense of humor can be macabre at times, but I don't mean to spoil your day."

Squaring her shoulders, Jade forced a grin. "That's a very pretty dress...."

"Oh, this old rag?" Leah smoothed the flowing skirt. "I've had it for ages." Giggling, she added, "I'm surprised it still fits." She patted her flat tummy. "Middle-aged spread, y'know?"

The doorbell rang for the twentieth time, announcing the arrival of yet another guest. There would be fifty in attendance, counting Jade's family, Riley's family, and Leah's friends from church.

"I saw Pastor Jones out back," Jade said, glancing at the clock. "I guess it's time we went outside."

❦

The moment Jade took her place on the lawn, Riley's palms began to perspire.

His best man gave him a playful elbow jab to the ribs. "Keep that ticker of yours quiet, will ya?" Pete teased. "We don't want anybody dialing 9-1-1."

Grinning, Riley rolled his eyes. "Put a lid on it." Of course, his brother couldn't *really* hear his heart beating...

...Could he?

Riley took a deep, calming breath just in case.

Despite the distance between the deck, where Jade was standing, and the makeshift altar, and despite the gauzy veil that covered her face, Riley could see that she'd fixed her blue-eyed gaze on him.

He'd heard women described as dazzling. Pretty. Handsome, even. The only word Riley could come up with to describe Jade had been worn thin by overuse. Still, it was the only word that would do: *beautiful.*

Riley had never been a vain man, so the thought that ran through his mind made him frown. "Do you think I look okay?" he asked his brother through clenched teeth.

"What do you mean?" Pete whispered back.

Annoyed, he snorted, "I mean, do you think she thinks I look all right?"

Shrugging, Pete said, "Sure."

"Sure, what?"

Pete leaned back and, grinning, said, "Sure, you look okay."

Riley expelled a grateful sigh. "Thanks."

"Thanks for what?"

Rolling his eyes, Riley said, "Never mind."

Chuckling, Pete elbowed him again. "You're welcome, little brother."

Riley tugged at the sleeves of his tux as the music started—Leah had even seen to that—and he thought his heart might leap out of his chest.

Leah rolled down the aisle, grinning like the Cheshire cat as she scattered rose petals left and right. She parked her wheelchair and turned to watch Jade, who floated toward Riley like an angel riding a soft, white cloud. The satiny sheen of her knee-length suit reflected the sunlight. Riley blinked. He rubbed his eyes, hoping she was real and not another of the many dreams he'd had over the years.

She was real, all right. More real than any woman he'd known to date. The way she'd described the suit Leah had ordered from a catalog had made it sound attractive enough. But to see it now, wrapped around her... well, even Robert Frost couldn't have written a description to do it justice.

The wedding procession ended, and Mr. Nelson left Jade there, standing beside Riley under the arbor. The pastor read from the Good Book and led the guests in a heartfelt prayer, then said a blessing on the couple, who stood trembling before God. He felt a little sorry for Jade. Riley's fear wasn't visible, but Jade's was apparent by the constant quaking of the roses in her bouquet. As though she could read his thoughts, Jade turned and handed the flowers to Leah.

The pastor's droning voice penetrated his frightened fog. Squaring his shoulders, he blinked.

"Riley Steele, do you take this woman, Jade Nelson, to be your lawfully wedded wife?"

He turned to face her. Took her hands in his. "I do," he said softly, staring deep into teary blue eyes that shimmered like a babbling spring. *Tears?* he remarked with silent confusion, then frowned slightly. *Is the prospect of a lifetime with me that unbearable to face?*

Riley's heart ached. *Or is she wishing it were Hank Berger standing here instead of me?* He'd thought about little else the night before as he'd tossed and turned the hours away. For while, on the night of her arrival, she'd said that Hank never loved her—never would—Jade hadn't said how she felt about Hank.

But she had come home to stay.

So, the tears in her eyes now...they *could* be tears of joy....

...Couldn't they?

"And do you, Jade Nelson, take this man, Riley Steele, to be your lawfully wedded husband?"

Even through the veil, he saw her long, lush lashes flutter, sending two tears down her cheeks. She sank her teeth into her lower lip, then whispered, "I do."

She had hesitated for a fraction of a second, at most, but the infinitesimal tick in time was enough to cut him to the quick. Riley had hoped that Jade secretly wanted this marriage every bit as much as he did.

"I now pronounce you man and wife." The pastor turned to Riley and smiled. "You may kiss the bride."

Riley lifted the filmy fabric that veiled her face and laid it gently atop her hat. She seemed so small, so vulnerable, standing there and blinking up at him. Setting aside his own dashed hopes, he listened to his male instinct, which made him want to wrap her in a protective embrace and shield her from all harm, from all pain, for a lifetime. He'd tried for years to convince himself he didn't love her, wouldn't love her.

But he did.

Gently, Riley pressed his palms to Jade's cheeks and let his thumbs tilt her face up to receive his kiss. He'd intended it to be a light brush of lips, nothing more. But the moment his mouth met hers, Riley's spirit soared, and the gloom that had enveloped him since learning of Leah's illness lifted as if carried away by angels. "I once was lost, but now am found" had always been Leah's favorite line from the hymn "Amazing Grace." *Ironic*, Riley thought....

A male guest shouted, "Attaboy, Riley!" Another whistled. Everyone else applauded. And the noise shattered the moment. Riley ended the kiss and stood back, his palms still cupping Jade's lovely face. Slowly, her eyes fluttered open and met his. For a moment, he thought he saw love sparkling there amid the green and gray flecks that deepened the blue of her eyes, and his heart pounded harder still.

There was a chance that she loved him already. But even if he was mistaken, and what he saw in her eyes was relief that this arranged wedding was over at last, he would do everything in his power to take good care of her...

...for the rest of his life.

In the receiving line, Riley's sister-in-law told Jade that she had it on good authority the groom hadn't eaten a proper meal in days. "Is that right?" Jade asked, one brow high on her forehead.

Later, at the reception, Jade insisted on performing her first official wifely duty, and she forced Riley to sit at the picnic table. "Now, you wait right there," she instructed him, laughing. "Don't move. I mean it!"

She filled a plate with food prepared by the Ladies' Auxiliary and set it down before him, a polished knife and fork beside it, and tucked a linen napkin into his collar. "If you don't eat every bite," she said, winking, "I'll just have to force-feed you!"

He folded his arms across his chest. "Is that so?"

She inclined her head and grinned. "You think I won't do it?"

Riley glanced around at the friends and relatives who'd gathered to wish them well. Meeting Jade's eyes again, he shook his head. "Not a chance."

Jade looked around, too. She'd known most of these people her whole life. There was no reason for the flutter in her stomach, and so she sat down beside him. Never taking her eyes from his, she slowly and deliberately removed her gloves, one lace-covered finger at a time.

Ignoring the lazy heat smoldering in his dark eyes, she laid the gloves carefully on the tabletop, patting them flat and smooth before lifting the fork she'd placed beside his plate. Spearing a slice of ham, she leaned in close and whispered, "Open wide, Riley, and let the yummy food inside."

As though they were being controlled by some benign force, his lips parted. It amazed Riley that he so quickly did as he was told. But he saw the warmth glowing in her eyes as she slipped the chunk of meat past his teeth. The glow intensified as he closed his lips around the fork tines and clamped down, allowing her to withdraw the empty utensil. She pierced a piece of potato next, and this time, her own lips parted as she aimed the food at his open, waiting mouth.

Bite by bite, Jade fed Riley every scrap of food on his plate, stopping occasionally to hold a glass of sparkling water to his lips. She hadn't said a word through the entire meal, and neither had he.

But, oh, they'd communicated in those moments....

Unable to resist another minute, Riley wrapped his fingers around her delicate wrist and forced her to take the fork from his mouth. He chewed and swallowed, watching as the tip of her pink tongue slid over her lips, mimicking his movements. They were nose to nose when he said through clenched teeth, "For two cents, I'd kiss the livin' daylights out of you, right here, right now."

Emboldened by the intimacy of the meal, Jade looked away only long enough to open her tiny white satin purse. Withdrawing two coins, she slapped them on the table and, meeting his eyes, said in a mere whisper, "A wedding gift from me to you, Mr. Steele. Now, why don't you put your money where my mouth is?"

Everything in him warned Riley to stand up. To walk away from the table and pretend to visit with the wedding guests. But she looked so gorgeous sitting there, her curvy torso leaning close and her full, slightly parted lips beckoning him. What choice did he have but to lean forward himself and press his mouth to hers?

He hadn't expected the silken sigh that escaped her lungs, nor the soft purr that rumbled deep within her chest. Hadn't expected her hands to comb through his hair before coming to rest on his shoulders. Nor was he prepared for the sight of her thick-lashed, closed eyes, right there near his, or the way she tilted her head back, inviting him to have another taste.

Riley was aware, suddenly, that the atmosphere around them had changed. Grinning, he placed both hands on Jade's shoulders and gently pushed her away. "You don't know how it pains me to do that," he admitted, gazing longingly at her, "but it seems we've got ourselves an audience."

Jade's eyes fluttered open, and the gleam of passion they showed quickly became a teasing glimmer as she looked around and took note of the curious onlookers around them. She stood up, gathered her purse and gloves, and bent over at the waist so that she was eye to eye with Riley.

He nodded toward the dessert table. "I sure could go for a big, fat slice of cake."

She raised an eyebrow and left him sitting there alone, wide-eyed and gap-jawed.

A smattering of laughter floated around them as the guests who'd gathered disbanded. Jade pretended not to hear it, pretended the flush in her cheeks had been put there by the hot July day rather than the tantalizing kiss she and Riley had just shared.

She'd never behaved with such wild abandon!

But then, she'd never been Mrs. Riley Steele before....

They'll be calling you the Shameful Mrs. Steele, she told herself, and you'll deserve it, after that brazen behavior!

Halfway to the dessert table, she turned and looked over her shoulder, mildly stunned to find Riley still staring after her. Jade didn't know what possessed her to do it, but she held up her hand and sent him a flirty little wave, then added a merry wink and a saucy smile for good measure.

Put that in your pipe and smoke it was her silent message to him as she plopped a thickly iced slice of wedding cake onto her plate.

When all of the guests had gone and Fiona and Leah were tucked in bed, Jade and Riley sat together on the back deck, staring up at the stars. They were still wearing their wedding clothes, but both had kicked off their shoes.

"About that little scene at the table," Jade began, breaking the silence, "I—I don't know what came over me."

Chuckling under his breath, Riley said, "Darlin', I enjoyed every lip-smackin' minute of it. Believe me!"

Jade shook her head. "But what must people be thinking? What are they saying about the way I behaved?"

"How did you behave?"

"Like a wanton hussy, right there in front of the preacher and all our friends! We'll be the talk of—"

"I was the envy of every man in the yard," he said, "and I was proud as a peacock to have you paying so much attention to me."

"Really?"

"You betcha. But I have to warn you...."

"What?"

"Well, if I wasn't sure before, I'm sure now!"

"Sure? Sure of what?"

He clasped both hands behind his head and looked back up at the star-studded sky. "Nothing. Forget I mentioned it."

Jade sat up, planting both stockinged feet on the deck. "I didn't mean to put you on the spot that way, Riley. I mean...." She stared at the boards beneath her feet. "I mean, the deal was to get married. We never talked about what we'd do about the...about...." She took a deep breath. "I'm sorry."

"Jade, there's absolutely nothing to apologize for." He turned slightly to face her. "Honest."

She was crying quietly, and he didn't for the life of him know why. But it wasn't like Jade to give in to tears without a good reason. Riley remembered her moment of hesitation during the ceremony...were these tears connected somehow to that?

He hoped not. Because he wanted to believe that she'd consented so quickly to marry him not only for Leah and Fiona's sakes, but also because she loved him. Or, at the very least, that she believed she might love him...someday.

Riley wanted to promise her that nothing in life would ever make her cry again. But that was impractical, at best.

It had been a long time since a woman had stirred anything in him—since his high school graduation, to be exact, when Jade had given him that delicious kiss of congratulations. Her sassy behavior at the reception had reminded him of that night. Would she be worried that her actions had embarrassed him if she didn't care, if she didn't love him...or at least believe she could?

Riley got up and sat down beside her on the patio chaise, wrapping her in his arms. She melted against him like honey in hot tea, and it felt right, felt good, having her head nestled in the crook of his neck.

It had all happened so fast that neither of them had had a chance to sort it out, to make sense of it. But there would be time for that....

"That was some day, wasn't it?" Riley asked.

Nodding, Jade said, "Mmm-hmm."

"Good thing we only have to do something like that once. I don't think I'd survive another wedding."

She laughed softly. "Oh, it wasn't *all* bad. I got a couple of neat pot holders out of the deal."

Riley harrumphed. "No fair. All I got was a chef's hat that's two sizes too big for my head."

Sighing again, she sat up. "I'd better check on Leah."

"I'll come with you. We're in this together from here on out, remember?"

The moon had slipped behind a cloud, leaving just enough light to illuminate Jade's sweet, grateful smile. Oh, how he loved her! And one day soon, he'd have the freedom to admit it.

Somehow, he would show her that he'd loved her for years. He didn't know how, but Riley wasn't worried. He had the rest of his life to find a way. "Sit with me a minute longer," he suggested.

She snuggled against him as a clap of thunder sounded in the distance. "Looks like we're finally gonna get that storm the weatherman promised on the Fourth."

"Think it'll be an all-nighter?"

"I hope so. I love the sound of rain on the roof."

He hugged her closer. "That breeze feels good."

She tilted her face heavenward. "Smells good, too."

Gently, Riley kissed her. And, chuckling, he said, "Aren't you supposed to close your eyes when you kiss?"

"Hmm?"

"Isn't that what you gals say...that it's more romantic that way?"

Jade closed her eyes and puckered up. And stayed that way until he gave her another kiss. She combed her fingers through his hair, and he wondered how in the world he was going to keep his distance until they'd discussed the...*incidentals* of their marriage.

She wrapped her arms around him, pressing her lips to his bearded cheek. Riley's blood ran hot and fast; his pulse pounded.

"I've never been kissed that way before," she whispered.

Her admission kindled something in him, fanning the flames already burning in his heart. "Neither have I."

When his lips found hers again, her mouth softened beautifully for him. He felt her desire like the taut and trembling strings of a violin. And she'd make music with him now, if he asked it of her. *Nothing wrong with that,* Riley thought. *We're married, both legally and in the eyes of God....*

But he owed her more than that. Owed her the time and patience to believe in their love. And before that could happen, he had to earn it.

Lightning sliced the sky, brightening her features. If she didn't love him, Jade was certainly a talented actress, Riley thought. He'd never felt so treasured. Surrounded and overwhelmed by the obviousness of it, he buried his face in her hair. His eyes were moist with emotion when he whispered, "Ah, Jade...," a soft smile playing at the corners of his mouth.

Her next kiss came at the same moment as a violent clap of thunder, and Riley couldn't be sure which had caused the furious beating of his heart...nature in the sky, or nature in his arms.

"We'd better get inside," she said, "before we're electrocuted."

Chuckling, he held her at arm's length. "Too late for that," he said under his breath. "I can already feel the electricity...."

"What?"

He sighed. "Nothing.... I'm a lucky guy, is all."

"Lucky?" she repeated, standing up.

"How many men are so blessed?"

"Blessed?"

"Polly want a cracker?" he teased.

Jade held out her hand. "It's starting to rain. Let's go in, now."

"What's the matter, sugar?" he asked, closing the door behind them. "Afraid you'll melt?"

"No," Jade said, smiling. "I'm not *that* sweet."

They stepped into the hall. "Says you."

"Shh, you'll wake them."

"Sorry," he whispered. "I don't mean to behave like a hyperactive brat, but I can't help myself." He did a little jig outside Leah's door. "I'm happy, Jade. Really happy."

She took his hand. "Me, too, Riley. Me, too."

Then, pushing the door open, Jade held a finger over her lips, signaling silence.

"No need to tippy-toe," Leah said. "I'm awake."

"How ya doin', kid?" Riley asked first thing.

Leah patted the mattress. "Sit down here, both of you."

Jade perched on the edge of the bed while Riley leaned both palms on the footboard.

"Did you have a good time at the wedding?" Riley wanted to know.

"I—I had a...terrific time."

"Leah," Jade said, taking her hand, "what's wrong? Are you having trouble breathing?"

"Yes, I'm afraid I am."

Immediately, Jade reached for the oxygen tank and fastened the breathing tubes to Leah's nose. "There you go. Nice, deep breaths, now. Slow and easy, that's it."

"Thanks, sweetie."

Leah closed her eyes, and for a moment, Riley and Jade thought maybe she'd fallen asleep...or was unconscious....

Jade smoothed the hair from Leah's forehead as Riley tucked the covers up under her chin. Then, exchanging melancholy smiles, they headed for the door.

"Where...where do you...think you're going?"

"Get some sleep, Leah," Jade instructed.

"I will," she promised, "as soon as I say this...."

They moved closer, waiting.

"H-help me sit...up."

Riley got behind her and propped her upright. "There y'go, dollface. Go ahead, spill the beans."

"I just...wan...ted to...thank you." She managed a weary smile. "Y-you're swell."

"We know," Riley said, trying to sound lighthearted. "And we think you're swell, too."

"You're gonna be...gonna be great for...for Fiona. She's lucky, so lucky to have—"

"Leah," Jade interrupted her, joining the hug, "please be quiet. Just rest, okay?"

"Okay. I'll rest. But first...." She grabbed Riley's hand and pressed it to Jade's. "First I have to know...."

"Have to know what, Leah?" Jade asked around a sob.

"That you'll try. Just say...just say you'll try...."

Their eyes met, locked, and overflowed with tears. *Try? Try* what? was the question that passed between their gazes.

"Oh, Jade," Leah whispered. "Don't be sad. Please don't cry for me."

"All right, Leah. I won't. Not if you'll promise to go to sleep."

She gave a feeble nod and closed her eyes. "Okay. Okay, I'll sleep. And don't worry. I'm not gonna croak on your wedding day. What sort of memory would that be?"

Gently, Riley lowered her down. She was asleep even before they walked out the door.

In the kitchen, under the halo of the overhead lamp, Jade fell into Riley's waiting arms. "She's so weak and pale. It's as though she was holding on all this time, just to bring us together."

"Yeah," he choked out. "And now that we're married...."

Jade pressed her fingertips over his lips. "Shh. Don't say it. Please don't say it."

He held her tighter. "Think we oughtta call Peterson?"

She nodded against his chest. "Maybe...yeah. I don't know what he can do for her, but—"

"To make her more comfortable, you mean?"

Another nod. "Every breath is a struggle for her now. Why didn't I see it before? Was I so wrapped up in my own—?"

"Stop it, Jade." He held her at arm's length, his hands gripping her shoulders, and gave her a gentle shake. "We didn't see it because she didn't *want* us to see it."

She stepped out of his embrace and dialed the doctor's number, then quickly rattled off pertinent information about Leah's condition.

"What?" she nearly shouted into the receiver. "But you're the *specialist*...."

Riley watched her lovely face crinkle with anger.

"Tell me something—anything—that'll help till you get here!" she insisted.

A moment later, Jade hung up. "He's on his way."

Tenderly, he cupped her face in his hands. "What did he say to get you so riled up, kiddo?"

"He said there's nothing we can do...but pray."

Riley slid his arms around her, but this time, the hug was more for his benefit than Jade's. "Dear God," he said, "let her last till morning, because she'll want—"

A sob strangled the words from his throat.

"She'll want to see Fiona," Jade completed for him, "so she can say...."

"...good-bye," they said together.

Chapter Seven

On the Fourth of July, Ron Peterson had worn shorts and a T-shirt. When he stopped by on Saturdays and Sundays, he was usually in blue jeans and collarless shirts. Once, as an afterthought, he'd dropped in on his way to the track, outfitted like an Olympic runner. Without exception, the doctor had always looked as though he'd stepped straight from the pages of a catalog.

Not so tonight.

His maroon and gold football jersey didn't match his pale blue sweatpants. One white sock bore a popular tennis logo; the other was light green. His shoelaces were untied, he hadn't shaved, and his eyes were puffy. "I got here soon as I could," he said when Jade opened the door.

"I brewed a pot of coffee," she told him, stepping aside to let him in. "Care for a cup?"

The doctor nodded. "Double-double."

Jade smiled sadly. "Except for adding the coffee, your mug is all ready for you—two sugars, two creams, just the way you like it."

"She's a born caretaker, isn't she, Doc?"

It was the first time since his arrival that Riley had acknowledged Ron's presence. Like Jade, he'd changed out of his wedding garb.

"Yeah," Ron said, stuffing his hands into the pockets of his sweatpants, "a natural."

"It's no wonder she went into nursing...."

"Doesn't mean a thing," Ron said, running a hand through his hair. "Some of the worst housekeepers I've ever known have been nurses. Couple of my buddies married nurses, and about all the care they get from their wives happens on payday." His gaze seemed to take in everything...Jade's white-socked feet, Capri-length stretch pants, baggy T-shirt, and loose braid holding her blonde tresses back from her face. "Either you're a nurturer," he said, smiling, "or you aren't." Resting a hand on her shoulder, he added, "Jade would have been this way no matter what line of work she chose."

Jade frowned. "The coffee," she reminded the men, "is in the kitchen."

They followed her down the hall and seated themselves hastily at the table. Jade placed napkins and spoons beside their mugs, then slid a slice of cherry pie in front of each of them.

"We're sorry you couldn't make it to the wedding," Jade said to Ron, sitting down beside Riley. "How's your sister?"

His cheeks turned nearly as red as the fruit when he said, "She's fine, just fine."

Riley looked from Jade to Ron. "Your sister? What happened to her?"

Ron's blush deepened. "She...uh, her...um, her dog ran off. She's really attached to the mutt now that the kids are grown and on their own...."

Frowning slightly, Riley said, "Ah-ha. So, did you find him?"

"Her. Yes, we found her."

"Well, good. I'm glad she's safe and sound." Harrumphing, he added, "That's more than we can say for Leah."

Ron tucked in one corner of his mouth and met Jade's steady gaze. "You said her breathing has been labored?"

Jade nodded. "She was fine all afternoon. Fine this evening, too. And then...." Her voice faltered, then faded.

"She's sleeping now, I presume?"

"If you want to call it that."

He took a sip of coffee. "It's perfect," said Ron. "Like you."

And before either Jade or Riley could respond, he scooted his chair back and stood up. "I'll just go and have a look at her."

Jade started to join him, but he held a hand level with the tabletop. "No," he said, "you've had a—" He looked away, then cleared his throat. "You've had quite a day. Take it easy...while you can." And then he was gone.

"Well, well, well," Riley said, staring after him.

"Well, well, what?"

"Looks to me like the good doctor has a crush on you," he began, focusing on Jade, *"Mrs. Steele."*

She frowned. "He's here for Leah. Period."

"Mmm-hmm. And that's why he turned beet-red when you acknowledged that he missed the wedding."

She was about to ask him if he realized how ridiculous he sounded when Ron poked his head in the kitchen. "I think you guys better get in here...*now.*"

Riley leaped up so fast, his chair toppled over. The feet of Jade's chair screeched across the tiles like fingernails on a chalkboard. "What?" she asked breathily, joining Ron in the hall. "Is she—?"

"She's still with us," he said gravely, "but just barely...."

Leah looked so tiny and fragile in the middle of her queen-sized bed, it was difficult to determine where she ended and the starched white linens began. Lifting her hand, Leah reached for Riley's. "You have a birthday coming up. I haven't missed one of your birthdays since we were little kids."

He feigned a smile. "I'm too old to celebrate birthdays."

"Thirty-one isn't old, you big-bearded goof."

"I suppose not," he said with a shrug. "I guess I've lived alone so long, I feel ancient sometimes."

"Well, Fiona will be good for you, then. By the way, is she asleep?"

"For an hour already," Jade answered for him.

An almost indiscernible sigh escaped Leah's lungs. "Amazing, isn't it?"

"What's amazing?" Jade wanted to know.

Leah took Jade's hand, too. "The way God brings people together exactly when and where they need each other most." Her blue eyes bored hotly into Jade's, into Riley's. "You'll be good for each other, too."

Deliberately, they averted their gazes.

"I'm so happy Fiona will be growing up in a house with a mommy and a daddy who love each other."

Jade looked toward the door as Leah added, "It gives me an incredible sense of peace, knowing that."

Taking Leah's brush from the nightstand drawer, Jade perched on the edge of the bed and began gently running it through her thin, blonde strands. "That feels nice," Leah sighed, closing her eyes. "Reminds me of how my mother used to do it." And within seconds, it seemed, she was asleep.

The only sound in the room was the hushed hiss of oxygen.

The doctor had been standing by, quietly and unobtrusively, at the foot of the bed. "She seems to be resting peacefully," Jade said to him. "She must have allowed you to give her something for the pain."

He shook his head. "She said there were things she had to say, that morphine would cloud her judgment."

Suddenly, Leah opened her eyes. "That's right," she said. And then, "It's time."

"Time? Time for what?" Jade ventured. But it was obvious from her solemn expression that she already knew the answer. Jade bit her lip and Riley clamped his teeth together as Ron's fingers tightened around the bedpost.

"I have something...." Leah winced with pain. "...Something to tell the two of you...."

When Leah motioned for them to come closer, they got on their knees and leaned in toward her.

"Don't feel guilty anymore, okay?"

"Guilty?" Riley repeated, gently patting her hand. "What do we have to feel guilty about?"

"I've been watching...." Another grimace. "I've been... watching the both of you. You're so oppressed by guilt, it's a wonder you can stand up straight." She raised one eyebrow, lifted a frail hand, and pointed—first at Riley, then at Jade. "You have nothing to feel guilty *about*. The love you feel for each other? I've been *praying* for it. Get this through your hard heads: It's *God's will!*"

Jade stood up and straightened her shoulders, as if trying to summon the self-control required to hold back her tears. "Leah, rest, why don't you, so that—"

"Sweetie," Leah interrupted her, "you know that I love you, but...." She gave Jade's hand an affectionate squeeze. "All too soon, I'll be resting for eternity." Another squeeze and a smile, and then, "So shut up, will you, please, and let me have my say?"

Nodding, Jade smoothed back Leah's sparse bangs.

"There's a good girl—" Leah took a quavery breath and winced, squeezing her eyes shut and biting her lower lip.

"Let Ron give you something for the pain, kiddo."

A frail smile curved her pale lips. "No, Riley, and he already told you why."

When she coughed, Jade helped her sit up a bit, then held the plastic straw from her drinking glass between her parched lips. After two tiny sips, Leah lay back, breathless from the effort. "Now then, what was I saying?"

A second passed, maybe two, before she focused on Riley. "Would you wake Fiona, please? Bring her in here, so I can...."

Placing one hand on either side of her head, he leaned down and kissed her cheek. "Lie still now. I'll be right back." He pressed a second kiss to her forehead, then started for the door. When he hesitated in the doorway, Leah said, "Don't worry, I'll hang on...till you get back...."

Though Leah was smiling bravely, Jade knew that Ron had been right: the end was near. Very near. And the proof was in Leah's joyless monotone. It broke her heart to see such sadness in her friend's eyes. Jade wanted to fling herself across the bed and sob about the unfairness of it all.

But Leah deserved to be surrounded now by the same kind of strength she had displayed throughout her ordeal. "Did you hear Fiona tonight?" Jade asked, tidying Leah's covers. "Every time I read the word *beauty*, she pointed at Belle." Plumping the pillows, she continued in a bright, cheery voice, "She's so smart that it's a little scary. I mean...." She repositioned the water glass, the alarm clock, and the telephone on the nightstand. "...If she's recognizing words already, and she's barely two, well," she said, forcing a laugh, "I'd hate to be her kindergarten teacher!"

Riley entered the room, carrying the tousle-headed little blonde. One chubby cheek, still pink from the warmth of sleep, boasted brighter pink sheet wrinkles, and the other rested against his shoulder. He tenderly eased her under the covers to nestle beside her mother. "Mama," Fiona whimpered, snuggling close and rubbing her eyes with her fists. "Fee seepy...."

Leah drew her little girl close. "I know you're sleepy, sweet girl," she whispered, kissing her temple, "and you can go back to bed in a minute. Mama just wanted to hug you for a moment, that's all."

Jade had no idea how much time passed as the two of them cuddled quietly—Leah humming a sweet lullaby as she wound strands of flaxen baby hair around a forefinger, Fiona contentedly sucking her thumb—for she wanted to memorize this moment, wanted to fuse it to her memory for all time.

Grinning slightly, Fiona began to sing the words to her mother's tune: "Rock-a-bye bay-bee inna twee top...."

It must have been too sweet for Leah, because she bit her lip and closed her eyes, ending the song. "Aw, sweetie," she sighed, hugging Fiona tighter still. "My sweet girl.... Everything is going to be all right," she whispered into her daughter's ear. "I promise. Mama asked Jesus to take care of you, and He did. He made sure you'd have a mommy and a daddy to love you and watch over you after...when...."

Tears filled her eyes as she kissed Fiona's forehead. "Oh, how I love you, my sweet Fee. Mama's going to miss you, going to miss you so much!"

Suddenly, Leah cleared her throat. "Put her back to bed," she instructed Riley in a voice that belied her condition. "It's bad enough she's had to see me fall apart like an old toy. I don't want her to see what's about to happen."

He made a move to scoop the girl into his arms, but Ron stepped forward and laid a hand on Riley's forearm.

Nodding, he said in a soft, cracking voice, "I'll take her. You stay here with Leah."

A brusque yet sincere "Thanks, Doc" scraped from Riley's throat as he handed over Fiona.

The minute Ron and Fiona were out of the room, Riley cupped Leah's face in his hands. His voice trembled when he spoke. "You know what you remind me of?"

She gave a fragile laugh. "A dishrag? A wet noodle? A—"

He placed a finger over her lips. "Shh.... I'll tell you what you remind me of. Remember my mother's Christmas angel?"

Nodding weakly, Leah smiled. "The one she topped the tree with every year?"

"That's the one."

"I always thought she was so beautiful...."

"And she was," he agreed. "She was really nothing more than a china doll with a halo and wings and a white dress. And her smile...sometimes I'd stare at her so long, I imagined her lips were moving. Even now, I can't help but—"

"Careful," Leah teased, "or your tough guy routine will be exposed for the sham that—" Her words, caught on the ragged edge of pain, stuck in her throat. "Oh, Lord," she prayed aloud. "It hurts, guys. Hurts bad...."

"I'll get Ron," Jade said. "I'm sure he brought something to ease the pain."

"No!" Leah rasped. "I want to be awake and aware, right to the bitter end...."

Riley straightened and turned his back to the bed. Jade watched as he ran both hands through his hair, then stood up, fingers clasped at the base of his skull. She wanted to go to him, throw her arms around him, console him as he'd consoled her so many times. But there would be time for that later. Right now, Leah needed her more.

Climbing onto the bed, Jade stretched out beside Leah and held her in her arms. "We're here," she said, hugging her gently, "right here with you, all the way."

One corner of Leah's mouth turned up in a weak smile. "Did you have onions for supper?"

Despite the moment, Jade grinned. "Leave it to you to make light of a heavy situation."

"Well, the joke's on you," Leah teased, "'cause I'm not goin' anywhere just yet. I promised not to die on your wedding day, and, by golly, I won't."

She was quiet for a long moment, and then she said, "Your turn."

"For what?" Riley asked.

"A promise." She didn't wait for them to respond. Instead, Leah said, "I know you'll take good care of Fiona… but I want you to take care of each other, too."

"Done," Riley said without hesitation.

"Ditto," Jade agreed.

Leah exhaled a long, relieved sigh. The furrows that had wrinkled her brow smoothed as if her pain had been overpowered by their simple, heartfelt pledge.

"Thanks, guys," she sighed, patting their hands.

It was happening right before their eyes, and they were helpless to prevent it. "Oh, Leah," Jade cried, gathering her closer. "I love you…."

With her eyelids fluttering, Leah met Jade's gaze. "Love you, too, sweetie." And, turning to Riley, she added, "You, too…."

"Yeah, yeah," he said, trying unsuccessfully to smile past his own tears. "Let's put a cork in all this mushy stuff, shall we?"

She looked at each of them long and hard, then smiled serenely. "Is it after midnight yet?"

She was too weak to lift her head and read that the clock said 10:30. "Almost seven minutes after," Jade said.

"Good, 'cause I promised not to go toes-up on your wedding day...." Then, "It's been quite a life, hasn't it, guys?"

"That it has, kiddo," Riley said, meeting Jade's gaze. In a broken voice, he began to recite 1 Corinthians 15:51–52. "*Lo! I tell you a mystery....*"

"*...In the twinkling of an eye...,*" Jade continued, "*the trumpet will sound....*"

"*...And the dead will be raised imperishable,*" they prayed together, "*and we shall be changed.*"

Tears trickled from the corners of Leah's eyes. "Don't let Fee forget me."

"We won't," they assured her.

They clung together for those last moments, forming a three-way hug as they'd done so many times in the past.

"It's...it's been...pure pleasure," Leah sighed, "loving you both, having you love me."

When her eyes fluttered shut, they knew her spirit had left her, yet Jade and Riley continued to hold her for a long, silent moment, their tears dampening the soft cotton flannel of her blue-flowered nightgown.

"The pleasure was ours," Riley said. "All ours...."

If Leah had said it once, she'd said it a hundred times: "Wakes are a barbaric pagan ritual. I don't want people gawking at what used to be me when I'm gone. And I don't want 'em sending flowers that I won't be able to enjoy!"

So it was no surprise that she'd arranged a private memorial service, to take place immediately before the burial. "Amazing Grace" played in the background as the preacher's booming voice recited her favorite Bible verse: 1 Corinthians 10:13. "*No temptation has overtaken you that is not common to man. God is faithful, and he will not let you be tempted beyond your strength, but with the temptation will also provide the way of escape, that you may be able to endure it.'"* Leah had lived by that verse and, as it turned out, died by it, too.

She'd thought of everything, right down to her black-and-white photographic portrait, which appeared beside her obituary in the Saturday edition of the *Baltimore Sun*. The plain, gray casket, picked out and paid for long before she'd left them, was slowly lowered into the deep, dark rectangle carved into the earth beside John's grave. And the headstone she'd commissioned read simply, "Leah Marie Jordan, 1978–2008, beloved wife, mother, friend."

"It's supposed to be raining," Jade said glumly as they stood there, stock-still and stiff, watching the groundskeepers prepare to fill the gaping hole. "It's supposed to be bleak and cold...ugly as death itself."

Riley scanned the lush, green cemetery lawn. Ancient, stately oaks shaded cherubs and archangels carved from white marble that guarded the tombs. And in the branches of birch and willow trees, birds tried to outsing one another. Flowers of every color and variety bloomed along neatly trimmed hedgerows that were home to chorusing crickets.

A sweet, summer breeze riffled Jade's blonde hair, lifting it like a butter-yellow cape that fluttered behind her. The sunshine shimmered down, its golden fronds stroking them like the warm, reassuring fingers of a loving parent.

It was anything *but* a dreary day.

"Leah planned everything else," Riley said, smiling. "If she could have ordered the weather, it would have been a day just like this."

Jade heaved a deep sigh. "I suppose you're right. It's just that I'm so tired of being stoic, of pretending everything's all right, of behaving like I'm willing to go along with...." She pointed at Leah's grave. "...with *that*."

He slipped an arm around her waist. "Come on. Let's go and pick up Fiona."

Jade let him walk her to the car. "She's a smart little thing. She's sure to know."

Nodding, he said, "For a while. But she's awfully young...."

She stepped back as he opened the passenger door for her. "Well," she said, "we'll make sure she never forgets. We'll show her pictures, and tell her stories, and—"

He wrapped her in his arms and held her tight, his tears dampening her hair, hers soaking into his shirt. "'Course we will," he sobbed. "'Course we will."

A man in a dark suit stepped up beside them and removed his aviator-style sunglasses. "Sorry to intrude," he said, pocketing the shades. He extended his right hand. "I'm Jules Harris, Leah's attorney." He shook Riley's hand, then Jade's, and held out the manila envelope he'd been holding in his other hand. "She asked me to wait until after the funeral to give you this."

For a moment, Jade merely stared at the envelope, as if she expected it might explode. When she finally accepted it, she frowned slightly. "It feels like a DVD or a CD...."

"That's exactly what it is," Harris said, running a hand through his dark hair. "Don't ask me what's on it, because I haven't looked." He glanced toward the navy sedan parked across the way and gave a little wave to the red-headed woman in the passenger seat. "Well," he said, putting the sunglasses back on, "I'd better go." He smiled. "My wife's eight months pregnant, and if I know her, she's in desperate need of a ladies' room."

His wasn't smiling when he added, "Leah was some terrific lady. Wish I'd known her better...and under better circumstances...."

Riley nodded.

Jade smiled sadly.

Jules started to leave, then stopped and faced them again. "She thought the world of you two. But I guess you already knew that...."

Another nod from Riley.

A second sad smile from Jade.

Without another word, he turned and walked away.

Jade slumped into the passenger seat, and Riley closed the door. They drove back to Leah's house—the one she'd signed over to them—in total silence.

The lawyer's mustard-yellow envelope sat on the seat between them....

Riley had moved a few of his things into the main bathroom, hung a few shirts and several pairs of trousers in the hall closet, and stuffed some jeans, rag-knit socks, and colorful T-shirts in the antique bureau in the den.

He slept on the couch in the family room, which was too short and too narrow to provide a decent night's rest. But he couldn't bring himself to sleep in the master bedroom, in the brass bed that had been Leah's. He thought about bringing his own mattress from home, but it would still be Leah's room....

The big, ugly hospital bed was gone now, and when several attendants from the medical supply company had come to pick it up, they had also taken away the tanks and clear plastic tubing that had carried oxygen to Leah's exhausted lungs.

Still, the memory of her was everywhere....

She smiled at him from the family portrait taken of her and John and baby Fiona. Her favorite books filled the shelves in bookcases that flanked the flagstone fireplace, and her thriving houseplants stood in every corner and on the hearth. The pink-and-cream afghan she'd knitted in her high school home economics class was draped over the arm of the loveseat. Her collection of ceramic vases adorned end tables, the mantle, and window ledges. The well-worn family Bible she'd always kept within easy reach lay on the coffee table.

And the plastic case holding the DVD sat atop the TV.

Riley and Jade had been too tired that first night to watch it. And in the two days that had passed since, one thing or another—Fiona's out-of-character fussiness, friends stopping by to pay their last respects, phone calls from people who hadn't made it to the memorial service—kept them from seeing the last-minute message Leah had recorded for them.

How she'd recorded it in her condition and without anyone knowing was anybody's guess. But Leah had thought of everything else. Riley suspected that when they finally got around to watching it, that question, too, would be answered.

Any minute now, Jade would finish up in the kitchen. Fiona was sound asleep—she had been for nearly an hour now. There would be no more excuses, no more procrastinating. Difficult as it would be, they would watch it. Together.

As Riley prepared the DVD player and the TV, a piece of paper fluttered to the floor and landed face-up on the carpet. Immediately, he recognized Leah's oversized, child-like script. The date above the salutation read January 5.

It's August tenth, he thought. *Had she really started preparing for the end that far in advance?* Squatting, he picked up the single sheet of pale, pink stationery and read, "Dearest Jade,...."

Riley read no further.

Standing up, he slid the disk and accompanying note back into the envelope, which he was about to put back on top of the TV when Jade entered the room. She took one look at the package and said, "I guess we've put it off long enough."

"That's what I was thinking when I found this." He handed her the envelope. "It's addressed to you."

She turned it over, then over again. "But there's no writing on it. How do you know it's addressed—"

"There's a note inside. When I read 'Dearest Jade,' I put it right back." Fighting tears, he rubbed his beard with his hand. *What in tarnation is wrong with you? he demanded of himself. It isn't as though you've never dealt with death before....* He'd lost a beloved grandparent, an elderly aunt. When he was ten, his favorite cousin died in a car accident, and a little more than a year ago, his college roommate had passed on after a month-long bout with pneumonia. Disgusted with his weakness, Riley shook his head. "I'll be in the kitchen. If you need anything, just—"

"Please don't leave," Jade whispered, extending her hand. Grinning slightly, she added, "We've always shared everything. I see no reason to start keeping secrets just 'cause we're married now."

Returning her smile, he gave her hand a little squeeze and sat down beside her on the sofa.

Jade dumped the envelope contents into her lap. "I'm doubly glad Fiona was sound asleep when I checked on her just now." She rolled her eyes. "If I thought she might see my reaction...."

Placing the DVD on the coffee table, she held the letter in trembling hands. "'Dearest Jade,'" she read aloud, "'I got some bad news this morning, and if my suspicions are correct, it's going to affect Fiona, and Riley, and you, too.'"

Jade covered her face with one hand. "I can't believe what a weakling I've been through this whole thing." She held out the note. "Would you mind?"

"What makes you think I'll do any better?" Riley asked, one side of his mouth lifting in a sad grin. But he took the note from her, smoothed it flat, and picked up where she'd left off.

"'You know how terrible I've always been at things like this. That's why I've made a little movie of sorts for you to watch. And if you're reading this, it means I was right...and the worst has already happened. (Well, not the worst; the worst would be if something happened to my sweet little Fee.)'"

A ragged sigh escaped his lungs as he pinched the bridge of his nose with his thumb and forefinger. "'Anyway,'" he continued, "'please don't be sad, because I'll be watching you....'"

He stopped, a pent-up sob preventing him from reading the last words aloud.

"'...from heaven,'" Jade finished.

"'Love you always, Leah.'"

Jade held the note to her chest and bit her lower lip. "I'm almost afraid to look at the recording," she said, folding the note neatly. She took a deep breath. "But knowing Leah, there's a list of instructions five feet long on it." Sighing again, she stood up resolutely and turned on the TV and DVD player. Holding the disk in one hand, she said, "We may as well get it over with, right?"

Riley nodded. He scooted to the edge of the sofa, preparing to stand. "You want me to fix you a cup of tea or something first?"

She smiled understandingly, lovingly. "No, but we'll probably need something soothing when it's over...."

Chapter Eight

The bright-blue TV screen flickered, then gave way to a hodgepodge of black-and-white haze before the fuzzy image of Leah's family room came into view.

She'd aimed the camera at the couch, where Jade and Riley were sitting now. "Bear with me...," came her bubbly voice from behind the tripod. The picture clouded further, then came into sharp focus. "There. I think that's it...."

A moment later, she hop-skipped in front of the lens and flopped onto the center sofa cushion, her blonde waves spilling over her shoulders and catching the sunlight filtering in through the windows. She was wearing her customary violet eye shadow and black mascara to highlight her beautiful blue eyes, along with a coat of coral lipstick to emphasize her perky smile. A sheer cover of powder did nothing to hide the freckles that had always dotted the bridge of her nose, and when she smiled, a dimple dented her right cheek.

"She looks beautiful," Riley said, smiling wistfully. "So healthy and—"

Leah spread her arms wide and wiggled her well-arched brows. "Well, sweetie, feast your eyes. I don't imagine you've seen me looking like this in a long, long time!"

Sitting cross-legged, Leah leaned elbows on knees and took a deep breath. "Well, now. Where to begin...?" Squinting, she tapped a forefinger against her chin, then rolled her eyes. "At the beginning, right?" She giggled. "Okay, here goes. I saw the doctor today...."

"She never could sit still when she was nervous," Jade observed, smiling sadly. "Just look at her fidgeting...."

"Anyway," Leah continued, "he seems to think there's no hope for me." She held both arms akimbo again. "As you can see, I've already lost about twenty pounds. Under other circumstances, I'd be giddy with glee to be stuffing my carcass into size six jeans, but...."

Riley bowed his head. "God bless her take-it-on-the-chin attitude, huh?"

Jade nodded in silent agreement.

"From the moment I learned about the, uh, the cancer," she said, looking away from the camera, "I've been giving a lot of serious thought to Fiona's future." She wasn't smiling when she added, "I came up with this idea, see, and I've been praying and praying about it, and I believe my plan has God's blessing...."

Fiona's voice, coming from her room down the hall, interrupted them. "I'll get her," Riley offered. "You go ahead and watch the rest. I'll catch the end later."

Ordinarily, she would have stopped him, would have gone to Fiona herself. But something about Leah's choice of words made Jade believe this film had been intended for her eyes only.

The temporary distraction caused her to miss the part when Leah heaved a deep sigh and folded both hands in her lap. But by the time Riley had gone down the hall and into Fiona's room, Leah was looking straight into the lens again. "I won't pussyfoot around, Jade," she said in that no-nonsense way of hers. "We both know how you feel about Riley."

You were right; the note was addressed to you, be-cause the recording wasn't intended for Riley's eyes...or ears. Her heart hammering, she grabbed the remote and quickly turned down the volume.

"If you weren't so proud and stubborn, *he'd* know it, too, because you would have told him by now. And more than likely," she said, wagging a finger in the air, "you'd be married and have a couple of kids already!"

Children? Her and Riley's? The image of it, sweet and warm, flashed in her mind's eye, making her heart beat faster.

Leah's voice called her attention back to the TV screen. "You're a sweetie," she was saying, rolling her eyes, "but you sure can be frustratingly bullheaded sometimes!"

"Puppy to the root," Ron had said....

Jade smiled as Leah gave a little laugh. "Like I said, I have this plan, see—one I'm certain will be best for ev-erybody." She tilted her head slightly and tucked in one corner of her mouth. "Knowing you and Riley, it's gonna take a while for either of you to admit it, but, trust me, you'll thank me in the end."

I hope you're resting easy, Leah, because everything went exactly according to your plan, Jade admitted to her-self. Riley and I are married, your house is legally ours....

Leah propped the soles of her shoes on the edge of the sofa cushion and smiled, hugging her legs. "So, you're married! Isn't it just the most wonderful thing?" She bobbed her head from side to side, grinning like a school-girl as she said in singsong, "There you are in your own little house, with the baby sleeping down the hall, waiting for your good-lookin' husband to come home from work.

"And he's across town, watching the clock and count-ing the minutes till he can go home to his little family...." She heaved a wistful sigh. "It's so-o-o ro-*man*-tic...."

Leah retied the laces on one of her sneakers, patting the neat bow. "Can you hear that?" she asked, looking down the hall toward the bedrooms. "No, I don't suppose you can. Well," she whispered, her gaze directed at the camera again, "Fiona is waking up from her nap, so I'm going to have to make this short and snappy.

"I hope I had the presence of mind to tell you in the, uh, at the end, that you shouldn't feel guilty about loving Riley. And he shouldn't feel guilty about loving you, either."

Leah had said pretty much the same thing on her deathbed. But how had she known they'd feel this way?

"I've known the pair of you a lifetime," she said, as if cued by Jade's thoughts, "and I'd be surprised if you *weren't* feeling guilty. So, stop it. Stop it right now! It's okay to need each other. In fact, it's better than okay. It's *good*. Really, it is!"

Leah went into singsong mode again. "You're probably thinking there's something bad about wanting a happy future with Riley because it seems selfish or self-centered to want that, considering, well, y'know...how I'm *dead* and all. But Jade, honey, that's nonsense, just plain nonsense. The love you feel for Riley is anything *but* selfish or self-centered. In fact, it's proof of your loyalty to me. I mean, you went through with the wedding, without knowing for sure if he loves you...if he'll *ever* love you...to fulfill my last wish." She held out her hands and used her fingers to draw quotation marks in the air at the words "last wish." "You wouldn't be looking at this movie if you hadn't, 'cause I instructed Jules to give you the envelope *only if* you and Riley got married before I... before...." She took a breath. "Before I died.

"There. I said it." A little giggle popped from her mouth, though Jade noted that the smile didn't quite make it to her eyes. "That wasn't as tough as I thought it'd be."

Completely straight-faced, she gazed into the camera lens. "Things won't be as tough as you think they'll be, either. You have my word on it. Because whether you know it yet or not, Riley loves you. Always has, always will."

Jade rolled her eyes. *Yeah, right....*

"Don't roll your eyes, missy. You'll see...I'm right. Besides, he told me so!"

Jade could only shake her head in awe as Leah suddenly stood up, crossed the room, and disappeared behind the camera. She leaned in front of it for a moment, her lively, loving face filling nearly the entire TV screen. "And a second 'besides'...you have *God's* word on it!"

The grainy snow that had preceded the recording returned, followed by an annoying hiss and crackle. Jade hit the remote's Stop button, then turned off the TV and DVD player. Later, when Riley and Fiona were asleep, she'd sneak the package into Leah's room and watch it again....

"Our girl completely unmade her crib," Riley announced, marching into the room with Fiona on his shoulders. "But not to worry," he said, wincing as she filled her hands with his hair, "we put it back together, didn't we, Fee?"

At Leah's suggestion, they'd both been calling her Fee, practically since the day Jade had come back from California. She'd never actually *heard* Leah telling Fiona to call them Daddy and Mommy, but how else was she to explain why the little girl referred to them in exactly that way?

As for herself, despite how sweet it felt to have the title of mother associated with her name, Jade had always corrected the toddler. "Jade," she'd say sweetly, one hand pressed to her chest. And, pointing at Leah, she'd add, "*There's* Mama." Until now, she'd thought Leah's annoyance was proof she didn't like another woman scolding her child, even in the gentlest voice.

Riley, on the other hand, appeared completely comfortable with his role as surrogate father, so natural and confident that it seemed he thrived on the label and the duties that went hand and hand with it. Like a boy shoving to be first in line at the movie counter, he always volunteered eagerly to feed Fiona. Every day, as Jade had bathed Leah or massaged lotion into her skin to prevent bed sores or changed the linens, she could count on Riley to be there, entertaining Fiona. He didn't even mind changing dirty diapers! When Fee called him "Dah-dee" in her exuberant, loving way, he positively glowed. And Jade had to admit, the title *fit*.

As she watched him now, blowing air bubbles on Fiona's chubby cheek and provoking gales of baby giggles, she loved him. Could Leah have been right about Riley loving her, too? Or had he said it because it was what Leah needed to hear?

Perhaps romantic love would one day be a part of their marriage. But even if it wasn't—and they continued to live as they'd been living, devoting themselves to Fiona—it would be a deep and abiding relationship. No doubt *thousands* of couples had gladly settled for that. How could their relationship be an exception, when it had been built on a godly foundation?

But what was it that William Wilde Curringer had said? Something like, "The thing that really separates human beings is the gap between what each of them wants...and what each is willing to settle for."

She'd been saying this an awful lot lately: *That should be enough. So why isn't it enough?*

❧

It had been a week since Jade viewed Leah's video, and she hadn't been herself since. Riley couldn't help but wonder what message Leah might have taped that would have such a strangely sobering effect on Jade's normally upbeat and energetic personality. One thing was certain: Leah had intended it for Jade, and Jade seemed resolved to honor that intention.

It was more proof, as he saw it, that Riley's girls (as they'd often affectionately referred to themselves) sometimes shared things that didn't include him. Because even if they *had* tried to explain why some things got them giggling and other things started their eyes to leaking, he had a feeling he wasn't supposed to understand....

Besides, to whom had they turned for answers to their "really important" questions, such as whether or not boys *really* liked girls to wear makeup and fingernail polish, as the teen magazines claimed? And when their feelings were hurt or they were scared, to whom had they gone for comfort and protection?

That Leah would make a movie just for Jade hurt, but admitting it hurt worse. The confession made him feel small and shallow and, worst of all, like a milksop....

Riley had prayed on it long and hard and had come to the conclusion that the best way to deal with his feelings was *not* to deal with his feelings. He would concentrate on Fiona. And on Jade, which wouldn't be difficult—she'd been the center of his life since that night he'd picked her up at the airport.

Leah's illness had required round-the-clock care, and that had put her front and center, whether she liked it or not. But *Jade* had been the one to give that care—whenever, wherever, and however long it was needed—and she'd given joyfully, generously, and without a word of complaint. He'd watched her smile as she hand-fed

Leah when she was too weak to feed herself; he'd heard her laughing and making jokes, as if watching a loved one die was no hardship at all.

But, of course, it had been hard. Not just the back-breaking day-to-day work that was necessary to nurse a terminally ill patient, but the fact that *this* terminally ill patient had been Jade's lifelong friend, perhaps more beloved than a flesh-and-blood sister. Yet she had saved her tears for the moments when Leah couldn't see them, and Riley greatly admired her for that.

Jade stood no more than five feet two inches and weighed in at barely 115. And yet, she had more strength of character than any man he could name—and at times like this, that included him.

He'd taken a course in veterinary school—"Dealing with Grief," or something along those lines—to learn to help people cope with the loss of a beloved pet. Only when an individual acknowledged how he felt about death could his healing begin. Good advice was good advice, no matter who gave it, to whom it was given, or why.

Riley's first experience with loss had come at the age of ten, when his grandfather had died. Family members and close friends had celebrated together after the funeral, leaving him to wonder what all the good cheer was about. Shouldn't they have been crying? Shaking their fists at the heavens, demanding to know why Grandpa had been taken from them? If they'd loved him, wouldn't it show by the depth of their mourning?

Nearly a week had passed before the angry and confused boy had posed those very questions to his grandmother. There had been tears in her eyes and a loving smile on her face when she said, "Ah, but there's good reason for the joy y'saw, Riley, m'boy. Yer gran-da has gone on to a better world, where he can sing with the angels an' talk with Jesus, face-to-face."

His grandfather had loved to sing, and the life of Jesus had always been one of his favorite topics.

"There's no more pain in his bones, 'cause in Paradise, y'see, there ain't no sufferin', and man is perfect for the first time in his life."

Gran had been fifty-one when the title of widow had been forced upon her, and though Riley knew for a fact that she'd been asked, his Gran never remarried. Many years after his grandfather's death, her still-inquisitive grandson had asked why. "Oh, but 'twouldn't be fair, 'cause I'd always be comparin' the poor bloke to yer gran-da, and since there's no way he could measure up, he'd be miserable!"

She missed her man. The proof was in her eyes, in her voice, in the spellbinding stories she'd tell when a chip in a tabletop or a tree in the yard or a song on the radio reminded her of a moment in the life they'd shared. She seemed content to focus on their years together rather than the moment of his death.

Maybe that's what Jade needed—an opportunity to talk about Leah, about the good times the three of them had shared...about the sorrow he and Jade shared now that they'd lost her.

Minutes later, he barged into the kitchen and found Jade at the sink, holding her face in her hands. "What's wrong, kiddo?"

She nodded at the table, which she had set for supper. On the table sat three placemats, three napkins, and three sets of silverware. Fiona's baby cup and matching plate and spoon lay on the tray of her high chair. "I set a place for Leah," she said, her voice cracking. "I must be losing my mind. It's the second time I've done that since...."

Hugging her from behind, Riley rested his chin on her shoulder. "Don't worry, 'cause if you're goin' nuts, you'll have company. Not more than an hour ago, I walked into her room to see if she was hungry."

She turned her tear-streaked face to him.

"And a few days ago," he said, focusing on Leah's place setting, "I could have sworn I heard her calling my name."

Jade collapsed in a kitchen chair. "I know the mind can play tricks at a time like this. I took a course in grief management, and—"

"Grief management," he repeated dully.

She sighed and rattled off the list: "Anger, sadness, depression, hopelessness, guilt, loneliness, helplessness, frustration.... I know not everyone goes through every stage; I know we don't go through them in order...but at some point, you have to get to the hardest one."

"Acceptance," he said quietly.

Jade propped both elbows on the table as Riley sat down across from her. Resting her chin in one hand, she said, "Good thing I'm not being graded, 'cause I'm not doing this very well, am I?"

He tucked a few strands of her hair behind her ear. "You're doing fine. *We're* doing fine. It's been only a couple of weeks, and for Fiona's sake, we're living in her house, surrounded by her things. Give yourself a little cred- it where credit is due. You see her everywhere, all day long...." Riley paused, then said pointedly, "Do you realize this is the first time we've actually talked about her?"

Her eyes met his. "I suppose you're right."

He raised both eyebrows. "You *suppose*?" Tenderly, he touched her cheek. "Remember what I told you the night you agreed to marry me...?"

A half-grin brightened her face, telling him she knew exactly what line of dialogue he was referring to. But "Hmm...I'm not exactly sure" is what she said.

Riley chuckled. "Well then, let me refresh your memory. I said we'd get along fine, as long as you—"

"—continued being so agreeable."

"Exactly."

"Then I have a piece of advice for you, Mr. Steele...."

He read the teasing glint in her eyes and matched it with one of his own.

"I'll be agreeable...when you're right."

"Seems to me the true test of a wife's devotion is to be agreeable...when her husband is wrong."

Standing up, Jade tucked in one corner of her mouth. "I never did like tests," she said humorlessly, picking up the extra place setting.

He came to stand beside her, combing his fingers through her silken locks and kissing the top of her head. "It's going to take a long time, I think."

"What?"

"Getting used to life without her."

Jade wiped her eyes with a paper napkin. "I feel like such a monster," she said, slamming doors and drawers as she put away Leah's plate and silverware. "Why didn't I call her more often? Why didn't I visit more than once a year? Why—"

"I was right here," Riley said, "and I saw her only a couple times a year...."

"At least you called a couple times a week."

"So did you." Then, "Wait...how'd you know that?"

"Because," she blurted out, "she told me so."

"When?"

Biting her lower lip, Jade looked away. "It wasn't enough...." She huffed and shook her head. "I didn't have her responsibilities. I could've done more."

"Leah was happy, Jade. She didn't need us in the same way after she married John."

"That's exactly what I'm talking about. Why didn't I visit more *after* John's accident?"

"You stayed with her for more than a month after his funeral, as I recall."

She shrugged. "What's your point?"

Three, perhaps four, feet of space separated them, so why did she seem miles away? "Jade, honey, look at me," he said softly.

A second passed before she did as he asked.

He held out his arms, fully expecting her to take those three or four steps and press up against him, as she'd done earlier.

Instead, she walked to the stove and began lifting lids, stirring the contents of each pot and pan. "Well," she said in an artificially cheerful voice, "supper is ready. Would you mind getting Fee for me?"

"Jade, don't—"

"She shouldn't need a diaper change. I checked her before I put her in the playpen a few minutes ago."

"—Don't shut me out," he finished.

"I—I'm not. It's just...I can't talk about it right now, okay?"

"Can't? Or won't?"

She turned her back to him and began filling serving bowls. "Fee had a doozy of a nap this afternoon. She'll probably eat like a horse!"

"Yippee," he muttered, then plodded from the room.

"So, how's married life?" Jade's sister Amber wanted to know.

Jade recalled their near-silent dinner the night before.

Amber handed her little boy another cookie. "I always knew the two of you would get together eventually."

Gently, Jade wiped a blob of jelly from the corner of Fiona's mouth and raised an inquisitive brow. "You did?"

"Didn't everybody?"

"Everybody...?"

Laughing, Amber rolled her blue eyes. "Well, it was never a big secret, was it, that you and Riley were crazy about each other? I mean, we used to make guesses about when he'd pop the question."

She tucked in one corner of her mouth. "'We' who?"

Grinning mischievously, Amber shrugged. "Mom, Dad, me...." She counted on her fingers. "Riley's folks, and his brother, Pete...." She leaned forward and giggled. "I *love* how-we-met stories. But since you guys have practically known each other since the cradle, I guess I'll have to settle for a when-I-knew-I-loved-him story. Come on, you can tell me. When did you know Riley was Mr. Right?"

Jade met Amber's steady gaze and smiled. "I think I always knew."

Her sister's hand shot into the air, two fingers forming the victory sign. "Ha! I was right!" But she sobered suddenly, laying a hand atop Jade's. "Listen...I know you miss Leah. She was a great lady." She patted her hand. "But so are you. You helped make her last days as happy and comfortable as possible." She held up a finger and added, "And let's not forget that you've changed your whole life to grant her last wish!"

"What makes you think—"

"Leah swore me to secrecy. Remember that time I came to visit her, and you went to the kitchen to make sandwiches? Well, that's the day she told me. I've always looked up to you and admired you, Jade, but never more than now. What you did for Leah...well, you're a hero in the truest sense of the word."

"You ought to concentrate a little less on me and a little more on your hostess duties," Jade teased, blushing as she pointed at her empty mug. "I've been out of coffee for nearly two whole minutes."

Damp eyes and trembling smiles made it clear that, pleasant though it was, hot, fresh coffee was not what the sisters were most grateful for....

Chapter Nine

After leaving Amber's, Jade decided that she *would* pull herself together. It hadn't been a hard decision to make, really, once she got on her knees and asked for God's help. She hadn't been in prayer a full minute when the question flitted through her head: *What would Leah do under similar circumstances?*

The answer came almost as quickly. She'd throw back her shoulders and square her chin, that's what, and keep on keeping on, just as she had when her family was taken from her, when John died, when she learned her own death was certain. She'd endured so many losses in her short life, and she'd done it matter-of-factly, with courage and fortitude Jade had seen no one else exhibit, to date.

"Forgive me, Father," she prayed, "for forgetting what You instructed us to do through the words of Paul in Philippians 2:14: *'Do all things without grumbling or questioning.'*" Next, she quoted Psalm 130:7: *"'For with the LORD there is steadfast love, and with him is plenteous redemption.'"* Secure in the knowledge that Jesus had atoned for her sin of self-centeredness, Jade got to her feet as the back doorbell chimed.

"Ron," she said, smiling as he stepped into the kitchen, "what a nice surprise. What brings you by?"

"I was just in the neighborhood and thought I'd say hi." He hesitated, as if he didn't know what to say next. "It's good to see you. How've you been?"

"Fine." And for the first time since Leah's burial, she meant it.

"You look a little pale, if you don't mind my saying so...."

She waved his concern away. "Can I fix you a glass of something?"

"That'd be nice." He settled himself at the kitchen table. "Where's Riley?"

"At the clinic." She sent him a wry grin. "Life must go on, or so the sages say...."

Ron nodded. "And how's Fiona?"

Jade put two napkins and two glasses of fresh-squeezed lemonade on the table, then sat down across from him. "It's amazing, really, how resilient children are. I mean, it's obvious she realizes something is drastically different, because she asks for Leah all the time. But she doesn't seem the least bit sad. I like to think it's because she knows her mommy has gone to a better place that's free of pain, and—"

The look on his face stopped her. Jade didn't know him well enough to determine if it was outright anger or utter sadness that had furrowed his brow. Jade leaned an elbow on the table, resting her chin in her fist. "We haven't known each other long, Ron, but what we went through together because of Leah...." She smiled slightly. "I like to think the one positive thing to come of it was that you and I became friends."

He met her gaze and tucked in a corner of his mouth. "That's good to hear. Because since Leah died, I keep asking myself what I could have done differently...if I overlooked something...whether I accepted the claims of 'science' too soon...."

"I saw her chart; all the tests said the same thing: There was nothing more on earth you could have done for her."

"Nothing on earth," he repeated dully.

"She was in God's hands."

"Which raises a very important question."

"Which is?"

"You were praying, Riley was praying, both of your families and Leah's fellow parishioners were praying. If He's up there, all merciful like He wants us to believe...," Ron began. His eyes narrowed, and his lips thinned in outrage. "Why didn't He save her?"

"Who can know the mind of God?"

"Don't add insult to injury by spouting biblical maxims. They're about as useful as lips on a chicken at a time like this, if you ask me."

"Whew," she said, fanning her face, "and I thought *I* was angry."

He frowned. "You? Angry? You're one of the most even-tempered people I've ever met."

She quirked an eyebrow. "You think you're the only one who questions God?"

"So what keeps you believing, then, since you admit you can't get satisfying answers from Him?"

"I never said He didn't provide satisfying answers."

"He didn't save Leah...."

"No," she said softly, "He didn't."

"And you accept that?"

"Yes."

"Why?"

"All He asks of us is that we have faith."

"Ah, yes," he said, imitating W. C. Fields, "the ever-present, super-popular, all-powerful faith...."

"I'm sure you didn't stop by today to make fun of me because, despite the fact that I'm a nurse, I've chosen to put my faith in a Being more powerful than your precious science."

"I want to believe, Jade; I want to have faith, but—"

"But you've seen where it gets people."

"Right. They put all their hopes and dreams in God, and where does it get them?"

"It gets them *faith*. Faith isn't something you order from a catalog. It's a gift, and it's yours, if you'll merely ask for it."

"In my experience, the minute you ask for faith, something ugly happens to test it. How can people keep looking to heaven like wide-eyed, trusting children who expect miracles, knowing that?"

"Because sometimes, they *get* miracles."

"Or they get kicked in the head."

"You said it yourself a moment ago—we look to the heavens like wide-eyed, trusting children.... *That's* where we get our faith—from our childlike belief that God is our Father, who will watch over us and do what's best for us, even though we might not see eye to eye with Him when He does." She paused. "*I* don't know why Leah got cancer, why she suffered, or why she died, but *God* knows." She took a deep breath. "Like it or not, you're a child of God, too, you know."

He looked genuinely surprised. "Who, me? No way."

She grabbed his hand and gave it a squeeze. "Yes, you...with a head full of scientific facts and a heart hardened by the suffering and death you've seen. Why *not* you?"

"Because...I'm a self-centered know-it-all."

Jade laughed softly. "God has a special place in His heart for arrogant, hardheaded know-it-alls like you."

"Hardheaded?" he repeated. Grinning a bit, he added, "Arrogant?"

"Well, you have to admit, you don't exactly take to new ideas easily, especially if they can't be worked out on a calculator or measured in a lab experiment."

He glanced at her hand resting atop his. "I declare, Jade, if you weren't Riley's wife...."

She read the gleam emanating from his eyes and realized for the first time that what he felt for her had very
little, if anything, to do with friendship. And it certainly
had nothing to do with faith! She pulled her hand away.
"Drink your lemonade, Ron," she instructed him. "The
ice is melting."

"Then again," he continued as if she hadn't spoken,
"it's not like you guys are really married. You only went
through with that sham of a wedding to make Leah happy in the end. I mean, it's not like you're in love with the
guy or anything...right?"

Jade stood up so fast that her chair teetered before
coming to rest on all four feet again. She hadn't been eating
properly, hadn't been sleeping well, either, and so standing
up quickly sent a rush of dizziness coursing through her,
making her stagger and stumble. She didn't speak at first.
Didn't dare, for the words churning in her head would likely have singed his ears. Then, she said, "I'm Riley's wife in
the eyes of God, according to the State of Maryland, and,
most important of all, in my *heart*. I love him more than
life itself, and that isn't going to change. Ever."

He shrugged one shoulder and held out his hands,
palms up. "Well," he said, grinning, "you don't hate me
for trying, do you?"

She returned his smile. "How could I hate the man
who tried so hard to save Leah?"

As Ron quietly let himself out the back door, Jade
dropped onto the seat of the nearest chair and sent yet
another prayer heavenward: *Lord, give me the wisdom to
know when I should tell Riley what I just told Dr. Peterson!*

❦

Riley had thought it might be fun to stop off at the
local burger joint on the way home and buy a couple of

bags of those French fries Fiona seemed to love so much. He grinned like a fool as he imagined the look little Fee would make when he handed them to her....

And then he saw Ron Peterson's car in the driveway.

Glowering, Riley's heart began beating like a parade drum. *What's he doing here?* he demanded silently, slamming the car door.

Leah's house—correction, his and Jade's house, now that he had his condo on the market—was a tri-level affair with a layout that pretty much guaranteed that if Jade was in the kitchen and he came in through the laundry room, he could tap-dance on the washing machine and she wouldn't hear it. So, he'd taken to whistling softly when he entered so as not to startle her.

Riley didn't even bother puckering up today....

He had every intention of barging into the kitchen and making it clear to Ron Peterson that this was *his* house; that Jade was *his* wife.

But her soft, sweet voice stopped him cold.

"I like to think the one positive thing to come of it was that you and I became friends...."

The one positive thing from Leah's death was not Fiona or their marriage but a relationship with Ron Peterson? Holding his breath, Riley ground his molars together. *I oughtta march in there and deck that fatheaded cretin. I oughtta—*

Their conversation turned suddenly to God, of all things, and he listened, grinning with pride as Jade appeared to be putting the pompous Dr. Know-It-All in his place. Her soft laughter, like a magnet, pulled Riley forward a step or two, and he almost allowed himself to be drawn into the kitchen by the warm, inviting sound of it.

"I mean," he heard Ron say, "it's not like you're in love with the guy or anything, right?"

Riley took a chance and peeked through the fronds of the Boston fern at the bottom of the stairs just in time to see Jade leap up from her chair. It seemed she was about to fall over in a dead faint when Ron reached out and steadied her...as Jade pushed the doctor away. "I'm Riley's wife in the eyes of God, according to the State of Maryland, and, most important of all, in my *heart*. I love him more than life itself, and that isn't going to change. Ever."

Riley's heart swelled with relief and pride and love, and he wanted to wrap her in his arms and press a grateful kiss to her lips.

The doctor shrugged. "Well, you don't hate me for trying, do you?"

Jade's back was still to him, but Riley knew from her tone of voice that Jade was smiling when she said, "How could I hate the man who tried so hard to save Leah?"

And she was right, Riley admitted to himself. There was that reason, at least, to keep from hating Ron Peterson. And, grinning, he told himself that if the doc hadn't already let himself out through the kitchen door, he might just have given him a great, big, grateful hug.

Riley headed back through the house, intending to go out the way he'd come in and make a second entrance, this time the way Ron Peterson had done it. He'd take Jade in his arms and confess all—that he'd fallen feet over forehead for her the first time he saw her, and that every day that had passed since, he'd only loved her more. And if God saw fit to answer his most current prayer, tonight, Riley would make her his wife in every sense of the word.

The burgers and fries would no doubt be cold after they'd exchanged their latest vows. *But hey*, he said to himself, grinning, *isn't that why the microwave oven was invented?*

Jade was wide-eyed and frantic when Riley walked into Fiona's room, beaming as he held out the white paper bag filled with burgers and fries. "Oh, Riley, thank God you're home early. I was just about to call her pediatrician!"

He dropped the sack on the changing table and took the little girl from her. "She's burning up!" he said, one big hand covering Fiona's forehead.

"I read in the morning paper that a little boy died of meningitis just last week," Jade said, half running into the kitchen. "It really isn't the season for it, but...." She shook her head. "The virus that causes it can be terribly contagious. Just yesterday, Fee and I went to the grocery store right up the street where he lived." Jade grabbed Leah's personal phone directory and looked up Fiona's doctor's name.

If she'd been in the same neighborhood as the boy who'd died, it was entirely possible Jade and Fiona had come into contact with the airborne germs that caused the potentially deadly disease. "What's the incubation period?" he asked.

She finished dialing. "Could be hours, could be days; depends on how healthy you are when you're exposed."

Fiona continued to snooze against his shoulder. "But she hasn't been sick...."

"Hasn't been her usual self, either. Remember how she's been pushing her food away the past few days?"

It was true. Ordinarily, Fiona had a voracious appetite, but lately, she'd been barely eating a bite at mealtime. She'd been sleeping in fits and starts, too. They'd sloughed it off as the result of the drop-in guests, the interrupted naps, and missing Leah. "Couldn't she be teething, like we figured?"

"Sure, but we can't take the chance. Not with something like that going arou—"

"Yes," Jade said into the phone. "I'm...." She hesitated, but for only a moment. Leah had seen to it that all of Fiona's records had been changed, including those on file at the pediatrician's office. "I'm Fiona Steele's mother. She's burning up with a fever, and I'm leaving for the emergency room as soon as we hang up. I want you to get a message to Dr. O'Dell to meet her father and me at the hospital as soon as possible."

She listened for a moment, then snarled, "I don't care if he's about to shoot a birdie; get him off the golf course and over to the hospital, stat!"

Riley had never seen Jade this way before. Normally, she was cool under pressure and gentle as a deer. During Leah's illness, and even as Leah lay dying in their arms, Jade had held her emotions in check. She'd given in to tears—who wouldn't have, under those circumstances?—but never to the point that the job didn't get done, and never in front of Leah or Fiona. *There must be something to this maternal stuff,* he thought, because she'd turned into a fire-breathing dragon right before his very eyes at the mere possibility of her child being in danger.

"I'll rev up the car," he said, heading for the garage.

She hung up the phone. "I'll be right out; I just want to grab a few diapers, her Teddy and favorite blanket...."

Fiona hadn't said a word since he'd taken her in his arms, and that wasn't like her. What worried Riley most wasn't the high temperature itself—he'd seen her spike a fever before—but her silence. Nothing, not even that bout with croup, had managed to keep her from chattering like a chipmunk. *Lord Jesus*, he prayed silently, *lay Your healing hands on our girl....*

They drove to the hospital with the emergency flashers going and the headlights turned on bright, Riley honking as he zoomed around other drivers who were obeying the posted speed limit. "Where's a cop when you need one?" he wondered aloud. "If we got stopped for speeding, we could get a police escort."

"We're nearly there," Jade assured him, patting the hand with white knuckles that operated the gearshift knob, "and you're doin' swell."

"You sounded like Leah when you said that."

She nodded. "I thought the same thing the minute the words came out of my mouth. I'm going to take that as a good sign."

Fiona snuggled a little closer and held Jade a little tighter. "You'll be fine, sweet girl," she cooed, kissing the child's temple, "just fine. Mommy and Daddy are going to take you to the doctor so they can fix you right up," she added, smoothing soft, silken locks from her feverish forehead.

Mommy and Daddy.

Suddenly, it didn't sound at all foreign. Instead, it sounded normal and natural...and strangely comforting. "And before you know it," Jade continued, "you'll be all better again, and Mommy and Daddy will take you home, and we'll eat cookies!"

"Coo-kie?" Fiona whimpered.

It was the first word Riley had heard her speak since he'd arrived home. He took it as a signal—a sign from God that all would be well, just as Jade had promised.

Riley steered the car under the protective overhang at the emergency room entrance. "You go on in," he instructed Jade with an encouraging wink, "while I find a parking space."

She quickly gathered the little girl and her things, then stepped onto the concrete ramp that led to help— and, hopefully, to healing. "Don't be long," she said meaningfully. "We need you."

He nodded and drove off, his nerves jangling and his muscles tight as a tambourine. Something told him he wouldn't feel calm, or complete, until he was with them again.

It seemed to take hours instead of moments for Riley to park the car, which struck Jade as odd in more ways than one....

For one thing, she'd always prided herself on being independent, self-sufficient, reliable. Plus, she had extensive training as an emergency room nurse. This was very familiar territory, from the ebb of calm moments to the tide of critical ones, and she should feel comfortable surrounded by the lifesaving staff and equipment.

But today, Jade was just another frightened mother hoping that these people and their machines could save her child.

Riley's presence had a calming, soothing effect on her, especially lately, and she didn't quite know how to feel about that. Because, on the one hand, her training should have provided her with the strength to do what had to be done on the night that Leah died; by all rights, she should have been the steadfast one, the one doling out assurances, because she had been there at the end for hundreds of strangers.

On the other hand, it was pompous and arrogant to presume that just because the suffering Riley saw every day in his practice was of the animal rather than human variety, he didn't understand the full ramifications of a life lost....

There was another, very real element to consider: His nearness had seemed all she'd needed to keep her emotions in check on that harrowing, horrible night when Leah had left them. One look at his intense self-control had been enough to gird her own fortitude, an unfair position to put him in, especially considering that he had loved Leah every bit as much as she had.

She would not put him through such an ordeal this time. He adored Fiona, and she'd seen the fear in his dark eyes the moment he'd realized how serious her condition might be. He'd certainly earned the right to let his guard down, to accept rather than constantly give comfort, and while it terrified Jade more than she cared to admit to see Fiona in this state—frail, feverish, afraid— she would hide her worries...for Riley's sake.

Jade recalled the passage from Isaiah, chapter 40, verses 29–31, that she'd memorized as a child as a Sunday school assignment. "*He gives power to the faint, and to him who has no might he increases strength,*" she recited mentally, tightening her hold on Fiona as they awaited a doctor's attention. "*...They who wait for the LORD shall renew their strength, they shall mount up with wings like eagles, they shall run and not be weary, they shall walk and not faint.*"

She had God's assurance that the strength required of her would be available when she needed it.

Just then, Riley shoved through the doors and walked toward her in that sure, solid way that was uniquely his. Their gazes fused, and his eyes warmed her, overpowering the air-conditioned temperature of the waiting room. They were connected by threads of honor and respect, and he managed a shaky smile, which she returned with a hopeful, confident look.

"How's our girl doing?" he asked, sitting down beside her.

"No better, but no worse, either," Jade answered as he slid his arm across her shoulders.

Riley nodded toward the double doors that barred entrance to the emergency room itself. "How much longer?"

"Five, maybe ten, minutes, according to that nurse over there."

He followed her gaze, then looked into her eyes and raised both dark eyebrows. "Ten whole minutes? And she's still walkin' around with a head on her shoulders?" Giving Jade a sideways hug, he grinned slightly. "I'm surprised you didn't bite it off and threaten to stuff it into her pocket for making Fee wait even ten *seconds*."

Jade recalled the brief set-to between the admitting nurse and herself when she'd walked up to the counter. She'd explained in no uncertain terms that, as one who had walked emergency room halls, she knew procedure and would not be kept waiting unnecessarily long. "Oh, trust me," she said, "she understands the seriousness of the situation."

Riley pressed a kiss to her cheek, then laid a hand on Fiona's forehead. "I sure do wish they'd hurry up back there. Fee's not getting any better sitting out here in this drafty waiting room...."

This was the way God had intended marriage to be, Jade believed—each partner intent upon working at full throttle so that when one half of the team wasn't up to it, the other could pull the load temporarily. *That's* what the Lord meant when He described equality in a love-filled marriage through the apostle Paul in Colossians....

"*Little children,*" John had written in 1 John 3:18, "*let us not love in word or speech but in deed and in truth.*"

One of Jade's favorite Bible passages had always been 1 Corinthians 13, and she started to whisper it to herself, beginning with verses 7 and 8: "'*Love bears all things, believes all things, hopes all things, endures all things. Love never ends....*'"

Riley pressed a gentle kiss to her temple, then whispered in her ear, "If I have not love, I am nothing."

She leaned her head on his shoulder, and, together, they hugged Fiona's feverish, shivering body. Despite the fear—or perhaps because of it—they shared a curious calm, as though God Himself had blessed the moment.

"Mr. and Mrs. Steele," the nurse called, "will you come with me, please?"

Relieving Jade of Fiona's limp weight, Riley guided her toward the entrance with his free hand. "*'So faith, hope, love abide, these three,'*" he whispered as they walked, "*'but the greatest of these is love.'*"

It would, perhaps, be a long and harrowing night, yet Jade was filled with a sense of peace and contentment like none she'd known before. God was with them, right here in the emergency room.

And she knew that He would be with them, no matter what, for the rest of their days.

Chapter Ten

Cerebrospinal meningitis," the neurologist on duty explained, "is an acute inflammation of the membranes of the brain or spinal cord...or both." He held the X-rays in front of the window and used the tip of his silver ballpoint pen as a pointer. "We'll know once we see results of the blood work if its cause is bacteria, viruses, protozoa, yeast, or fungi."

"Cut to the chase, Doc," Riley interrupted him. "How bad is it?"

The white-haired gent peered over the rims of his half-glasses to study Riley's face. "Sorry," he said, "didn't mean to pontificate." He smiled apologetically. "I've become a spoiled old man, I'm afraid, whose work these days consists mostly of teaching at the University of Maryland. When I volunteer for ER duty, I don't get the sleep I'm accustomed to, and sometimes, frankly, I forget where I am."

He cleared his throat and turned to Jade. "Now then, young lady, when did you first notice the symptoms?"

"Ordinarily, Fiona has a very pleasant disposition. It isn't like her to be so fussy, but then...these aren't ordinary circumstances...."

Frowning, he tilted his head. "Circumstances?"

Jade explained how she and Riley had become Fiona's parents, and how they had been attributing the child's recent behavior on changes in the household.

Nodding, the doctor said, "Easy to see why you'd think it was emotional rather than physical."

Riley took Jade's hand and gave it a supportive squeeze as she continued. "But then I noticed she was putting her hands to her head, moving as though she might have a stiff neck. Her temperature only registered 102, which I know isn't as dangerous for a child of two as it might be for an adult, but because of the story in the papers, I decided there were enough warning signs to warrant a trip to the hospital."

She glanced at Fiona, who'd been sleeping quietly on a high, narrow cot in the ER cubicle for the past few minutes. "I'd rather be labeled a fussbudget by the hospital staff than risk her taking a turn for the worse. I'm well aware that meningitis has a tendency to worsen quickly...climbing temperature, projectile vomiting, convulsions, coma—"

"It's not every fussbudget who knows so much about meningitis," the doctor said, smiling gently. "Don't tell me you teach at Maryland, as well?"

Flushing slightly, Jade explained her lecture. "Until very recently, I worked at LA General; we handled a meningitis epidemic some years back. For the patients who got to us in time, we managed to control it with sulfa and antibiotics, but not everyone was so lucky." Shaking her head, she continued. "Some lost their hearing or went blind because of infections of the iris; a few developed arthritis, and a few—the ones with extensive spotting of the skin—became delirious, went into comas."

"How many did you lose?"

"Half a dozen or so, total. Two on my shift." Another sigh. "Give me boring lectures in the gallery, complete with gory slide presentations, over actual human suffering any day. That was no way to get an education...."

"Well, you did a fine job diagnosing your daughter, a splendid job. And as soon as we can have a look at the lab work, we'll know how to proceed. Meanwhile," he said, looking over at Fiona, "it's a good sign that she's resting quietly."

"How soon will you know something?" Riley wanted to know.

The older man slid a gold pocket watch from his vest and popped open the lid. "It shouldn't be long now." Winking, he snapped it shut again. "But just to be sure," he said, putting the timepiece away, "why don't I just call down there and see if I can't hurry things along?" He gave Jade's shoulder a paternal squeeze. "Would that help you rest easier?"

Nodding, she smiled. "Yes, it most certainly would. Thank you so much, Dr.—"

"Stewart."

"Not *Anthony* Stewart...who separated the twins connected at the skull back in the sixties?" Riley asked.

The physician removed his half-glasses and nonchalantly shrugged one shoulder.

"You invented the process that doctors today are—"

Chuckling good-naturedly, the doctor held up a hand to silence Riley's praises. "I don't know as I'd go as far as to say I 'invented' anything," he said. He dropped the glasses into his lab coat pocket. Glancing at Fiona's chart, he said to Jade, "If you ever decide to come to work at Howard General, Nurse Steele, I'd very much appreciate it if you'd arrange to work on my shift."

She smiled appreciatively. "That's quite a compliment." She glanced at Riley before focusing on the doctor again. "When my husband and I decide it's time for me to go back to nursing, you'll be the first to know."

"*The prayer of faith will save the sick man, and the Lord will raise him up,*" Riley prayed, quoting James 5:15.

While Jade was rocking Fiona to sleep, he'd gone to the hospital chapel. On his knees at the simple little altar, he recited every verse he'd ever memorized that dealt with healing and medicine.

"'He...gave them authority over unclean spirits, to cast them out, and to heal every disease and every infirmity.' 'The LORD sustains him on his sickbed; in his illness thou healest all his infirmities.' 'This illness is not unto death; it is for the glory of God, so that the Son of God may be glorified by means of it.'"

At the end of it all, weary yet strangely energized, Riley stood up and faced the cross. Leah's death had taught him many things, among them that life is fleeting, at best. He had no idea why Leah had been taken, but he knew this: Fiona would not join her. Not for a very long time, at least. Riley believed this as strongly as he believed Leah had been right when she'd said his marriage to Jade was the Creator's handiwork, and Riley would not waste one more precious moment waiting for....

What *had* he been waiting for? A voice from on high, thundering permission for him and Jade to live as man and wife? A message written in the clouds, granting authorization to become one?

He loved Jade with all his heart. If she didn't know that already, well, he had the rest of his life to demonstrate it, didn't he?

Riley remembered their wedding day, when he'd wondered if her tears were the outward symbol of inward aversion to the marriage. He couldn't have been more wrong! The signs of her love for him were everywhere—in the special and loving things she did for him every day of his life; in the warm, affectionate light that glowed in her eyes only when she looked at him; in the sweet lilt that brightened her voice when she talked to him. Jade was devoted to Fiona, but not even her deep affection for the child could stir the one-of-a-kind expressions reserved only for him. Besides, he had a feeling the loving looks and warm words and gentle gestures she'd been showering on him were but a fraction of what Jade had to give her friend, life mate, and lover....

The Lord had not brought them together to share a home and years and life as mere pals; friendship was all well and good, a necessary part of marriage, but it was only one thread in the colorful fabric God had woven for husbands and wives.

And as soon as Fiona recuperated, Riley aimed to see that they started living married life—all of it—to the fullest.

He headed back to Fiona's room, stopping at the vending machine down the hall to buy a cup of steaming coffee for Jade and himself. He was about to turn the corner and enter the room when a soft, sweet voice stopped him.

Jade's voice....

"Peace is flowing like a river," she sang, "flowing out of you and me, flowing out into the desert, setting all the captives free...."

He hadn't heard her sing in nearly a decade—not since that night, a week or so before graduation, when she'd played her guitar so he could hear the newest song she'd written. One line still stuck with him, even after all these years: "In your eyes, love, I see my destiny; when you smile, my whole world is at peace. I have one dream, for all eternity...that you'll wrap your lovin' arms 'round me...." At the time, he'd thought she'd written it for Hank Berger, and the idea had made him grit his teeth and clench his fists. He knew better now. She'd written down and sung in her heart words that expressed how she felt about *him*—Riley.

Think of all the years you've wasted...years you could have lived with her, loved her, and been loved by her.

They could have had three, maybe four, kids by now. And a house in the country...like the one Jade had always talked about.... *If only you hadn't been so blind, so all-fired dense.*

Riley vowed, right where he stood, not to let another precious second tick by!

Jade had started a new song as he stood musing in the hall, and even without musical accompaniment, her melodic voice sounded angelic and pure. "We hold a treasure, not made of gold; in earthen vessels wealth untold. One treasure only: the Lord, the Christ, in earthen vessels...."

Silence, then nothing but the quiet creak of the rocker. "Riley," she called softly, "is that you out there casting the giant shadow I see?"

Chuckling, he looked down at the floor, where a six-foot silhouette of himself slanted across the industrial-grade, orange-and-green-flecked carpeting. "I didn't want to disturb you," he explained, coming around the corner and setting a cup of coffee on the nightstand beside her. "Your voice is even more beautiful than I remembered."

"That's sweet of you to say," she said, smiling. Then, looking at Fiona's sleeping face, she said, "But *this*—this is real beauty."

"Our sleeping beauty," he agreed. The cherubic face, relaxed in contented slumber, was indeed flawless, with the innocent lift of tiny blonde brows and long, lush lashes that dusted round, rosy cheeks. The sweet smile on her tiny pink mouth told them that Fiona must have been dreaming happy baby dreams.

She stirred in Jade's arms, frowning slightly in her sleep.

"She wants another song," Riley said.

"*She* wants another song?"

"She was fine till you stopped singing...."

Grinning, Jade shook her head as Fiona's tiny fingers wrapped around hers. "Well, all right," she acquiesced. "She loves the tempo and actually knows some of the words to this one...."

"Maybe when we get her home, the two of you will sing it for me."

She nodded. "Not maybe. Definitely," Jade said, her grin softening into a loving smile.

His heart swelling and pounding with love for her, Riley grinned. "Well, go on," he coaxed, "sing!"

"Bloom, bloom, bloom where you're planted, and you will find your way. Bloom, bloom, bloom where you're planted, you will have your day....

"Look at the flowers, look at them growing; they never worry...they never work. Yet look at the way our Father clothes them, each with a beauty all its own.

"Bloom, bloom, bloom where you're planted, and you will find your—"

The sight of a starched white lab coat silenced her.

"Please don't stop. That's by far the loveliest thing I've heard in a long, long time."

Jade blushed and covered her lips with her free hand. "Dr. Stewart," she said, smiling as she nodded at the clipboard he held at his side. "I hope that's good news you're holding in your hands."

He raised the clipboard and perched on the edge of Fiona's empty bed. "My dear, I can tell you this: Nothing I can do for that child will equal the healing properties of what you were doing just now." Looking over at Riley, he shook his hand. "Your wife is quite a talented lady."

"Jack-of-all-trades," Jade said, her blush deepening.

"That's a lot of hooey, and we all know it," Riley countered. "She can draw, too, and make roses grow in sand. And you ought to taste her lasagna!"

The doctor nodded approvingly. "Now *there's* something you don't see very often these days...."

"A perfect woman?" Riley asked.

"The genuine, unbridled love of a man for his wife."

Riley met Jade's gaze and smiled. "Guilty as charged."

Shaking his head, Stewart chuckled.

"Well, it isn't like I was trying to hide it," Riley said, winking at her. He turned to the doctor. "So, what's up, Doc?" he asked, pointing to the clipboard. "Good news, I presume?"

"Seems we have been blessed. Little Fiona's meningitis is not severe, and because it's bacterial in nature, we can address it with antibiotic therapy." He looked from Riley to Jade and back again. "If all goes as expected, you ought to be tucking her into her own little bed by this time tomorrow."

"Praise God!" Jade sighed, bowing her head.

"Boom, boom, boom," Fiona said, attempting to sing the notes Jade had just concluded. She thrust a fat little finger between Jade's lips and, frowning slightly, said, "Mommy sing?"

A moment of relieved adult laughter bounced from every wall in the tiny room before Jade picked up where she'd left off:

"Look at the love that lies deep within you. Let yourself be! Let yourself be! Look at the gifts you have been given, let them go free; let them go free....

"Bloom, bloom, bloom," she sang as the doctor headed for the door.

"Boom, boom, boom," Fiona crooned in an off-key voice.

"Bloom, bloom, bloom," they sang together, their voices blending in a mellifluous duet, "and you will find your way...and you will find your way...."

❧

"She looks wonderful, Jade," Amber whispered, peeking in Fiona's room. "She had us all very worried there for a while. Neil and I prayed for her every chance we got."

Jade closed the door quietly. "Thanks, sweetie."

"So tell me," her sister said, settling on the family room sofa, "what do you hear from Hank lately?"

"Nothing. In fact, the last time I talked to him was before I left LA."

"You're joking."

Jade shook her head. "I'm as serious as a judge."

"Have you called him? Maybe something happened to him...."

Jade had poured them each some iced tea before letting Amber peek in at Fiona. She picked up her glass and took a sip. "Nothing has happened to Hank Berger." She put the tumbler back on the coffee table. "I called him the night I got here, and the next night, and every night after that for a full week."

"Wasn't he home?"

Another shake of the head. "Nope. Wasn't in the office, either. I left messages with the receptionist at the TV station, on his voice mail at work, on his answering machine at home, on his cell phone...."

"Sounds like he was avoiding you. And lately?"

"Not a peep."

"Ha. That makes sense, since I always thought he resembled a plucked chicken."

"Amber!" Jade scolded, laughing. "I'm tellin' Mom!"

Shrugging, Amber grinned. "What can she do to me? She's the one who taught me I should always tell the truth."

"She also said, 'If you don't have anything nice to say about someone,....'"

"...'don't say anything at all,'" Amber finished for her.

The sisters shared a moment of warm laughter that waned into companionable silence.

"So how're you doin', big sister?"

Jade sighed. "I miss Leah, but I'm happy, really happy...."

"Why do I hear a 'but' in that statement?"

Another sigh, deeper this time. "If only our marriage was...."

"If only it was *what*?"

Shrugging, Jade fidgeted, searching for the words that would help her explain.

"Jade!" her sister shouted. "Don't tell me the two of you haven't.... You mean you're not...? But it's been three whole months! How can that be?"

Pouting slightly, Jade shook her head. "I sleep in the guest room, and Riley sleeps right here on the couch."

"Now I'm tellin' Mom. You know how she feels about teasing."

"It's true, every word of it."

"But Jade, the two of you are so much in love. It's written all over your faces. Everyone who knows you sees it."

"How can I explain something I don't understand myself? It isn't something we've discussed, that's all."

"That's all? *That's all*?!" Amber clapped a palm to her forehead. "Jade, when *are* you going to discuss it?"

She shrugged. "I don't know."

"Do you realize that you're missing out on one of the most beautiful things God gave husbands and wives?"

She sighed.

"What about Fiona?"

"What about her?"

"You don't want her to be an only child, do you?"

"I'd love a houseful of children!"

Amber buried her face in a throw pillow to muffle her bellow of frustration. "Well, how do you expect to get them," she said, throwing the pillow at Jade, "if you're sleeping there," she pointed down the hall, "and Riley is sleeping here?" she pointed at the couch. "Osmosis works only on *plants*, y'know!"

"I know, I know; I've been praying for a solution...."

"How do You stand it?" she asked God with a look up at the ceiling. Then, rolling her eyes, Amber growled with frustration. Suddenly, she leaned forward, grinning mischievously and wiggling her eyebrows. "Want some advice, big sister?"

Jade laughed at her sister's shenanigans. "I can use all the help I can get."

"You'd better pray harder, or oftener, or *something*, because I want some little tyke to call me Auntie Amber!"

Several hours later, after Amber had returned home to her husband and little boy, Jade put Fiona in the playpen in the corner of the kitchen, where she could keep an eye on her while she prepared supper.

"Mind if I join you?" Riley asked, flopping the evening paper onto the table. "The light's better in here," he explained as he sat down.

"Of course, I don't mind," she said without thinking. "I love having you so near...."

She had her head in the fridge when the phone rang.

"Whatever they're selling," he teased from behind the paper, "we don't want it."

"Not interested in aluminum siding and tilt-in replacement windows?"

"Not interested in lifetime lightbulbs that barely last a month or trash bags that can't hold a pound of feathers, either," he added after the second ring.

Jade recognized the voice immediately.

"I can't believe you're still out there," he said. "When are you coming home?"

"Why, I'm just fine, Hank, thanks. And how are you?"

Hank? Riley mouthed. *What does he want?*

Grinning, she held a finger over her lips as Hank said, "I see you're still the Queen of Sarcasm."

"Now there's a nickname I haven't heard in a while. Can't say I was overly fond of it." Jade paused, then said, "Odd, isn't it, you called me that only when I disagreed with you, and I don't believe you've said anything I can disagree with...yet...."

He groaned, and she could almost see him rubbing his face with his hand. "Look, I'm sorry. Let's start over, shall we? So, how are you, Jade?"

"Fine. You?"

"Can't complain. How's your girlfriend?"

"Leah?"

"Yeah. That's the one."

"She's—"

"Did you hear? I won the party's nomination. I'll be running for state senate...."

Yes, she'd heard. It had been on the cable news network the week before Leah died. And she knew very well what message his lengthy pause meant to imply: He'd run, despite the fact that Jade had left him high and dry out there, to do everything for himself. "Congratulations," she said, and meant it. "I'm happy for you."

"Thanks."

"You're welcome."

Another pause. This one, she knew, was supposed to convey criticism—no doubt of what he saw as her blatant self-centeredness.

"You're going to make me say it, aren't you?"

"Say what?"

She heard his deep, exasperated sigh.

"I want you to come home, Jade."

"I *am* home, Hank."

Riley knit his brows. *Hang up*, he gestured, pointing at the empty telephone cradle on the counter.

Jade shook her head, wagging a finger under his nose.

"You lived here for ten years!" Hank was saying. "*This* is your home."

"I sold my condo, remember?"

"There are hundreds of properties for sale, and—"

"That doesn't mean I'm in the market to buy."

"Come on, Jade. Surely your girlfriend doesn't expect you to—"

"Leah," she interrupted, angry now. "Her name was Leah. And she—"

"*Was*?"

"That's right. Leah died three months ago."

"Oh. Sorry." He cleared his throat again. "Why in the world didn't you call? I would have flown out there to—"

"I did call, Hank. But, to misquote an old movie, we seem to have developed a failure to communicate. Besides, we managed just fine without you," she said curtly.

"We?"

Smiling, she held out her hand, and Riley took it. "Riley and Fiona and I."

"Riley? Not Riley *Steele*...."

"Yes, Riley Steele. I'm surprised you remember him."

"How could I forget him? He was in every issue of *The Wingspan*, and the football coach paraded him out at every school assembly. I don't think there was an election he didn't run for...and win. I was grateful to be a senior when you guys were sophomores, let me tell you, 'cause it got me out of that school!"

A moment of silence ticked by, which he ended with, "Look, Jade...maybe I can arrange to take a few days off and—"

"Before you book a flight and reserve a hotel room, I think you should know...Riley and I are married."

For the first time, Jade had no idea how to interpret the silence. She felt a little guilty for being so abrupt. And just as she was about to apologize, Hank said, "I... uh, I guess I'm not surprised." He took a deep breath. "Are you...are you happy?"

She smiled at Riley. "Yes, I'm very happy."

"Answer me something...."

"What?"

"If I had asked you to marry me, would you have said yes?"

She laughed softly.

The hiss and crackle of the poor connection punctuated his admission. "You should have nagged me to set a date," he said, misinterpreting her reaction.

"Isn't my nature. Besides, it wasn't like we were engaged or anything."

"I suppose I should have taken you more seriously...."

When she'd been there for him, day after day? Or when, on the morning she had left California, she'd said that she wouldn't back?

"Where's Riley?"

"He's right here. Why?"

"Put him on the line for a minute."

With eyebrows raised, she held out the phone. "Hank wants to talk to you."

Matching her surprised expression, Riley took the phone. "Hank, hey. What's shakin'?"

"You'd better be good to her, Steele."

Frowning, Riley said, "That's the plan, *Berger*."

"Because she's a prize."

"A treasure," he corrected him. "Not something to be won, but something that, if you're lucky enough to find it, you cherish."

Hank hung up, and none too gently, either. Wincing, Riley put the phone to his other ear. "Gee," he said past the buzzing dial tone, "I dunno, Hank; that's an awfully big commitment."

"What's a big commitment?" Jade whispered.

Grinning roguishly, he waved her away. "Naming our first kid after you—"

Jade gasped.

Riley continued the charade. "I'm sure it'd make a great campaign slogan. Yeah, I can see the bumper stickers now: 'Vote for Uncle Hank.' Tell you what—we'll keep you posted. The minute we're, uh, in a family way, you'll be the first to know."

Riley replaced the handset in the cradle and gathered Jade in his arms. "Fiona asleep?" he asked, pulling her closer.

Smiling, Jade glanced at the playpen. "It appears so...."

"Good. 'Cause I just promised your old boyfriend that we'd consider naming our first kid after him."

She nodded. "I heard."

Tenderly, he kissed her eyelids, her cheeks, her chin. "And we can't very well do that," he whispered against her lips, "unless we *have* a kid...."

Holding her gaze, he linked his fingers with hers, lifted her hand to his lips, and kissed her knuckles one at a time. "Although, if we *did* have a kid, I don't know if Hank would be my first choice in boys' names...."

"Riley...."

His fingers caressed her face. "Hmm?"

"Shut up and kiss me."

Epilogue

Seven years later

"Mommy," Fiona called, "Zach is crying...."

Blinking into the darkness, Jade and Riley disentangled themselves from each other's limbs.

"He probably needs more of that pink stuff on his chicken pox," Riley said around a yawn. "You want me to take care of it?"

"No," she said, stretching. "I'll go. You went last time—"

"Mommy? If you don't make him stop, he'll wake Leah...."

Jade smiled and shook her head. "We can't let that happen, now, can we? I declare, it seems that child has been talking nonstop since birth. I think the only time she's quiet is when she's sound asleep."

"Even then, her mouth is open," he teased.

"But Fiona's right, you know; if I don't quiet him down, he'll wake the baby."

Riley murmured sleepily against her lips, "Stop calling her a baby. She'll be three in less than a week."

Jade sighed. "I know, I know, but it's a hard habit to break." She climbed out of bed and shrugged into her robe.

He opened one eye. "Hey, it's pretty chilly out there... aren't you gonna tie it up?"

She laughed softly. "I would if I could, but the belt isn't long enough anymore."

"Hang in there, kiddo. A few more weeks and you'll have your flat tummy back again."

"Yeah, right," she said, gently tucking the covers under his chin, "and the sun's gonna shine in exactly one minute."

He opened the other eye and glanced at red numerals of the alarm clock glowing in the darkness. "But it's only—" He chuckled. "Oh, I get it."

He sat up in bed and held out his arms.

"But Zach is—"

"Zach is six years old. He'll be fine for one minute more."

Jade climbed back into bed and let him draw her close.

"You're the most beautiful creature I've ever seen," he told her, "especially when you're pregnant." Gently, he pressed a palm to her swollen belly. "But if you never got your hourglass figure back again, I'd still love you like crazy."

"Really?" she asked, grinning drowsily.

"You know the answer to that as well as I do." He kissed the tip of her nose. "Now, you stay put. I'll dab some more calamine lotion on the boy."

"Thanks, sweetie."

It was his turn to tuck the quilt under her chin.

"Riley?" she said as he stepped into the hall.

"Hmm?"

"I love you."

"And I love you."

"Hurry back," she added, yawning again, "because I'm feeling a little crampy."

"Crampy?" He all but ran back into the room. "You don't mean...?"

"This one's going to be early, I think."

He slipped his arms around her. "But—but we haven't picked a name yet."

"I have a feeling it's going to be a boy. And you still haven't fulfilled your promise...."

"What promise?"

"To Hank Berger, when he called from California all those years ago, remember?"

Grinning, he hung his head. "You know as well as I do that the promise was bogus. Hank hung up long before I said anything about naming a kid after him."

"I know," she said, lifting his chin with her forefinger.

"You know?"

"I've always known."

"But...how?"

She tapped her ear. "Dial tone...."

"You heard it?"

She nodded. "I heard it."

"And you let me...?"

"I'd been praying God would help us, um, finalize our marriage vows."

"You'd been praying for...?"

Another nod.

He wrapped his arms around her. "Jade?"

She snuggled close. "Hmm?"

"Shut up and kiss me."

Montana Sky

Chapter One

Sky sensed the sniper's crosshairs centered between her eyebrows and crouched behind a boulder, one arm protectively encircling her Irish setter's neck. The last rifle shot, so recent that the scent of sulfur still hung in the air, had killed the she-wolf instantly. The dead wolf's lifeblood slowly seeped onto the parched earth beneath her as her cubs trembled in the open space between the carcass and Sky's refuge.

Sky estimated the pups at twelve to eighteen weeks... weaned, but far from old enough to survive the wilderness. They seemed to understand that cruel fact, and they whimpered pathetically, nudging and pawing at their mother's lifeless body. The mournful whining escalated as they learned one of life's hardest lessons: the cold finality of death. Too many times, Sky had been a student of that same cruel teacher, and she recognized the sorrow that burned in their round, golden eyes.

Pebbles cascaded down the rock face, and Sky knew it meant the gunman was repositioning himself up there, searching for the angle that would guarantee a successful triple wolf kill—and add thousands to his bank account. What the cubs needed more than anything else right now was time. Time to find their pack. Time to practice skills that would protect them from beast and nature and the most dangerous enemy of all: man.

But, for weeks, *The Messenger*'s headlines had screamed, "Wolf Wars Rage between Animal Activists and Ranchers." Time was the one thing the cubs didn't have.

Sky looked into their sad, innocent eyes and swallowed hard. Chances of another she-wolf adopting them were slim, at best. And without a mother to protect them from pack hierarchy, they'd be outcasts, subject to slow, vicious deaths. Even the sniper's way was gentler than that.

But it didn't *have* to be an either-or outcome....

Her heart pounded with fear as she made a life-altering, possibly life-threatening decision. "Hey, little guys, it's gonna be all right," she said softly. "I won't let anything happen to you. I promise."

With heads cocked and ears pricked forward, they froze, stunned into terrified silence by their first direct encounter with the human voice.

The unmistakable crack of gunfire shattered the quiet end-of-summer morning, and the bullet stopped with a sickening *thoomp* in the bark of a nearby tree. The little wolves cowered near their mother's dead body. Without a moment's hesitation, Sky dumped out her backpack, grabbed one yowling cub, then the other, and stuffed them into the bag, zipping it up despite their terrified, confused cries.

She clapped her hands to summon her Irish setter. "Face, c'mere! Down, girl!" she ordered. Her ears flat against her head, the dog, unaccustomed to such harshness in her mistress's voice, immediately did as she was told.

Cringing, Sky hunkered down behind the boulder, put on the backpack so that it nestled against her chest, and secured its stabilizing strap across her lower back. The cubs squirmed near her heart as she began what was as near a belly-crawl as her whimpering front load allowed. Beside her, Face mimicked her movements. "*'The Lord is faithful in all his words, and gracious in all his deeds,'*" she whispered. "*'The Lord upholds all who are falling....*'" Sky sent a silent prayer of thanks heavenward that her dad had made her memorize Bible passages such as this one, Psalm 145:13–14. "Never know when one will comfort or give you hope," Wade Allen had always said.

Another bullet zinged past, creating a tiny cloud of dust as it embedded itself in the rocks beside them. From where she lay hiding, Sky could see the angle of the bullets. Being able to hit what you aimed at in these parts could make the difference between life and death. It was no accident, she knew, that the marksman had missed again. But murder wasn't his goal. *Her* dead body wasn't worth thousands of dollars to him.

Just yesterday, *The Messenger*'s front page had read, "Rumored Wolf Bounties Reach Record Heights." Montana authorities, succumbing to pressure from powerful animal activist lobbies, had taken a hard line, threatening steep fines and jail time for anyone caught trading wolf skins for dollars. That fact underscored her assessment that the gunman's second and third shots had been intended only to scare her off, to enable him to finish the job—unwitnessed—and to exchange soft, warm bodies for cold, hard cash.

Sky crawled faster. Well-worn buckskin gloves protected her hands, but the elbows of her flannel shirt and the knees of her blue jeans were torn and bloodied by the time she reached her pickup. Oblivious to the cuts and scrapes, Sky reached up and opened the driver's door. Face didn't need an invitation; she immediately leapt into the cab. Sky was in the truck within seconds, the backpack still pressing against her chest. She drove like a maniac down Route 212, glancing in the rearview mirror every few seconds.

Through the windshield, Sky could see the fading glow of the moon, hanging high in the Montana morning sky, and recalled another Bible verse: *"Out of Zion, the perfection of beauty, God shines forth"* (Psalm 50:2). She found it hard to believe that the celestial view harbored a cold-blooded killer.

It seemed to take hours to drive the six winding miles home from the foothills. One last peek in the rearview mirror satisfied her that no one had followed. For the moment, at least, she and the cubs were safe. But just in case, Sky gave the steering wheel a sudden jerk to the left, her tires creating a ten-foot wave of grit as they gripped gravel, before careening down the winding, tree-lined drive that connected her home with the rest of the world.

The shooter's vantage point had provided him numerous benefits, including the element of surprise. Now, Sky had an advantage of her own. During "The Frightening Fifties," as Gramps had dubbed them, her grandfather had built a bomb shelter that he had disguised as a tool shed. He'd equipped the underground room with every modern convenience of the day. Being virtually soundproof, it would be the perfect hiding place for her cubs.

Inside the shelter, she removed the backpack and put it gently on the floor. Then, slowly, so she wouldn't catch the cubs' wooly fur in the zipper's teeth, Sky opened it. Yawning, the cubs poked their pointy noses through the opening and timidly sniffed their surroundings.

The time they'd spent pressed against her must have sped up the acquaintanceship process, for they boldly trotted side by side, sniffing out the perimeter of the shelter before christening each corner with a small yellow puddle. "Going to need a lot of newspapers down here," Sky said, wrinkling her nose, "and there's not a moment to lose."

Her watch beeped. Seven o'clock. In two hours, her veterinary assistant would arrive to assist in neutering the calico. There was a lot to do between now and then to make the shelter a proper temporary home for the little wolves. Sky made four trips between the house and the shelter, her arms loaded with things that would ease their adjustment.

Never-used quilts, piled in the far corner, would serve as their bed. An old clock radio, set to an all-music inspirational station, would play soft melodies to soothe them when she couldn't be there. She replaced the harsh white ceiling bulb with a yellow bug light that cast a warm, comforting glow. And after feeding them a hearty meal of warm, milk-softened dog chow, she filled a bucket with water for them to drink, then left to resume life as a small-town vet.

Though it was cool in the operating room, Sky was perspiring behind the sterile mask. Deft hands maneuvered scalpels and clamps as she mentally reviewed her decision to ready the cubs for a return to the wild. She knew precisely the level of commitment required to prepare them for freedom, because during her internship at the Atlanta Zoo, she'd worked with three wolf cubs brought back to the University of Georgia by students who'd gone hiking in Alaska. Back then, she and two other veterinary assistants had worked with the able yet aging Dr. Manfred Williams. This time, since complete secrecy was the only way Sky could guarantee the cubs' safety, she'd bear the time-consuming responsibility alone.

When she had returned home after the end of her workday, Sky sat down on the shelter floor and quietly invited the cubs to come to her. She knew that if they were to learn how to fend for themselves in the wild, they must transfer dependence on their mother to dependence on her. But they didn't budge. Side by side, they sat on the thick, old quilt, each keeping a wary eye on her.

Sky talked—a lot. To God. To Face. To them. The sooner they grew accustomed to the sound of her voice, the sooner they'd associate it with food and comfort. But much to Sky's dismay, neither cub came near her.

At the end of that frightening, frustrating, fascinating day, she slept the hard, deep sleep of the exhausted and awoke before the alarm buzzed at five. Instantly wide awake, she felt like a child on Christmas morning who'd asked Santa for a puppy. Sky dressed hurriedly and headed for the shelter, balancing a mug of steaming coffee on the hard-backed journal in which she'd track the cubs' progress. They didn't cower when she entered the room. Rather, they stood on all fours, heads low and eyes staring as she poured food and water into stainless-steel bowls. Sky refused to step aside once their meal had been prepared.

"*'He opens their ears to instruction,'*" she said, quoting Job 36:10. Her voice was gentle but stern when she added, "'Cause this is the way it has to be if you're to get what you need!" For several moments, the pair blinked their eyes and licked their lips. By five-thirty, they'd edged forward, one cautious step at a time, to eat their moist breakfast.

Sky yearned to tousle their thick, soft fur. To hug their fuzzy necks. To pat their flat little foreheads. "All in good time," she said, taking her affections out on Face, who greedily ate up the attention. "When I get back," she told them as she closed the door shut, "you guys are going to get some proper names. What do you think of that?"

Doggy brows rose and ears pricked forward in response to her question. The cubs' expressions made it hard to stay put. She wanted to stoop down and gather them up in a big, rough-and-tumble hug. "Let's go to town," she told Face, locking the cubs in the safe solitude of the shelter, "and get those pups some real food."

Face understood the word *town*, and because she loved riding in the truck, she bounded toward it at top speed, her high-pitched, excited bark leading the way.

"Patience," Sky told the dog, as her father had often told her, "is obviously one virtue you don't possess."

❧

When Martha Peebles' 1957 red Cadillac rolled up in front of The Grainery at eight, Sky had already been waiting on the old green porch swing for fifteen minutes. "G'mornin'," her old friend said. "Now, ain't you the early bird today!"

Sky grinned. *"The way of a sluggard is overgrown with thorns, but the path of the upright is a level highway,"* she quoted Proverbs 15:19. "Someone very wise taught me that at least twenty years ago."

The hoarse sound of Martha's laughter tickled Sky's ears, just as it always had. "Wise, my foot!" she said. "It's just plain good sense, is what it is."

Inside, as Sky piled the items on her list onto the worn, red-flecked Formica counter, Martha gossiped. If it had been any other way, Sky would have felt something important was missing. Half an hour later, Sky was paying for her supplies when a blue-jeaned cowboy slipped up and tugged a lock of her hair. "Well, I'll be. If it ain't Sky Allen."

She turned and met the clear blue eyes of her childhood friend. "Dale Rivers," she warned, returning his teasing grin, "you'd better have your running shoes laced up real tight if you plan to do that again."

Thumbing his black Stetson to the back of his head, Dale laughed. "Shoo-eee," he tooted. "Just like when we were young'uns...still full of spunk." With that, he reached out and tweaked her cheek.

Sky responded to his playfulness as she had since both she and Dale were four years old and put on a false show of fury. "I'll thank you to keep your mangy mitts to yourself, cowboy."

"And you're still as cute as all get-out when you're riled." But this time, when Dale reached for her, a large, tanned hand clamped around his wrist and stopped it in midair. "I think your hat must be too tight, Rivers," said a gravelly male voice, "and it's affecting more than your hearing."

His grin still intact, Dale said, "Relax, Chet. Sky knows I was just funnin'."

Sky glared, for real this time, at the so-called white knight who'd interrupted her reunion with Dale.

"Can't you see the little lady wants to be left alone?"

Little lady indeed! Sky hadn't needed a man to protect her since her father had been killed, nearly ten years ago. For an unblinking moment, she stared at Chet Cozart, owner of Four Aces Ranch—and Dale's boss. She'd heard a lot about this man in the weeks she'd been back in town, but this was her first face-to-face glimpse of the ex-rodeo star.

Crossing her arms over her chest, she inventoried the man who had taken it upon himself to be her rescuer: jet-black hair, sun-bronzed skin, and eyes that silently, broodingly said, "I know what's best for you." Sky knew it would be pointless to tell the big lummox she'd dealt with Dale's tomfoolery every summer day of her young life, so she turned on her heel and stomped away without so much as a howdy-do.

"What's gotten into *you*?" she heard Dale ask as she reached the door. "Sky's been like a sister to me since we were knee-high to gophers. Why—"

"Well," interrupted the in-charge voice, "try and mind your manners from here on out."

Sky slammed The Grainery's screen door, clenched her teeth, and headed for the skid that Martha had loaded beside her truck. "'Can't you see the little lady wants to be left alone?'" she muttered, mocking his slow drawl.

As she stacked cases of canned dog food onto the truck, she pictured him: jeans that hugged muscular thighs, a cuffed white shirt that exposed beefy forearms, dark-lashed, glittering gray eyes....

Dale's happy-go-lucky words interrupted her reverie. "You've been in town for weeks. Why haven't you made time for your old buddy? You want folks to think you're still mad about that nickname?"

It said "Lottie Marie Allen" on her birth certificate, but thanks to Dale, everybody called her Sky. What had started out as an innocent game of peekaboo with a bear cub had ended abruptly when its mama bear had appeared...and treed then ten-year-old Sky. If not for Dale, yelling as he banged a soup ladle on a pot, only God knew how long she'd have clung to that old pine. "Bet you can touch the sky," he'd teased once his noisemaking had scared off the bear; "think I'll call you 'Sky-High Lottie' from now on." Before her feet had touched ground, he'd abbreviated it to just plain "Sky," and the name had stuck.

Sky filed the sweet memory away and stepped into Dale's outstretched, welcoming arms.

"Well, why didn't you call me?" he asked.

The decision to return to Mountain Gate hadn't been an easy one. She'd put off looking up old friends, afraid and uncertain about the memories each reunion might conjure. "I've been awfully busy setting up the clinic," she explained. "Besides, since when do you need an invitation?"

Grinning, he glanced at his watch. "Shoo-eee! I'd better get a move on before Chet fires me and you end up supporting my sorry self." He dropped a brotherly kiss on her cheek and, walking backwards, added, "Tell ya what. I'll pick you up at five, take you to our favorite restaurant. My treat." With that, he disappeared into the cowboy crowd near The Grainery's porch steps.

Sky hopped up onto the pickup's tailgate to rearrange supplies on the truck bed. Mentally, she listed Mountain Gate's eateries: the Silver Bullet Diner and

Big Jim's Beef-o-Rama. As kids, she and Dale and little
Ella Houghton had spent a lot of time at Big Jim's. The
summer they turned twelve, the trio started a business
called "Anything for a Buck." Together, they shoveled
manure, mowed lawns, babysat kids and dogs and even
a goldfish or two—and spent every penny of their earn-
ings on Big Jim's burgers and fries. She was still smiling
to herself when she noticed his reflection in the truck's
rear window.

Dale, she thought, grinning, *back for more fun and
games*. In the mirror-like glass, she saw his arm rise
up, reach out.... If the big goof thought he'd get a second
chance to pull her hair, he had another thing coming!

She'd meant only to slap his hand away. Instead,
the back of her hand met his left eyebrow and sent him
sprawling. Her father had always said she was as strong
as an ox. "Don't know your own strength," he'd tease in
a perfect Bullwinkle imitation. She started to tell Dale
she hadn't intended to knock him down, but she stopped
short when she saw that it wasn't Dale but her would-be
rescuer. Chet had looked powerful and intimidating in
The Grainery. Now, sitting there in the dust, he seemed
small and vulnerable, and the sight tweaked a maternal
chord in Sky's heart. She jumped down onto the ground,
landing squarely on both booted feet, shook her hand,
and feigned pain. "Whew! That's some hard head you've
got there," she said.

He touched his already-reddening left brow as a slow
grin slanted his thick, dark mustache.

Sky rested gloved fists on her hips. "I'm sorry, but if
you hadn't snuck up on me—"

"—and if you hadn't been up on that tailgate...." His
grin broadened.

"Guess I did have the upper hand...."

"You pack quite a wallop...for a woman."

Ignoring his sexist remark, Sky stuck out her hand to help him up. Taking it, he unfolded all six feet and three inches of him. "No hard feelings?"

"Nah." He brushed street grime from the seat of his jeans as she lifted the last bag of cedar chips from the skid. "But if you'd-a popped Rivers this way in there," he suggested, gesturing toward the store, "maybe I wouldn't have felt obliged to protect you."

The sack hit the truck bed harder than Sky had intended, splitting the bag and scattering sweet-smelling wood curls across the liner. Chet's tone, the way he casually leaned against her fender, that smart-alecky lift of his slightly-swollen left brow.... "If you'd bothered to ask," she snapped, dark eyes flashing, "I'd have told you I didn't need protecting."

His right forefinger drew a small circle in the air. Sky thought for a moment that he was about to point it at her before diving into some kind of male chauvinist lecture. Instead, he touched his swollen brow, winced, and pushed his black cowboy hat to the back of his head. "Don't I know it."

Stubbornly, Sky stretched to her full five-foot-nine-inch height and set her jaw. *If it's a staring contest he wants*, she decided, *I aim to win it.* To her relief, he blinked and looked away first.

He held out his hand. "Name's Chet. Chet Cozart."

"Sky Allen," she said, pumping his arm.

The casual get-acquainted touch became a crackling connection that sizzled between gloved palms and traveled on an invisible current that fused brown eyes to gray. "Guess I'll see you around," he said, releasing her hand. He turned around as if to head back to The Grainery but swiveled on his heels.

"Say...what do you need with all that dog food? Your dog here," he said, patting Face's head, "is as slim as a dime." Face nuzzled his gloved hand. When he bent down to pet her, she slurped his chin.

Her heart pounding, Sky licked her lips. If he'd been the rifleman in the foothills, he already knew why she'd purchased so much dog food. "Maybe you haven't heard, but I'm a veterinarian...."

The mustache slanted again, this time in a cocky smirk. "Yeah, I've heard." He shrugged one shoulder. "What's one thing got to do with the other?"

Those clear gray eyes seemed friendly. Inviting, even. And just intimidating enough to be the eyes of a sharpshooter. "I can't very well let my patients starve while they're at my clinic, now, can I?"

His puffy left brow arched as he considered her answer. Then, sliding his hat forward again, Chet saluted. "If you say so." Then, "Have a nice day, now, y'hear?"

She teetered between fear and fury until she noticed his limp and wondered what horrible accident had marred his otherwise perfect physique. She slammed the truck's tailgate shut, grabbed the rusty, metal skid's handle, and rolled the skid alongside the others near The Grainery's steps. Martha knew everything about everyone in Mountain Gate. After a few well-aimed questions in her direction, Sky would know exactly what had caused Chet's limp.

And if Sky knew anything about Martha, she'd probably learn a lot more than that!

Chapter Two

That evening, because she knew better than to tell her overprotective childhood friend about finding the cubs, Sky refused to discuss anything but old times with Dale as they ate burgers and fries at Big Jim's. Once they were caught up, Sky told Dale about her second meeting with Chet, calling it "The Grainery Fiasco."

"Chet's a great guy." Leaning closer for effect, Dale whispered, "You could do worse, y'know."

Smiling, Sky pulled her soda straw in and out of the opening in the cup lid. *Hee-haw*, it protested, *hee-haw*.

"You and your soda can laugh if you want, but the truth is, Chet's one of the most respected men in Montana. I think you two would make a right handsome couple."

Sky frowned. "Cut it out, Dale. You know what I always say: Nothing ventured—"

"—nothing lost," he finished, rolling his eyes. "That motto of yours is getting a mite boring, if you don't mind my saying. Your daddy's been dead ten years now, Sky. You can't live in the past forever. And Wade would whoop your britches if he knew you'd been trying." He paused, giving his advice a moment to sink in. "You know I'm right."

Pouting, she tried to knot a French fry. Her mother had run off and left her and her dad before Sky had turned five. By the time she was fifteen, both of her beloved grandparents had passed away. Finally, when her dad was killed two days before her seventeenth birthday, her solitary lifestyle prompted her to rewrite the maxim, "Nothing ventured, nothing gained."

Dale shook his head. "I think it's mighty sad, that's all. You're a great gal, and you deserve to be happy."

Popping the knotted fry into her mouth, she looked up quickly. "What makes you think I'm not?"

His blue eyes glowed with warmth borne from years of friendship. "You can't kid a kidder." Then, wiggling his blond brows, he began counting on his fingers. "You're both devout Christians; both bull-headed and tall as trees; you both love animals and kids; you're both *available*...." Winking, he said, "You're perfect for each other."

Long after Dale had brought her home, Sky sat on her front porch, relaxed by the knowledge that she'd accomplished a great deal during her long, hard day. Sipping lemonade in Gramps' old rocker, she remembered Dale's praises of Chet and smiled. His insistence that she get better acquainted with his boss puzzled her, since Dale had never been much of a matchmaker.

His boss.

His rich, know-it-all boss.

Martha had told Sky that Bud Houghton still lived at Four Aces Ranch, even though the property now legally belonged to Chet. And rumor had it that Bud, not Chet, had initiated the hefty bounty that had cowboys all over the territory lining up wolves in their gun sights. But it stood to reason that if Bud hated wolves that much, so did Chet. *Birds of a feather, and all that*, she thought. *And this bird*, she decided, recalling the scene at The Grainery, *is 100 percent peacock.*

Actually, Sky thought it rather charming that Chet had chosen to play the gallant protector. In a day and age when such efforts were often considered demeaning to liberated women, the hero role could very well be a dangerous one. And the poor guy now sported a bruise to prove it. A tinge of guilt made Sky shift in her chair, pulling the worn old cardigan more tightly around her to ward off the night's chill.

Certainly, she'd acknowledged handsome men before, but only in a passing, offhanded kind of way. Her reaction to this man, however, stirred a strange and foreign emotion deep inside her.

She'd worked long and hard to earn the scholarships that had allowed her to attend Virginia's prestigious School of Veterinary Medicine. Worked even harder to graduate at the top of her class, deliberately filling every hour of every day with work and study and still more work, which left no time for the parties and romance that were such important parts of her classmates' lives. Oh, she'd dated some. Even "went steady" once. But no one had inspired Sky to alter her life motto in the slightest, so the fact that the handsome cowboy had come to mind dozens of times that day unsettled her.

Leaning back in the comfortable rocker, she pictured Chet yet again: rugged and hard-bodied, with hair that caught sunlight like black velvet. A mustached, flirty grin. And those sexy, smoke-gray eyes. "Ain't exactly chicken feed, is he, Face?"

The Irish setter woofed once as if she understood and agreed. Sky smiled fondly at the intelligent, loving dog that had become her full-time companion and remembered how she'd earned her name.

One day, Sky had returned to her Atlanta apartment building to find a dog sitting on the steps and staring in that noble way of Irish setters, as though waiting dutifully for her master to return home. "Just look at that face," Sky had said, extending a friendly hand. "C'mere, you big serious-looking thing, you." The dog's brows had risen, first one, then the other, before she'd stepped up to sniff Sky's fingertips. "I like that face," Sky had said, searching for a license, dog tags—anything that might tell her whom this gorgeous pup belonged to. Finding no identification, she had taken her inside, cleaned her up, fed her leftover meatloaf, and tacked flyers to every telephone pole in a two-mile radius. "We'll give it two weeks," she'd said after placing an ad in the local paper. "If nobody claims you by then, you're mine." They'd been together nearly three years when Sky decided to move back to her homestead, Magic Mountain, in Mountain Gate.

Though the dog had never so much as growled at a living thing, neither was she overly friendly. Yet she'd walked right up to Chet outside The Grainery, rolled on the ground at his feet, and rewarded his attentions with a lick that had left his chin damp. Sky glanced at Face, who lolled contentedly on her back. "Traitor," she said, smiling and nestling deeper into the oak rocker. Its *squeak, creak, squeak* kept time with the crickets' chirps.

The phone brought the tranquil moment to a jangling halt, and Sky carried her lemonade inside as she went to answer it. *Dale*, she thought. *Calling to aim a few more Cupid arrows in my direction.* Smiling, she sang a merry hello into the mouthpiece.

"We know you've got those wolf cubs," said a low, rasping voice. "Turn 'em loose—or you'll be sorry."

Chapter Three

The tumbler slipped from her hand and crashed to the floor, scattering shards of glass across the black and white tiles. "Who is this?"

A quiet click was his answer.

Her heart pounding, Sky latched the lower half of the Dutch door separating the kitchen from the dining room to keep Face from coming in and cutting her paws on the broken glass. Where had she heard that menacing voice before?

Up there on the plateau the previous morning, she'd been fairly certain the gunman had recognized her, thanks to her unruly Allen curls, and the threatening call was proof of it. "*The Lord is my light and my salvation; whom shall I fear?*" she quoted Psalm 27:1 as she swept up.

Today's *Messenger* reported that hybrid wolves had killed Digger Henson's prized bull. The animal had been worth thousands. Certainly Digger had good reason to fear and hate wolves. But he hadn't been the only victim. Matthew Wilson's favorite pony had been attacked by hybrids just last week. The rancher had spotted them and fired several shots that scared them off, but not before they'd done enough damage to require him to put the animal down. And because the horse had been a family pet, its death created quite a stir in Mountain Gate.

Pete Miller's horse had also been killed, but it had been a horse of a different worth. Never one to trust anyone else to do what he could do himself, he insisted on keeping the thoroughbred on his ranch, where he could oversee its feeding, exercise, and training between races. Panache had won numerous titles...and plenty of money. But the hybrids had put an end to all that.

And Sky blamed the wealthy Baltimore-based developer Mike Rowen for every scrap of trouble. If he hadn't come out West, tearing up the landscape to build tract houses on the once-wild terrain, the elk and moose wouldn't have moved farther north, leaving the ranchers' livestock as the canines' only food source.

But such thoughts were pointless. These were the prices humans and animals alike paid for progress. Still, Sky couldn't help but wonder who had paid the biggest price.

She filled a bucket with warm, sudsy water and, as she cleaned up the sticky lemonade spill, avoided looking at the windows. When she'd scrubbed and polished them during her first week back on Magic Mountain, she'd packed up Gran's frilly white curtains because they interfered with her panoramic view of Granite Peak. She wished now that she'd left them in place, for the black, mirror-like panes reminded her of two unblinking eyes, watching her every move.

Times, as Gramps had often said, they were a-changin'. And life had taught Sky the futility of fighting it. That's why she dumped sixteen window latch sets on the counter at The Grainery first thing the next morning.

"I thought you Allens didn't believe in locks," Martha said.

Sky's heart hammered as she recalled the two fuzzy reasons for her purchases. If the gunman knew how to reach her by phone, he knew how to reach her in person, too. "We do now."

Martha had grown accustomed to hearing about people's troubles. When Sky offered no more information, she began stuffing the lock kits into a big paper bag. "Chet was in here this morning asking about you," the older woman said, winking.

Sky's brows drew together. "Chet Cozart?"

"One and the same." Martha sighed dreamily. "Land sakes, but he's a good-lookin' fella. If I were twenty years younger...."

The gunshots and the eerie phone call gonged in Sky's memory. Had Chet asked about her out of simple, friendly curiosity? Or had he been seeking information that would tell him whether she was harboring the cubs? "What did he want to know?"

"Oh," Martha began offhandedly, "how long you'd been away from Mountain Gate, why you stayed away so long, whether or not you had a boyfriend...."

Sky's brows rose. "If I had a boyfriend!"

Martha had told her yesterday that Chet had first come to town with the rodeo. He'd been trampled by a bull, hence the limp. No doubt, the woman had given Chet every juicy tidbit about Sky, too. "Okay, so he knows my entire life story," Sky said, grinning. "But fair's fair. What about *his*?"

"Chet hasn't had a woman in his life since Ella died." She dropped another lock kit into the bag. "Oh, he takes a gal to the movies from time to time. And I hear tell he's gone into Livingston a time or two for dinner at Pablo's. But so far, no woman's turned his head like Ella Houghton did." Martha stopped loading the bag. "You knew he married her, didn't you?"

Sky nodded. Dale had told her all about what the folks of Mountain Gate had dubbed the "romance of the decade."

"Happened a couple of years after your daddy died and you stopped spending summers with your grandparents," Martha continued. "He met her in the hospital after the rodeo accident, don't you know. Ella was his private-duty nurse, see." She slid the bag toward Sky. "They'd just celebrated their second anniversary when their little girl was born." Martha peered over her bifocals and shook her head. "It was sad the way Ella died givin' that child life. She never was the sturdy sort, if you'll recall. Guess the poor little thing just couldn't handle...."

The woman's voice faded into the background as Sky pictured the petite, blue-eyed blonde who'd always reminded Sky of delicate porcelain. It didn't surprise her in the least that a function as natural as having a baby had killed her sweet childhood friend. What *did* surprise Sky was that Ella had married Chet. She wondered what Ella had seen in Chet to make her change her mind about cowboys. "How old is their little girl now?" *Their little girl.* It was both pleasant and painful to discover that a part of Ella lived on in Chet's child.

"Sally? Oh, I reckon she'd be about five by now. Wait till you see her...a miniature Ella, she is. Chet dotes on that girl like she's the last child he'll ever have."

Driving back to her ranch, Sky compared Chet's life to her father's. Her heart ached for Chet, forced by circumstances beyond his control to face parenthood alone. *Treats her like she's the last he'll ever have*, Martha had said. *Just like Daddy treated me* was Sky's bittersweet thought as she drove home.

It took half the morning to install the lock sets. As she worked on the last window, she realized she'd been thinking about Chet the whole time. She forcibly turned her attention back to the screwdriver and power drill she'd dug out of Wade's big red toolbox. He'd taught her how to use almost every tool in it. And what he hadn't taught her, Gramps had.

She wondered if Chet would someday teach his little girl to be self-sufficient and independent, as Wade had taught her to be. Sky tried to picture the tough cowboy gently explaining to his tiny daughter how to hammer a nail or back out a screw. Somehow, she found it hard to believe he had a gentle bone in his big, hard body.

Sky caught herself thinking of him again as she fed and exercised the cubs and later as she pulled a splinter from the paw of Billy Miller's basset hound. In fact, for days, Chet's slanting gray eyes and flirty grin seemed to follow her everywhere she went. Each time she went into town, Sky looked for his black-windowed grey truck. And each time it was nowhere to be seen, a note of disappointment rang in her heart.

For the life of her, she didn't understand her interest in Ella's widower. Sky had a heart as big as the Montana sky and a fun-loving streak just as wide. Ella had been pretty and petite, and Sky doubted the top of her head had even reached the big rancher's shoulders. After loving a woman like that, what would he see in all-arms-and-legs Sky?

Shrugging, she put the toolbox back on the laundry room shelf. She didn't have time for anything but work. Besides, *nothing ventured, nothing lost.*

Dale walked away from the circle of laughing men because he couldn't stomach another minute of their bragging. Digger Henson, Matthew Wilson, and Pete, Marty, and Bart Laurence stood outside The Grainery, each proudly adding up his wolf kills. Pete claimed to have shot four hybrids. Matt said he'd bagged two, maybe three if his last shot had hit its mark. Every man, it seemed, had done his share to rid the Wild West of the ravenous pests...except Bart.

"He couldn't hit the side of a barn with a cannon," Marty teased. "Didn't you see him at last year's turkey shoot?"

Bart bristled under their good-natured ribbing. It wasn't true, after all. He *was* a good shot. He'd missed that target only because he'd been carousing the night before the turkey shoot. But Bart knew that protesting aloud would only ensure their continued kidding.

"I hear Sky Allen has two cubs up on Magic Mountain," said Matt. "I heard tell she was out in the foothills when Duggie took down the mama. Says she took 'em home, like they was French poodles or somethin'!"

The men laughed. "Ain't that just like a woman!"

"Say, Bart," Marty said, "*there's* some easy pickin's for you. Duggie says they're penned up. You could just walk right on up an' pop 'em. Like fish in a barrel...."

Sober, Bart would have walked away from the cowboy's ridiculous taunts. But Bart hadn't fully recuperated from last night's bout with a bottle of red-eye. "Seems to me they'll be harder to hit now than ever," he replied. "You remember what an animal lover she was as a kid. I don't reckon that toned down any as she grew up." Bart crossed both arms over his chest. "Even if what you say is true, I ain't hankerin' to get arrested for trespassing."

"You can bet your pearly whites on it," Matt said, elbowing the man beside him. "What say we make this interesting...?" He pulled a wad of wrinkled currency from his pocket and smoothed a hundred-dollar bill against his thigh. "This dead president here says you can't bring us even one cub carcass."

Frowning, Bart shook his head. "You're out of your mind, man. I don't have anything against Sky. If she wants to raise a couple of flea-bitten—"

"Your pa would roll over in his grave if he heard you right now."

The alcohol still swirling in his mind, Bart pictured the way Sky had looked when he'd seen her at The Grainery... tall and trim and more gorgeous than ever. She'd suffered plenty, if rumors about the way Wade Allen had died were true, and Bart didn't see any reason to add to her misery.

"C'mon, put your money where your mouth is, Laurence. Let's see what kind of stuff you're made of."

Ever since they were boys, Matt had tormented Bart with one childish provocation after another. And he'd always won, too, a fact that had often prompted angry glares from Bart's father. He'd been a major disappointment to his dad—academically, athletically, as a ranch hand, as a man. Bart believed that, but worse, Matt believed it, too. Anger mixed with the whiskey that still ran strong in his veins, and he showed his own hundred-dollar bill. "You're on," he said, though he knew it was the whiskey, not he, that had accepted Matt's challenge.

Every man joined Matt's bet. "We know how hard it is for you rich boys to do any real work," Matt said, "so we'll give you a month to bring us a wolf hide." He slapped Bart's back. "Think you're up to the challenge, buddy?"

"Don't need a month," Bart grated, "and you ain't my buddy." With that, he stormed off, feeling exactly as he had at ten, when a dare of Matt's had prompted him to cross the Ruby River in a canoe. He'd nearly drowned, but at least he'd showed Matt what kind of stuff he was made of. Showed his dad, too, and his reward had been a brand-new saddle.

He was pretty drunk, but not so foggy that he didn't know he'd have to use Sky Allen to prove himself this time. He licked his lips, then swallowed a gulp of the cola he'd bought from the soda machine on The Grainery porch. He'd seen her before she left Mountain Gate all those years ago, surrounded by half a dozen wobbly-legged kittens and at least as many potbellied pups. It hadn't surprised him to learn she'd become a veterinarian. What *had* surprised him was the way the knobby-kneed girl with the wild red curls had grown into a woman who could give any cover model a run for her money.

Matt had been right, much to Bart's dismay. Sky *was* harboring two wolf cubs on Magic Mountain. He'd seen them from his well-hidden perch near the top of Granite Peak. For her sake, Bart promised himself their deaths would be swift and painless. At least he'd have that much to salve his conscience when he turned their hides over to the cowboy gang. Maybe he'd take their "dare" money and buy something nice for Sky's clinic....

Sitting in his hiding place now, watching her through a spyglass, he quickly learned Sky's routine. And, as he watched, he remembered the terror in her lovely voice when he'd made that first call from the throwaway cell phone.

She'd grieve when the cubs turned up missing, but she'd go on, as she'd done when her grandparents, and then her father, had died. And why shouldn't she? Sky Allen had a lot to look forward to: Magic Mountain Ranch, a successful career, memories of a loving family, and the respect of every Mountain Gate resident, to boot. Maybe once he'd completed this dirty deed and had rid the town of two more wolves, he'd turn over a new leaf and start earning himself a share of that respect.

Every cloud has a silver lining, he told himself. His reputation for being a poor shot would save him, should anyone decide to finger him for killing the cubs. And maybe, when the whole sorry mess was over, he could be the one to comfort her in her time of loss....

❧

The evening had always been Sky's favorite time of day at the ranch. Snuggled deep in the red gingham cushions of Gramps' rocker, she focused on Granite

Peak, standing proud and bold against the inky sky, then closed her eyes and inhaled crisp mountain air.

Face's chin warmed the toes of her boots as crickets harmonized with the chair's steady creaking. She hadn't slept more than a few fitful hours since rescuing the cubs, and she was determined to enjoy these moments of relaxation, despite the conflicting thoughts that swirled in her brain: fear of the gunman, the threatening call, work...and the effect Chet was having on her.

"You're mighty pretty in the moonlight...."

Jumping with fright, she gasped as Face welcomed the speaker, her tail wagging as he tethered his horse to the gate. Sky leapt to her feet—too quickly, she realized, when dizzying waves shot through her head.

In a whipstitch, Chet was beside her, one big hand supporting her elbow, the other planted firmly against her lower back. "Sorry, didn't mean to scare you," he admitted, his soft breath tickling her ear. "We like to ride after supper," he added, nodding toward his big black mare. "You looked so peaceful, I didn't want to disturb you."

At first, being in his arms seemed as natural as inhaling and exhaling, but when Sky heard her own ragged breaths, she stepped quickly back and nearly tumbled down the porch steps. Again, Chet steadied her. So, twice in less than a minute, he'd saved her from falling. Then, as though sensing her discomfort at his nearness, Chet pocketed his hands. "Say, that looks tasty."

She followed his gaze to where her half-filled glass of lemonade sat in a dewy puddle on the table between the rocking chairs. "Would you like some?" A gnawing cold spot pulsed where his hand had touched her back.

"Love some."

She left him and Face alone on the porch. In the kitchen, picturing the fading bruise she'd caused above his eye, she missed the mouth of his glass and splashed lemonade onto the countertop. When she tried to sop it up, she knocked the ice tray to the floor. Sky was on her hands and knees, muttering angrily under her breath, when Chet joined her in the kitchen.

"One of those days?"

A nervous giggle popped from her mouth as she scrambled to her feet. She prided herself on being organized. Capable. Calm in a storm. So the rapid beating of her heart and the heat in her cheeks annoyed her. She reached to hand him his glass just as his fingers closed around it. His skin was work-roughened yet surprisingly warm. She snatched back her hand and watched him drain, then refill, the glass of lemonade.

His long, satisfied sigh made her stomach flip.

"Can't remember when I last had homemade lemonade."

Face woofed, took Chet's shirtsleeve in her teeth, and tugged gently. "Guess she's trying to tell me I've overstayed my welcome," he said, laughing as he stooped to follow the dog onto the porch.

The screen door slammed behind them, reminding Sky of the gunshots that had zinged past her the day she rescued the cubs. When they weren't winking flirtatiously, those glittering, black-lashed orbs could very well be the eyes of a sharpshooter, she realized, now more suspicious of his intentions than ever. From the doorway, she said, "What brings you all the way out here?"

Chet had just settled into Gran's rocker. Shrugging, he flashed a shy half-smile in her direction. "Like I said, Sugar and I always ride after supper." Blinking, he looked at the floorboards. "Well, that's not entirely true."

His admission quickened her heartbeat.

"It's been a long time since.... Haven't much felt like...." He cleared his throat and flexed both hands, then added, "Thought it might be nice to get better acquainted, since we're practically neighbors, that's all."

Sky sat beside him in Gramps' chair. Small talk had never been her forte, but she decided she'd better try some on for size if she hoped to find out what, if anything, he knew about her cubs.

Before she could say a word, Chet said, "I met a lady vet in Butte, once." Leaning back, he rested his booted feet on the railing. "Reminded me of old Miss Grundy from the *Archie* comics." He grinned over at her. "I got that picture in my mind every time I heard about a lady doctor after that. Until I met you."

His sideways compliment put a small smile on her face.

"What made you decide to become a veterinarian, anyway?"

She rocked slowly. "Well, when I was six, I found a kitten beside Route 212. Somebody had tossed it from a car, no doubt, causing compound fractures in both forelegs. She was coal-black with snow-white forepaws, so I named her Mittens." Sky took a deep breath, remembering. "She died even before my dad could drive me into town to see the vet. Somehow, I sensed that if I'd known more—known *something*—Doc Adams might have been able to save her." She shook her head. "When I buried her, I swore I'd never let myself feel that helpless again. I went to the library the very next day and checked out two of James Herriot's children's books. From that moment on, I was hooked."

Chet smiled and nodded, and those warm gray eyes told her that he understood. But she needed to forget about his gorgeous face and get back to her detective work. "Martha tells me you're not originally from Montana."

Both his feet hit the floor, and he rested his glass on his knee. "Born and raised in Wyoming. Fort Washakie, to be precise." Moonlight lit his face, spilled down his chest, and landed in an icy-white pool between the pointy toes of his dusty cowboy boots. "After my dad died, my mother and I struck a deal—I'd finish college, and she wouldn't raise a ruckus when I signed on with the rodeo." He put his glass on the table between them and met her eyes. "That's how I got this limp, you know."

In response to Sky's silence, he continued. "I was hot to win first prize riding Black Devil, meanest Brahma I ever set eyes on. He was pitching and snorting even before we got out of the chute," Chet said. "Guess I oughtta be thankful he didn't leave me with worse than a limp."

Sky wondered if Chet was aware that his big-knuckled hands were gripping the arms of Gran's chair so tightly that his fingertips had turned white.

"I held on nearly six seconds before he threw me." Chuckling softly, Chet added, "Thought he was gonna stomp me into dust. I spent three long weeks at County General with broken ribs, a punctured lung, my arm in a sling, my leg in traction, and a headache the size of the Grand Canyon. That was the end of my rodeo career."

Sky barely knew him, yet the pain in his eyes was as obvious as the mournful coyote song carried down from the mountains on the calm evening breeze. "I'm sorry," was all she said.

He shrugged. "I'm not. If it hadn't been for that accident, I'd never have met my Ella." A full minute passed before he said, "She died a while back." He took off his hat and hung it on one knee. "She talked about you all the time. Wanted you to be her maid of honor, you know."

No, Sky hadn't known that. If she hadn't been so busy wallowing in self-pity to involve herself in Ella's life, she might have been there for her childhood friend.

Chet's soft voice interrupted her thoughts. "Martha told me you spent all your summers here on Magic Mountain as a kid."

When he looked at her with that gentle gaze, Sky found herself holding her breath. She hadn't known what to expect when she'd started her mini-investigation to see how—if—he might be involved in the shooting, but opening old wounds sure hadn't been part of the plan!

He'd said "my Ella," not with the voice of a man who considered his wife property but with the soft, sweet tones of genuine love. Sky made a mental note of that and added it to her rapidly growing list of reasons to like Chet Cozart.

"She left me the prettiest little daughter a man could hope to have."

According to Martha, Ella had died nearly five years ago, but the slight catch in his voice made it apparent to Sky that to Chet, it seemed like yesterday. The tenderness in his eyes and voice when he spoke of her friend only made Sky like him all the more.

Suddenly, he sat up and leaned forward, elbows on his knees. "So, tell me, what're you doing way out here? You'd make a lot more money if your clinic was in the city."

"True," Sky said, nodding, "but I wouldn't have that to look at."

Together, they gazed toward Granite Peak, cloaked by the deep-purple night sky. The hazy, mystical view was responsible for the name her soft-hearted, poetic grandfather had given to the property.

"You've got a point there," Chet agreed, his voice a near whisper.

Spending so much time with animals had honed Sky's ability to analyze demeanor and attitude. She sensed that Chet was a good and decent man. A man who could be trusted with any secret. She wondered what he'd say if he knew she was raising two wolf cubs, and what he'd do if he found out that she intended to continue working with them until they were old enough to survive on their own in the wild.

Quickly, she came to her senses. His whole life was livestock, in one way or another. Martha had told her that Chet now owned Four Aces Ranch. Maybe it was at his command that Bud Houghton, Ella's father, had posted the steadily rising wolf bounty in the first place. *Just stick to the plan*, she warned herself, *and keep your mouth shut about those cubs!*

Several moments ticked by as they watched the night sky, content, it seemed, to enjoy the awesome beauty and silence that surrounded them. Sky's wristwatch beeped, cracking the stillness and startling them both. Their eyes locked, and they burst into a tension-reducing round of laughter.

Face woofed.

"My sentiments exactly." Chet patted the dog's head, then stood up. "Guess I'd better head on out."

Sky couldn't convince herself that it had been Chet who'd been shooting at her that day in the foothills. In fact, something made Sky want to share her secret with him. In that moment of weakness, she almost quoted Mae West: "Come on back and see me some time." But before her tongue could form the words, old ghosts reared their ugly heads.

"Thanks for the drink...and the company."

Her life motto clear in her mind, Sky realized she'd better keep a safe distance from this man if she hoped to continue living by it. In a deliberately steely voice, she said, "You're quite welcome."

Chet tore his gaze from the horizon to meet her eyes. The furrowed brow and tight-lipped pout, visible thanks to a shaft of moonlight slanting across his rugged features, told Sky that her cool response had stung like a slap. *Well*, she asked herself, *what did he expect? A big, juicy good-night kiss?*

As if he heard her thoughts, Chet licked his lips. "Guess I'll be on my way, then." His boots thumped down the wooden porch steps and over the flagstone walk.

Though he tried hard to hide it, the effects of his run-in with the Brahma were obvious. Sky wondered if he limped because it hurt to walk or simply because the bull's hooves had permanently damaged muscle and bone. She preferred to think the latter; having lost the love of his life, he'd already suffered enough pain.

From the other side of the fence, he climbed into the saddle. "G'night," he said, sending her the Cowboy Salute. "Maybe I'll see you in town sometime soon." With that, he rode away.

Face jumped up, rested her front paws between picket points, and watched until he disappeared from sight. She cast a backward glance in the direction of her mistress and whined.

"Oh, don't give me that," Sky scolded halfheartedly. "It isn't *my* fault your new best friend left."

In response, Face barked and trotted past Sky onto the porch, where she flopped in a graceless heap. Her actions made it very clear who, in her opinion, had been responsible for the sudden departure of her pal.

Hours later, Sky was dreaming of Chet's handsome half-grin when the phone woke her. The clock on the nightstand said 3:47.

When no one responded to her groggy greeting, Sky sat up. "Hello?" she said again.

"Do yourself a big favor, Doc. Turn those critters loose before somebody gets hurt."

Since there had been just one call in the days that followed the cubs' rescue, she'd allowed herself to slip into a comfortable, confident routine. Told herself that maybe the caller had paid a visit to Magic Mountain and, after quick investigation, had satisfied himself that no wolf cubs lived there.

Suddenly, anger doused her fear. How dare the cowardly bully threaten her this way! But before she had a chance to put her fury into words, the dial tone droned in her ear. She hung up wishing she could talk to the marksman, could tell him she understood how apprehension of man had been bred out of the half-dog, half-wolf hybrids. How, pressed by hunger, they sometimes attacked livestock and pets. And how ranchers, after getting no help or support from the government, adopted a credo that said, "The only good wolf is a dead wolf."

Sky knew only too well that her cubs' mother had been a hybrid and very well may have been a part of pack activity that had cost some rancher a prized bull or a favorite horse. Knew that the ranchers' vigilante mentality had turned brutal and ugly. Now, purebred wolves—whose fear of man made sightings rare—were on the hit list, too.

But none of that mattered now. The cubs were as defenseless as the ranchers' livestock, and Sky intended to give them a chance at survival in the wild—nothing more.

Roaming through the darkened house, Face close at her heels, Sky peered out the living room window into the shadowy yard, wondering if the caller and the shooter were one and the same person, or if his use of first-person plural meant that the ranchers had banded together. A creepy-crawly "somebody's watching" feeling prickled the back of her neck, and, crossing her arms over her chest, she cupped her elbows to ward off the resulting chill. Sky prowled the house all night, stopping only now and then to sit stiff-backed in a chair or lie rigid on her bed, wide awake, listening, aware....

At first light, she grabbed her dad's police binoculars and positioned herself in the middle of the yard. Rotating slowly, she examined the horizon. Finding no evidence that anyone had set up a lookout anywhere beyond Magic Mountain's property lines, she headed for the shelter to feed and exercise the cubs in the tiny, fenced-in space behind the house.

Gran used to say, "Idle hands are the devil's workshop." Sky supposed the old saying could just as easily apply to a worried mind. Long hours and hard work had helped her survive Wade's violent death. The same medicine would see her through this ordeal, she reasoned. So, she got up a little earlier every day, worked a little longer and harder with the cubs, and extended her clinic hours. A weed wouldn't dare show itself, and dust barely had time to settle in the house before she wiped it away, leaving Sky just enough energy after falling into bed every night to pray the phone wouldn't ring.

Because she'd found the cubs near a gnarled pine growing from a boulder, Sky named the female Piney and the male Rocky. Daily, she scribbled wolf-related statistics under column headings she'd printed on the left side of the ledger-style book: *Exercise. Play. Instinctual Behavior. Learned Behavior. Weight. Meals.* On the right-hand pages, Sky charted more specific observations: *Three weeks before, they'd climb up and down the shelter stairs.*

Her med school work with Alaskan wolves had taught her most of what she needed to know about the species. The shelter, as it turned out, was the perfect home for the cubs, for it protected them not only from being seen but also from seeing the things they would need to avoid once she'd returned them to the wild. Cars, airplanes, farm equipment, and other machines of man would still terrify them long after they'd been released in the foothills. Most important, the sight, scent, and sound of humans other than herself would send them hightailing for cover. And because most domestic animals carried human scent, the cubs would be equally wary of live-stock and pets—with the exception of Face.

For the past two days, Sky wrote in the journal, *Rocky and Piney have responded to handclapping by running to me*. She then clapped and waited for the customary *clickety-clack* of toenails as the cubs scrambled down the narrow wooden staircase that led into the cool, cavernous shelter. Giving each cub a hearty hug, she laughingly endured their damp smooches.

"You guys have bad breath," she said, ruffling their soft, silvery fur. "Haven't you ever heard of a little invention called a toothbrush?"

The Irish setter, insinuating herself into the fuzzy circle, licked Sky's cheek, then slobbered on each cub.

"They sure grow on you, don't they, girl?"

Face answered with a happy bark and a doggy smile. All three canines growled and rolled playfully on the cool concrete floor as Sky laughed at their noisy, affectionate display of cousinly love.

"Are you lookin' to get *shot*?" thundered an angry male voice.

Chapter Four

C het looked like he owned the place, leaning casually against the doorframe, his dark brows drawn together above gun-metal gray eyes.

The sight of him intimidated yet thrilled her. "W-what are you doing here?"

A slight grin lit his eyes. "Now, what kind of a greeting is that?"

His voice, so smug and self-assured, grated in her ears. "The only kind you're gonna get when you sneak around and scare people half to death."

"Well, at least you have the good sense to *be* scared. Are you ready to let me help you load up those critters and put 'em back where they belong, before somebody gets hurt?" he asked, nodding toward the cubs.

Before somebody gets hurt.... Sky sent a silent prayer heavenward that she had been correct in her conclusion that the caller's voice and Chet's were completely different. For a reason she couldn't explain, she didn't want to believe the worst about him. Ignoring his question, she posed one of her own. "Exactly who do you think you are, coming over here uninvited and barking orders like a drill sergeant?"

Shifting a toothpick from the left side of his mouth to the right, he held his calm stance, as if willing her to realize how foolish it was to try to raise a pair of wolf cubs. "What do you want?" she demanded.

He held the toothpick between his thumb and fore-finger and inspected it for a long, silent moment before returning it to his mustached mouth. Crossing one boot-ed foot in front of the other, he hooked both thumbs into his belt loops. "Let's just say I'm a very curious fellow." The toothpick travelled right. "I saw fur on your shirt the other night in your kitchen, and it's been bugging me ever since."

Sky pointed at Face, who looked up adoringly at him. "*And* I'm a veterinarian."

He shook his head and grinned. "That you are, pret-ty lady. But Face here is a redhead, like you," he said, using the toothpick as a pointer. "And the fur I saw was gray. Coarse." His grin disappeared when he added, "Like wolf fur." He stared at her for a full minute before speaking again. "Yesterday, I overheard a couple of my cowhands talking about a she-wolf they'd shot a while back. Seems Digger Henson gave 'em five hundred bucks for her carcass." He squatted in the doorway to drape an arm around Face. "They've been looking for her cubs ever since."

He met her eyes with such intensity it caused Sky to blink. She swallowed. Hard.

"Too much coincidence, or could that wolf have been mama to these guys?" he asked, his voice surprisingly gentle, despite the steely glow emanating from his eyes. "You think you're fooling them, Sky? Think about it from their point of view. If anybody was going to rescue a cou-ple of orphaned wolf cubs, it'd be you."

Across the room, the cubs sat side by side, staring at Chet. Oddly, they didn't seem the least bit afraid of him. *Quite the contrary*, Sky noted as their dog lips pulled back in matching canine grins.

She simply didn't get it. She'd saved their lives. Made a safe haven for them here in the shelter. Fed and watered and exercised them regularly, showered them with attention and affection, and yet they'd only just begun to respond to her as she'd hoped. So why did it appear that they trusted Chet already? What had he done, she wondered, to earn their instant trust?

Sky adjusted the glow of the lamp near the door. "Let's take this discussion outside. I don't want you to upset them. Upstairs, Face," she ordered, snapping her fingers. The dog obeyed immediately and dashed up the steps, followed closely by Chet, while Sky stayed behind to bolt the shelter's thick metal door.

"Unreasonable, ridiculous...," Chet muttered as he walked past, his arms flapping like a giant blue-jeaned bird, "...afraid to talk...in front of animals!" In the shed, he had folded his arms over his chest, planted his booted feet shoulder width apart, and watched her drop the trap door into place. Outside, as she snapped the padlock shut, he assumed the same stance.

Sky dropped the key into her shirt pocket and said, "This way, Mr. Clean," then led him into the kitchen, where she filled two big mugs with coffee. In half an hour, the sun would be up, but right now, the house was still early-morning dark. Sky turned on the overhead light. "Milk and sugar?"

"Just black, thanks." Chet put his hat on the corner of the table, turned a kitchen chair around, and sat down, resting his big arms on its back.

Sky sat down across from him.

"How could anyone so smart do something so stupid?" he demanded. "Don't you know there's a bounty on their heads?"

"It's precisely *because* of the bounty that I'm doing this! I was there when their mother was killed. I couldn't very well let them be shot, too, could I?"

Chet's dark brows knitted with worry. "Did you stop to consider, even for a minute, that letting them die might have been the most humane thing you could have done for everybody concerned?"

Exasperated, she blew a stream of air through her lips.

"Look," he said, folding his huge hands on the table-top, "I know it's your business to protect and care for animals. But be realistic, why don't you? If certain people find out what you're doing, you could be in as much danger as those pups out there."

Her eyes met his, and it surprised her to find such honest concern there. Still, something made her say, "Certain people? People like *you*, maybe?"

He let the question pass unanswered.

"I won't let them die for a few measly dollars."

"*'A prudent man sees danger and hides himself; but the simple go on, and suffer for it,'*" Chet said.

"Dale seems to think you're a pretty decent guy," Sky began, drumming her fingers on the table. "So, let me ask you a question...."

Chet's shrug invited her to continue.

"Why'd you post that bounty in the first place?"

His brows rose so quickly, Sky was afraid they'd collide with his hairline. "I didn't post it. It was Digger Henson, and Bud followed suit."

"Well, it's *your* ranch, so I'd think...."

"If you were a thinking woman, you wouldn't be in this fix." Then, his eyes darkening and his voice lowering dangerously, he said, "And you don't know diddly about me and my ranch, lady, so I suggest you stick to discussing subjects you *do* know something about."

His flinty-eyed scrutiny unnerved her, but to keep him from seeing it, Sky took a long, slow drink of her coffee.

Chet ran both hands through his thick, dark hair and held them there a moment, then sucked in a deep breath, as if trying to decide whether or not to stay. Sky watched his forefinger slide back and forth on the black felt brim of his hat, raising and flattening the velvety material. Sky thought he looked incredibly handsome, lost in thought like that.

When he met her eyes again, his left brow lifted. "Here's the way it happened: the Houghtons and the Laurences have been battling over the boundary between Four Aces and the Lazy L for generations. One night, Bud and Bart Sr. got involved in a poker game, and the two old fools bet land instead of money. Bud lost, and the acreage he lost just so happened to have on it the only water supply for miles. He'd have gone under for sure without that parcel.

"So, I waited till old Bart sobered up. I couldn't just stand there like a fence post and watch my Ella suffer a lifetime for one night of her father's drunken stupidity. I had saved nearly every dollar of rodeo prize money, figured it'd help her."

A flash of pain crossed his face, interrupting the story. Chet took a swallow of the coffee, then continued: "So, I made Bart an offer he couldn't refuse—twenty thousand if he'd forget the bet. The land was worth five; the other fifteen grand guaranteed he'd keep his big yap shut about my part in it. But they got tanked up again a couple months later, and old Bart spilled the beans.

"Call it pride, call it ego, call it *stupidity*—Bud called it charity, saying, 'No Houghton has ever taken a handout!' So, he drew up some papers and insisted the place was mine, since it was my money that had saved it.

"The ranch had been losing money every year for more than a decade. Four Aces was this close to bankruptcy," Chet explained, putting an inch of air between his forefinger and thumb. "I have a master's in economics, so I promised Bud that if I couldn't get the place humming again within the year, I'd tear up the paperwork."

"And did you save it?"

The well-arched left brow rose again as he grinned. "Turned a profit that first year, and despite this stinking economy, we've been holding our own ever since."

"So, Four Aces is yours, to run as you see fit."

An angry grimace replaced his grin. "There you go again, yammerin' about things you know nothing about." He took a swallow of coffee. "When Ella died, Bud lost all interest in the place. Said he'd rather see me at the helm than watch the land go fallow. So, I've been doing just that. For Bud—in Ella's memory—so Sally would have something of her own one day. Her mama loved that place," he said with a softer tone in his voice. Then, straightening his shoulders, he added, "Four Aces is mine on paper, but it's really Bud's. If he ever comes to his senses, Four Aces will be his again."

"How very generous of you."

Chet laughed at her caustic remark. "You don't know me well enough to have such a low opinion of me, Doc." The smile in his eyes dimmed when he added, "What kind of man would I be if I kicked the old coot out just 'cause I *could*?"

Sky didn't have a low opinion of him. In fact, she admired and respected him for what he'd done. And the fact that she thought so highly of him, all things considered, unnerved her. "What does any of that have to do with allowing Bud to post a bounty?"

Chet's stare hardened. "First of all, nobody *allows* Bud Houghton to do anything. And, second, I'm half Cheyenne, for crying out loud. I probably know as much about wolves as...as even a fancy-schooled *veterinarian*."

She ignored his sarcasm.

"They're beautiful, intelligent beasts. And most of the time," he continued, his face and attitude gentling, "I wish we still lived back in the days when 'survival of the fittest' was the law of the land. I'd never stoop as low as to pay to have one killed, but I'd shoot in a heartbeat if I caught one makin' a meal outta one of my cows. I'm no different from any other rancher that way—we do whatever it takes to protect what's ours."

As a rancher, Chet was duty-bound to protect the livestock that were the financial support of his family and employees, yet he respected the rights of wild creatures. Handsome. Intelligent. Honest. Big-hearted to a fault. Sky liked him, doggone it—too much, perhaps. "Nothing justifies killing innocent anim—"

"Innocent?" he interrupted her. "Those hybrids will kill more than their share of cattle in a single season. That's hardly my idea of innocent."

"But they kill by instinct, and only then to survive."

"That's all the ranchers are trying to do."

His quiet logic reminded her that her grandparents had spent a lifetime striving to eke out a living on a meager rancher's income. She knew exactly how hard life could be out here. But that didn't change one thing in her mind. "Survival of the fittest," she murmured.

Chet could only smile and shake his head.

"I need to know what your intentions are," Sky said.

Grinning, he raised both brows this time. "My intentions? I'm sure not ready to tie the knot, lady!"

Waving away his ridiculous comment, Sky focused on the issue at hand. The cubs deserved to live as God intended. If, upon their release, they couldn't survive the weather, other wolves, or the bounty hunters, so be it. But she intended to give them at least a fighting chance. "I can't let you tell anyone that I'm trying to save them." She hoped the desperation in her heart wasn't evident in her voice.

One corner of his mouth lifted in wry amusement. "Like I said, anybody with half a brain already knows what you're up to." Leaning forward, he added, "But even if they didn't, exactly how would you stop me from talkin'?"

Sky lowered her eyes, wondering if he could hear her hammering heart. She gulped her coffee and took her time swallowing it. Whether it was his penetrating gaze or his titillating grin or his loyalty to Bud, Sky couldn't say, but something deep inside her said she could trust him. "Maybe you're wrong. Maybe nobody else *is* smart enough to have added two and two, and if that's the case, I just need a little time to teach them to fend for themselves."

"How much time?"

Hope filled her heart. "Four months," she said, no longer caring if he heard the pleading note in her voice. "Give me four months, and I'll release them in the foothills."

Face padded into the kitchen and sat beside Chet. "She wants to keep them safe until they're old enough to fend for themselves," he told the dog. "I say she's plumb loco. What do you think?"

The dog barked once, then laid a paw on Chet's thigh.

Ruffling Face's fur, Chet looked deep into Sky's eyes. "You're either as dumb as they come," he said slowly, "or the bravest woman I've ever met."

Shifting uncomfortably in her seat, Sky didn't know whether he'd just paid her a compliment or slapped her with an insult. "Does that mean you won't tell anyone? You'll keep my secret?"

Chet smoothed his mustache with his thumb and forefinger. "Big risk you're taking, assuming I'm the only one who's figured things out." A pause followed, then, "Could be right interesting to watch you teach 'em how to behave like proper wolves."

Feeling simultaneously safe and elated, Sky impulsively covered his hands with her own. "Thanks," she sighed.

He looked at the tiny mountain their fingers had created. After a long moment, he met her eyes again. "Don't thank me just yet, Doc," he said, his voice soft and somber.

Readjusting their hands so that his blanketed hers, he added, "You'll need to be very careful from here on out, 'cause there's no way you can convince me I'm not the only one who can—as you so astutely put it—add two and two." He focused for a moment on their hands, still entwined on the table. This time, when he looked up, he said, "Okay, I'll keep your little secret...on one condition."

It took a moment for Sky to let this sink in. First, Chet had scared her half to death by listing the reasons she was a target. And then, with no warning whatsoever, he'd done a complete turnabout and tacked a condition on to his agreement to keep his mouth shut. Sky snatched back her hands. "I might have known you were the type who'd go back on your word. But you've got me between a rock and a hard place, and we both know it, so go ahead, cowboy. Name your 'condition.'"

The barest hint of a smile glimmered in his eyes. "Dinner," he drawled.

Sky blinked. She'd expected him to ask for free veterinary services. Maid service, maybe. But...dinner?

As if he'd read her mind, Chet nodded once. "Dinner." Then he stood and branded her with that smoky gaze.

"I don't get it."

"You don't have to get it. You just have to be ready at seven. We're going to Livingston."

Livingston was an hour's drive north of Mountain Gate. Mentally, Sky calculated the evening hours: one to get there, at least another for the meal, one more to get home.... She didn't know if she could stand being alone with him that long. But since her cubs' lives depended on his silence....

Chet thrust out his right hand. "Deal?"

Hesitantly, she put hers in it. "Deal."

Chet squeezed ever so gently before releasing her hand. Without another word, he grabbed his hat and headed for the back door. Then, as if he'd overlooked something important, he stopped, one hand on the door-knob, and faced her.

Here it comes, she told herself. *The real condition....*

"This restaurant I have in mind," he said, "is pretty classy. In case you're wondering how to dress, I mean...." And as quickly as he'd said it, he was gone, black hat and all.

Face stared at the closed door and whimpered.

"Yeah, I know," Sky said. "There he goes again, riding off into the sunset." She noticed the bright fireball rising slowly in the morning sky. "I stand corrected: into the sun*rise*."

All day long, Sky found herself wishing she had more to keep her mind occupied so that she could stop thinking about the evening ahead. Unfortunately, it was a slow day at the clinic. She spent a few hours in the gardens, pulling up the last of the spent flowers and the half-dead stalks of the vegetables she'd planted during her first days in Mountain Gate. But no matter how hard she tried to keep her mind elsewhere, her thoughts returned to her early-morning conversation with Chet. A grating voice in her head whispered, *He could be the shooter*, while a gentler, sweeter voice in her heart sighed, *You can trust him*.

Sky wanted to believe in Chet, but by now, she'd spent so many years living by her motto that she wondered if she remembered how.

Chapter Five

S ky barely recognized Chet when he arrived wearing a navy suit and a starched white shirt. His maroon tie was in such sharp contrast to his eyes that they looked more rainy-day gray than ever.

"Well, look at you," he said, walking a big circle around her. "I must admit, you clean up real good."

She grinned at his sideways compliment. The peach chiffon had always been Sky's favorite dress. She had spent most of her life wearing jeans and T-shirts under her lab coats—hardly feminine attire. But in this dress, she'd always felt ladylike. A little bit pretty, even. "Do we have reservations?" she asked as he helped her into her coat.

"Don't need 'em," he said. "I have...uh...connections at this particular establishment." With that, he bowed low and opened the front door for her. "Your chariot awaits, m'lady."

In place of the dark-windowed truck he usually drove, a silver Porsche convertible sat in Sky's driveway. "Christmas present to myself last year," Chet explained as Sky locked the front door behind her, "when I decided it was time to start living my life again. Hope you don't mind the inconvenience of a lowrider."

Ella's face flitted through Sky's mind at Chet's mention of living again. Sky hadn't expected to enjoy the evening, but for the cubs' sake, she'd decided to pretend. His mood was contagious, though; already, she was grinning. "I hope you don't plan to put the top down."

"Maybe on the drive home," he said, winking as he opened the passenger door, "when it won't matter if you get...mussed."

She slid onto the leather passenger seat, carefully avoiding his eyes. The tone of his deep voice alone had been more than suggestive enough. If she'd found the same message in his eyes, Sky would have blushed, as sure as she was sitting beside him.

He'd chosen a classical string concerto to entertain them on the car's CD player as they drove, and from time to time, he drew her attention to sights that hadn't been part of Montana's scenery years ago, when she'd spent every summer on Magic Mountain.

His "connections," as it turned out, were the restaurant owners. "Thees place, she is all mine and Maria's, thanks to Meester Chet," Pablo explained when Chet introduced him to Sky. "You see, the bank, she refuse to make a loan." He winked at Chet. "But Meester Chet, he know I can cook, and that my Maria, she can bake fine cakes and breads." He shrugged. "Weethout him, Maria would still be the cook at Four Aces, and I would still be the gardener."

Sky had never seen a man blush before, but there Chet stood, all six-foot-strapping-three of him, as pink cheeked as a schoolboy on his first date. He tried to shush Pablo, but the shorter man ignored him, took Sky's arm, and led her to a table in a quiet corner of the restaurant. "Meester Chet, he would not even charge us *eeenterest!* He is one fine man, for sure. You must be sometheeng special for him to choose you, *sí*?"

Smiling, Sky glanced at Chet, whose tanned cheeks still glowed. That he'd tried to keep his wonderful deed a secret only made him more appealing. "Yes," she admitted, "I suppose I am a lucky girl."

"I leave you now," Pablo said, "but I return *un minuto* with menus. And dinner, she is on me."

When Chet opened his mouth to protest, Pablo wagged a finger in the air. "I know you are a very proud man, Meester Chet. But you must allow Maria and me to show our gratitude. Thees place, she is mine, and I am boss, no? Let me do thees kindness for you, because what I say, she is law!"

Reluctantly, Chet agreed. "It was the only way I knew to get rid of him," he whispered to Sky, holding out her chair.

During dinner, as Chet entertained her with stories about his life as a rodeo star, Sky found it increasingly difficult to think of him as a hard-hearted, wolf-hating rancher. And when he pulled out his wallet to show off photos of his little girl, the warmth in his voice and the pride in his eyes made Sky recall her relationship with her own father. Wade had taught her how foolhardy it was to judge people by first impressions. If she'd allowed herself to form an opinion of Chet based on their first encounter, she'd never have discovered what a warm, witty, wonderful man he was.

In the ladies' room after dinner, Sky couldn't help thinking what a lucky little girl Sally was to have a father like Chet. Sky had grown up surrounded by that same huge kind of love...until a bank robber killed Wade days before her seventeenth birthday. He'd been so much more than her dad. He'd been her adviser, her protector, and, most of all, her friend. Ten years had passed since his death, yet the ache of missing him was as painful as ever.

"Is something the matter, honey?" the heavyset woman at the next sink asked. "Looks like you've seen a ghost."

Sky smiled stiffly, trembling as she stuffed her lipstick back into her purse. "I'm fine, thanks." Her emotions were dangerously close to the surface, and Sky squared her shoulders, determined, as always, to keep the memories in their proper place.

The minute she rounded the corner, Sky realized Chet had been watching for her. The closer she got to their table, the wider his grin grew. "I thought maybe you'd fallen in," he said, standing as she took her seat. "I was about to have Maria go in and fish you out."

Her father had possessed the same gift for turning cloudy moments sunny. "Why cry over spilt milk," Wade would say, "when it's so much more fun to lap it up?" Sky wanted to forget her moment of weakness in the ladies' room. Wanted to concentrate on being with Chet. He'd made a great effort to see that she thoroughly enjoyed the evening. Why, he hadn't mentioned the cubs even once! As they'd exchanged philosophical and political opinions, she'd discovered they had many things in common. They'd voted for the same candidate in the last election. Both became outraged at the mention of flag burning. And both loved kids and dogs and lemon meringue pie.

Sky was wondering what sorts of women Chet had seen since Ella's death when the lady from the restroom walked by, reminding Sky where her mind had been only moments ago. She took a deep breath and said a quick prayer that her melancholy mood would soon pass. She owed him at least that much for not subjecting her to a lecture on cub safety.

"Dessert?" the server asked, rolling the sweets-laden cart up to their table. Sky smiled as Chet rubbed his palms together.

"I'll take a slice of the lemon meringue pie," he said, grinning. "Sky, what'll you have?"

He'd never said her name before. It sounded lyrical and poetic coming from his lips. "I'm not very hungry," she admitted. "Maybe I'll just have a bite of yours?"

His flirty grin made her stomach flip and her heart lurch. Chet turned to the server and held up one finger. "One pie," he said. And when the second finger popped up, he added, "Two forks." When the tuxedoed young man moved on to the next table, Chet placed his hand atop hers. "You're awfully quiet all of a sudden. You okay?"

She took a sip of water. "I'm fine," she assured him. "It's just...the way you were talking about Sally reminded me of my dad. We were close, the way you and Sally are. Made me start thinking about how much I miss him, that's all."

"Martha told me he was a cop. A sheriff, I believe she said." His brow furrowed. "Killed in the line of duty?"

Sky nodded. "Took a bullet intended for a bank teller." The telling of it sounded so cold and mechanical that she quickly added, "He died in my arms. I felt so helpless, watching the life drain out of him." Two tellers and one bank patron had witnessed the grisly scene. Those facts had gone into the police report, of course, but she'd never told another living soul about the moment Wade died. Sky grabbed her water goblet again and hoped sipping from it would stop her trembling lips.

Chet's gentle grip on her free hand tightened, and his gray eyes said what he needn't have. "I'm sorry, Sky."

Shrugging, she sat up straighter and put the glass at the high noon spot above her plate. She drew a W in the condensation on its bowl. "There isn't a person alive who doesn't have a sad story to tell. You know that as well as I do."

He withdrew his hand and, for a moment, busied himself by adjusting his tie, examining his fingernails, straightening his silverware. Then, he smiled. "Not one to beat around the bush, are you?"

Sky was beginning to like the way his left brow lifted when he asked a question or stated an opinion. In fact, she was beginning to like a lot of things about him. She realized that if she hoped to continue abiding by her life motto, she'd have to exercise a lot of caution when dealing with this charming man.

When the server returned and put the dessert plate in front of him, Chet accepted only one fork. Carefully, he cut off the pointed end of the pie and held it in front of Sky's face. "You first."

She'd seen this in the movies, and she hesitated, afraid she might open her mouth too wide or not wide enough and that pie would end up on her face—or, worse, in her lap. But Chet skillfully slid the bite into her mouth, his lips parting slightly as he watched hers open to accept his offering.

"Thnk-ym," she mumbled around it.

He'd already popped a sizeable chunk into his own mouth. "Ywr wrlcm."

They seemed to share one thought: all dressed up like respectable adults but talking with their mouths full like a couple of unruly kids. Their laughter brought inquisitive stares from nearby diners. "I do believe," Chet said between snickers, "we're making public spectacles of ourselves."

He chose that moment to reach out and remove a tiny crumb of pie crust from her lower lip. The pressure of his thumb, lingering there, seemed natural and normal. Their eyes fused on a familiar sizzling current, reminding Sky of the day they'd met, when she'd vowed to win their staring match. Though she broke the visual connection this time, Sky sensed she and Chet were still attached mentally.

She began a deliberate search for things to dislike in order to make living by her motto easier. But try as she might, Sky couldn't find a single thing wrong with Chet. In fact, she felt as though she'd known him for years.

"I can't believe my big mouth tonight," Chet said as they crossed the darkened parking lot to his car. "I don't think I've talked this much, all at one time, ever before in my life." He slipped an arm around Sky's waist. "I hope you won't think I'm a complete boor for dominating the conversation."

Teasing and flirting had never been part of Sky's personality. Yet with Chet, the two went hand in hand as naturally as the stars went with the velvety black sky above. "Well, not a *complete* boor, anyway," she said, looking up at him.

The pleasant chatter they'd enjoyed in the restaurant continued during the hour's drive home. He'd chosen a collection of old country and western classics to listen to this time and occasionally joined Willie or Patsy for a line or two. Sky enjoyed every note, though his singing reminded her more of a rusty hinge than of any melody she'd ever heard.

When he parked the Porsche in front of her house, he turned in the seat and placed a big, warm hand on her shoulder. "How about a cup of coffee?"

Sky's heart fluttered. She could barely make out his features in the darkness, yet somehow she knew those crisp, gray eyes were boring into her, hoping for an affirmative answer. As she'd been dressing for dinner, Sky had told herself she'd behave graciously and politely, and nothing more—no matter what he did or said to rile her—for the cubs' sake. But he hadn't mentioned them once...or anything else that might have been construed as negative.

As they walked slowly up the flagstone path toward her house, Chet draped an arm across her shoulders, his big fingertips hanging down like a general's trim.

Sky liked the warm weight of his hand and resisted the urge to lace her fingers with his.

While she prepared the coffeepot, Chet sat where he had that very morning. "So, tell me, are you a good cook?" With his thumb, he dusted some pepper powder from the top of the shaker on the table.

"I'm no gourmet," Sky said, pulling two cups and saucers from the cupboard, "but I can whip up a respectable meat-and-potatoes meal when I've a mind to."

He nodded approvingly. "Most professional women I've known aren't very comfortable in the kitchen."

She wondered what it was about him that brought out this outrageously flirtatious side of her personality. Grinning, she said, "There's not a gadget in this room that scares me, cowboy."

Suddenly, the friendly light in his eyes dimmed. "Yeah. You're just all kinds of brave, aren't you?"

Here comes the speech, she thought.

In response to her stiff-backed silence, Chet held up his hands in mock surrender. "Hey, far be it from me to tell you how to live your life."

"I appreciate your concern, but I've been on my own for a long time. I know how to take care of myself."

He rubbed the spot above his eye where she'd hit him the day they'd first met. "So I've heard."

At least his mischievous grin was back. Sky hadn't realized how much she enjoyed looking at it until it disappeared. Finally, the pot hissed, its signal that the coffee was ready. "You take yours black, right?"

Face sat beside him, panting for a pat on the head. "Brave as a lion, with a memory like an elephant. She's in the right line of work, wouldn't you say?" he asked the dog, who answered in a happy, breathy bark.

Chet took his time drinking the coffee, then helped himself to a second cup, warming Sky's when he did.

For the next twenty minutes, he talked nonstop about the various consequences of trying to raise two hybrid wolf cubs. Finally, when his cup was empty and he was lectured out, he stood up. "Promise me something," he said, holding her hand as they crossed her wood-floored foyer. "Be careful anytime you go to the shelter. You never know who might be watching."

"I'll be careful," she said, her voice a bored monotone.

Placing both hands on her shoulders, he stopped her. "I'm serious, Sky. You're totally unprotected out here. Somebody with binoculars could be watching from any direction, and you'd never know it."

Narrowing her eyes, she regarded him with sudden suspicion. She thought she saw him blush, but he moved toward the door so quickly, she couldn't be sure.

"For your information," he volunteered, "I was looking for a stray the other day. I was miles away, yet I saw you go into that shed." His eyes darkened and his brows knitted together. "You're just lucky I wasn't one of the bounty hunters."

Sky frowned. "Oh, why don't you just call off the stupid bounty?"

"I didn't post it, remember? Besides, it's too late for that. There're enough side bets to make up for any bounty Bud or Bart could afford to pay."

"Side bets?"

He took a deep breath and stared at the ceiling for a moment. Whether he sought the explanation up there or the patience to tell it, Sky didn't know.

"You make it sound as if we're at war!"

"Haven't you been reading the papers?"

"Intelligent people don't pay any attention to that kind of news."

"Intelligent people don't harbor wolves on their property and risk being drummed out of business."

She was about to respond to his "intelligent people" remark when the rest of his statement caught her attention. "Do you really think it's that serious? People might...might boycott my clinic?"

"You bet I do."

Sky wanted to wish the whole sorry mess away. But she'd always been a woman of her word. For better or for worse, she was all the protection the cubs had. "If I let them go now, they'll die for sure. Even if the bounty hunters don't get them, the coyotes will. Or they'll starve to death. And they'll never be accepted by a pack, because they don't know the first thing about—"

With no warning, he gathered her in a warm, protective embrace. Automatically, her arms went around him.

"What am I gonna do with you?" he sighed into her hair. "You're as bighearted and pigheaded as they come," he added, kissing the top of her head. "And while that's a mighty delicious combination, I have a ranch to run and a daughter to raise. I can't be running over here morning and night to stand guard while you tend those critters."

She broke free of his hold and stood with her hands forming fists at her sides. "So who asked you to? I can—"

"—take care of yourself," he finished, rolling his eyes. "I know, I know." It was his turn to sound bored. Chet opened the door slightly, then clicked it shut it again. "I never meant to insult you, Sky. I hope you know that. It's just that I'm worried about what could happen to you, all alone, way out here in the middle of nowhere. I wish I was smart enough to make you understand that you could be in real danger."

No one had really cared what happened to her since Wade. Sky was touched by his concern. "I'll be fine."

Chet grabbed her wrist and pulled her to him. "You're a stubborn, infuriating woman, Sky Allen," he rasped, his lips fractions of an inch from hers.

In the dim light of the foyer lamp, his eyes glittered like hard, gray diamonds as they flicked from her mouth to her throat to her eyes. She wondered what that thick, dark mustache might feel like against her lips, and she held her breath as she waited for his kiss.

Chet inhaled deeply and stepped back. "You'd better be careful. That's all I can say. Because if anything happens to you...." He cupped her chin in his palm. Shaking his head, he repeated, "I mean it. *Be careful.*"

As his Porsche roared off, Sky touched the spot where his fingers had warmed her skin, still wondering how his lips might have felt against hers.

After she'd fed and exercised Rocky and Piney and secured them in the shelter, Sky made her night rounds in the clinic. She'd neutered a fat Siamese cat that morning, and Spuds glowered at her now as she inspected his incision. "You're healing up nicely, fella," she said, smoothing his soft, multicolored coat. "And don't look at me like that. You're getting a longer, healthier life for what you gave up."

Across the room, Fuzzbucket yipped for Sky's attention. "How many pecks on the snout will it take before you learn to leave that old rooster alone?" she asked the poodle. Max, the happy-faced German shepherd, sat calmly in his kennel cage, oblivious to the fact that in the morning, he'd share the cat's fate. "Okay, kids," she announced, yawning, "lights out. C'mon, Face. Let's go to bed."

Sky was halfway between the clinic and the house when she noticed a shadowy figure dart between two pines, causing their needled boughs to bounce lazily. "Stay, girl!" she ordered Face. Despite the dog's low growls, Sky forced herself to keep moving at a steady pace, straining her eyes to see what had caused the movement. She'd grown accustomed to an occasional coyote or raccoon ambling into her yard, but something told her that whatever lurked in the trees was far more ominous than any creature that called the woods home. The eerie sensation suddenly became too much to bear with respectable calm, and Sky bolted for her porch. Locked safely inside her house, she breathed a sigh of relief. "Chet has me scared of my own shadow," she said, and Face woofed her agreement.

She lay awake in bed for a long time, watching the alarm clock's numbers change from 11:40 to 12:00 to 12:30. The wispy white curtain rose and fell on the breeze that slipped through the tiny opening she'd left in her bedroom window. It was well after one o'clock when she finally drifted off to sleep.

At first, she thought it was helicopter blades chopping in the distance. Or soft jungle drumbeats. Maybe the thud of Face's paws padding across the braided rug in the living room. Sleepily, Sky lifted her head from the pillow, trying to identify the sound that seemed to be coming from just outside the window.

Footsteps?

Face whimpered as Sky tossed the covers aside and glanced at the clock: 3:34. Wide awake now, she tiptoed to the window in time to see a dark-clothed figure running alongside the tree line precisely where she'd seen a shadow earlier. In an instant, the figure was gone, swallowed up by the deep murk of darkness.

Soundlessly, Sky opened the nightstand drawer and drew out her father's big, black flashlight. She walked through the hall and into the foyer, the unlit implement resting on her shoulder like a baseball bat.

Sky stopped dead in her tracks and nearly collided with Face when she saw the inky rectangle, silhouetted by moonlight, in the center of the front door's etched window. Keeping her back to the wall, Sky sneaked closer. Holding her breath, she peeked through the narrow, beveled pane beside the door. Satisfied no one was on the porch, she released the dead bolt and cringed as it echoed in the wide, uncarpeted space. Old brass hinges squealed mercilessly as she opened the heavy oak door. Quickly, she grabbed the piece of paper that had been taped to the glass, slammed the door shut, and locked it tight.

Weak with fear, she dropped to her knees, hands trembling violently as she held the scrap of paper under the flashlight's beam and read:

> *You're not fooling anyone. Get rid of them, or we'll do it for you.*
>
> *Your neighbors*

Chapter Six

P anic rose in her throat as she read and reread the messy, maniacal handwriting and its menacing threat. Racing across the lawn with the note crumpled in the palm of her hand, she prayed the writer of the note hadn't already gotten to the cubs. She tugged the padlock on the shelter door.

Amazingly, it was still locked tight. Her hands trembled as she shoved the key into the lock. When she stepped inside, the cubs were roused from a deep sleep and yawned. She'd taught them that bright light and warm words meant mealtime; anything else could be ignored. For a moment, their eyes, glowing red in the dim shaft of moonlight that spilled down the steps and into the underground room, blinked sleepily at her. Realizing she wasn't there to provide fun or food, they snuggled together once again and closed their eyes. Satisfied with their safety, Sky relocked the doors and headed back to the house.

She decided to call Dr. Williams. He'd been her guide and her inspiration as she was preparing the Alaskan wolves for their return to the wild. Surely, when she told him what was going on in Montana, he'd consent to take Piney and Rocky far away from Mountain Gate, Montana....

In the kitchen, Sky's hands trembled as she thumbed through her personal phone book, then dialed the long-distance number. His phone rang once. Twice. The clock above the stove said 3:55. In Virginia, it was nearly six in the morning, and Sky hoped he was still an early riser. A husky-voiced woman answered on the fourth ring, and Sky immediately apologized for calling so early. "Steven has retired due to ill health," the woman said. "He's not to be disturbed under any circumstances."

"Let me leave my name and number, then," Sky suggested, "and the professor can return my call at his convenience."

"I'm afraid that's impossible," she said. "Dr. Williams's family has hired me as his full-time nurse. He's had a stroke, you see, and can't speak with anyone." With that, she hung up.

Sky ran her hands through her hair and paced the brightly lit kitchen. She had shared two years with the elderly professor. What had begun as a teacher-student relationship had become a durable friendship, which made the news of his illness especially difficult to hear.

Face, staring at the moon through the uncurtained kitchen windows, whimpered. Suddenly, Sky remembered what Chet had said: *Someone with binoculars could be watching from any direction....*

Her property, as he'd so astutely pointed out, sat in the middle of nowhere, nestled in a gently sloping valley. Her closest neighbors were the Rockies, a canyon, a prairie, a thick pine forest...plenty of hiding places from every angle.

Sky shivered as she wandered the house. Even curled under Gran's flowery afghan on the living room sofa, she couldn't relax, because every window in the house seemed like a black, soulless, unblinking eye that watched her every move but never allowed her to see more than her own reflection.

Before the wolf mess, Mountain Gate's very location had made it a haven. Now, it made Sky feel exposed and vulnerable. She rode an emotional seesaw, swinging between panic and rage—panic that someone unknown could bring harm to her or the cubs, and rage that his secrecy made her powerless to stop him.

Wide awake, Sky headed back into the kitchen. After she'd tacked several towels over the windows, she began doing what she always did when sleep eluded her. She'd memorized Gran's chocolate chip cookie recipe long ago. The mechanics of measuring and sifting and stirring had always calmed her, no matter how upset she was. By the time the clock told her it was time to feed and exercise the cubs, she'd baked six batches of cookies.

The cubs greeted her with their customary damp kisses. "You guys give a whole new meaning to the term *tongue-lashing*," she said, enduring their affections. Today, she would begin teaching them to howl, and she prayed for success. The week before, she'd spent hours sitting in the wilderness with her handheld recording device, capturing the bloodcurdling howls of the pack that lived beyond the foothills. She'd spent considerable time covered in creek slime to disguise her human scent and watching from her perch behind the thick brambles beyond the rocks.

She'd seen the black alpha male, huge and formidable, several times before. The first time, she hadn't prepared herself with the creek disguise. A camera in one hand and her trusty backpack dangling from the other, Sky had been perched on a rock, hoping to catch a glimpse of the mountain goat family that often tiptoed up and down the steep incline that skirted the foothills near Magic Mountain. She'd sensed the wolf before actually spotting him, posed majestically atop a craggy overhang. Eye contact had been at once scary and satisfying as his golden gaze had studied her.

Though fewer than thirty yards had separated her from the mighty beast, something in his demeanor had told Sky she had nothing to fear. So, she'd sat, motionless, to revel in his magnificence for as long as he'd allow it. Five minutes had ticked silently by before he'd sat back on his haunches. Ten minutes later, he had assumed the position of the sphinx. But never in those moments had his eyes left hers.

Knowing too much eye contact could be read as a sign of aggression, Sky had occasionally lowered her gaze. Each time she'd looked at him again, he'd lifted his chin as if to say, "Go ahead. Feast your eyes." She had so enjoyed her study of him that she'd grinned. He had stood up when she'd done that and, much to her surprise, had sent a doggy grin of his own down the mountainside to where she was sitting. Then, suddenly, he'd left her, moving with the grace of a doe and the power of an eagle. Sky had decided to call him Raven, and it was his pack she'd recorded.

By now, the cubs were down to two meals a day, eating not dampened dog chow but raw meat. Soon, Sky would face the difficult chore of feeding them only every third or fourth day, for if she hoped to teach them to hunt on their own, they'd have to start out hungry. The measure was a necessary and important part of their survival training, since feast or famine was part of life in the wild. It was little consolation that they'd received far better care from her than if they'd been with their own kind. She had assumed the role of their mother, and, as it would be for a true parent, refusing them anything—especially food— would be a difficult and heartbreaking task.

Though the air was warm and the sky sunny on that fall morning, Sky didn't dare let the cubs outside to play in the fenced-in yard, and they protested loudly. She wondered exactly how she'd accomplish the hunting aspect of their outdoor education, knowing that the gunman could take a potshot from any direction at any time.

Sky decided to take the Scarlett O'Hara approach to that problem and worry about it when the time came.

The steak bones she'd brought back from Pablo's restaurant appeased them for a while, but even before she'd finished cleaning up their newspaper mess, the pair were whimpering and scratching at the big metal door. "Sorry, guys," she said, drawing them into a hug, "can't let you out there till I'm sure it's safe."

And who knows how long that might be? she wondered. Side by side, Piney and Rocky sat in the middle of their now-tattered quilt, heads cocked and brows raised in canine confusion.

Sky turned on the recording device, hoping to distract them from their yearning to be outdoors. The moment the first howl echoed through the shelter, both cubs stood on all fours, ears pointed toward the sound of their kin. Piney was the first to respond, her little mouth opening and closing as she tried to figure out how to duplicate that peculiar, haunting sound. But it was Rocky who cut loose with the first near-howl. It surprised him that he'd produced such a cry, and he jumped back, momentarily startled at his own prowess. But the caterwauls that came from the small device made him quickly forget his apprehension. Male ego wouldn't allow him to be outsung by another!

Rocky lifted his head with eyes closed and mouth open, his black dog lips covering his white teeth as his pink tongue lolled to the back of his throat. This time, his wail sent shivers down Sky's spine. With a little more practice, she knew that he'd have a howl as powerful as Raven's—and might earn the title of pack leader one day.

"What's the matter, Piney?" Sky asked, ruffling the she-wolf's furry neck. "Jealous that your brother's one up on you?"

Piney made a habit of butting Sky, as if she thought herself a billy goat instead of a wolf. She butted Sky now, emitting a low, playful growl. She cocked her head and whimpered at the mournful howls coming from the re-cording device—and from her brother. "Don't you worry, girl," Sky said, hugging her. "Before you know it, you'll be hollering with the best of them."

Panting, Piney sat back on her haunches, looking at Sky as if to say, "But...only if I'm in the mood."

Sky glanced at her watch. She had a surgery sched-uled for 8:30. She hated to leave them, because being sequestered with them in the shelter and teaching them to behave like proper wolves was one of the only real joys she derived from life these days. In the cool, quiet un-derground space, she could forget about scary notes and threatening phone calls and loved ones lost. Regretfully, she left the cubs to play with their new toys: two teddy bears and a big blue rubber ball.

As she'd been baking cookies the night before, Sky had decided that a "business as usual" attitude was saf-est. For now, at least. The phone jangled as she walked into the clinic, and she prayed it wouldn't be the sharp-shooter. "I was about to hang up," Chet said when she finally answered. "Is everything all right?"

It amazed her that the mere sound of his voice could provoke a smile, even amid the cub-related turmoil on Magic Mountain. For a fleeting moment, she considered telling him about her terrifying, sleepless night. "Every-thing's terrific," she fibbed. "Why wouldn't it be?"

"I don't know. You sounded...odd...when you an-swered."

"Probably because I took your advice and didn't let the cubs outside for their morning romp in case someone might be watching. They cried like babies. I'm afraid I won't be a very good mom. I didn't like seeing my kids' disappointment."

His soft laugh filtered into her ear. "Look at it this way: at least they're alive to *be* disappointed."

Silently, she agreed.

"What are you doing for lunch?"

Sky glanced at the clock. It wasn't even eight yet. "I have surgery in half an hour, and back-to-back appointments from ten till noon. Why?"

"I promised Sally I'd take her to Big Jim's. It'd be a good way for you two to meet."

When he'd shown her Sally's picture at dinner, Sky had said she'd like to meet his little girl—but the very next day? The threatening note crinkled in her pocket, and Sky hesitated, afraid for a moment to leave the clinic and the house vulnerable to the shooter. Then, she remembered the promise she'd made to herself, elbow-deep in flour, the night before: she wouldn't give him the satisfaction of knowing he'd frightened her into altering her normal routine.

"So what do you say?" Chet asked. "We could pick you up at 12:30."

Sky loved his musical, masculine voice. *Pity his singing voice isn't as melodious*, she thought, grinning as she remembered the way he'd harmonized with Willie Nelson. "I guess I can be out of my scrubs and into jeans by that time."

"Time's gonna drag till then," Chet said, then hung up.

Chapter Seven

C het and Sally arrived ten minutes early, and Sky was still buckling her belt when the door-bell rang. Halfway down the hall that ran the length of her rancher, she paused at the mirror to check her hair. Then, smiling, she opened the door wide. "Well, hey! Come on in."

Wearing a crisp white shirt and black trousers, Chet looked as handsome as he had the night before. Grinning, he said, "You look...rested."

Her smile faded slightly as she closed the door behind him. She hadn't told him she'd been up all night worrying about the shadow in the pines, or that she'd found a note taped to her door. And she hadn't told him she'd been baking like a maniac. Again, a horrible, suspicious sensation crowded her mind. "Why wouldn't I look rested?"

Chet only shrugged. "Sally, this is Dr. Allen. Sky, I'd like you to meet the love of my life."

"Pleased to meet you," Sally said. "Do I smell chocolate chip cookies?"

Just as Martha had said, Sally was a smaller version of Ella, from her sparkling blue eyes to her honey-blonde hair and her ballerina-like frame. Warm summer days of hide-and-seek, picnics invaded by ants, and

Barbie-doll tradeoffs flashed through her memory, and Sky wanted to wrap the child in a bear hug. Instead, she smiled warmly. "As a matter of fact, I baked some last night. Would you like one?"

Sally nodded, causing her golden ponytails to bob up and down. "They're my favorite," she said, following Sky into the kitchen. "Oh, my goodness," she exclaimed upon entering the room. "It's...it's like a cookie factory!"

Chet's gray eyes scanned the stovetop, counters, table, and chairs. "Is there a place in here that *isn't* cookie-covered?"

Sally giggled and pointed at the trash can. "There's one!"

Following Sally's finger, Sky noticed the note lying in a crumpled ball on the floor beside it. "Guess I get a little carried away when I bake." She'd angrily pitched the note toward the garbage but obviously had missed. Quickly, she scooped it up. "I don't think your dad will mind if you have just one cookie before lunch," Sky said, nonchalantly stuffing the note into the garbage can before Chet had a chance to see it. "Right?"

"Okay," he said, "one cookie. But then we'd better get a move on. You know how crowded Big Jim's is this time of day."

Sally tugged Chet's hand, and when he bent down, she whispered loudly into his ear, "You're right, Daddy; she's very tall and *very* pretty." To Sky, she said, "Are you really a am-nal doctor?"

Smiling, Sky nodded. "Maybe you'd like a tour of the clinic when we get back from lunch."

The ponytails bobbed again. "Can Daddy come, too?"

Sky met Chet's gaze. "Well, maybe if he promises to stay out of our way...."

He seemed to be sending a silent, secret message by way of those crystalline gray eyes, and Sky wished for the power to read it. Then, he blinked, ending the trancelike connection, and looked at his watch. "Everybody ready for burgers and fries?"

Like her mother, Sally knew dozens of knock-knock jokes, and she told them all during the drive, making Sky wonder if bad joke-telling was an inheritable trait. As Chet munched his steak sandwich and Sky her salad, Sally offered them French fries from her kids' meal. Later, while she romped in the children's playroom among monkey bars and soft, colorful balls, Chet barely took his eyes off her. "She's something else, isn't she?"

"It's easy to see why you're so proud of her."

His eyes met hers. "It's not pride, Sky. At least, that's not all it is. It's...Sally's all I have."

Sky considered pointing out that he had more. So much more. He owned one of the largest cattle ranches in the state. Lived in a mansion. Had earned the love and respect of friends, relatives, and employees. He was robustly healthy, despite his limp, and good-looking, to boot. But because he believed his little girl was his only connection to a happy past, the house, the ranch, and the money were worthless without her. Sky realized that behind Chet's tough-guy exterior beat the heart of a man who melted at the mere sight of one tiny blonde.

"Until my dad was killed," she said, "I thought I had the world on a stick—my very own big blue lollipop. The world isn't the same without him, but it's still spinning...."

Chet gazed at her for a long time, and Sky wondered what sad thoughts had dimmed the vibrant spark in those gleaming gray eyes. "Is there any particular time you need to get back to the clinic?" he asked.

In response to his formal tone of voice, she replied, "Why do you ask, Mr. Cozart?"

Sally skipped up to the table just then. "You don't have to call him Mr. Cozart," she said, one hand on Sky's arm. "You can call him Chester if you want."

Sky tried to meet his eyes, which he'd hidden behind a large, work-hardened hand. "Chester?"

Sally slid into the booth beside Sky. "Uncle Dale and Grandfather call him Chet, but Grandmother calls him Chester. That's his real name. Isn't that right, Daddy?"

Chet sighed and came out of hiding. He looked from Sky to his daughter and back again. "That's right, honey." Nodding and wearing a silly, tight-lipped grin, he patted Sky's hand. "Please, call me Chet," he encouraged her. "All my *friends* do."

Sky took one last sip of her soda, then busied herself by gathering burger wrappers and French fry cartons on the red plastic tray in the middle of their table. She didn't quite know how to react to being included in the exclusive circle of Chet's friends.

She'd been watching Sally, and when Sky looked up, she realized Chet had been watching *her*. "What do you say we bring Dr. Allen home to meet Tootsie?" Chet asked his daughter, never taking his eyes from Sky's.

The child clasped her hands together and beamed. "Would you like that, Dr. Allen?"

Sky couldn't help it; she was doing a lot of beaming of her own lately, it seemed. "Sounds like a great idea."

As they drove to Four Aces Ranch, Sally told a few more knock-knock jokes, then chattered endlessly about her horse. She had been a Christmas gift last year, she said, when her daddy had bought himself a new car. "She's very big, but very gentle. Daddy lets me ride her when he rides Sugar."

In the barn, perched on the stall's gate, Sally brushed Tootsie's mane. "Do you know how she got her name, Dr. Allen?"

Sky squinted at the mare and gave the matter some serious thought. "Because she's the same color as a Tootsie Roll?"

Sally's awed gaze swung toward Chet, who was holding his precariously balanced daughter's waist. "Wow, Daddy, she's *smart*, too!"

"Mmm-hmm. And brave." His eyes bored hotly into Sky's. "Too brave for her own good sometimes, I'm afraid."

Sally, busy with her horse's hairdo, paid the adults' conversation no mind. Sky glanced at her watch. They'd been at Four Aces less than ten minutes, and already she felt trapped. "You know, I just remembered that today is Lisa's early day, and Max will be needing some one-on-one."

"Who's Max?" Sally wanted to know.

"He's a dog. He had an operation this morning, so he's not feeling very well right now."

Sally wrapped her arms around Chet's neck. "You'd better take her right home. She has 'portant work to do."

"Sometimes, you're smarter than your old dad, kiddo." He lowered her gently to the hay-covered floor.

"Is it two o'clock?"

"Almost."

"Oh, no!" she gasped, both hands over her mouth. "I'll be late for my riding lesson!"

"You won't be late, sweetie. Run on up to the house and take off that pretty dress. Then, ask Grandmother if she'll help you find your riding clothes. Now give us a great big kiss." Chet squatted down and held out his arms, and Sally pressed a loud, wet kiss on his cheek.

In the doorway, she stopped. "Dr. Allen, can I visit the animal hospital tomorrow, since we didn't have time today?"

Sky looked at Chet but, unable to read his mood, said, "If it's all right with your dad, it's fine with me."

"I think we can squeeze in a few minutes."

Waving, Sally ran toward the mansion. "See you tomorrow, Dr. Allen," she called over her shoulder.

Sky grinned. "How old is she, Chet? Twenty-four; twenty-five?"

"Almost five," he said, laughing. "Bright as a new penny, isn't she?"

"Takes after her dad in the brains department."

He shoved both hands into his pockets and blushed like a boy. "Well, she's the spitting image of her mother in every other way. Sometimes, when I look at her," he said, staring after her, "I see Ella looking back at me. It's...." Chet shook his head as if shaking off a painful memory. "I think you must be part psychiatrist, 'cause you have a way of making me tell you things I've never told...." He took a deep breath. "Guess we'd better get you home before your assistant turns into a pumpkin."

Impulsively, Sky grabbed his hand and squeezed it gently. "Sally does look a lot like her mother. And I'm glad, because she reminds me of all the good times Ella and I had together when we were kids." Sky's cheeks flushed, and tears stung her eyes. "When I lost my dad, I wouldn't come back to Montana because it was nothing but memories of him. I never realized until today how much more I lost by staying away."

Chet stared at the hay-strewn floor.

She squeezed his hand again. "Memories are all I have of my dad, but you have Sally to help you remember Ella. That shouldn't make you sad."

He met her gaze for an instant, and in that instant, Sky saw those long, black lashes blink away unshed tears. He coughed, then looked toward the door. "It doesn't make me sad," he said with an angry edge to his voice. "The good Lord's seen fit to bless me with that little angel to replace the one He called home, and I'm thankful every day of my life for that. I don't want you to get the idea that I've spent these last five years feeling sorry for myself." Then, clearing his throat, he added, "Ready to go?"

Eleven miles separated Four Aces and Magic Mountain, and they drove five of them without saying a word. Chet stayed busy playing with the radio dials and the rearview mirror. Every now and then, he'd open his mouth as if about to say something, but then he'd quickly close it.

Finally, he said, "When were you planning to tell me about the note, Sky?"

Chapter Eight

She'd been staring out the passenger window, amazed that the sky and the cattle and the trees looked as bright from inside the black-windowed truck as they did outside. She knew it had been a mistake to tell Dale about the note. No doubt he'd run straight to Chet with the information, thinking he needed to protect Sky from herself. "What note?"

His right hand slapped the steering wheel. "The one Dale told me about. The one somebody delivered while sneaking around your place in the middle of the night." He shot her a wary look. "Why? Have there been others?"

Dale, Sky thought, *needs to learn to keep his big yap shut.* "He's making mountains out of molehills, as usual. It's awfully close to Halloween. I'm sure it's just a silly prank pulled by some teenagers."

Sighing loudly, Chet turned off the radio. "You seem to have a mental block where this wolf stuff is concerned. I wish I could get it through your beautiful head that you could be in danger."

Sky smoothed nonexistent wrinkles in her jeans. "I'm beginning to sound like a broken record, I know, but I'm going to say it again: the cubs have no one but me. So, in danger or not, I'll take my chances. Besides, it's too late to back out now."

"If I've learned one thing in life, it's that it's never too late."

Sky twisted slightly to face him. "But if I release them, your bounty hunters will...."

Slapping the steering wheel again, he shouted, "Confound it, Sky! Why do you insist on calling them *my* bounty hunters? I had nothing to do with it!"

"It's *your* ranch—"

"That's right. It's my ranch," he interrupted, "and I'll run it any way I see fit. And if I see fit to let an old man hold on to what little pride he's got left, then that's what I aim to do."

"At what cost?"

A thick cloud of dust swirled around them as Chet brought the truck to a jerking halt on the side of the road. "What's that supposed to mean?" he demanded, turning off the engine.

"You allow 'poor old Bud' to play boss, and everybody suffers. The cubs, me...."

Chet leaned his forehead against fingers wrapped tightly around the steering wheel. After muttering a string of unintelligible words under his breath, he turned sideways on the bench seat. "There's no getting through to you, is there? How will I make you understand?"

Sky focused for a moment on the padded ceiling of his truck, then sighed. "I understand perfectly: half-breed wolf packs have attacked some cattle because they're not terrified of humans like the purebreds are. And the ranchers are reacting by shooting every wolf on sight—half-breed and purebred alike—whether the wolves are in the middle of a meal or not. I don't have to agree with their vigilante mentality to understand it!" She turned in the seat, too, so that now they faced each other. "What I have in my shelter are *cubs*. They couldn't take down a horse or a steer if they tried."

Chet only stared at her.

Feeling helpless, she raised her hands, then dropped them in her lap. "I know the cubs are at least half-hybrid, that they'll very likely wander from the foothills looking for easy pickings in a herd of cattle when they're grown. If they're struck by lightning or attacked by a moose or shot by a bounty hunter, well, that's awful, but that's life in the wild. But they deserve a fighting chance. That's all I'm trying to give them, Chet—a fighting chance."

He took her hands in his. "But not everybody out there," he said, nodding toward the endless, rolling acres beyond the windshield, "can afford your mind-set of 'expect the worst, then do your best to prevent it.' Weather, coyotes, rustlers…it's a code ranchers have learned to live with."

Sky couldn't look into those steely, dark-lashed eyes a moment longer, afraid they had the power to convince her to turn the cubs loose, after all.

Chet took a deep breath, let go of her, and restarted the engine. They drove the remaining six miles to Magic Mountain without even the radio to distract them from their separate yet similar thoughts.

Sky watched his jaw flex in anger, and when they had pulled into her driveway, she half expected him to plant the sole of his cowboy boot in the middle of her back and shove her out onto the gravel drive. Instead, he walked around to her side of the truck and, with all the decorum of a proper English butler, opened her door.

"I want to see that note," he said before her feet hit the ground.

It was most definitely not a request, and Sky almost told him to get lost. To mind his own business, once and for all. But despite all her outward appearances of bravado, the note—and the way it had been delivered— had scared the living daylights out of her. If she showed the note to Chet, maybe he'd recognize the handwriting and the whole stupid mess would be over and done with before nightfall.

Sky unlocked the front door and invited him to wait inside. "I'm going over to the clinic to tell Lisa she can lock up and go home. The note is in the kitchen," she said, leaving him alone on the porch.

"I know exactly where it is," he called after her. "It's in the trash can. Right where you put it earlier. My leg doesn't work like it used to, but there's nothin' wrong with my eyes...."

She thought she'd disposed of it smoothly. *Evidently not smoothly enough to fool the likes of one Mr. Chester Cozart*, she told herself.

When Sky returned, Chet was clearing a space for them at the cookie-covered kitchen table. "Okay, so let's see it," he said around a mouthful of chocolate chip cookie.

Grinning, she held back the swinging trash can lid, retracted the note, and handed it to him. "I thought you knew exactly where it was."

"I don't make a habit of digging through other people's garbage." He snatched the note from her, read it, then read it again. "Now, here's a friendly greeting if ever I saw one."

"Would you like some coffee to wash down that cookie?" she asked, ignoring his sarcasm.

Chet threw his hands in the air. "No, Sky. I wouldn't like some coffee to wash down this cookie. What I want is for you to tell me how you plan to accomplish this spectacular cub-rearing feat without getting yourself killed!"

She willed her lower lip to stop trembling. When it wouldn't obey, she bit it. Hard.

"Look," he said, crossing the room to where she was standing, leaning against the sink, "it's obvious I was right." He waved the note in the air. "You're in big trouble.

You could get hurt. There's no point denying it anymore. Like it or not, you've got to get rid of those animals. The sooner, the better."

She looked up at him. The stern yet compassionate light in his eyes made her remember how safe she'd felt in his arms the night before, how disappointed she'd been when he'd left without giving her a chance to discover how that wonderful, mustached mouth would feel against her lips.

Chet must have read her mind, for he wadded up the note and tossed it over his shoulder. "Something is happening here," he whispered, stepping closer and lifting her chin, "and I don't know whether to run from it or straight at it."

Sky trembled as his muscular body pinned her to the counter. She inhaled crisp aftershave and his sweet cookie breath. *Nothing ventured, nothing lost*, she chanted in her head. *Nothing ventured, nothing—*.

Chet groaned. "Oh, why not...?"

When his lips touched hers, Sky gasped. The soul-stirring taste of him—chocolate chips and all—sent silent shockwaves straight to her heart. Weak-kneed and light-headed, she felt his arms encircle her, providing steady, much-needed support. Slowly, his fingers combed through her hair, then traced down her shoulders and her back. He gently caressed her flushed cheeks as the mustache she'd been so curious about skimmed, feather-light, from her earlobes to her throat to her forehead, leaving a sizzling trail in its wake before sliding back to her slightly parted, waiting lips. Between kisses, he stammered and stuttered, and his words made no sense to her. "It's been...never thought...so long...." Then, he sighed. "Sky...."

When Chet said her name, it was like a soft spring breeze, rustling the pines and floating dogwood petals through the air. Liking the way he'd warmed her lonely heart, she wanted to learn more about this strong-willed man.

Until her life motto sliced the moment short.

He seemed to sense her sudden mood swing and gradually ended the deliriously delicious kiss. "I don't know what's gotten into me," he murmured shakily near her ear, still holding her close. Then, looking long and deep into her eyes, he said, "That's a lie. I know exactly what's gotten into me."

A tightrope walker could have balanced on the taut thread that melded their gazes. Chet stood back slightly, his eyes sliding over Sky's facial features, reminding her where his lips had been just seconds ago. She waited for him to tell her exactly what had gotten into him.

"I sure could use that cup of coffee now," he said instead.

Small talk over the mountain of chocolate chip cookies was companionable, as it had been on her porch, at the restaurant, at Big Jim's, in his barn. When Chet stood up to leave, she wanted to beg him to stay. Wanted to feel his big, protective arms around her again, making her forget the horrible, frightening threats. She wanted him to prove to her that her life motto was a worthless, silly cliché and nothing more. "Wait...."

He'd made stacks of cookies as they were talking, and now he was straightening the teetering columns. "Wait?"

Sky thought he seemed pleased—happy, even—that she wanted him to stay. But she wasn't ready. Not yet. "Just let me pack up some cookies to send with you. For Sally."

He grinned. "Do you do this often?" His big hand waved over the cookie pile.

"Only when I'm upset. Baking soothes me."

Chet chuckled softly and surveyed the cookie-strewn room. "From the looks of things, that note must have upset you a lot."

Sky was stuffing a grocery sack with the sweet treats when Chet bent over to pick up the note. It seemed to have developed a life of its own, appearing and disappearing, flaunting its threat. He folded it into his shirt pocket and patted it. "Never know when it might come in handy—as evidence."

Sky's hands froze above the bag. "Evidence? Evidence of what?"

Shrugging, he said, "Don't rightly know. But it's better to be safe than sorry, I always say."

Sky's heart raced.

"Aw, c'mon now," he said. "Don't look like that." He hugged her, pinning the bag between them and crumbling a few cookies. "I didn't mean to scare you," he added, kissing her forehead. "It's just that my tongue wags like an old woman's when I'm around you. There's an old Indian legend warning that some women have the power to cast spells. I'm beginning to believe you're one of those women...that you've cast a spell on me."

"Mmm-hmm," Sky said, calmer already now that she was standing in the warm circle of his embrace. "It's my favorite hex: 'Chocolate chips, loose lips,'" she chanted.

Laughter from deep in his chest rumbled against her. "I'd better get home before Sally's grandmother calls the sheriff and reports me missing."

He took her hand and led her into the foyer. Standing in the open doorway, Chet said, "I'm as near as the phone. You know that, right?" Then, before she had a chance to answer or tell him that she could take care of herself or ask him not to go, he clutched her to him and kissed the top of her head.

"Lock up tight, hear? I don't know what I'd do if anything happened to you."

He'd been gone nearly an hour before she finished cleaning up the evidence of her baking frenzy. As she scrubbed cookie sheets, Sky's mind seesawed from his parting comment to the note he'd taken with him. She hoped its writer had poked around Magic Mountain long enough to convince himself that no wolf cubs lived there. The shelter was soundproof; he couldn't possibly have heard the cubs as he was prowling. And unless he'd seen them from a distance while she was exercising them in the yard, as Chet had suggested, the vile man had left the note on a hunch as a warning of what might happen if she didn't comply with his demands.

Sky forced the horrid thought out of her mind and rummaged through the cupboards for containers to store the cookies in. Like a ghost, the memory of Chet's kiss followed her every move. She floated on that cloud of blissful remembrance until every cookie was sealed up tight, save for the plate that sat in the middle of the kitchen table.

She was sweeping cookie crumbs from the black and white tiles when the idea first struck. Sky hated her suspicious mind as it wondered if Chet had pocketed the note...to protect *himself.*

She stood stock-still in the middle of the room, gripping the broom handle like a protective weapon. *Chet's a wealthy man,* her heart said; he certainly wouldn't need the bounty money he'd earn if he killed her cubs. *Still, he always seems to show up in conjunction with some frightening event,* insisted her brain. *But he's part Cheyenne,* her heart argued, *and he respects all things in nature.*

Picturing his slanting, black-lashed eyes, she remembered again the romantic scene in the kitchen.

Distractedly, she resumed sweeping. Her instincts told her that Chet had nothing to do with the terrifying phone calls and the threatening note. No man who'd done what Chet had done for Pablo and Bud, who was the kind of father he was to Sally, could threaten a woman one minute and kiss the living daylights out of her the next.

As she emptied a dustpan of cookie crumbs into the trash can, the battle between her heart and her brain ended, but she sensed that the war was far from over.

Chapter Nine

When Sky was a child, Gran had taught her that praying and reciting Bible verses could make almost any situation seem minor. But not even repeating the Twenty-third Psalm calmed her enough to get that vicious note out of her mind. Long before the alarm clock sounded at five o'clock, she'd dressed and headed for the shelter. The extra two hours with the cubs would do them all a lot of good. Every day, the cubs grew more restless within their cramped quarters, prowling and growling and behaving like caged zoo animals. Sky knew she had to get them out of there, fast. But how, with the shooter lurking...somewhere?

She decided that tonight, she'd sneak on foot into Beartooth country. She believed the cubs would stay close to her, since they thought of her as their mother. She'd learned some low growling tones of her own by watching the wolf pack from her hiding place in the trees and then mimicking the mother wolves' behavior and calls. So far, her attempts at sounding wolflike had been effective in keeping the cubs in line...at least in the shelter. Whether they'd be as obedient in their natural element remained to be seen. Sky had no choice but to give it a try. "Tonight's the night," she announced when she entered the shelter.

Face, Piney, and Rocky picked up on her excitement, howling and woofing and running small circles around their "mom." She'd take them to her favorite spot, miles from the ranch and high in canyon country, where she and her father had gone so many times. There, the cubs would have an opportunity to commune with nature, and the likelihood of their tormenter following or finding them was slim.

Since there were no appointments scheduled that morning, Sky decided to give the clinic a thorough cleaning to help the time pass more quickly. That done, she caught up on her filing. She'd skipped breakfast and lunch, and her stomach was growling as she walked back to the house. The red blinking light of her answering machine told her she'd received three calls. Her heart skipped a beat as she pressed Play. "Maybe your pal called," she said to Face. "Wouldn't that be nice?"

Wagging her tail, the dog barked.

"Dr. Allen...."

Immediately, Sky recognized the intimidating drawl.

"We've just about run out of patience with you. You've got till Sunday to turn those wolves loose." One second, then two hissed by before he added, "*Sunday.*"

Sky searched her memory. Why was the voice so familiar? The answer had better come soon, she knew, because with each threat, he grew bolder and more brazen. Sky couldn't imagine why he'd give her this second piece of physical evidence. Was he that stupid? Or simply that sure he could carry out his threats without getting caught? Sky shuddered at the thought.

She listened to the message four more times, hoping each time to match a name or a face with the raspy voice. But it was no use. She held her head in her hands, unable to focus on anything but the tiny red light. Just when she reached out to block it from view, the phone rang, scaring her so badly that she nearly leapt out of the chair.

"Dr. Allen?"

"Sally?" Sky couldn't imagine why the child would call her, especially in tears.

"Oh, Dr. Allen," the girl wailed, "Tootsie's bleeding. I don't want Tootsie to die...."

Sky heard Chet's patient yet authoritative voice in the background. "Give Daddy the phone, sweetie." Several thumps and bumps later, his voice came on the line. "We were out riding and her horse got tangled in some barbed wire. I've stitched up stuff like this dozens of times, but Sally won't have anyone touch Tootsie but you." He paused. "I don't know who's more hysterical—Tootsie or Sally."

"Immobilize that animal any way you can," Sky instructed him. "Tie her up if you have to. I'm on my way."

Sky raced back to the clinic, called the owners of the two pets she was to inoculate that afternoon, explained the situation, and promised to reschedule their appointments soon. She flung back the supply cabinet door and stuffed sutures, gauze, a powerful tranquilizer, and a hypodermic of antibiotic into her medical bag, then ran out of the clinic, stopping only to lock the door. Face had seen this flurry of activity before. Bored with the high-tension atmosphere, she ran around to the backyard and climbed into her doghouse.

From the clinic porch, Sky could see the answering machine through the slats of the mini-blinds in the front window of her house, its winking light sending a last taunting reminder of the frightening message. But she couldn't dwell on that right now. She'd never shirked duty in her life, and she didn't intend to start now.

Four Aces' tree-lined drive ribboned from the road to the five-car garage, then forked toward the barn. Sky brought her mini-pickup to a screeching halt when she saw Dale approaching. "Chet's got her bandaged up fairly well," he said, running alongside her toward the horse stalls, "but we're having a time keeping her still."

Four pairs of eyes greeted her: Bud's, wary and stern; Sally's, brimming with tears; her grandmother Stella's, distant and haughty; and Chet's, filled with concern.

Sky barged into the stall, followed by Dale, and dropped her medical bag, dodging Tootsie's high-kicking, pounding hooves. With one deft movement, she grabbed the horse's reins, wrapped the leather twice around her hand, and yanked. "Thanks, but I've got her," she told Dale. "The fewer people in here, the better." Once Dale had moved outside the stall walls, Sky said in a strong, steady voice, "C'mon, now, Tootsie. Calm down, girl, so I can have a look at that cut." The horse had worked herself into such a frenzy, she'd all but kicked off the bandage Chet had so carefully applied, and the whites of her eyes were visible around the entire perimeters of her chocolate-brown irises.

Though Dale stood by, ready to assist, it was Chet's eyes Sky sought out. "Looks like she's nearly severed an artery," she said, patting the horse's sweaty shoulder. "I'm going to need you."

In an instant, he was beside her. "Doesn't look good, does it?" he whispered. "Not good at all. We could lose her."

Sky smiled slightly. "Maybe not."

Chet focused on his little girl as Sky maintained her firm grip on the horse's reins. Her quiet, in-charge voice had slowed the horse's whinnying and stamping, but she knew better than to let go now. Perseverance and speed were of the essence.

"There's a hypodermic in my bag," she told Chet. Most ranchers had to be part-salesmen, part-farmers, and part-vets to keep a place running. "Ever given an injection?"

"Sure. Plenty of times. Why?"

"Because if I let go now, there's no telling how long it'll take to calm her down again. It's the white hypodermic with the blue label."

"Is Tootsie going to die, Daddy?"

Sky said, "Maybe you ought to hold Grandma's hand, Sally, so she won't be so scared." In response to Sky's not-so-veiled hint, Stella's icy glare turned hot. But Sky refused to look away until she saw the woman take her granddaughter's hand.

Chet's position facing the stall's back wall helped hide his half-grin from his mother-in-law, but not from Sky. In less time than it takes to blink, he'd sent an "attagirl" message her way, and despite the tension of the moment, Sky's heart fluttered. Then, as if he'd been doing it for a lifetime, he removed the needle's protective cap and held the hypodermic in midair.

"Ready when you are."

He met her eyes, tucked in one corner of his mouth, took a deep breath, and did the deed. After he'd withdrawn the needle, he looked at Sky and grinned.

Sky smiled, too. "Good job."

Almost immediately, Tootsie began to relax. Sky turned to Dale. "C'mere and help us guide her to the floor, pal o' mine."

That done, Sky gently removed what remained of the bandage and saw that the barbs had nearly sliced to the bone. "Take Sally outside," she told Chet. "In fact, get everybody out of here. We've got to keep her calm, and we can't do that with this audience." More for Stella's benefit than for any other reason, she added, "Besides, this could get messy, real messy." Then she unceremoniously poured isopropyl alcohol over her hands.

By the time Chet reached his daughter, Sky had threaded the surgical needle, and without looking up, she knew that no one had made a move to leave the barn. In a stronger voice, she said, "I mean it, Chet. Get them out of here. Now."

"Well, I never!" she heard Stella say.

"It's *my* barn...," Bud added.

"But Grandmother, teacher says we should *always* do what the doctor says," Sally announced, sniffing.

From the mouths of babes, Sky thought as Chet's in-laws stomped away.

"We'll be in the kitchen," Stella said to Chet. "Come, Sally. Let's leave the animal doctor here in the barn...." Under her breath, but loud enough for Sky to hear, she added, "...where she belongs."

Once Sally and her grandparents were gone, Dale snickered. "Shoo-eee! I haven't seen her that mad since we were fourteen and broke the terrace window. You could freeze a side of beef on that lady's stare."

Chet grinned and shook his head. "I'll say one thing for you, Sky: you sure know how to win friends and influence people."

"I can take just about anything from anybody," she said, taking another stitch, "but I can't stand a person who thinks she's better than everybody else."

"Believe it or not," Chet said, "she's got a heart as big as Montana. Trouble is, she won't show it to anybody but family."

Sky admired his loyalty, even if she didn't agree with it. But Stella's character was quickly forgotten as she got to the business of repairing the horse's leg.

It took nearly half an hour to complete the intricate patchwork, and when Sky finished, Tootsie snorted softly and lifted her head. Instinctively, Dale stroked her long, white-streaked nose. "It's okay, girl. You're in good hands."

"The best," Chet added.

Sky blushed but hid it by digging in her bag.

Dale whistled. "I thought old Tootsie here was a goner for sure, way she was bleeding. I've seen Chet sew up plenty of cuts, but not like you stitched up that one." He gave Sky a sideways hug and kissed her cheek. "Now I'm sorry I cancelled our date. I'd rather spend the evening with a hero than a pretty blonde any day."

Chet's eyes went from rainy-day to stormy gray. "You guys are...*dating*?"

Dale laughed. "You've gotta be kidding. We're like siblings." He ruffled her hair. "Right, sis?"

Playfully, Sky poked him in the ribs. "Yeah, well, you owe me dinner and a movie, *bro*." Smiling, she couldn't help but wonder if the merry gleam had returned to Chet's eyes in response to the friends' teasing or because it relieved him to learn she and Dale weren't a twosome.

"I've had to put down animals that were hurt as bad," Chet said. "You really think she'll be all right?"

"She won't be jumping any fences in her future, but she'll live."

"Sally's going to be relieved."

"Yeah. Sally," Dale said, chuckling as he lightly punched Chet's shoulder. "And her daddy wasn't sweating worry bullets ten minutes ago...."

Chet's left brow did its rising act. "'I'll thank you to keep your mitts to yourself, cowboy,'" he quoted, reminding Sky of the day they met. For the moment, they had eyes only for each other.

Dale looked from Sky to Chet and back again. "Okay. I'm outta here. A brick doesn't have to fall on my head." Walking backwards toward the door, he added, "I know when I'm not wanted. I'll just leave you two lovebirds alone."

Chet took Sky's hands in his own. "Dale's right. I've done patch jobs before, but not like that one. You did a terrific job," he said, looking from her bloodied fingers to her shining brown eyes. "Makes me right proud to be your...friend."

His arms slipped around her waist and he drew her to him. As his lips met hers, Tootsie struggled to her feet with a mighty puff of air.

"Where was Dale supposed to take you on this so-called date of yours tonight?"

Sky shrugged. With his lips still this close to hers, she couldn't think of much else. Even her best friend. "It was his turn to pay, and he's usually good for a burger and fries."

"How would you feel about another trip to Livingston?"

I'd feel like I'd died and gone to heaven. Her secret thought shocked her. *What kind of woman are you, to have fallen for your dead friend's husband?* But the better question was, what had happened to her life motto? "Face is home alone," she said, "and I left so fast I didn't even put fresh water in her bowl. Besides, I have to—"

"—take care of the you-know-what," he droned.

Sky turned from the disappointed look in his eyes and stepped out of his embrace. "Is she an evening feeder?" she asked, petting Tootsie's nose.

Chet pocketed his hands. "Morning. Why?"

"Good. She won't need to miss a meal."

"How long till your boarders have finished theirs?"

Sky's eyebrows rose in confusion.

"Pablo serves dinner till eleven...."

She'd intended to keep the frightening message on her answering machine a secret, more determined than ever to display an "everything's normal" façade for everybody.

Going to Livingston would underscore that things were fine on Magic Mountain. Still, Sky couldn't bring herself to leave the house—or the cubs—unprotected. She had no explanation for the feelings bubbling inside her. "Are you any good with charcoal?"

It was his turn to look puzzled.

"I took a pound of hamburger out of the freezer this morning; I couldn't possibly eat it all by myself. I could whip us up a bowl of potato salad, and you could put some burgers on Gramps' brick oven."

Chet grinned and followed her out of the stall. "Just tell me what time to fire up the coals."

Sky glanced at her watch. "How's six sound? And bring Sally. It'll get her mind off Tootsie."

He grasped a wayward red curl by her temple. "I hate mustard in my potato salad."

Wrinkling her nose, she said, "Me, too."

Chet walked her to the truck and leaned into the open window as she cranked up the motor. His nose was no more than an inch from hers, and she wanted to run her fingers through his soft, shining hair, kiss the worried look off his handsome face. Instead, she contented herself with inhaling the masculine scent of fresh hay and hard work.

"Can I bring anything?"

"Just Sally," she said, shifting into reverse. "See you soon."

"Soon," he whispered. His lips lingered longer than necessary on her cheek, making what should have been an ordinary good-bye extraordinarily memorable.

Chapter Ten

T hey arrived at Sky's house fifteen minutes early, Chet carrying a bag of charcoal under one arm and holding a bouquet of white daisies in his free hand. "Sally's idea," he said to Sky as he handed her the flowers.

Sky took the child's hand and smiled. "Thanks, little one," she said. "Daisies are my favorite flowers. How did you know?"

Sally grinned and looked at their hands. "Grandfather said Mommy loved daisies. And Daddy said you and Mommy were best friends. Best friends like the same things lots of the time." She shrugged her tiny shoulders and held her other hand out, palm up. "That's how I knew."

Sky had wanted to hug this kid since the first time she'd set eyes on her. The spur-of-the-moment gesture didn't seem to surprise Sally at all. The child hugged Sky's neck with a power that belied her size. "Thanks, kiddo."

"You're welcome. Are there any chocolate chip cookies left?"

As she munched a sweet treat, Sally helped Sky set the picnic table. When the meal was over, she helped her father clear the dishes. The feast left them pleasantly sated, and as the sun began to set, the new autumn air turned bitingly cool.

The party moved inside, where the threesome sat side by side on the living room sofa as they watched an Andy Griffith rerun on Sky's tiny TV. Face, sprawled on the floor at their feet, sat up now and then to receive a pat from Sally or Chet. When the program ended, they moved into the kitchen, and Sky made sundaes for dessert. It was dark when she packed up another bag of chocolate chip cookies for Sally. "You still have enough to feed an army," Chet observed as Sky closed the door on the half-dozen still-full containers lining the pantry shelves. "Next time you can't sleep, give me a call. I'll talk you through it."

"Chocoholics Anonymous?" she teased.

"Something like that," he said, laughing as he slipped his arm around her waist. Taking Sally's hand, he looked from the girl to the woman and grinned. "I could spend the rest of my life like this, right here between my two best girls."

Sally tugged his arm. "C'mon, Daddy. I want to see Tootsie before bedtime."

Chet let himself be led into the foyer but refused to let Sky out of his grasp. In the open doorway, he pulled her closer still and lightly brushed his mustache across her lips. "Sleep tight," he sighed. "Don't let the chocolate chips bite."

Side by side, Face and Sky watched until the red glow of his taillights were no longer visible. "Off he goes into the wild black yonder. Again."

She sighed, and Face barked in agreement.

Sky had planned to leave with the cubs for Beartooth at dark. But, being exhausted, she decided to wait until the following night instead. After a good night's sleep and a long, restful day, she'd be far better prepared to tackle the wilderness, anyway.

Two hours later, snuggling under Gran's afghan as she lounged on the living room sofa, Sky was able to blot the threatening note and phone calls from her mind by thinking of Chet and Sally's visit. A pianist's rendition of Chopin's *Prelude in C Minor* tinkled from the stereo speakers, and the latest issue of *Health* magazine sat open in her lap. "Don't ever fall in love," she said, petting the dog beside her. "It'll turn you into a featherbrained twit who can't get through one paragraph without thinking of—"

Face sat up and cocked her head toward the front door.

Tires crunched up the gravel drive, followed by the slam of a car door. A second later, footsteps thumped across the porch, followed by three hard knocks. "Some watchdog you are," Sky said as the Irish setter slunk into the foyer. "Where's your ferocious bark when I need it?"

But the dog didn't seem the least bit frightened. "Well, I'm scared enough for the both of us," she whispered. It never dawned on her that Face's reaction meant "friend, not foe" on the other side of the front door.

Sky's heart drummed with fear, and the blood in her veins ran cold. She headed for the foyer, turning out lights as she went, and grabbed Wade's police flashlight from its new storage spot on the table beside the door. Resting it on one shoulder like a rifle, she tiptoed to the door, instantly recognizing the massive silhouette through the oval of etched glass. Sky controlled the urge to throw open the door and leap into his arms.

"Sky...it's me."

"Why are you whispering?" she whispered back, grinning as she opened the door.

Chet stared at her as Face, her tail wagging, whimpered for his attention. Distractedly, he patted her head, but his eyes never left Sky's. "Just had to stop by to make sure you were all right."

"Wouldn't it have been easier to phone?"

"You have a lovely telephone voice," he said, stepping into the foyer and closing the door quietly behind him, "but it pales in comparison to the in-person thing." He took the flashlight from her hand and placed it on the foyer table. "Planning to bop me with that, were you?"

She glanced at it, then back at him. "No. It's.... I thought.... I was—"

Sky stopped talking when his dark brows inched together.

"So, Miss Brave-and-Able *does* have fears," he said, scooping her up and carrying her into the living room, where he gently deposited her on the couch.

The house was totally dark except for the dim lamp glowing on the end table.

Chet sat down beside her and took her hands in his. Clearing his throat, he said, "I, uh, I'd like to know if you'd...."

His sigh, long and loud, hung in the air for several seconds, making Sky wish she knew what to say to ease his discomfort.

"It's been a long time since I've felt like this," he murmured, staring down at their hands, "about a woman, I mean...."

If she'd had one measly ounce of courage, she'd have admitted she'd *never* felt this way about a man.

He turned a little to face her, draping an arm over her shoulders. "So, I was wondering...."

She watched him intently, patiently, and waited.

"I was wondering if...if you'd consider...."

He stared across the room at the wide picture window and blew a stream of air through his teeth. "I prayed about this all the way over here," he admitted, shaking his head. Then, meeting her eyes, he grinned. "Been prayin' about this for days, if you want to know the truth. You'd think all that conversin' with God would make things easier, wouldn't you?"

Sky didn't speak. Didn't even nod. Was he about to *propose*?

"Guess the best way to do this is just to spit it out." He took another gulp of air, then faced her again. "Would you be my girl, Sky?"

Blinking, she repeated the question in her mind. Repeated it again. The tremor in his voice, the worry lines on his brow, the serious way his eyes held hers inspired slow laughter to bubble from her.

"What's so funny?" he wanted to know, his frown intensifying.

"I thought...," she began, giggling harder, "...it sounded like...well, like you were revving up to propose."

Chet's eyebrows rose high on his forehead. He chuckled. "Man. If asking you to go steady was that hard, I can't imagine what asking you to marry me would've been like!" Then, "So, will you? Be my girl, I mean?"

"Since I can't think of any reason to say no, I guess that leaves yes."

Lost in the moment, Sky and Chet didn't notice the quiet crunch of gravel in the driveway, and they ignored Face's whimpering. They didn't hear the footsteps that thumped across the yard or see the shadowy figure crouch beside Chet's truck.

The dark figure had hidden his beat-up old Jeep deep in the pines on the other side of the highway, more than a mile away, but even the jog down Sky's long, winding drive had done little to warm him from autumn's cold night air. For weeks, he'd been showing up this way, always at a different time, hoping to catch a glimpse of her with the cubs. He'd grown accustomed to the irregular stream of visitors who showed up at the clinic while the sky was bright, but so far during his surveillance, no one had come to Magic Mountain at this hour.

He'd heard Chet's truck long before he'd seen the vehicle, and he'd hidden behind a large tree. The moment the truck had passed, he'd recognized it as Chet's, and he'd wondered what had brought the rancher all the way out here so late at night....

Chapter Eleven

C het had been gone for less than a minute when the grandfather clock chimed twelve times. Sky stood alone in the foyer, hugging herself and humming happily.

Scuffling and shouts interrupted her song, and suddenly, Chet was on the porch again, hollering for her to call the sheriff. Sky opened the door and gaped in fear. When he'd left only moments ago, warmth had been glowing in his eyes. Now, they blazed with violent, barely controlled rage. At the end of one beefy arm, he held a very rumpled, very terrified Joe Peebles by the scruff of the neck. "I was almost at the end of the drive when I saw him slinking around in the trees," Chet thundered.

"I jus' w-w-wanted to see fer myself," Joe stammered. "I ain't never seen no w-wolf cubs before."

As long as Sky had known Martha's lanky, middle-aged son, he had never been anything but gentle and kind, and he cowered under Chet's angry glare. "You're hurting him, Chet. Let him go!"

Chet turned his glowering gaze on Sky. "Let him go? Are you crazy? I find him skulking around in the middle of the night, and you say, 'Let him go'?"

Sky pried Chet's fingers from Joe's shirt collar and straightened the thin man's eyeglasses. "What are you doing out here at this time of night?"

Dumbly, Joe shrugged and shook his head. "I j-jus' wanted to see the w-wolves."

"How did you know there were wolves here?"

"Heard in town. Some of the Lazy L guys were talkin' in Ma's store. They hang 'round The Grainery all the time, y'know."

Chet shook his head, anger still brewing in his eyes. "Have you been calling here and writing notes?" he demanded.

The fury in his voice alone was enough to make Joe take a step back. "Ma don't let me use the phone, on account of the time I dialed H-Hawaii by m-m-mistake." He looked at Sky. "'M-member?"

She smiled gently and patted his hand. "Yes. I remember."

"Good grief," Chet grumbled, impatiently rubbing his eyes. "Are you going to call the sheriff, or do I have to do it?"

Sky leveled a look of impatience at Chet. "Will you please calm down and just think about this for a minute? You know Joe as well as—or better, even—than I do. You've been doing business with him and his mother at The Grainery for years. Have you ever known him to be anything but honest?"

The heat in his eyes dimmed slightly. "Well, no. But—"

"But nothing!" Sky insisted. "I'd know that voice on the telephone anywhere, and it definitely wasn't Joe's. Besides," she added, looking back at her slow-blinking friend, "He doesn't *write* notes. He prints them. Isn't that right, Joe?"

Joe nodded so quickly, he momentarily lost his balance. "'C-cause this hand don't w-work too good," he explained, flexing the withered appendage.

Sky sent Chet an I-told-you-so look that defused his remaining wrath. He lifted his chin defiantly and crossed both arms over his chest. "That may be so, but it doesn't explain what he's doing here at midnight."

Blushing, Joe stared at the toes of his loosely tied sneakers. "I-I already tol' you...s-some of the cowboys in Ma's store s-said Sky had c-cubs on Magic M-Mountain." He looked at Chet. "I ain't n-never seen no b-baby wolves. N-not up close, anyways. So I borrowed Ma's Jeep." He patted his pocket, where the keys jangled quietly. "Those cubs s-sure are cute. Are they as soft as they l-look, Sky?"

Chet stepped up beside Sky and slid his arm protectively around her waist. "Did you actually *see* the wolves, Joe?"

When he nodded, his glasses slid down his nose. "Uh-huh. An' I h-heard 'em, too. They sure sound s-scary when they howl, d-don't they?"

Sky and Chet exchanged "What are we gonna do now?" glances. "But why so late at night, Joe?" Chet pressed.

Joe's flush deepened and he grinned crookedly. "On account o' Ma's asleep. She can't ask n-no questions if she's asleep. 'Sides, b-baby animals need to eat every t-two hours. Y-you taught me that, Sky. You t-taught me," he said, excitement making his voice rise in pitch and volume. "I saw you g-go down by the shed at t-ten o'clock. I s-saw with my b-bin...binoculars. You p-put that big light on, and I could see real g-good. I was g-gonna wait two more hours, so I could s-s-see 'em again." Joe held up his arm and showed Sky his wristwatch. Then, staring at the toes of his sneakers again, he added quietly, "Only... only I f-fell asleep."

His hazel eyes, magnified several times by the convex lenses of his eyeglasses, focused on Chet. "That's w-why I was in the woods when your t-truck woke me up."

Giggling, Joe covered his face with his gnarled hand. "I know what *you* two were doin'. You g-guys were *kissin'* an stuff, like in the m-movies, weren't ya?"

Wry amusement crinkled the corners of Chet's eyes when Sky glanced up at him. She sighed, relieved that this particular bomb, at least, had been diffused. "I don't know about anybody else," she said, "but I sure could use a nice cup of hot tea."

"Me, t-too," Joe said. Holding up three fingers, he added, "I like m-mine with this m-many sugars."

Chet squeezed her hand. "I'd better head on out. You gonna be okay?"

She returned the squeeze. "I'll be fine." To Joe, she said, "The teapot is on the kitchen counter. Would you mind filling it with water for me and putting it on the stove to boil?"

Joe shuffled toward the kitchen. "Sure, Sky. S-sure...."

Once Joe was out of earshot, Chet took her in his arms. "I'll call you first thing in the morning."

Sky felt so warm and safe that she forgot for a moment about the cubs. About the threatening note. About the scary phone calls. "It *is* first thing in the morning."

"Then I'll call at an hour rational people consider morning." He kissed her, then added, "Because I'm certainly not rational around you." He gave her a long, meaningful look. "Don't stay up too long. It's been quite a day."

A monumental, momentous, unforgettable day, she thought, smiling. The sight of him reaching for his keys made her heart ache. She didn't want him to leave. "I wish you could stay," she admitted, her voice softly pleading. If he did, she'd tell him about her plans to turn the cubs loose....

"So do I."

The tenderness on his face was almost as comforting as one of his big bear hugs. And it kept her warm inside for a long while after he had left. He'd been gone nearly half an hour when Sky refilled Joe's teacup. She'd told him the whole story by then. Joe may have been slow, but he wasn't stupid.

"I don't like this," he said, his bushy brows knitted in a concerned pout. "Nope. Don't like this one bit. That bad guy wants those cubs real bad. He could maybe try to hurt you to get them, Sky."

She noticed that he hadn't stammered once during his warning. Suddenly, Joe's fist crashed onto the table. "I have a great idea!" he shouted. "Why don't we put 'em in my secret place! Nobody knows 'bout my secret place!" He jumped up and ran around and around the table, looking like a giant flamingo as he flapped his long arms. Face, who'd been half asleep at Sky's feet, yipped with glee and joined his circular romp.

The clock said 3:55, meaning Sky had been up for nearly twenty-four hours. She didn't know what caused it—Joe's silly display or her sleep deficit—but she laughed long and hard, and it took her a full minute to get control of herself. Wiping tears of laughter from her cheeks, she patted the seat of Joe's chair. "Sit down and tell me about your secret place, Joe. Is it far away? In town, maybe?"

Joe bounced up and down in his chair, hardly able to contain himself. "No, no; not in town. In the foothills. On Beartooth Plateau. It's a cave, see. I found it after Pa died. I used to go there when I missed him. It helped me stop being sad." Joe pushed his glasses higher on his narrow nose. "Now I go there when I'm tired of workin' in the store."

Sky remembered Martha's complaints: *"Guess you'll have to load your own skid. Joe's missin' again."* And whenever he returned, Joe stubbornly refused to discuss his absences. The fact that he'd kept this secret place under wraps for nearly twenty years told Sky that Joe could be trusted with her secret.

As he began listing the features of the place, his usually drowsy eyes glowed with life and intelligence. "It's very big. I could stack stuff over the entrance so they couldn't get out. And so them bad guys couldn't get in there. I keep lanterns and flashlights and a sleeping bag up there. Sometimes, I cook, too." Joe explained that he'd built a stove from cinderblocks and rocks and an oven rack he'd bought at the junkyard for a nickel. "It never gets smoky," he continued, his forehead wrinkling as he scratched his head. "I don't know why, but it just never does."

Moving the cubs to Joe's cave might solve a few of her problems, Sky realized. It would place them smack-dab in the middle of the very place where she'd eventually release them. They could grow slowly accustomed to the sounds and scents that would be typical of their home. And, she could teach them to hunt there.

Only one problem plagued her mind. Involving Joe would place him in the very same danger she'd been in since rescuing the cubs.

Chapter Twelve

The kitchen clock said 10:15 a.m. Sky had told Chet as he'd left that she'd stop by the ranch before lunch to check on Tootsie. If she hurried, she could shower and change before heading out to Four Aces. It had been a busy morning, what with delivering the cubs to Joe's cave—and taking care not to let the man in the hills see—and her busy clinic schedule. Surprisingly, she wasn't the least bit tired. She chalked it up to knowing the cubs were finally safe.

What more could you ask for?

Only one thing came to mind: Wade. He'd have been proud of what she'd accomplished in her twenty-seven years.

Driving to Four Aces, Sky saw the rocky cliffs and the broad fields through new eyes. She'd always cherished the vast beauty of Montana's landscape, but because it had been Wade's birthplace, bits and pieces of his life seemed to echo from the hills and valleys: the big rock where he'd taught her to tie her shoes, the giant pine in whose trunk he'd carved her name, the mountain peak that he'd said was her very own castle in the sky. Suddenly, memories that had once caused pain now brought pleasure. She felt as though her smile began deep in her soul and radiated outward.

When she parked her truck outside Chet's barn, Dale greeted her, saying, "Looks like you just swallowed a gallon of happy juice. Love sure does agree with you."

Sky sent her friend a slice of that whole-body smile she'd been showing. She dismissed her life motto and prayed that this time, things would be different.

Sky was on her hands and knees examining Tootsie's leg when Chet appeared out of nowhere. "How's our patient, Doc?"

She hadn't thought it possible for her spirits to soar any higher—until she heard the sound of his voice. "No infection," she announced, carefully applying another sterile dressing to the wound. "But I'm going to give her another dose of antibiotic, just in case."

He rested his arms atop the stall gate as he watched Sky administer the medication. He was still watching as she packed up her supplies. "How do you feel about pot roast?"

Looking into his eyes made her feel helpless and small, like she'd been swallowed up by a deep gray ocean. Her heart swelled with emotion. "You have a talent for asking left-field questions," she said, getting to her feet. "Pot roast, huh? Well, Gran made a roast once that nearly choked me, but I'm not the kind of woman who'd judge 'em all by the bad behavior of one."

Chet rested his chin on the back of his hand and grinned. "We eat at seven, and Stella likes us to 'dress' for dinner."

Stella. Hard-nosed, tight-lipped, thick-skinned Stella. The mere mention of her name cooled the space between them. As kids, Dale and Sky had put Stella in the same fear-inducing category as Dorothy's wicked witch and Jack's giant. Bud may have done all the barking at Four Aces, but everybody in Mountain Gate knew it was Stella who had the bite. Sky had never seen her hug Ella. Bud, either, for that matter. In fact, she couldn't remember hearing her utter a kind word to man or beast. She couldn't imagine eating a peaceful meal at the same table with the Ice Lady—and her bounty-hunting husband.

Sky grimaced. "I don't know, Chet. I didn't exactly win any Brownie points with Stella yesterday. Maybe you could just drive over to my place after sup—"

"Nonsense." He walked over and affectionately tucked some of her hair behind her ears. "I'll pick you up at six-thirty." That said, he took her medical bag from her hands and put it on the floor beside them, then drew her into a loose embrace.

Being in his arms felt so right and so good that Sky wondered why she'd fought it at first. Looking up into his handsome face, she smiled. She'd never noticed the freckles that flecked the bridge of his nose, and she let her fingertips linger there as if counting them one by one. And as the thick, soft mustache above his upper lip swept across her cheeks, she discovered it wasn't just black, but mahogany and cinnamon and gold, too, just like the luxurious hair on his head. He had the high, angled cheeks of a Cheyenne and a strong Irish nose, and her hands molded to his sun-kissed skin the way a sculptress puts the final, gentle strokes on firm, fresh clay.

Sky knew she'd never tire of looking at him, but she closed her eyes to test her memory of that noble face. She inhaled deeply, wanting scent and sight to create a singular image when she slept alone that night.

He must have been doing the same thing. "You smell like a cowboy," he said, grinning. "A woman after my own heart."

❦

The moment she opened the front door, Sky knew she'd chosen her outfit wisely. Chet's eyes widened, and he uttered a low whistle of approval. Her hair fell in soft waves and just touched the shoulders of her long-sleeved black dress. The fabric clung subtly to her torso and flowed freely and loosely from her waist to her knees. At five feet nine inches, Sky usually wore flats or pumps so she wouldn't tower over male dinner companions. But even in two-inch heels, she felt petite beside Chet.

"Mmm, mmm, mmm," he said, nodding. "You look good enough to eat."

You will not blush, you will not blush!

He seemed to favor starched white shirts, which was fine with Sky, since she loved the way they accented his tanned complexion. His gray sports coat matched his eyes, and the legs of his navy trousers had such sharp creases, Sky feared they might draw blood if she stood too close.

"Don't want to mess your makeup," he whispered, "but I just gotta have a predinner treat." And after one savory kiss, he whisked her away in his silver Porsche.

Stella sat stiffly in her teal wingback chair as Chet made reintroductions. "Be nice to her," he whispered in his mother-in-law's ear. "She was a good friend to Ella."

At the mention of his daughter's name, Bud's dark eyes brightened. "That's true enough. Sky, here, spent many a summer day in this house, didn't you, Sky?"

Sky smiled, hoping it would hide the quivering of her lips. It didn't. During the ride to Four Aces, she had promised herself there'd be no talk of wolves or bounties. She thought she'd prepared herself for the Ice Lady's reception, knowing full well she'd never been one of Stella's favorite people. In fact, she'd once overheard her telling Bud that she wasn't sure Sky was a suitable playmate for their only child. She'd run off crying before hearing

Bud's response, but Sky was fairly certain from his over-all grumpy attitude what that response had been. She'd prepared herself for more of the same attitude tonight but hadn't figured on anybody mentioning Ella. Her heart ached as she spoke to no one in particular, "Some of my fondest childhood memories were made right here in this house."

Stella harrumphed and adjusted the hem of her silk dress.

You get more flies with honey, Sky could hear her father saying. She ignored Stella's haughty attitude and grinned. "You look lovely in that shade of blue, Mrs. Houghton. It brings out the color of your eyes."

Blinking, the older woman touched a hand to her well-coiffed, cotton-white hair. "Yes...well.... Thank you, dear." She looked at Bud. "Is it seven o'clock yet?"

He held up a gold watch that dangled at the end of its sparkling, thick-linked chain. It made a quiet *click* as he popped open the lid. "Not for five minutes yet," he said, snapping it shut.

Sally dashed into the room and wrapped herself around Sky's knees in a hug. "Dr. Allen! I'm so glad you're here!"

Minutes later, in the dining room, Stella dictated the seating arrangements so that Sky sat alone facing Chet. Sally sat to his right, and Stella and Bud took their places at either end of the long mahogany table. China dishes, crystal goblets, and silver flatware gleamed atop a hand-embroidered, white-on-white tablecloth, and a second chandelier, smaller than the one in the huge foy-er, rained aurora borealis-like light down upon them.

Chung, the Houghtons' manservant, grasped Stella's water goblet with a white-gloved hand. "Missy rike wa-tah?" he asked, his pitcher hovering above her glass. He didn't wait for a reply, and after filling it, he returned it to the two o'clock position above her plate. He then flapped a crisp white napkin and draped it neatly across her lap. Chung repeated the process with each person until everyone had been watered and napkined. "I be back in jiffy," he said, bowing as he backed into the kitchen. When he returned moments later, he was pushing a food-laden brass cart. "Got rotsa good stuff here. All-a you peoples gonna eat prenty, okay?"

"Not until we say grace," Stella said. "Sally, please fold your hands. Bud, put down that glass. Chester," she said, "since she's your *guest*, you'll do the honors." Stella said "guest" as though Sky had crashed through the roof in a pink flying saucer, and since the question was more an order than a request, Sky marveled that Chet didn't seem to even notice Stella's belligerent attitude. Sky bowed her head and resisted the temptation to peek up at Chet as he prayed.

"Lord, we ask that You bless this food and those who prepared it. Bless also those of us who sit together at this table. We thank You for this glorious bounty, and for our good health, happiness, and material successes. In the name of the Father, and of the Son, and of the Holy Ghost...whoever eats the fastest gets to eat the most." When Chet lifted his head, he winked mischievously at Sally, then at Sky, and rubbed his palms together. "Pass the spuds, Doc."

Stella groaned, Sally giggled, and Bud rolled his eyes, as if Chet's shenanigans were a daily affair.

It was thanks to his constant, lighthearted banter that the dinner conversation remained reasonably pleasant. By the time Chung had handed out the last plate of homemade apple pie, even Stella was wearing a relaxed smile on her rigid face.

Sally invited Sky to help Chet tuck her in for the night. She gave her a huge hug and kiss and thanked her for saving Tootsie's life. Sky was so overcome with emotion at the child's display of affection and gratitude that tears prevented her from responding verbally.

Half an hour later, when the Porsche's headlights illuminated the big wooden sign at the end of her drive, Chet asked Sky, "Where'd you Allens get a name like Magic Mountain, anyway? Sounds like an amusement park ride."

The similarity had never even occurred to her before, but he definitely had a point. "Leave it to you to find the ridiculous in the sublime," she said, laughing. "Unfortunately, there's no poetic story to explain the name. Gramps always said the view of Granite Peak was magical. After he'd said it a couple thousand times, the name just kind of stuck."

He was still chuckling as they stepped into her foyer. He didn't even give her time to hang up her coat before wrapping her in a hearty hug and kissing her soundly. "I've been dying to do that all night." Face insisted on some attention, too, and Chet obligingly doled it out. "Did I tell you that I fell asleep last night thanking God that you said you'd be my girl?"

Blushing, Sky stepped out of his hug. "I've never been the answer to a prayer before. I hope I'm worthy."

The little red light of the answering machine on the desk in the living room was blinking, telling Sky she had missed one call. "Let me make sure nobody has a sick cow or anything," she said, grinning. Standing beside her, Chet hugged her as she pressed the message button.

"Just one more day, and you're gonna find out that we're not foolin'," said the raucous, gritty voice. "Get rid of those cubs, or you'll be sorry."

Chapter Thirteen

C het gently pushed her aside and pressed the button again, and after listening to the message a second time, he paced between the couch and the coffee table. "He said he wasn't fooling, so he's called before? How many times?" he demanded, ripping off his tie and flinging it onto the couch. "How many times has he called? And just exactly how long were you planning to hide this from me?"

Sky picked up his rumpled tie and draped it neatly over the arm of the couch. "I never saw a need to involve you in my personal problems," she said, smoothing the navy silk.

Chet leaned back against the desk and crossed both arms over his chest. The grandfather clock in the foyer chimed ten times as he stared at her. When the last hollow note stopped echoing, he shook his head. "Your personal problems," he repeated, his voice a raspy whisper. "That hurts, Sky. I thought...." But he never finished his sentence. Instead, he massaged his temples.

Sky inhaled deeply and fiddled with her watchband, then removed her earrings and put them on the end table. This whole wolf thing had become a maddening, frustrating mess. What had started out as a simple attempt to right one wrong had gone all wayward and cockeyed, getting more dangerous and more frightening by the minute. It dawned on her that anyone associated with her was at great risk. Chet, his innocent little girl, Joe, and even her patients and their owners.

The day she'd sequestered the cubs in the shelter, she'd decided that no one else would be involved—that no one else *should* be involved or endangered as a result of her choice. But she hadn't stuck to that decision, and only God and the maniac who'd killed the cubs' mother knew what might happen next.

"Sally has already lost one parent," she began, her voice quaking with emotion. "I'll not make you a part of anything that might cost her another."

He looked up so suddenly that a lock of dark hair fell over one eye. The fierce scowl on his face softened, and in two long strides, he was beside her, holding her close. "You're forgetting that I'm part Cheyenne. And a believer," he whispered into her hair. "That gives me special protection from evil." Tenderly, Chet kissed her forehead. "I'm touched that you're worried about Sally and me, but knock it off, will ya?"

When her eyes met his eyes and she saw the familiar, teasing glint sparkling there, Sky's heart lurched. It was clear that he would put his life on the line for her. And Sky could not—would not—allow that!

"I'm stronger than I look," Chet said, a grin slanting his thick, dark mustache. "Why, just this afternoon, I lifted a veterinarian into the air with my bare hands."

Sky saw in her mind's eye the way he'd scooped her up as though she weighed no more than a rag doll. But she saw the red flash of the answering machine, too—a steady reminder that the more time Chet spent with her, the more likely he was to be hurt. Tears filled her eyes, and she swiped angrily at them. *Be strong*, she told herself. *Be strong and do the right thing!* "I think you'd better leave."

Chet's brows knitted with confusion. "You...you can't mean that." His smile faded, and the lusty light in his eyes dimmed when he saw how serious she was.

Tearing herself from the wonderful warmth of his arms was one of the hardest things Sky had ever done. She turned her back on him and, hugging herself, bit her lower lip to keep from crying.

"You have every right to be afraid," he said. "In fact, I'm glad you're afraid, because it tells me you've finally come to your senses and admitted how serious this wolf situation is."

Sky guessed the distance between them to be less than a yard, though at that moment, it seemed more like a mile.

"Sky," Chet said softly, "c'mere. Please?"

She wanted to run to him, to throw herself into his arms and hold on for dear life. Wanted it more than anything. But Sky stood her ground. The only way to protect him—and his little girl—was to reject him. "I'm awfully tired. I'd really appreciate it if you'd just go now." Better that he see her as a moody, fickle female than risk another moment in her company.

Ticktock, ticktock went Gran's clock, the only sound in the room.

Face padded up to Sky and sat down, her coppery eyes filled with concern and compassion at her mistress's discomfort. When the dog whimpered, Sky stooped over to hug her. "Everything's okay, girl. Don't worry, all right?"

Face glanced at Chet, then sauntered over to him. "Don't believe a word she says," he told the dog. "She's got herself in so deep, she can't even see her way out."

Face barked and whined as she stood between them, looking helplessly from Chet to her mistress and back again.

Ticktock, ticktock....

Suddenly, Chet was behind Sky, turning her around and wrapping her in those big, strong, comforting arms. "Beat me with a stick," he sighed. "Jab a needle in my eye. Burn me with a hot poker. Shoot me in my *good* leg, even. Just don't send me away...."

It was the last thing on earth Sky wanted to do, but, like it or not, it was the very thing she had to do.

"We can beat this thing together," Chet insisted.

Together.... The word said *two as one* and *happily ever after* and *till death us do part.* Sky closed her eyes and pictured Sally—wide-eyed, innocent, and very much dependent on her daddy—and deliberately focused on the "death" part....

Ticktock, ticktock, ticktock....

"Look...I'll talk to the sheriff. I'll have Dale camp out here with a loaded shotgun," Chet said. "We'll call out the National Guard if we have to—"

"This is best for everyone involved," she said. "You know that as well as I do."

Oh, how it hurt to look into his bewildered face! If she'd obeyed her life motto, none of this would be happening now. Her heart wouldn't be breaking, and there'd be no reason to break his. "Any time now, I can let the cubs go, and this whole thing will be over." Her left brow arched slightly—a trick learned from an expert conversation manipulator. She added, *"Until* then, I...don't... want...you...here."* She put extra emphasis on the word *until* and prayed he'd hear and understand.

With that, she stepped into the foyer and opened the front door. With one hand on the gleaming brass handle and the other on her hip, Sky willed Chet through the door and out of her life—for now, just for now. Her breaths came in short, shallow gasps, and her heart was racing, but she pressed her lips tightly together to give the illusion, at least, of determination and strength.

Chet's bulk filled the living room doorway. He'd gotten that far but couldn't seem to take those final steps into the foyer and out of her life, even temporarily. She recognized the pained look in his eyes. It was the same expression she'd seen the night on her porch when he'd explained what it had been like to lose Ella. Sky would deal with her guilt and remorse later. Right now, she had to send him home, where he'd be safe.

"Confound it, Sky. This isn't necessary, I'm telling you."

She took a deep breath. "It's absolutely necessary." And with a wave of her hand, she invited him to walk through the door.

"Fine," he snapped, "if that's the way you want it. Two can play this game."

The moment Chet was on the porch, Sky slammed the door behind him and locked it. Leaning against the smooth, cool glass, she listened to the silence. No boots thumped across the porch or thudded down the steps. He was standing there, she knew, hoping she'd change her mind, waiting for her to open the door.

Ticktock, ticktock, ticktock....

At last, she heard the roar of the Porsche's engine, followed by the grating of tires against gravel. She guessed he'd made it down the drive and onto the highway in half the usual time, leaving her to listen to the endless silence that screamed, "He's gone!"

Several times that night, Sky awoke with a start, thinking she heard his car. His voice. His boots on the porch. During the few restless hours that she managed to doze, she dreamed of him. Of his laughing gray eyes and his wide, winning smile. When she awoke for good at 4:30, she dismally admitted that she very well may have saved him...only to lose him forever.

Chapter Fourteen

W hat are you doing here?"

Sky had been out all morning visiting Joe and the cubs, making house calls, and running errands. It shouldn't have been difficult to sound tired and cold, hard and unfeeling. But it was. She tried to look angry and put-out as she walked toward the porch, her backpack slung over one shoulder. "I thought I made myself clear last night."

"You did a lot of yammering," Chet drawled, chewing on a toothpick. "I don't know if I'd say you were 'clear.'"

Dark circles beneath his beautiful eyes told her he hadn't slept much, either. She wanted to kiss each worry line from his brow. Instead, she glanced at her watch. "I've been up since dawn and have a very full day ahead of me," she said stiffly. "Whatever brought you here...., make it quick." She reminded herself that he'd never said he loved her. He'd come close, but as Gramps used to say, "no cigar." It wouldn't have made any difference if he had.

Face wagged her tail and insisted on a pat. Obligingly, Chet gave her one, then plopped down in Gran's chair. "Have a seat, Sky."

She dropped her backpack on the porch floor and sat down in Gramps' rocker. "Pull up a chair. Make yourself at home. Have a seat, Sky," she said sarcastically.

Chet scowled as he sat down. "Why do you always crack jokes when you're scared out of your wits?"

Sky sat up straighter. "I don't!" she insisted. "I'm not...." She hesitated. "*You* certainly don't scare me."

He took a deep, exasperated breath. "I feel like I'm talking to Sally," he said to the porch ceiling. "Well, all right," he added, meeting her eyes, "if you insist on behaving like a spoiled brat, that's the way I'll deal with you." Chet leaned forward and balanced his elbows on his knees, that arrogant left eyebrow cocked high on his forehead. "I'm not going to say this more than once, so pay attention. I care what happens to you, though for the life of me, I don't know why—with all your flip-flopping changes of mind—and I want to help pull you out of this hole you've dug yourself into, so we can begin living some kind of normal—"

Sky held up a hand to silence him. "I'm doing fine, all alone in my hole."

"So you've said. 'I'm kicking you out for your own good until the cubs are gone,'" he paraphrased, his voice thick with sarcasm. Wagging his forefinger inches from her nose, he added, "Well, get this through your thick skull, missy, 'cause I'm not that easy to dismiss."

In a flash, he was on his feet. "Wake up, Sky. Stop thinking like an animal-loving tree hugger for a minute and admit that those wolves of yours are tearing apart more than just us. They're tearing the whole *town* apart. If I had the key to your grandfather's shelter, I'd shoot the little beasts myself just to put an end to this whole sorry mess, once and for all!"

Fury flowed from his eyes like molten lava, and she believed he meant it...at least at that moment. "And that," she said, brewing up a little fury of her own as she stood to her feet as well, "is precisely why I asked you to stay away. You see me as a helpless female, desperately in need of the protection of a big, strong male. Well, I'm not helpless, and I certainly don't need your protection!" *Quite the opposite*, she thought, knowing that even now, the gunman could be perched on a boulder, this time with *Chet* in his crosshairs.

Chet pursed his lips, then grinned crookedly. Oh, how she loved that face! She stood there silently, her hands clenched into fists at her sides, trembling with love and frustration. Two steps. That's all it would take to put herself in his arms, welcoming the kisses that would make her forget the cubs and the note and the calls. Just two steps. Sadly, she admitted to herself that it might as well have been a hundred miles.

He locked her eyes in a hot gaze and refused to let go, daring her to deny her true feelings. "Lord help me, but you're gorgeous when you're mad. For two cents, I'd kiss you right where you stand."

Sky didn't know what possessed her to do it, but she reached into her pocket, drew out two pennies, and tossed them at his feet.

Chet stared at the coins for a moment, then looked up at her, a dazzling grin on his face. He took a step. Sky took a step. And the hundred-mile gap between them closed. "You make me crazy! Do you know that?" he asked, hugging her tight. "Don't ever do that again. Don't you ever say you don't want me around."

You're a weak, pathetic pushover, she told herself, closing her eyes as he dotted sweet kisses across the bridge of her nose, over her cheeks, and on her chin and lips. "I wanted you to stay away only until...."

She'd seen a leaf float into a whirlpool once. Watched it whirl round and round, down and down, untouched and unharmed, until it disappeared into the deep, fast-rushing river. In his arms, Sky felt a lot like that helpless little leaf.

"I'm crazy about you."

He'd said "crazy." She heard "love."

The phone rang. And rang. Sky couldn't ignore it, yet she had no desire to go into the living room to answer it. She didn't want the happy moment to end.

Chet seemed able to read her mind, and he led her by the hand into the living room, where he picked up the receiver and placed it gently beside her ear. "I'm going to get us some cookies," he mouthed, pointing toward the kitchen.

She nodded and smiled, happier than she'd been in a long, long time.

"It's Saturday...."

Instantly, the tranquility of the moment vanished, and now she felt like a leaf in a hurricane. "I'm sorry," she said, sitting down on the arm of the couch, "I'm afraid I didn't hear you."

"I said, it's Saturday. I gave you till Sunday to get rid of those cubs. Doesn't leave you much time."

"But I don't have any cubs," she said truthfully, thankful he'd given her a chance to speak this time.

"You have them. Don't deny it."

"I have a dog. An Irish setter. But there are no wolves here." It was true, after all. The cubs were safe and sound at last, in Joe's cave.

"You're a terrible liar, Doc. You have two gray wolves. Four months old, give or take a week. A male and a female. The male's a good bit bigger than the female. You write stuff about them in a blue and maroon journal. You were feeding them every two hours at first; then every four. Then a morning and an evening meal. They're down to every other day now. And just a few days ago, you took two big brown teddy bears down into that hole in the ground where you've got 'em stashed." He paused, then snickered sickeningly. "Need more proof that I know what I know?"

She trembled with terror. "I don't know where you're getting your information, but there are no—"

"Straight from the horse's mouth, that's where," he interrupted her. "I'll call you in a couple of days and let you know what kind of deal we're gonna make."

Maybe, if she chose her words carefully, she could convince him that the cubs were gone. "But I took your advice. I already let them go. If you watch as carefully as you say, surely you remember that I left here the day before yesterday with a big box in the back of my truck. The wolves were in it."

"I'll be in touch," he said, and hung up.

Almost immediately, the phone rang again. Chet walked back into the room carrying a tray with two glasses of milk and a stack of chocolate chip cookies. "Don't answer it," he said, winking playfully.

She hoped he wouldn't read the panic in her eyes. "I have to. It could be a client."

"I forgot to tell ya earlier," the voice grated in her ear, "it won't do any good to keep that cowboy around all the time. He can't protect you."

She thought her heart might leap straight out of her chest.

"Hey, what's up?" Chet asked, setting the milk and cookies on the coffee table. "You're pale as a ghost." He sat down beside her on the couch and took her hand in his. "You're trembling." Suddenly, understanding dawned on his handsome face. "That's *him*, isn't it?"

Sky nodded.

Chet leaned his head close to Sky's in order to listen in. "...I had him in my sights while he was sittin' in that stiff-backed old chair on your porch a little while ago.

Would have been a shame to bloody up that pretty blue shirt of his...."

"Gimme that phone!" Chet roared. But by the time he put it to his ear, the caller had left him holding a dead line.

"Did you hear that?" Sky demanded, looking at Chet. "Do you get it now? Do you see why I don't want you around here?"

He hugged her. "I see why you're scared. Anybody would be, under the circumstances. But this guy is more than we can handle on our own. You have to call the sheriff. He'll know what to do." He paused, then stood up and started pacing. "I know that voice. Why do I know that voice?"

If he recognized it, too, it must mean that the gunman is someone we both know. Suddenly, Sky felt completely exposed. She pulled Gran's afghan onto her lap and shook her head furiously. Chet had said *we* and *our*. Just last night, she'd successfully removed him from harm's way, and now, thanks to her spinelessness, he was directly in the line of fire.

She hugged the afghan to her. "You have to leave, Chet. And don't come back again. I couldn't live with myself if anything happened to you. I...I...." Tears choked her words. Shamed by her display of weakness, she hid her face in the blanket.

Again, Chet sat down again and gathered her into a warm, protective embrace. "Shhh," he soothed her. "Once the cops are involved, everything will be just—"

She leapt up from the couch. "Don't call the police, Chet, and don't come back here. Stay away from me. I can—"

"The only way this guy's gonna keep me away from you, pretty lady," he said, "is to put a bullet right here." He put his fingertip between his eyebrows.

Sky gasped, and her eyes filled with fresh tears. "Don't say things like that!" She grabbed his hands and pulled him to his feet. "I'm not kidding," she said, shoving him toward the door. "I want you out of here right now, and I don't want to see you again until I've cleaned up this mess."

"I can't stand to see you like this." And, as if to prove it, he kissed her tenderly.

Sky refused to reciprocate the kiss. She concentrated instead on what he'd said earlier about the hole she'd dug herself into. It gave her an idea, and if she played it out smartly, she just might be able to save the cubs, Chet, and herself, too....

Chapter Fifteen

P roperty developer Mike Rowen loosened the knot of his tie and waited for his secretary to refill his coffee cup. "That'll be all," he said, smiling condescendingly. His casual wave made further words unnecessary. He had been summoning and dismissing people for so long, it was second nature to him now.

Rowen inhaled deeply from the cigarette between his fingers, then watched the gray-blue stream of smoke float from his lips toward the window wall. "So, the good doctor isn't cooperating?" Crisp-blue eyes bored into Bart, demanding an explanation.

Bart had been picking nervously at the brass brads that held the supple red leather of his chair armrest in place, but his hands froze when he noticed that Rowen's icy glare had zeroed in on the activity. Showing weakness around this guy was as dangerous as wearing a coat made of honeycomb and standing in front of a half-starved grizzly bear. Bart took a long, slow sip of his coffee, buying time, trying to calm down. Trying to think up an excuse that would appease Rowen. "We're not dealing with one of your blonde bimbos here, Mike," he said. "Sky Allen is smart, and she's got guts."

Rowen leaned his elbows on the glass-topped mahogany desk. "Then *you'll* just have to be smarter...and braver." He clenched his teeth, making a thin line of his lips as his blue eyes narrowed. "You'd be wise to keep that temper of yours in check, Bart, my boy. You're into me for half a million, don't forget."

How could he possibly forget when the creep reminded him of the debt every chance he got? Bart sighed and ran a hand through his hair. He'd come to despise that smirking, tanned face. Rowen hadn't earned his color with long hours of hard work, sweating in hot, sunny fields, as he had. No. Rowen's golden glow was a rich man's tan that came from baking in a tanning bed. A *gilded one, probably*, Bart thought, grinning slightly, *with his initials etched on it.*

"You find something amusing about our conversation?" Rowen demanded. "Maybe I'm making this too easy for you." He lit another cigarette and stared for a long time at the sterling lighter. "Obviously, this job has been hard on you. I've noticed a few gray streaks in those shining brown waves, of late," he said with a wink. "You're beginning to look a little rough around the edges, m'friend."

Rowen's perfect, practiced smile vanished, and Bart flinched involuntarily.

"I'm running out of time, and out of patience, too. Now, let's not kid ourselves.... Your ranch is a solid property. But it's not worth a tenth what Sky Allen's is worth, and we both know why. We made a deal. Shook hands in front of witnesses, need I remind you...?"

Bart's hatred for this man intensified, but he swallowed hard to keep it hidden. When this sorry mess was over, he'd tell the fool to drop dead. Might even tell him with a doubled-up fist. But until then, he had no choice but to be Rowen's whipping boy. Gambling and drinking had made him a target, and he had no one to blame but himself for the mess he was in.

At that moment, Bart was glad his daddy had died last year. Because if he'd lived to see what a muddle his youngest son had made of his life, he'd have died of a broken heart instead of a heart attack. Bart sipped his coffee. It was cold. And bitter. Like his life.

Rowen laughed softly, then walked around to the front of the big desk and perched on its corner. "I want you to listen to me, Bart, and listen good," he said, flapping a thick envelope. "I'm holdin' your family's ranch right here in the palm of my hand. You wanna save it, you do things my way, and you do 'em quick. Got it?"

The suave, sophisticated voice and proper grammar had disappeared. Bart had always suspected that Rowen's upper-class demeanor was nothing but a façade. Years of the man's bullying boiled up and put him on his feet. With one fist, he grabbed the wrist of the hand holding the deed to the Lazy L, and with the other, he wadded Rowen's two-hundred-dollar silk tie. "No, *you* listen, you cocky stuffed shirt. I don't like you. In fact, I've met mangy coyotes I like better." He shook the blond man for emphasis.

Rowen's face was turning from tan to beet-red as Bart twisted the delicate fabric tighter against his throat.

"I'm gonna get you that Allen property because I said I would. I owe it to my daddy to protect the Lazy L. But I'm warning you...you'd better show me a little respect." He looked down at his fist, and then, as though repulsed that he'd touched someone as vile as Rowen, tossed the man backward on his desk. "You'd be wise to remember that desperate men do desperate things."

Rowen smoothed his rumpled tie. His "How dare you?" look infuriated Bart, who stared back through slitted eyes. Then, he grinned. Laughed. Spread his big arms wide. "I've got no wife. No kids. No family." He looked at the deed, still clasped tightly in Rowen's greedy hand.

"And maybe, thanks to you, no home. You're lookin' at a man with nothin' to lose, *my boy*."

"Get out," Rowen rasped, returning to the other side of his desk. "And don't you dare show your face around here again until you can give me something that says the Allen ranch is *mine*." He jabbed his appointment book with his forefinger as he added, "Or on the first of next month, the Lazy L will be mine, and nothin' will give me more pleasure than tossing your sorry carcass off your daddy's land."

Bart sauntered toward the door, grinning as he pulled his hat lower on his forehead. But his smirk died even before he'd pushed the elevator's Down button, because Rowen had him over a barrel, and he knew it. He'd done a lot of miserable things in his life, but losing the Lazy L definitely topped the list. If it was the last thing he did, he'd get that deed back.

Desperate men do desperate things, he'd said. "Find their weaknesses," his daddy had always said. To save his ranch, he had no choice but to give Rowen what he wanted. And to do that, he'd looked for *Sky's* weakness....

Studying her had taught him they had a lot more in common than she'd ever know. Of their shared traits was the fact that she, too, had very little to lose. But his surveillances had taught him something else....

She owned something that meant more to her than just about anything else.

And Bart was just desperate enough to use it.

Sky heard Face's familiar whimper on the other end of the line but couldn't accept what the grating voice had said. He *couldn't* have taken the dog captive. Why, Face had been dogging Sky's heels no more than an hour ago....

Placing her hand over the phone's mouthpiece, she hollered, "Face! C'mere, girl!"

Silence.

If the dog had been within earshot, she'd have bounded onto Sky's bed in a whipstitch. But no happy feet came running. No friendly bark sounded at the end of the hall. No smiling doggy face greeted hers with adoring, damp kisses.

"You gotta be more careful, Doc," he advised. "This here's one purty little pup you've got. I bet I could get a hunnerd bucks for her in Livingston."

Again, Face whimpered.

"If you harm her in any way, I'll—"

"You'll *what*?" he snarled drunkenly. "*I've* got the upper hand, and don't you forget it!"

Wade's voice echoed from somewhere deep in Sky's memory: "*Talking to a drunk is like talking to a wall.*" As sheriff of Georgia's Fulton County, he'd arrested no fewer than a dozen drunks a week. "You got to let 'em ramble till they're sober, *then* you can let 'em have it." Trying to keep a calm, even tone in her voice, Sky asked, "What do you want?"

He laughed a wicked little laugh. "You remember that old TV show, Doc, called *Let's Make a Deal*?" he asked, then went on to explain his terms.

Sky didn't know which emotion rang louder—fear or anger. But she sensed that if he heard her fear, he'd use it against her. "I'm going to hang up and call the sheriff," she snapped, having no difficulty sounding angry.

"And tell him what?"

He was right, of course. By the time the officials figured out who this mysterious lunatic was, he'd have disappeared...with Face.

"Maybe you'd like a week or two to think it over," he said, interrupting her frenzied thoughts. "I'll be in touch." With that, he hung up.

The house seemed huge and empty without Face's constant companionship. Sky wandered from room to room, missing the dog's quiet panting and the *click-click* of her toenails on the hardwood floors. Again, Sky's life motto echoed in her head and taunted her. *If you'd followed the rules, it said, you wouldn't be in this position now.* But then, she wouldn't have enjoyed three years of Face's devoted affection, either....

Chet had been right—she'd dug herself in deep this time. But whenever trouble had touched her in the past, Sky had faced it alone...and survived. Still, difficult as some of those situations had been, none had included a madman. She'd have to exercise caution if she hoped to get Face back, safe and sound. She wanted this man to pay for taunting and threatening her, for stealing Face, and for possibly costing her the only man she'd ever loved.

She couldn't call Dale or the sheriff. She certainly couldn't call Chet. If this guy would take Face, there was no telling what else he might be capable of doing...or to whom. Sky recalled Romans 12:19: *"Vengeance is mine, I will repay, says the Lord."* As much as she would have liked to see him suffer for all he'd done, she preferred to see it all end.

At first light, Sky stood in the shower for a long time, letting the hot water pummel her weary body. She hoped it would wash the tension and fear down the drain along with the sweet-smelling suds.

As she towel-dried her hair, she reached a decision....

Get the deed to Magic Mountain.

He had spelled it out carefully: he'd trade Face for a "paid in full" bill of sale on the parcel of her land that bordered the highway, where the river snaked between her property and the Lazy L.

She didn't raise livestock, as her grandparents had, and she had no intention of doing so. The endless water supply was useless to her. Sky saw no reason to hold on to it. Especially when handing over the property rights to it would free Face and get this madman out of her life.

Suddenly, Sky remembered reading in last week's paper that Rowen Construction, the same company that was building tract houses on former wilderness land, was strong-arming farmers and ranchers in and around Mountain Gate to get control of their properties. The huge development corporation had built ski and beach resorts all over the country, and this time, it had set its cap on Yellowstone territory.

Because Sky's property paralleled Route 212, it had a second distinct advantage: easy access for construction equipment during the building process, easy access for tourist traffic later. Without it, Rowen would be forced to wait out the procedures of the county government as it began the lengthy legal process of approving and issuing permits.

Everything made sense, and now that she understood the stakes, making the decision was easier than ever. It would all be over soon, and nothing would please her more.

"Morning, Sky," Mrs. Warfield said. "What can I do for you today?"

Sky showed the old woman her key. "I need to get into my safe deposit box."

Chet stepped into line behind her, but Sky didn't notice him.

"That might be a problem," Mrs. Warfield said. "They're laying new tiles back there, you see, and no one can walk on them just yet."

Sky frowned. "Why didn't they plan to do that before or after normal banking hours?"

The teller shrugged. "Nobody else seemed to mind."

"Well, I mind," Sky snapped. Then, in reaction to Mrs. Warfield's disdainful expression, she added, "I'll be in there only a minute or two. I promise to be careful...." She sighed and then tried a different approach. "It's very important, Mrs. Warfield," she said. "I'd never consider putting you to all this trouble if it wasn't."

Mrs. Warfield, appeased by Sky's kinder, gentler attitude, gave it a moment's thought. "I'll need to see what Mr. Harper says. You wait right there." With that, the woman disappeared into the manager's office.

In the teller's absence, Sky's nerves twitched. She hated banks and conducted business in them as seldom—and as quickly—as possible. Her head aching and stomach churning, she leaned on the polished marble counter and watched the camera on the opposite wall pan the bank's interior.

The camera at First Atlanta Savings and Loan had been making that same grinding noise on the day her father was gunned down. Here, the vault behind the counter stood ajar, just as the one in Georgia had. Computer screens were blinking. A telephone rang. The black marble floors reflected the dim glow of the chandeliers. And there was the unmistakable scent of metal money... all reminiscent of the day her dad was killed.

Ever since that horrible day in August, just before her seventeenth birthday, Sky couldn't enter a bank without connecting everything inside to the smell of gunpowder. Wade had died a slow, painful death, right before her eyes....

She recited Acts 2:24 aloud: "*'But God raised him up, having loosed the pangs of death, because it was not possible for him to be held by it.'*" She took comfort in knowing that the Lord would gently cradle her father through eternity, just as she'd gently cradled him on that fateful day.

Sky's stomach growled embarrassingly, reminding her that she wasn't in Atlanta at all but in Mountain

Gate, Montana. She hadn't been eating properly, choosing instead to work through meals as she had done in college and med school. Back then, hard work had helped her forget the things that haunted her, and she'd hoped it would help her forget what was haunting her now...the man in the hills who seemed to know her every move, who'd taken Face. And Joe, so innocent and dependent, alone in the cave with the cubs. And the awful fight she'd picked with Chet....

She wanted the man in the hills to see the anger, the pain, the resolution on Chet's face as he watched the dissolution of Sky and Chet's budding romance. *So maybe I did say every hateful, spiteful thing I could think to say. If I had to hurt him to save him, so be it*, she'd decided.

Well, she'd hurt him, all right. That much had been evident in his clear, gray eyes. Even knowing she'd done the right thing didn't make it any easier. Her well-intentioned deed had come with a hefty price tag: long, sleepless nights spent alone with her empty, aching heart.

Exhaustion and fear and frustration mounted as Sky waited for Mrs. Warfield to return from the bank's back room. What started as a quiet ringing in her ears became a loud, underwater sound. A cold, clammy sensation gripped her entire body as waves of dizziness swept over her. Sky gripped the counter for support, hoping it would pass.

Instead, she began trembling. Her teeth chattered as her palms and brow and upper lip grew sticky with sweat. She was dizzy. So dizzy....

She'd never fainted before. A silly grin spread across her face as she began to melt onto the hard, polished floor.

There's a first time for everything was her last conscious thought.

Chapter Sixteen

Chet had been standing there listening, trying to send Mrs. Warfield a telepathic message to let Sky into the vault. The sooner Mrs. Warfield got Sky what she wanted, the less time he'd have to stand there looking at her—at those shiny, auburn waves...at the stubborn lift of her chin...at that way she had of squaring her shoulders.

At first, he thought it was his imagination when she began swaying at the counter. But when she started to slump toward the floor, Chet understood something was dreadfully wrong. When he took a step forward and held out his arms, Sky fell into them like a weak, willing child. He went to the floor with her, allowing his body to cushion hers.

Holding her in his lap brought suppressed emotions to the surface. Since her tantrum in her living room a few weeks prior, he'd stubbornly refused to call her. He hadn't pulled into her driveway, though his pickup seemed to lurch in that direction every time he passed Magic Mountain on his way to or from town. He told himself over and over that he had neither the time nor the patience for a woman whose emotions swung in such a wide arc. So, in the past few weeks, he'd spent more time in the barn. More time in the fields. A lot more time with Sally.

But daisies were Sky's favorite flowers, and the remnants of wild ones that grew along the highway awakened vivid images of her. She had called Sally "little one," and now, whenever the child used the endearment with one of her dollies or stuffed animals, his heart ached with longing.

Seeing her this way unnerved him. She'd always been strong. Determined to do everything all by herself, all on her own. Holding her limp body against his chest filled him with an incredible fear. If he were smart, he'd hand her over to Mrs. Warfield, who was babbling nonsensically as she fanned Sky's face with an "Open a New Checking Account Today" brochure. Yes, if he were smart, he'd hand her over, turn tail, and run, because he was scared to death that the moment she opened her eyes, he'd blurt out how much he'd missed her. Tell her that life without her these past few weeks had been dull and dreary, like the dark days following Ella's death.

He stared into her pretty face, his big hands brushing her lightly freckled cheeks and wiping perspiration from her brow. He'd tried telling himself she was all wrong for him. That her stubborn streak and independent nature made her too high-strung for the likes of him. But then he'd remember how quietly and calmly she'd soothed Sally the day of Tootsie's injury.

He'd tried telling himself she'd been alone too long; that she'd developed habits and traits that would make life with her a nightmare. And then he'd recall the ease with which she adjusted to new situations, despite all she'd lived through, and he knew that life with her would be a dream come true. It shamed him a little to admit it, but he loved this woman like he'd never loved anyone—even more than his precious Ella.

If Sky had never come into his life, he'd have gone right on missing Ella's happy chatter and sweet kisses, believing that what they'd shared had been the epitome of love. He'd have lived out the rest of his days totally unaware that something more existed, something deeper and more abiding, something that fulfilled a burning, yearning, never-ending need.

Chet's breath caught in his throat as Sky's long-lashed eyelids began to flutter. The moment her eyes met his, he had a profound desire to kiss her, for in that moment of unguarded confusion, he saw every ounce of the love he felt for her coming right back at him.

The only time he'd felt more vulnerable was when the doctor had grabbed his hand in the hallway outside Ella's hospital room and said, "We're sorry, Chet...."

Sky slowly looked around at the rest of the worried faces hovering above her. Then, after what seemed an eternity, she looked at him again. "Hi," she whispered with a silly, lopsided grin on her face. "What are you doing here?"

"You fainted," he explained, smiling and hugging her a little tighter.

"If it hadn't been for Chet," Mrs. Warfield said, "you'd probably have hit your head on this marble floor. Might have yourself a dandy concussion right about now."

Woozily, Sky interpreted the woman's words. So, he'd saved her again. She giggled, remembering that night on her porch when his strong presence had been the only thing between her and the hard board floor. The fog of the fainting spell began to lift slowly, and Sky became gradually aware of her surroundings.

That smell.

Those noises.

Suddenly, Sky remembered where she was. And why she'd come here. She tried to sit up. It surprised her when she couldn't, and she emitted a tiny, frustrated sigh.

"What's your hurry?" Chet asked, holding her tighter.

"The deed...."

The worry furrow on his brow deepened. "What deed?"

Sky frowned right back at him. "The one to Magic Mountain, of course."

"What do you need it for, Sky?"

"Because," she sighed, gripping his hand, "he has *Face*."

He'd wrapped his arms around her, and now he pulled her closer. "*Who* has Face?" he asked, a ferocious, protective note in his voice.

Sky sat up, hiding her face behind her hands. It all came back to her in a sickening, terrifying rush—what the man on the phone wanted, and why, and what he might do if she didn't give it to him. *Can't tell Chet*, she thought, her subconscious still sending choppy, fragmented messages to her conscious mind. *Have to do it alone. Get the deed...for Face.*

Mr. Harper and Mrs. Warfield had wandered away, and they stood near the counter, looking over at Sky and mumbling about the bank's liability in case of a lawsuit. Chet continued sitting cross-legged on the floor, cradling Sky's head in his lap. As he continued to hold her, his strength ebbed into her. Before long, her breathing had returned to normal, and the dizzying waves stopped crashing over her.

After a few moments, Sky managed to pull away, but only partially, because she didn't really want to break their close connection.

"What have you been doing to yourself? You look horrible," Chet said with concern.

Tucking in one corner of her mouth, Sky sent him a weak grin. "Wow, you sure know how to turn a girl's head."

Chet ignored her sarcasm. His stern glare told her he intended to get answers to his questions. "When was the last time you ate a decent meal?"

She shrugged. "I dunno. Day before yesterday?" She got onto her knees, waited to see if her legs would support her, then stood slowly. "Mrs. Warfield," she said, holding the counter with one hand and straightening her shirt and smoothing her hair with the other, "I have appointments, so if you'll...."

"What's all this nonsense about a deed?" Chet asked.

She rubbed her temples. "My head hurts," she complained aloud, hoping it might distract him. But one look into those serious gray eyes told her he wasn't that easily distracted. "Maybe you don't have enough to do over there at Four Aces," she snapped, "what with Bud and Dale around to do all the dirty work. Maybe you ought to get a job so you won't have so much time on your hands."

"Sky—"

"It's none of your business." Her words were strong, but her voice was small and weak. Her feet and hands felt lead-heavy, but she turned to Mrs. Warfield to resume her errand. "Mrs. Warfield, what do I have to do to get into my safe deposit box? Threaten to close my accounts?"

Chet stood beside her and leaned one elbow on the counter. "Planning to sell the homestead?"

He was so near that his breath rustled her hair. But she didn't dare meet his eyes; the image of the worried expression he'd worn just moments ago as he'd held her protectively was still too clear in her mind. Sky licked her lips. "Actually, I'm thinking of selling just one section."

Sky heard the smile in his voice when he said, "Well, good for you."

Mrs. Warfield interrupted them. "You'll have to come back later this afternoon. The glue isn't dry enough for you to walk on the tiles yet."

The thought of Face having to spend one more minute with that madman terrified Sky. She'd told Face's captor that the deed would be on her porch by ten. She gripped the edge of the counter and looked at the timepiece on the back wall of the tellers' cage. It was 9:30 already! "I *can't* wait until later this afternoon!" Sky seemed unaware that her voice had taken on a shrill, hysterical quality.

The teller frowned. "You make it sound as though it's a matter of life and death."

"Look, Mrs. Warfield. I mean no disrespect, but I know my rights. I have every right to get into that box any time during normal banking hours. And I don't owe you an explanation as to *why* I need to do it."

A scalding, withering look spilled over the silvery rim of Mrs. Warfield's spectacles as she tilted her blue-haired head. "I'll just have another word with Mr. Harper...."

"Maybe I'll just have a word with him myself," Sky muttered. Grabbing a brochure from the pocket on the counter, she started fanning her face. "And maybe I'll just tell him I'd like to withdraw all of my money," she said, loudly enough for Mrs. Warfield *and* Mr. Harper to hear. "I'm sure they don't replace tiles during business hours across the street at—"

"Right this way," the manager said.

As Sky followed him, she had an overwhelming need for air. A sip of cool water. She focused on staying conscious as she entered the vault. It took no more than a minute to unlock and empty the box, and the moment Sky held the deed in her hand, she shouldered her purse and half ran from the bank without so much as a "Thanks" or a "Have a good day."

"I've never known Sky to behave that way," Mrs. Warfield said, frowning. "What do you suppose got into her?"

Chet watched through the window as Sky climbed into her truck. "Don't rightly know," he said as she pulled away from the curb, "but I sure aim to find out...."

❧

Since the brute had chosen the place, Sky had insisted on being in control of the time. She hadn't understood why he'd been so agreeable. In fact, his suddenly kind tone made her more wary than ever. Why, he'd all but apologized for what he was doing!

But Sky had never been one to look gift horses in the mouth. She thanked the Lord for the madman's congeniality, sneaked out of the house, and hid in the pines along Route 212. From her vantage point, she'd be able to see him arrive. And when he stopped the truck and opened the door, she'd have him right where she wanted him. Sky had taught Face to respond to a series of whistles, some that sounded like bird calls, others that more closely resembled the signal for lunchtime in factories.

She didn't recognize the battered pickup that pulled up and stopped, and she was too far from it to recognize the driver. But the moment he stepped from the truck, she let loose with a whistle that meant "treats" and watched with joy as her dog bounded toward her... and as the man yelled obscenities.

"Good dog," she whispered when Face finally reached her. Holding tight to Face's collar, she watched as the pickup raced back down her driveway and made a screeching entrance onto Route 212. For now, at least, she was in the driver's seat. But her position was a precarious one, and common sense told her she wouldn't hold it for long. "C'mon, girl," she said. "Let's go home."

The best attack was a surprise attack, she decided. So the moment after Sky had bolted the front door behind her, she picked up the phone. "Martha, do me a favor and spread the word...I'm closing the clinic for a while. Dr. Mossman in Lincoln City will handle any emergencies." Before her friend had a chance to ask why, Sky hung up. Her dialing was fast and furious as she cancelled appointment after appointment. She couldn't take the chance of his trying another stunt like the one he'd pulled with Face while someone else's pet was on Magic Mountain.

Then, after locking her truck in the garage, Sky packed her gear and set out on foot for Beartooth Plateau by way of the place where she and her father had camped so many summers ago.

It was a hard day's hike to the top of Boulder Pass. As she'd done with her dad, Sky followed the Clearwater River west. Face trotted alongside her, stopping here and there to sniff out bear tracks and dig up miscellaneous buried treasures that she'd carry in her jaws until finding the next prize that enticed her. Sky followed Big Hole Trail from where Deerlodge Creek forked off to the north, across Beaverhead Plateau, and deep into Beartooth country.

Part of the beauty of this country was its never-changing nature. Sky recognized trees and trails that she'd marked with her Swiss army knife, under Wade's careful supervision, years ago. Finally, as the sun slid down the backside of Granite Peak, their special place opened itself to her.

She didn't even bother taking off the heavy backpack during those first minutes of intense scrutiny. Sitting down on a fallen tree trunk with her hands resting on her knees and Face at her side, she drank in the sight like a woman who'd been lost in the desert might suck at the wet lip of a canteen. Not until the dog nudged her damp nose against Sky's hand did she rouse from her trance and start the business of setting up camp.

The temperature here dipped low at night. Whipping around the mountain peaks, the wind sometimes pushed the readings below zero, even this early in the winter. But Sky had prepared for brutal weather. Besides, nature couldn't do anything to her up here to equal what the madman had done on Magic Mountain. That fact made it easy to trade the comfort of home for the barren wilderness of Granite Peak.

The two-man tent, poking up from the landscape like two green-gloved hands together in prayer, held her supplies. If it rained or the winds kicked up, she'd climb inside. Otherwise, she intended to sleep outside, staring up at the wide Montana sky with her faithful, furry friend snuggled close beside her.

Now, staring up at the shimmering darkness, she felt Wade's presence. Sky barely remembered her mother, having been only four years old when Wade's wife had left Atlanta on a sizzling August day.

Wade had more than made up for Sky's lack of a mom. Being sheriff, he could often whittle time into his workday to accompany her on class field trips. He'd never missed a school pageant or a parent-teacher conference, and he'd occasionally surprised her by showing up in the school cafeteria carrying a bag of Big Jim's Dimeburgers for her and her friends.

He'd taught her how to pick her way through a dense forest, how to find fresh drinking water in the wild, and how to tell which berries and mushrooms were edible— and which ones were poisonous. Out behind his office, he'd taught her to load and shoot a pistol, a rifle, and a shotgun, instilling within her a respect of not only the weapons but also the power behind them. In essence, he'd taught her to survive anything, anywhere.

He'd loved bluegrass and opera, Shakespeare and Twain, grits and escargot; and in his excitement to experience life, he'd taught her to be accepting and tolerant, to find enjoyment in the very things that made people *individuals*.

Wade had also enjoyed altering clichés. "Never met a kid I didn't like," he'd say, putting a new twist on the famous line. And, like a six-foot magnet, he attracted children of all shapes and sizes.

Sky missed her dad more right now than even during the first few hard days after the shooting. He'd have known exactly how to handle the crazy man in the hills. And he'd have told her how to fix the mess of things she'd made with Chet.

She snuggled deep into the down-stuffed sleeping bag. *They'd have gotten along famously*, she thought, missing both men more than she cared to admit.

That night, with her heart and head full of wonderful memories of Wade, she slept deeply and peacefully for the first time in weeks. When she awoke at dawn, she felt as though she'd slept six nights instead of one, and she sat up to stretch and breathe in the pure, sharp scent of spruce. Immediately, she got on her knees and faced the rising sun. "Dear Lord," she prayed, hands folded and face tilted toward the heavens, "thank You for a night of peaceful slumber. Thank You for this glorious morning. For this beautiful view. For all You've given me. Bless this day, and help me to do Your will throughout it. Amen."

When Sky was finished, Face gave her a good-morning doggy grin and wagged her tail. "You like it up here, don't you, girl?" Sky asked, ruffling the dog's thick russet coat. A quick, wet slurp across the cheek was Sky's answer. Laughing, she said, "How 'bout some breakfast?"

After rolling up her sleeping bag, Sky poked at the smoldering campfire. Carefully, she laid dry leaves and sticks atop the coals and blew gently across the pile until they glowed red. When tiny flames licked at the twigs, she added bigger branches until the fire was blazing hot and bright. She dumped two teaspoons of coffee grounds into the bottom of the blue-speckled percolator and poured fresh mountain spring water on top of them. While she waited for the water to boil, Sky emptied a pouch of dog food onto a metal plate. "There you go," she told the dog. "Eat up, 'cause we have a big day ahead."

Her own breakfast consisted of two strips of beef jerky and a crisp apple, washed down by hot black coffee. When she finished eating, Sky splashed icy water from a nearby stream onto her face and brushed her teeth. Piling the rocks higher around the campfire to prevent sparks from igniting the nearby brush, Sky grabbed her rifle and her mess kit and headed north toward the place Wade had dubbed "Bit o' Heaven." It took an hour to hike the trail, and when she arrived at her destination, it was clear that she and Wade had been the last to tramp here. The underbrush had grown thick and tall, all but erasing the spot from view. As though she still had Wade to guide her, Sky made her way to the rise on memory alone.

Tears stung her eyes as she surveyed the pristine scene. "How anyone could plant his boots on ground like this and say he doesn't believe in God is beyond me!" Wade would say. "'*Great is the* LORD *and greatly to be praised,*'" he'd add, quoting Psalm 48:1–2; "'*...His holy mountain...is the joy of all the earth....*'"

Sky couldn't help but agree, for only a powerful and mighty being could have created anything so vast and magnificent. The morning was an explosion of color and scent, from the sunlit mountain peaks to the twisting river below, from the pale, azure sky to the pillowy green of distant treetops.

An eagle screeched overhead as a white mountain goat skittered down a rocky slope, a fuzzy kid close on its heels. Cottony clouds sailed silently by, so close it seemed as if Sky could reach up and touch them. She stared with pride at the pink snow that dappled the mountaintop, knowing that this was one of a very few places in the whole world where the stuff existed.

Bit o' Heaven had certainly earned its name.

Face lifted her head and sniffed the wind, familiarizing herself with the odors of the wilderness. Moose and bear, bison and pronghorn shared the place with geese and ptarmigan and saw-whet owls. After the spring, nodding yellow bells and Shooting Stars made way for summer's daisies and fall's wild mums. Sapphires, garnets, and smoky quartz hid beneath the rich soil. Here was a ghost town, there an abandoned mining town. No matter which way Sky looked, she felt the *life* that was this land. *A few days here*, she thought, *and the world will feel right again.*

Sky waited until the sun began to set before picking her way back down the trail to her camp. Big, broad paw prints in the dirt around the campfire told her she'd had an uninvited guest during her absence. Storing her food in airtight metal canisters was the only thing that had stood between a bear's curious visit and the total destruction of the campsite. Funny, even knowing the bear might still be in the area wasn't as frightening to Sky as what had happened down the mountain in so-called civilization.... Sky laid her rifle on the ground and sat down on the cold, hard earth, leaning back against a tree trunk.

At lunchtime, she'd given half her mustard and bologna sandwich to Face, yet despite her long hike, Sky wasn't the least bit hungry. "Maybe we'll dig out the old liverwurst when it gets dark," she told the dog, and Face woofed at the mention of her favorite treat. Feeling lazy and tranquilized, Sky closed her eyes, hands folded loosely in her lap, and dozed. Only when the chill of the night set in did she rouse—just long enough to unroll her sleeping bag and climb inside.

The next day's sunrise was even more spectacular than the previous one. But as Sky watched the yellow sphere blot out the darkness on the third morning, she knew it was time to return to Magic Mountain. Though she loved life up here on the mountaintop, three days without a proper bath were about as many as she could take. Face loped along ahead of her, following their three-day-old scents, and Sky grinned. "We'll make a mountain dog out of you yet," she called after Face. At the sound of her mistress's voice, the dog turned and galloped toward her, ran a happy circle around her, and then dashed back down the trail.

When she got home, Sky decided, she'd shower and change, then invite Dale to meet her for supper in Mountain Gate so she could share this glorious mood with a dear friend.

When the house came into view, Sky was reminded of the label on a bottle of maple syrup. Old-fashioned and inviting, it popped onto the horizon like a WELCOME HOME sign, its wide porch like open arms outspread and waiting to greet each visitor with a big, warm hug. She remembered feeling the very same way at the start of each summer. The moment Wade would turn his big red truck into the entrance of Magic Mountain, her anticipation and elation would climb to such a high level of impatience that Sky would inevitably start bouncing up and down on her seat and wouldn't stop until he'd parked in front of the two-car garage door. She felt that same itchy eagerness now, and she broke into a full run, thirty-pound backpack and all.

Sky reached the porch feeling breathless but invigorated and sat down on the bottom step to get some air and scan the view. Behind her on the porch, Face whimpered, then barked. Sky turned to see what was causing the dog's unusual behavior. Face was growling and pawing at something on the floor, and Sky slipped the backpack from her shoulders. "What's up, girl?" she asked, climbing the stairs. "Find another chipmunk?"

Gran had always insisted that her porch floor gleam with bright, white enamel paint. Sky's peaceful mood died as her heartbeat quickened, for there, in the middle of those milky wood planks, was a message in bold, blood-red letters:

"Gonna have a hot time on the old town tonight!"

Chapter Seventeen

She'd promised to let Dale know the minute she got back—and she'd promised *herself* that she'd call the sheriff the minute they hung up.

But Dale informed her that Chet had left for Wyoming two days earlier. "He always heads north when things start eatin' at him," her friend said. "Sometimes he stays a few days, sometimes a month or more."

Just because it was best for all concerned didn't make losing him easier to bear. For the first time in her life, Sky gave in to self-pity and flopped onto the sofa. As tears pooled in her eyes, something cool touched her cheek, and, without looking, she knew exactly what it was: Chet's tie.

Sky snuggled against it, letting the smooth silk caress her skin. She sat up and, holding one end in each hand, studied the navy cloth. Impulsively, Sky gathered it in her palms, held it to her face, and closed her eyes, tears trickling from their corners as she inhaled his fresh, masculine scent.

Face leapt onto the couch. Whimpering, she licked the backs of Sky's hands, then sniffed the tie.

Sky hugged her. "I miss him, too," she admitted. She didn't fight the tears. Couldn't, it seemed. Soon, Face's fur was clumping where Sky's teardrops had fallen in a steady stream.

Long after the crying jag ended and the Irish setter's fur had dried, Gran's clock chimed ten times. Then eleven. At the stroke of midnight, Sky headed for her bedroom. Though exhausted, she never expected to sleep. Maybe, as she tossed and turned, she'd figure out a way to make the sheriff understand why she'd been so stupid and so stubborn, why she'd waited so long to report everything that had been going on....

She awoke with a start to the sound of Face's ferocious barking. She read the dial of her alarm clock: 2:38. The only other time she'd heard Face bark so viciously had been the day they'd found the cubs. Then, the dog had started running back and forth, sniffing the air and the ground like a bloodhound in hot pursuit. Now, she paced in front of the window, stopping every few seconds to look outside.

"What is it, girl?" Sky asked, running to the window. But even before she got there, Sky knew the answer.

Fire.

The air was thick with the unmistakable odor of burning wood. Outside, the night sky glowed bright from the yellow-orange flames that lapped at the clinic porch. Knowing she didn't have a minute to waste, Sky grabbed the phone as she stepped into her boots.

But instead of the customary *buzz* of the dial tone, Sky heard nothing. The silence was deafening. Terrifying. Deadly. She had no choice. If she wanted to save her clinic, she'd have to fight the blaze herself. Sky grabbed her sweatshirt jacket—the one Wade had always worn when he was off duty—which hung from the brass hook on the back of her bedroom door.

She knew better than to let Face go out there, and she slammed the bedroom door behind her, trapping the dog inside. Face's high-pitched barks rang in her ears as she raced out the front door and across the lawn, glad she hadn't had time to put the garden hose away in the shed. Sky turned the water on full blast, grabbed the nozzle, and aimed it at the clinic porch, where the inferno was burning the brightest. Fortunately, the flames seemed contained to this one area. If she could get it under control quickly enough, maybe it wouldn't spread.

For nearly an hour, it was all-out war between Sky and the flames. Finally, blessedly, the last spark dimmed, and Sky sat down in a murky puddle on the bottom porch step, soaked and shivering in the cold night air and still holding the spurting hose in one trembling hand. She heard Face still barking inside the house and hoped the frantic dog hadn't torn up her room too badly. Weak from fear and tension, she twisted the nozzle to stop the water's flow, then dropped the hose. It landed with a quiet splash in the puddle at her feet.

Holding her head in her hands, Sky thought of the first discussion about wolves that she and Chet had had in the wee hours of the morning, mere days after she'd found the cubs. "Leaving them out there might have been the most humane thing you could have done," he'd said. For a moment, she wondered if the two beautiful wild animals were worth all this misery. Then she pictured their shaggy, silver coats, big, clumsy paws, and round, golden eyes. They were worth it, all right. And then some.

Shaking from fear and exhaustion, Sky stood up, holding tight to the porch rail for support. Something crinkled beneath her damp, sooty palm. She grabbed it. Instantly, she was reminded of the red-lettered message on the porch floor. Another message, she realized, from her new pen pal. In the next moment, she understood that he'd set a small, controllable fire to send the message that his latest note needn't have spelled out: "Next time, I won't give you time to react."

Sky tucked it into the damp pocket of her jeans. If she had that first note to compare it to, she might have proof that both had been written by the same hand. But the first note was with Chet in Wyoming, where he was trying to forget her.

She headed for the house but stopped in the middle of the front yard to face Granite Peak. "I have nothing more to lose!" she screamed. Though she hollered for all she was worth, her voice seemed small and pathetic as it was swallowed up by the vast Montana sky. "Go ahead, you coward! Give me your best shot!"

Minutes ticked silently by. "Coward!" she shouted again, then turned on her heel and climbed onto the porch, where she sat down on the hideous red letters and prayed. "Lord, You've been with me through some hard times. Thank You, sweet Jesus, for being at my side through this one."

She recited her favorite Bible verse, 1 Corinthians 10:13. Then, armed with the knowledge that God would never inflict her with more trauma than He knew she was able to bear, Sky removed her wet boots as calmly as if she'd dirtied them planting petunias in the flower bed or hiking to pick a bucket of berries. Placing the boots neatly beside the front door, she went inside. The door swung quietly shut. Sky didn't even bother to lock it.

Face ran from the bedroom the moment Sky opened the door. She ignored the dog and fell onto the couch, exhausted, burying her face in the pillow on which Chet had leaned when he'd asked her to be his girl. Within minutes, she was asleep.

Sky awoke at noon, cold and wet and hungry. There'd be time for a shower, dry clothes, and a meal afterward....

"Good Lord, Sky, you look awful," Martha said when Sky plopped her list of lumber supplies on the counter. The woman reached out and touched Sky's cheek. "Why, this is...it's soot!"

"Gettin' a mite nippy for outdoor barbecues, don't you think?" Dale asked, using his bandanna to wipe the spot.

Sky's heart thundered. If she told them what had happened, they'd rally to her side...and she'd have the safety of two *more* people she loved to worry about. "That ancient coffeepot in the clinic shorted out, started a little fire." She shrugged nonchalantly. "No big deal."

"No big deal?" Dale repeated, looking stern and skeptical.

"I had it all under control in minutes," she said, flashing a wide grin to prove things were fine. "It did some damage to the railing, but I'll have that repaired in no time," she added, pointing to her list.

Dale's blue eyes narrowed. "You have a hammer?"

Sky nodded.

"And a power saw?"

"Gramps had a fully equipped tool shed, remember?" They'd built a tree house one summer—such a resounding success that they'd tried their hand at a rowboat the following year. Though the boat didn't survive even one dip in Gibson's Pond, the tree house still perched in the top of a big pine.

Dale shot a strange, worried look at Martha, who, contrary to her personality and character, only said, "Joe's gone missin' again, so I'll have Billy load your truck for you."

"No need," Sky said, heading for her truck. "I can handle it."

The moment she was out of sight, Dale turned to Martha. "I need your phone."

"Good idea. Maybe he can talk some sense into our girl."

After wading through the obligatory small talk, Dale heard Chet's mom hand the phone to her son. "Sky is fine," Dale said, "but that fire wasn't caused by any coffeepot. She says the porch is the only thing that was damaged...."

"Must be fifteen, twenty feet between that cart and the door," Chet agreed.

"The fire happened not long after she got home from her camping trip."

"What camping trip?"

"Up on Beartooth. Stayed up there three days...longest she's been out there alone since her daddy died."

"Is she out of her ever-lovin' mind? The bears are more ornery before they hibernate than at any other time of the year. Sky knows that. What could she have been thinking?"

"Said she needed to think. Seems to be goin' around...."

Chet cleared his throat, remembering the scene in her living room when she'd gone from warm and loving to cold and bitter in a heartbeat. Suddenly, it all made sense. She'd picked that fight to protect him, then headed for the hills—literally—to tell herself it had been the right thing to do. He hadn't thought it possible to love her more...but he'd been wrong. "If I leave now, I can be there by sundown. Don't tell anybody. Not even Martha."

Chet's mother had been standing in the doorway, blatantly eavesdropping. "This Sky," she said as he hung up the phone, "is she the Dr. Allen Sally talks about nonstop?"

Chet nodded and refilled his coffee cup.

Lucy Cozart sat down at the table and pointed at the chair across from hers. "Park it, son."

Smiling, he did as he was told, watching her left eyebrow rise on her forehead—a sure sign that he was in for one dandy lecture.

"You love her, you big galoot. Why, it's as plain as the nose on your face. So why haven't you told *her*?"

Chet ran one big finger around and around the rim of his cup. "I wish I knew."

"Loyalty."

"Loyalty?"

"To Ella." Lucy patted his hand. "I know how much you miss her. I miss her, too." She pursed her lips and tilted her head, causing her silver-streaked bangs to fall over one eye. "I came to think of her as a daughter in the years you two were together."

Chet smiled sadly.

"What do you suppose she'd say," his mother continued, "if she knew you had a chance at happiness but passed it up because of some long-dead memory?"

He blinked and said nothing. He'd never given the matter a moment's thought. Why would he have, when no woman but Sky had ever touched his heart as Ella had?

Lucy sighed. "Let me put it another way. If it had been you who'd died, would you want Ella spending the rest of her life alone? Unloved? Clinging to cold memories?"

"Of course not!" he bellowed suddenly. "I'd want her to—"

"—to be happy?" Just as she'd done when he was a boy, Lucy let silence teach the final lesson. After a wordless moment, she got up and refilled her coffee cup. "Sky must be some woman to have turned your head."

He'd been absently picking at the tiny nubs on the red-checkered tablecloth, and he looked up when she said that.

"But she's nothing like Ella," she remarked. "Is that what scares you?"

As always, Lucy had zeroed in on his biggest concern. He'd always been attracted to petite women— blondes with big, blue eyes and soft, womanly curves. "She's nearly as tall as me, Ma, with flaming red hair and brown eyes as big as your saucer there. And stubborn...." Chet whistled. "Strong as an ox, too, and independent to a fault." *But more a woman than any I've known in my lifetime,* he added to himself.

"Ella was just a slip of a girl when you two married, and you weren't much more than a boy yourself," Lucy said. "But you're all grown-up now, balancing big responsibilities on those shoulders of yours," she said with a teasing glint in her eyes. "Sally. The ranch. All those cowhands. And the good Lord knows Stella is a handful all by herself!" Lucy laughed. Then, sighing again, she added, "Your pa would be so proud of you."

Chet looked at her with new eyes and saw not just his mother, but also a beautiful woman, a woman who had been cherished and loved for nearly a quarter of a century by one man—his father. "Why didn't you take your own good advice?"

She returned to her chair as a dreamy, loving light put a youthful sparkle in her eyes. "And remarry?"

Chet nodded.

"Because I'm a fool, to put it plainly. Happiness came my way once, but, like you, I thought grasping it would tell the world I hadn't loved your pa enough." Her wistful smile shrank as she added, "He was a wonderful, patient man. Mooned around like a lost pup for years."

"Not Jesse Coolidge!"

"One and the same. Then, one day, he said he was just a flesh and blood man with flesh and blood needs. Told me he didn't have an eternity to wait till I came to my senses." She'd been staring off into space as she talked, eyes focused on some point in time that only she could see.

Their conversation had given Chet a later start for Montana than he'd planned, but his mother's advice traveled with him all the way back to Mountain Gate. Suddenly, he understood that what had attracted him to Sky in the first place had been a blend of the very things he admired most in his mother. Inner strength. Common sense. Too much pride to resort to the crybaby tactics most women seemed to favor when trying to wheedle what they wanted from a relationship. And an ability to love with a heart that knew no bounds, and for which no sacrifice was too great.

His mother had insisted on keeping Sally with her in Wyoming until things calmed down in Montana. She'd loaned him her car, kissed him good-bye, and handed him a roll of shelf paper to cover Sky's garage windows once he'd parked the Caddy inside. "Don't take no for an answer," she'd said when he'd shared his plan to bunk down on her sofa. "She might say otherwise, but it's not what Sky wants to hear, anyway."

At the end of Sky's driveway, Chet switched off the headlights, thanking God that Sky had left the garage doors open. Parking beside her pickup, he set about the task of covering the windows, then grabbed his duffle and sneaked out, locking the Dutch door behind him.

As he walked across the snow-dusted grass, he heard Face barking inside the darkened house. The dog was one of the best behaved he'd ever met, and he couldn't help wondering what task was occupying Sky so completely that she wasn't doing anything to hush the Irish setter.

The hood of her truck had been cold to his touch, telling him she hadn't driven it for hours. She wouldn't be with the cubs in the shelter at this time of night. Could she have returned to Beartooth? A scary thought....

And then Chet had an even scarier thought: *What if the crazy fool who'd been tormenting her had gotten into the house?* Chet broke into a run and reached the porch in seconds. When the front door swung open at his first touch, icy fear flowed through his veins.

He stepped cautiously into the gloomy foyer. "Sky?"

Face stopped barking, and he wondered what—or who—had stopped her. The silence was at once terrifying and deafening.

"Sky? Answer me!"

Chapter Eighteen

C het stepped hesitantly into the dark living room. All the ugly pictures he'd been conjuring in his mind disappeared when he saw Sky, snuggled on the couch beneath her favorite afghan. *Thank You, Lord*, he prayed silently. *Thank You....*

She looked so small and so vulnerable lying there. She must have been exhausted to have fallen into a sleep too deep to hear Face, to hear him calling her name....

Chet sat down on the edge of the sofa, fully prepared to take her in his arms, gently wake her, and tell her how much he'd missed her, how much he loved her, when Face put her forepaws on the cushion beside him, tail wagging, and yipped a happy greeting for him.

Surely she heard that, he told himself, frowning.

But Sky didn't stir.

"Sky," he said softly, shaking her shoulder. "Sky, wake up...."

Groggily, she rubbed her eyes, and he watched as she struggled to focus. Face's tail overturned a bottle of over-the-counter sleeping pills on the coffee table, and he grabbed it, rattled the remaining tablets. "How many of these have you taken?"

"What?"

"What were you thinking?" he shouted, standing up.

Levering herself up on one elbow, she removed two foam earplugs.

Relief flooded his being as he dismissed the terrifying thoughts the pills had aroused.

"Say...how'd you get in here?" Sky asked.

"Door was unlocked."

"Guess I was more exhausted than I realized."

"Don't go anywhere," he said, stomping into the kitchen. Knowing Sky probably hadn't eaten for days, he made her a sandwich. Made one for himself, too. Sliced an apple and stacked a few chocolate chip cookies on the plate, then poured them each a glass of milk.

"I'll ask you one more time," he said, thrusting the sandwich into her hand. "How many sleeping pills did you take?"

"Just one," she said around a mouthful of bologna and cheese. "As if it's any of your business." She took a sip of milk. "What are you doing here?"

He opened his mouth to answer, but the doorbell chimed and cut him off.

"Neat trick," she said. "Can you do choo-choo trains and airplanes, too?"

Ignoring her, Chet headed for the foyer and peeked out on the front porch. "You've got company," he said through clenched teeth.

Sky rose from the couch and tiptoed up beside him. "What's *he* doing here?"

"Why don't you just find out?" He headed back into the kitchen. "I'll be in here in case you need me...."

When Sky opened the door, her visitor stepped into the foyer, uninvited. "I know I should have called first," he said, removing his Stetson from his head, "but I was afraid you wouldn't see me at this hour."

Sky followed his gaze to the two partially eaten sandwiches and glasses of milk on the coffee table. "I was just having a little snack. Can I get you something?"

Bart shook his head. "No, thanks."

He seemed agitated. His nervousness confused and frightened Sky.

"Can I sit down for a minute?" He walked into the living room and flopped into her easy chair. "I don't know where to begin," he said, holding his hat in his hands.

Though she'd known him most of her life, Sky had usually avoided Bart Laurence. She couldn't quite put her finger on *why*, but she had always agreed with what Gran would say: "That young fella gives me the heebie-jeebies." She closed the front door. "Have you been drinking?"

He met her gaze. "No. For a change, I'm sober as a judge." He took a deep breath. "This is going to be hard...."

Sky sat down on the far end of the couch.

"I'm sorry, Sky," he said, turning his hat round and round in his hands. "It's been awful for you, and I'm sorry."

"Sorry for what?"

Staring at an invisible spot between his boots, he shook his head. "It was me. All of it. I have no excuse... no good excuse, that is." Briefly, his eyes met Sky's eyes. Then, shaking his head again, he placed his hat on the coffee table. Focusing on the enlarged photograph of Granite Peak that hung on the opposite wall, he repeated, more softly this time, "I'm sorry."

"But...why? I've never done anything to you."

"It's a long story."

"Thanks to you, I have nothing but time," she said coolly, crossing her legs and arms at the same time.

Bart took a deep breath and began his story. Half an hour later, he'd spelled the whole thing out. "If you want to call the sheriff, I won't put up a fight."

Chet walked into the room.

"You can shoot me later, Cozart," he said. "Right after you finish your milk and cookies. Right now, we have to figure out how we're going to stop Rowen and save Sky's land."

Sky was still sitting there, straight and tall, chin high, lips in a taut line. Chet was proud of her strength and assurance. Not until he sat down beside her and grabbed her trembling hand did he realize that her show of bravado was for Bart's benefit.

"You mean, how we're going to stop Rowen and save the Lazy L?" Chet interjected, reminding them all that Bart had just admitted to handing over the deed to his ranch during a drunken game of poker.

"Can't blame you one whit for not believing me," Bart said, "but I'm on the level."

Chet harrumphed. "You say you have an idea how we can help Sky?"

"Yeah, but it won't be easy, and somebody could get hurt." They had no reason to trust him, Bart acknowledged—no reason to believe he was really on their side. "You don't have much choice, as I see it."

Chet was on his feet in a heartbeat. "One phone call," he sneered through clenched teeth, "and you'll be behind bars so fast it'll knock the scales off those snakeskin boots of yours."

Sky grabbed his doubled-up fist. "I hate to interrupt all this macho confrontational stuff, but somebody has to be the voice of reason here...."

"And what's the voice of reason saying?"

"That we should hear him out, see if his plan will hold water."

Bart took that as his cue to spell it out for them. When he finished, he sat back as Chet glowered and jabbed his forefinger in the air. "Okay, but one false move and I swear—"

"When this is over, you've got my permission to beat me senseless. But right now, what say we get busy?"

Chapter Nineteen

I hoe art ish kee-in' owin izzy."

Sky's hands froze above the file drawer as she replayed his sentence in her mind. When it still made absolutely no sense, she whispered, "What?"

"I hoe art ish kee-in' owin izzy."

She looked at him, hunched over the tall metal filing cabinet on the other side of the dark room. If not for the small flashlight between his teeth, Sky wouldn't have been able to see him at all, as he was dressed in black from his long-sleeved shirt to his high-top sneakers. Only his brown knit gloves kept him from fitting the super-spy image he'd tried so hard to duplicate.

Sky looked a bit like a shadow, too, wearing a snug black jumpsuit over a black turtleneck. Pointing at her mouth and shaking her head, she whispered, "Can't understand a word you're saying."

His quiet laughter echoed in the file drawer. He removed the flashlight from his mouth and repeated, "I hope Bart is keeping Rowen busy."

The night Bart had surprised them with a visit, he'd told them that Mike Rowen had been paying a prominent Montana senator big bucks to approve illegal licenses and permits. Told them, too, how he'd managed to get ahold of Rowen's keys just long enough to get into his Baltimore office and locate the files that would back up his claims. The next morning, while Sky drove Face to Four Aces to stay with Dale, Chet had booked the first flight out of Butte, and immediately after he and Sky had landed at Thurgood Marshall Airport in Baltimore, he'd rented a boxy, black sedan.

Sky and Chet had already photocopied those incriminating documents and put the originals back exactly as they'd found them. Now, their objective was to find proof that Rowen never intended to turn the mountain into a wildlife preserve as the paperwork outlined. Government grants and tax-free incentives encouraged the nation's well-intentioned wealthy to invest in protecting and preserving the environment. But what Rowen really had planned for Granite Peak would preserve nothing but his bank account. Once the deeds had changed hands, it would have cost the state of Montana millions in court fees to prevent Rowen from doing whatever he wanted with his mountain...*if* the truth ever reached the governor's office.

Now, in Rowen's darkened office suite near the top of the World Trade Center, she glanced at the colorful lights of the Inner Harbor below, hoping that Bart hadn't led them on a wild goose chase. The only sound in the gloomy room was the quiet shuffling of papers as their fingers walked through file after file....

...until Chet yanked a folder from a drawer and rasped, "Eureka!"

They'd been sitting side by side in the front seat of the rental car for nearly fifteen minutes, chatting casually as they waited for Bart to join them, when Chet said, "I think we should build a new house once we're married."

Sky couldn't believe her ears. "But...what about my patients?"

"Mountain Gate isn't New York City. We'll see to it they'll find you, trust me."

And she did. Completely. Sky turned in the seat to face him. "Seems a little bizarre that we're discussing things like that when we've never said...you know...."

He looked deep into her eyes. "Ladies first, and all that."

"Let's compromise. No good marriage can survive without it."

He draped his arm over her shoulders. "Okay, start talking."

"We'll both start talking, on the count of three."

Chet opened his mouth as she said, "One, two, three...I love you!"

After a moment, he said, "That's the meanest, scariest look anybody ever gave me."

"What did you expect? You tricked me!"

"I asked you to marry me. If that doesn't say it, I don't know what does." He leaned back and shook his head. "I do, you know," he said, hugging her tight. "Always have. Right from the moment your fist connected with my eye. Love at first fight."

"Ditto."

"Didn't know you spoke Morse Code," he teased.

"That's what we'll name our first son!"

"Like that goofy kid in the comic strip? I won't hear of it."

"No, silly. Not Ditto. Morse."

"No son of mine is gonna have a name that rhymes with horse, no matter how many of 'em I own." He held her at arm's length. "Wait—our *first* son? How many are you planning to give me?"

"Two. But I won't give them to you. Nor the girls. They're gonna cost you, cowboy."

Chet counted the charges on his fingers. "Bribing public officials, falsifying court documents, fraud, extortion...the list goes on and on," he said, smiling as he watched Rowen sift through the file.

Rowen's tanned face paled as his practiced smile vanished. "Where did you get this?" he demanded, tossing the folder onto the desk.

Bart leaned casually against the wall, studying a toothpick. "From right under your uppity nose, Rowen," he said, voice dripping with sarcasm. "You gave me the keys. Told me to make copies." He chuckled. "Pity you weren't more specific about how *many* copies...or who I was allowed to show 'em to."

"I oughtta call the cops," Rowan growled, pacing in front of the window wall. "I oughtta have the lot of you arrested for breaking and entering. Burglary. Invasion of privacy...."

Bart calmly inspected the toothpick he'd been chewing as he nonchalantly asked, "Where's your proof of all that?" He used the toothpick to point to the folder. "In there?"

Rowen's fists opened and closed. "I have friends in high places," he threatened. "This won't mean diddly when they get through with—"

Bart crossed the room in seconds and filled his hands with Rowen's lapels. "You won't be able to do anything to anybody when I get finished with you, you low-life—"

"Let go of him," Sky said.

Bart's eyes widened with confusion. "But he was willing to do anything to get your land. *Anything.* How can you defend him?"

She placed a hand on his forearm. "I'm not defending him. I'm defending you."

"If it were up to me," he grated, tossing Rowen into his leather chair, "I'd string him up from the nearest tree."

The developer jerked his jaw left and right, then straightened his tie in an attempt to reclaim lost dignity. "I suppose you cowpokes made copies of those—"

Chet nodded and grinned. "Yup," he said with a deliberately exaggerated drawl, "a couple of copies, as a matter of fact. Sent one on down to the state attorney general's office. Sent another to the district attorney."

Rowen sat forward, his eyes widening with shock and fear. He focused on Bart. "You'll do time for this, too...."

Bart shrugged nonchalantly. "Yup, I reckon I will," he said, his drawl every bit as thick as Chet's. "The wages of sin come with a big price tag. I'm willing to pay my debt to society. How 'bout you, *my boy*?"

Chapter Twenty

As the weeks flew by, Sky barely had time to think about the wolves, let alone miss them. In her mind, they'd always be her cubs, even though they'd been nearly full grown when she'd set them free on Beartooth Plateau.

The only sadness that had touched her life in the weeks since she and Chet had broken the news of their wedding had been Bart's announcement that he'd sell the Lazy L and move East. He'd been sentenced to two years in prison for his part in the land-stealing scheme, but because he'd helped gather the evidence that convicted Rowen, and because Sky hadn't pressed charges, his sentence had been reduced to six months' probation. Sky had made him promise to return now and then, starting with the upcoming wedding.

Stella filled her days with wedding plans, Sally had already started calling Sky "Mama," and the traitorous Face had decided that she belonged to a little girl now.

Life couldn't have been more perfect...that is, until Stella took Sky into her closet after one of their planning sessions. "Ella wasn't tall enough to wear this," she said, pulling an ivory satin gown from a garment bag, "but it should fit you perfectly."

Sky touched the soft, billowing folds and, pressing the gown against her, pirouetted gracefully in front of the mirror. "It's beautiful, Stella, but—"

"When I wore that dress thirty-five years ago, something told me if I held on to it long enough, someone would get another wearing out of it," Stella said, her eyes damp.

Sky gently draped the gown over the bed and took Stella's hands in hers. "I know I'm a ghastly stand-in for Ella. She was so feminine and delicate, and I was always such a klutz," Sky said, her own eyes swimming, "but I'll try to make you proud."

"You mustn't ridicule yourself. It's very unbecoming," Stella said, smiling. "You'll be a beautiful bride."

The Ice Lady had melted when she'd seen how thrilled Sally was to have Sky as a mother, without leaving as much as a pool of cool water to remember her by.

Epilogue

On a bright April morning, Sky studied her reflection in Gran's oval mirror. Her father's silver chain of dog tags served as "something old," the shiny good-luck penny in her shoe was Dale's idea of "something new," Lucy Cozart's cameo was "something borrowed," and Joe's gift, a scrap of blue cloth from the cubs' blanket, was tucked into her bouquet of white roses as "something blue." The dress fit as though it had been designed especially for her. Sky felt beautiful and ladylike as she swished into the waiting white limousine.

Residents of Mountain Gate packed the tiny log cabin church in the center of town as Sally and Face marched down the aisle to Martha's off-key piano rendition of Wagner's "Wedding March." In the vestibule, Dale linked his arm with Sky's and proceeded to lead her slowly toward the altar.

When Chet lifted her veil, she broke with tradition and spoke to him—just long enough to whisper her new life motto into his ear: "Nothing ventured, everything lost."

He smiled, although his left brow arched with confusion.

"I'll have a lifetime to explain it," she said softly. "A lifetime...."

A Preview of
Beautiful Bandit

Book One in the Lone Star Legends Series
by Loree Lough

Chapter One

June 1888
San Antonio, Texas

The hot, sticky air in the banker's cluttered office made it hard to breathe. Josh ran a fingertip under his stiff collar as the image of cows dropping by the thousand reminded him why he'd come to San Antonio. Selling off the Rockin' N Ranch's uncontaminated acres would be the only way to protect the cows that remained—at least until they'd gotten the anthrax infection—under control.

He did his best not to glare at the decorous Bostonian sitting beside him. It wasn't the Swede's fault, after all, that anthrax had killed so many Neville cattle. In his shoes, Josh would have snapped up the land even more quickly. Trouble was, now this la-di-da Easterner would move to Eagle Pass, bringing his never-been-out-of-the-city wife and children with him. Worse yet, Josh had a sneaking suspicion that the former printing press operator would make a regular pest of himself by asking about Texas weather, irrigation, when to plant, and only the good Lord knew what else. If that didn't earn Josh a seat closer to the Throne, he didn't know what would.

Few things agitated him more than sitting in one spot. Especially indoors. How these fancy gents managed to look so calm and cool, all buttoned up in their dark suits, he didn't know. Wondering about it had only added to his restlessness, so he'd hung his Stetson on his left knee, mostly so he'd have something to do with his hands. Now, he moved it to his right knee as the banker explained the terms of the agreement.

He stared hard at the deep red Persian rug under his boots, searching his mind for something to else to focus on—anything other than the wretched document that would transfer ownership of Neville land to this foreigner. Moving his hat to his left knee again, he remembered the day he'd bought it, and how he'd picked up another just like it a year later, when Rockin' N business had put him in Garland, so he'd have one for riding the range and one for his wedding. He found it strange how Sadie's image could appear in his mind's eye from out of nowhere, even after two long, hard years without her....

Josh forced the thought of her from his mind. This get-together was more than painful enough without dwelling on the most agonizing episode of his life. He exhaled a harsh sigh, hoping the banker and the Swede hadn't heard the tremor in it. He blamed his pounding heat. His empty stomach. The ten-day ride from Eagle Pass that had left him too bone tired to sleep on the hotel's too-soft mattress. *A body would think that an establishment with Persian rugs and velvet curtains could afford to provide water for businessmen*, he thought, loosening his string tie as Griffin asked yet another inane question. *Father, give me the strength to keep from grabbing those papers and hotfooting it out of here!* he prayed silently.

Sadly, his woolgathering was doing little to distract him from the grim truth....

Josh had been the sole dissenting vote at the family meeting, and their loathsome decision had turned downright odious when he'd realized that, as the only Neville with a legal background, he would be the one responsible for transacting the sale. He groaned inwardly as grief engulfed him. *What a sorry state of affairs*, he thought, leaning forward to hide the tears that burned in his eyes. He loved every blessed acre that made up the Rockin' N, especially the acre where he'd built a small but solid home for Sadie and himself. He would hate letting it go, even if she *hadn't been* buried there!

Griffin, God bless him, had been the one to suggest that Josh hold on to that precious acre after Josh had asked permission to visit the graves of his wife and babies. "We'll build a fence around the land," Griffin had said, "to make sure your family is never disturbed." But Josh had known, even as he'd nodded in agreement, that crossing Griffin property to reach his little family would only heap one misery atop another.

With his elbows propped on his knees, Josh spun his hat round and round, watching through the window as three men dismounted sweaty horses outside. The lot of them looked as jumpy and agitated as he felt, and he wondered what ugly family business had brought *them* to the bank today. Maybe that explained the riderless horse....

"If you'll just sign here, Mr. Neville," Schaeffer said, redirecting Josh's attention to the transaction at hand.

Josh accepted the banker's fountain pen, and, as its freshly inked nib hovered over the document, a bead of sweat trickled down his spine. In that moment, he felt a disturbing kinship with the fat hen his mama had roasted for last Sunday's dinner.

Outside, the wind blew steadily, swirling street grit into tiny twisters that skittered up the parched road before bouncing under buggies and scurrying into alleyways. Even the burning breeze would feel better than the choking heat in Schaeffer's office. "Mind if I open the window? I'm sweatin' like a—"

Schaeffer peered over the rims of his gold spectacles. "I'd much rather you didn't. The wind is likely to scatter our paperwork hither and yon."

Hither and yon, indeed. Josh had read similar phrases in books, but what sort of person actually used words like that in—

Suddenly, shuffling footsteps and coarse whispers on the other side of the banker's door interrupted his thoughts. Inspired a stern frown on Schaeffer's heat-reddened face, too. "I declare," the man said through clenched teeth, "I can't take my eyes off that fool assistant of mine for fifteen minutes without some sort of mayhem erupting." Blotting his forehead with a starched, white hanky, he continued grumbling. "Looks like I'll have no choice but to replace him." Shoving his eyeglasses higher on his nose, he lifted his chin and arched one bushy gray eyebrow, a not-so-subtle prompt for Josh to sign the paper.

So, gritting his teeth, Josh inhaled a sharp breath and scratched his name on the thin, black line, then traded the pen for a banknote.

On his feet now, the Swede grabbed Josh's hand. "T'ank you," he said, shaking it. "Been a pleasure doing business wit' you, Neville."

Unable to make himself say "Likewise," Josh forced a stiff smile and pocketed the check. "You bet." God willing, perhaps the worst was behind for his family now.

The burnished, brass pendulum of the big clock behind the banker's desk swayed left with an audible *tick* as the men prepared to go their separate ways...and swung right as gunshots rang out in the lobby.

Schaeffer and Griffin ran for the door, but a flurry of activity drew Josh's attention back to the window.

Tick....

The three men he'd seen earlier were scrambling into their saddles. Only now, their faces were covered with bandannas, and a young woman had joined them. She climbed into the previously empty saddle as the biggest man hoisted a burlap sack over his horse's saddle horn, sunlight glinting off the pistol in his gloved hand.

Tick....

Josh grabbed his sidearm, pulling back the hammer with one hand, then pushed open the window with the other. He thought that maybe he could get off a shot or two before the robbers were swallowed up by the cyclone of dust kicked up by their horses' hooves.

Tick....

Perched on the sill, he took aim at the shoulder of the fattest bandit just as the woman's pony veered right, putting her square in the center of his gun sight.

Tick....

She looked back, and her green gaze fused to his. Josh released the pressure on the sweat-slicked trigger as fear traveled the invisible cord connecting her wide eyes to his.

Tick....

Josh didn't have time to make sense of the helpless expression on her pretty face, for, as quick as you please, she faced front again, her cornflower-blue skirt flapping like a tattered sail as she was swallowed up by a thick cloud of dust.

About the Author

Long before becoming a writer, best-selling author Loree Lough literally sang for her supper. She enjoyed receiving rave reviews and applause and touring the country but sensed it wasn't what the Lord had in mind for her. She tried everything from shrink-wrapping torque wrenches to spinning pizza dough to working as a chef in a nursing home kitchen, to name just a few, without finding one job that fit her. Then, while visiting her parents in Baltimore, Loree worked for an insurance corporation, where she met the man she would marry.

Loree began writing when her husband, Larry, had a job change that moved the family to Richmond, Virginia. She started out writing a neighborhood column and soon began getting assignments from the publication's editor—as well as the editors of other publications. But it wasn't until she penned her first novel, the award-winning *Pocketful of Love*, that Loree finally understood what the Lord had in mind for her: Seventy-three books (and counting) later, she's still touching the hearts of readers worldwide.

In addition to her books, Loree has sixty-three short stories and 2,500 articles in print. Her stories have earned dozens of industry and Reader's Choice awards.

Loree is a frequent guest speaker for writers' organizations, book clubs, private and government institutions, corporations, college and high school writing programs, and more, where she encourages aspiring writers with her comedic approach to learned-the-hard-way lessons about the craft and industry.

An avid wolf enthusiast, Loree is involved with the Wolf Sanctuary of Pennsylvania. She and Larry, along with a formerly abused, now spoiled pointer named Cash, split their time between a remote cabin in the Allegheny Mountains and a humble house in the Baltimore suburbs.

Loree loves hearing from her readers, so feel free to write her at loree@loreelough.com. To learn more about Loree and her books, visit her Web site at www.loreelough.com.